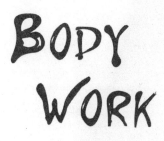

BODY
WORK

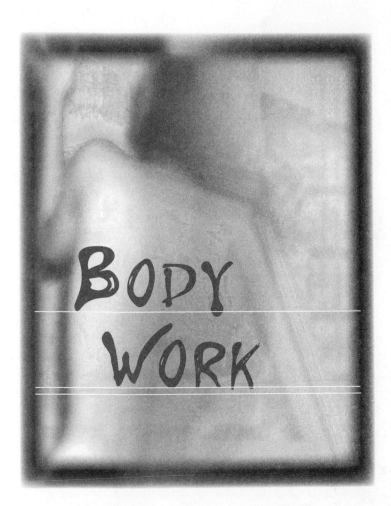

BODY WORK

Sara Paretsky

G. P. PUTNAM'S SONS   NEW YORK

PUTNAM

G. P. PUTNAM'S SONS
Publishers Since 1838
Published by the Penguin Group
Penguin Group (USA) Inc., 375 Hudson Street, New York, New York 10014, USA • Penguin
Group (Canada), 90 Eglinton Avenue East, Suite 700, Toronto, Ontario M4P 2Y3, Canada
(a division of Pearson Penguin Canada Inc.) • Penguin Books Ltd, 80 Strand, London
WC2R 0RL, England • Penguin Ireland, 25 St Stephen's Green, Dublin 2, Ireland (a division
of Penguin Books Ltd) • Penguin Group (Australia), 250 Camberwell Road, Camberwell,
Victoria 3124, Australia (a division of Pearson Australia Group Pty Ltd) • Penguin Books India
Pvt Ltd, 11 Community Centre, Panchsheel Park, New Delhi–110 017, India • Penguin Group
(NZ), 67 Apollo Drive, Rosedale, North Shore 0632, New Zealand (a division of Pearson
New Zealand Ltd) • Penguin Books (South Africa) (Pty) Ltd, 24 Sturdee Avenue,
Rosebank, Johannesburg 2196, South Africa

Penguin Books Ltd, Registered Offices: 80 Strand, London WC2R 0RL, England

Library of Congress Cataloging-in-Publication Data

Paretsky, Sara.
Body work / Sara Paretsky.
p.   cm.
ISBN 978-0-399-15674-8
1. Warshawski, V. I. (Fictitious character)—Fiction.   2. Women private investigators—
Illinois—Chicago—Fiction.   3. Artists—Crimes against—Fiction.   I. Title.
PS3566.A647B63   2010   2010016251
813'.54—dc22

Printed in the United States of America
10 9 8 7 6 5 4 3 2 1

BOOK DESIGN BY MEIGHAN CAVANAUGH

This is a work of fiction. Names, characters, places, and incidents either are the product of
the author's imagination or are used fictitiously, and any resemblance to actual persons, living
or dead, businesses, companies, events, or locales is entirely coincidental.

While the author has made every effort to provide accurate telephone numbers and Internet
addresses at the time of publication, neither the publisher nor the author assumes any
responsibility for errors, or for changes that occur after publication. Further, the publisher
does not have any control over and does not assume any responsibility for author or
third-party websites or their content.

John Vishneski and Karen Buckley are winners of a charity auction to have characters
named for them. The names are all that the fictional Buckley and Vishneski have
in common with the winners.

For Jo Anne, Jolynn, and Kathryn

Thanks for helping keep the rickety C-Dog ship
afloat all these years

CONTENTS

THANKS

Thanks to Dr. Bill Ernoehazy for his advice on forensic evidence, and on preparing autopsy reports. For reasons of the story, I didn't follow his advice to the letter, so please don't be dismayed if you think Captain Edwards should have acted differently.

On a happier note, thanks to Edwina Wolstencroft and the *Early Music Show* for advice on Jake Thibaut's song. Ms. Wolstencroft directed me to the *trobairitz*, who I'd never heard of before. The translation of Maria de Ventadorn's poem is taken from Meg Bogin, *The Women Troubadours*.

Thanks to Sue Riter for much more than I can say here. You made this book possible; you made it work.

Professor Israel bar-Joseph, an expert on nanoparticles at the Weizmann Institute, was kind enough to speak to me about gallium arsenide, among other matters.

Jolynn Parker provided crucial assistance in critiquing the book in manuscript form. Kathryn Lyndes's support was invaluable in helping with the final rewrites.

The title of Chapter 55 is an old Russian proverb: "Up a hill you push a cart; down a hill it rolls. There is some justice in this world, just not enough."

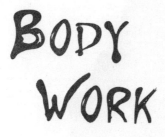

BODY
WORK

1

Dead in the Alley

Nadia Guaman died in my arms. Seconds after I left Club Gouge, I heard gunshots, screams, squealing tires, from the alley behind the building. I ran across the parking lot, slipping on gravel and ruts, and found Nadia crumpled on the dirty ice. Blood was flowing from her chest in a thick tide.

I ripped off my scarf and opened her coat. The wound was high in her chest—too high, I knew that—but I still made a pad of my scarf and pressed it against her. Keeping pressure on the pad, I struggled out of my coat and placed it under her. Left hand on chest, right hand underneath, pushing my coat against the exit wound. Without looking up or stopping the pressure, I shouted at the people surging around us to call 911, now, at once.

Nadia's eyes flickered open as I cradled her. The ghost of a smile flickered at the sides of her wide mouth. "Alley. Alley."

"Shhh, Nadia, save your strength."

I thought it was a good sign, a hopeful sign, that she spoke, and I kept pushing against her wound, singing snatches of a cradle song, trying to keep us both calm. When the paramedics arrived, and pried my hands free from her wounds, they shook their heads. She'd been dead for several minutes already.

I started to shiver. It was only when the medics forced me to my feet that I felt the January wind cut into my bones. The medics brought me into the ambulance but left Nadia lying on the ground, waiting for a tech team to photograph her. The crew wrapped a blanket around me and gave me hot sweet coffee from their own thermos.

"You did the best that could be done. No one could have done more." The tech was short and muscular, with wiry red hair. "She was bleeding out within minutes of being shot. I'm guessing the bullet nicked a major vein, but the ME will tell us more. Was she a friend?"

I shook my head. We'd barely spoken, and at that point, in fact, I only knew her first name.

A cop poked his head through the open ambulance door. "You the gal that put her coat on the dead girl?"

Dead woman, I started to say, but I was too exhausted to fight that battle tonight. Nadia was dead, and whatever one called her, it wouldn't bring her back to life. I didn't move from the bench facing the stretcher but croaked out a yes.

"Can we talk inside, ma'am?" the cop said. "The EMTs are going to take the dead girl to the morgue as soon as the photo team is through, and it's five degrees here in the parking lot."

I handed the blanket back to the ambulance crew and let the cop give me a hand as I jumped off the back. Nadia was lying where I'd left her, her face silver under the blue strobes, the blood on her chest black. My coat was still underneath her. I walked over and fished my car and house keys from the pockets, despite outcries from the evidence team. My handbag was lying a few feet from the "dead woman," I muttered out loud. I picked up the bag, also against the outraged shouts of the officer in charge.

"That's evidence."

"It's my handbag, which I dropped when I was performing first aid. You don't need it and I do." I turned on my heel and walked back into the Club Gouge. The bag was handmade from red leather, an apology of sorts from the friend of a dead missing person, and I wasn't going to risk losing it or my wallet in an evidence locker.

Everyone who'd been in the club or the parking lot, except those crafty enough to escape ahead of the team in blue, had been herded into the building. A minute before, I'd been too cold, but the club atmosphere, hot, nearly airless, made me ill. I started to sweat, and fought a rising tide of nausea.

The club staff, including my cousin Petra, were huddled by the bar. After a moment, when I decided I wasn't going to vomit, I shoved my way through the crowd to Petra's side.

"Vic, what happened?" Petra's blue eyes were wide with fear. "You're covered with blood."

I looked down and saw Nadia's blood on my jeans and sweater, on my hands. My scalp crawled: maybe her blood was in my hair.

"Someone shot a woman as she left the club," I said.

"Was it—who was it?"

"I heard her called 'Nadia,'" I said slowly, fixing Petra with a hard stare. "I don't know if that's her name, and I don't know her last name. If the cops, or a reporter, ask you questions about what happened tonight, you can answer only truthfully about things you actually know and saw. You shouldn't answer questions about things that are just guesses, because that could mislead the cops."

"It would be best if you don't consult the other witnesses," a voice said.

A female officer had fought through the shouting, texting, Twittering chaos to appear at my side.

Under the club lights, I could see her face, narrow, with pro-

nounced cheekbones, and lank black hair cut so short the ends only just
appeared below her cap rim. I read her badge: E. Milkova. E. Milkova
didn't look much older than my cousin, too young to be a cop, too
young to be telling me what to do. But—she had the badge. I let her
guide me to the small stage at the back of the club, which the police
had roped off with crime scene tape so they could use it for interrogations. She lifted the tape so I could crawl under, then dragged a couple
of chairs from the nearest table. I reached a hand out and took one of
them from her.

I was in that numb place you inhabit after you've been part of violence and death. It was hard to focus on Milkova's questions. I gave her
my name. I told her I'd heard gunshots and run to see what the problem
was. I told her I didn't know the dead woman.

"But you knew her name," Milkova said.

"That was just from hearing someone call her 'Nadia.' I don't know
her last name."

"Most people run away from gunshots."

I didn't say anything.

"You ran toward them."

I still didn't say anything, and she frowned at me. "Why?"

"Why, which?" I said.

"Why did you run toward danger?"

When I was younger and more insouciant, I would have quoted the
great Philip Marlowe and said, "Trouble is my business," but tonight I
was cold and apprehensive. "I don't know."

"Did you see anyone in the club threaten Nadia tonight?"

I shook my head. I hadn't seen anyone threaten her tonight. Earlier,
that was another story, but my years as a public defender had taught
me to answer only the question asked.

"Did you come here tonight because you thought there would be an
attack on someone?"

"It's a club. I came because I wanted to see the acts."

"You're a private investigator. They tell me you've been involved in a lot of high-profile investigations."

Someone had ID'd me to the police. I wondered if it was the club's owner, out of malice. "Thank you," I said.

Milkova pushed her short hair back behind her ears, a nervous gesture—she wasn't sure how to proceed. "But don't you think it's a strange coincidence, you being here the night someone got shot?"

"Cops have days off. Even doctors. And PIs have been known to take them, too." I didn't want to throw Petra to the wolves, and that's what would happen if I said anything about wanting to keep an eye on my cousin's workplace.

No one had bothered to turn off the Body Artist's computer, and the plasma screens on the stage kept flashing images of flowers and jungle animals. It made a disturbing backdrop to the interrogation.

"Vic, what are you doing here?"

I looked around and saw Terry Finchley, a detective I've known for a long time. "Terry! I might ask you the same question."

Finchley's been out of the field for five or six years now, on the personal staff of my dad's old protégé, Captain Bobby Mallory. I was surprised to see the Finch at an active homicide investigation.

He gave a wry smile. "Captain thought it was time I got my hands dirty again. And if you're anything to judge by, they're going to get mighty dirty indeed on this investigation."

I looked again at my stained hands. I was beginning to feel twitchy, covered in Nadia's blood. Terry climbed the shallow step to the stage and told Milkova to get him a chair.

"What have you learned, Liz?" Finchley asked Officer Milkova. So the *E* stood for Elizabeth.

"She's not cooperating, sir. She won't say how she knew the vic or why she was here, or anything."

"Officer Milkova, I've told you I didn't know the victim," I said. "It makes me cranky when people don't listen to me."

"Pretty much any damn thing makes you cranky, Warshawski," Finchley said. "But, out of curiosity, how did you get involved?"

"I was leaving the club, I heard gunshots. I ran across the parking lot and saw a woman on the ground. She was bleeding; I tried to block the wounds, so I didn't take time to follow the shooters. But on the principle that no good deed is left unpunished, I'm being treated as though I had something to do with the dead woman's murder." My voice had risen to a shout.

"Vic, you're exhausted. And I don't blame you." Terry's tone was unusually gentle, the sharp planes in his ebony cheeks softening with empathy. He'd felt angry with me for a lot of years—maybe I was finally forgiven. His voice sharpened. "The techs are annoyed because you took evidence from the crime scene. And, for that, I not only don't blame them but need you to turn it over to them."

Okay, not forgiven. He was just doing good-bad cop all in one paragraph.

"It wasn't evidence: these were my personal belongings that I dropped when I tried to administer first aid. I picked them up when Officer Milkova told me to leave the scene. I think your techs would be grateful to have extraneous items removed. Although I did abandon my coat."

My throat contracted, and I looked involuntarily at my hand, my right hand, which had been pushing my coat against Nadia's bleeding back. "You can keep the coat. I'll never wear it again."

Finchley paused briefly, and decided to let my handbag ride.

"Did you know the dead woman?"

"No."

"Why were you here?"

"It's a club. You can come in if you want a drink and want to see the show. I was doing both those things."

Finchley sighed. "You know, anyone else in this town, I'd nod and take your name and phone number and urge you to wash the blood off and try to forget the horrors you witnessed. But V. I. Warshawski chooses to come to a club the one night in the year a woman gets murdered at their back door? You know what the captain's going to ask when he hears that. Why were you here tonight?"

2

Performing Artist

Why had I been at Club Gouge the night Nadia Guaman took two bullets? Terry's question kept running through my head as I drove home. The simple answer had to do with my cousin Petra. Except Petra had been in my life less than a year, and I was rapidly learning that there are no simple answers where she's concerned.

In a way, that was unfair. It was really Jake Thibaut who first took me to Club Gouge, right after Thanksgiving. Jake's a bass player who moved into my building last spring; we've been dating for a few months now. He plays with a contemporary chamber group, as well as the early-music group High Plainsong. Trish Walsh, a friend of his from High Plainsong, was doing a strange blend of medieval music with heavy metal lyrics, accompanying herself on electric hurdy-gurdy and lute.

When Trish Walsh, singing as the Raving Renaissance Raven, got a gig at Club Gouge, Jake put together a party to hear her. A number of his musician friends joined us, but he also invited Lotty Herschel and Max Loewenthal, along with my downstairs neighbor, Mr. Contreras.

My cousin Petra wheedled her way into the invitation. "The Raving Renaissance Raven!" Petra's eyes glowed. "Jake, I didn't realize how totally cool you are. I have the Raven's Ravings on my iPod, but I've never caught her act!"

Club Gouge itself was one of a string of new nightspots that had taken over the abandoned warehouses under the Lake Street L, just west of downtown. Somehow, it had become the hippest scene on the strip, mostly because the owner, Olympia Koilada, apparently had a sixth sense for knowing when to book performers right before they became big.

The Raven, who was opening for an act billed as the Body Artist, sang and played for about forty minutes. Max was intrigued by her hurdy-gurdy, which was handmade of beautiful woods. The Raven had attached an amplifier to it, and the sound filled the club.

Jake and his musician friends didn't like the distortion that the amp brought to the musical line. Between sets, they argued about whether their friend could have achieved a better effect with a local mike. Petra and Mr. Contreras argued about the lyrics: she thought the Raven's songs were *awesome,* he found them disgusting.

It was Max who put my own reaction into words. "She perhaps never has had a wide audience in her early-music performance. Now she can show a young generation that even a gifted musician can shock, and thus build a market for herself."

"That's so *cynical,*" Petra protested. "She's just being brave enough to put herself out there."

"Where art and commerce intersect," Jake said. "You make art, you sell it—to make a living, to get some validation—you make compromises with your art to make a living—why not go the whole way? Which isn't to say she doesn't believe as deeply in heavy metal as she does in early music."

We had planned to leave before the Body Artist came onstage, but the lively arguments in our party—accompanied by the amount of beer and wine everyone was putting away—went on until the houselights were dimmed again for the evening's main event.

Young men at tables around us gave catcalls and stomped their feet in anticipation. During the intermission, I'd been watching a table in the middle of the room. The five young men sitting there were all drinking heavily, but two in particular had been banging their beer bottles on the tabletop, demanding that the Body Artist get going. When the lights went down, theirs were the shrillest whistles in a noisy room.

We sat in the dark for perhaps thirty seconds. When the lights came back up, the Body Artist had appeared onstage.

She sat on a high stool, very still. She was naked except for an electron-sized thong, but cream-colored foundation covered her body, including her face. Only her brown hair, swept up from her neck in a jeweled clip, belonged to the world of the living.

The Artist was completely at ease, her bare legs crossed yoga style, her palms pressed together in front of her breasts. It was the audience that was disturbed: little rustlings, as people crossed and uncrossed legs or fiddled with zippers. Explosions of whispered laughter.

Behind the woman, photographs of body art appeared on a series of screens: a field of lilies grew out of a vagina, with the flowers blooming across the breasts. A face painted like a tiger, magnified so that each whisker, each stripe around the muzzle, was visible. The tiger was replaced by a jungle scene that covered the back: elephants trumpeted on the shoulder blades, a giraffe straddled the spinal column. The jungle was followed by a giant blue eye, lid lowered, on an abdomen, seeming to wink at the vulva below.

The slides changed in time to a sound track of Middle Eastern music. At the front of the stage, two figures clad in burkas gyrated in time to the music. I hadn't noticed them at first, but the burkas somehow exaggerated the eroticism of the dancers' movements and made them almost as disturbing as the body art itself.

I was as uncomfortable as the rest of the audience. The spotlight on the Artist's breasts, the sense that this was a mannequin sitting there, not a woman, was both arousing and unpleasant, and I resented my body for responding to what my mind rejected. Jake Thibaut shifted away from me involuntarily, while Mr. Contreras said in a loud whisper, "This ain't right. It just ain't right!"

The Artist let the tension build until we were all ready to claw at each other, and then she lowered her hands, palms open toward us, in seeming invitation. "Art is in the hands of the maker, it's in the eyes of the beholder, it's in the air we breathe, the sunsets we admire, the dead bodies we wash and wrap in linens for burial. My body is my canvas, but tonight it's yours as well. Tonight is a night to let your imagination run free and to paint, the way you used to paint in kindergarten before you started worrying what someone might say about your work, your art. I'm your canvas, your—bare—canvas."

The five guys who'd been pounding their table, demanding the start of the Artist's act, now whistled and called out. One of them shouted, "Take it all off, girl, take off that thong thing. Let's see some pussy!"

I half turned to look at them. One of them was trying to signal for another round. All five were big guys, and the one shouting for the Body Artist to take off her thong had the kind of muscles you get from lifting heavy stuff all day long. The room was lit dimly, but I could make out a thicket of tattoos along his arms.

The woman on the stool smiled. Maybe she was used to drunken vulgarity. Maybe she enjoyed it.

"Can't we get a drink here?" the tattooed man cried, slapping the table.

"Cool it, Chad," one of his tablemates said.

I looked around for the bouncer and saw him at the back of the room, talking to the owner. They had their eye on the table and seemed to think the quintet didn't need professional attention just yet, but as I watched, I saw the owner shake her head at the waitstaff: No drinks right now, at least not in Chad's part of the room.

The Body Artist held out her arms to the tattooed man so that her breasts drooped forward, hanging like fruit above her thighs. "You and I both like body art, don't we? Come on up, I won't bite. Draw your heart's desire on my body."

"Go on, Chad," his buddies urged him, "go for it, do it. Like the lady says, she don't bite. Or at least not in front of all these other people she won't."

The group began to laugh and pound each other, and the tension eased out of the room.

The Body Artist picked up a brush from a tray of open paint cans on a cart beside her and began painting on her leg. For a moment, we forgot the strangeness of her nudity and watched as she picked up different brushes. She worked quickly, talking the whole time, about the body art convention she'd just attended, about gallery shows around town, about her childhood cat, Basta.

As she painted, the two burka-clad figures posed on the stage, periodically shifting legs or arms into new positions that mimed pleasure or excitement in the Artist's work.

After five minutes, the Body Artist stood, showing off her painting. Only people in the front of the club could see it, but they all clapped and cheered. The rest of us craned, and Chad and his friends got restive again. Before their complaints grew too loud, one of the burkaed figures picked up a camera from the cart that held the Artist's paints and other supplies. The Artist beckoned a man from the table directly in front of the stage. He had the embarrassed exchange with her that people often do when they're called up from the audience by the magician. After a moment, though, he joined her on the raised platform that served as Club Gouge's stage.

One of the dancers handed the camera to the man, and the Artist directed him to point it at her leg. The image appeared on one of the screens: a cat, elongated, disdainful, in the Egyptian style. Underneath it, the Artist had written "Let's see some pussy."

The room roared with laughter. Everyone had been upset by the catcalls from Chad and his drunk friends and was delighted to see them put down. Chad's face seemed to darken in the dim room, but his buddies kept their hands on his arms, and he didn't try to get up from the table.

The Body Artist kidded and prodded the man who'd joined her onstage into taking up a paintbrush. He drew a red stripe down her left arm.

"Now your work will be internationally famous," the Artist said. She handed the camera back to her dancers. One of them focused on her striped arm, which appeared on the middle of the three screens. "These go up in my picture gallery," she said. "You can sign it, if you want, or just tell your friends what to look for."

The man, who was as red as the stripe he'd painted, said he didn't need all that recognition. "You're the artist," he said, "you get the credit." He bowed to her awkwardly and left the platform, to another burst of applause.

After that, several other people felt bold enough to draw on the Artist. No one was able to match any of the elaborate paintings that kept flashing on the screens, but after a bit they'd covered her breasts with blue and green streaks, and someone had drawn a yellow smiley face on one of the Artist's shoulder blades.

Mr. Contreras grew more disturbed as the painting progressed. He wanted to have it out with Petra, but Jake persuaded him that a noisy club wasn't the place for an argument. Max, sizing up my neighbor's agitation, said he had a meeting in the morning, and Lotty had an early surgery call: they were leaving; they would take Mr. Contreras with them.

The old man grudgingly agreed, much to my relief. The thought of riding home with him while he vented his frustration on me was a treat I hadn't been looking forward to. I gave Lotty a grateful kiss, and returned to the table with Jake. Mr. Contreras tried to force Petra to leave with them, but she gave him her biggest, brightest smile and said she'd stay until the end of the act.

The Body Artist kept up a sort of patter while people painted on her. Occasionally, someone would say something that seemed to genuinely interest her, but most of her responses sounded aloof, almost amused at our expense, even while her words celebrated "the community of artists" in which we found ourselves.

One heavyset man walked up to the platform with a kind of rolling gait that made me think of a beat cop. In fact, as he bent to inspect the cans of paint I was pretty sure I could see the outline of his holster. I wondered for a moment if he was going to try to arrest the Artist for indecent exposure, but he dipped a brush into the can of red paint. After inspecting her body for bare spaces, he drew some numbers and letters on her buttocks—everyone else had been too squeamish to touch those. He picked up the camera himself and pointed it at his master-piece. Ignoring the applause and jeers from the audience, he rolled back to his seat.

Just as Jake and I decided we also had seen and heard enough, an-other woman stepped onto the small stage. She didn't say anything to the Body Artist or the audience, but began painting with the kind of focus none of the other volunteers had shown. The two dancers had mimed enthusiasm throughout the show, but now they seemed genu-lnely engaged by the work in progress. They began filming, and we all saw the woman's work: stylized flames that covered the Artist's back were overlaid with an intricate design, scrolls of fleurs-de-lis done in pink and gray. The painter was adding a face to her composition when the tattooed man began shouting again.

"Are you dissing me, bitch? Are you dissing me?"

Chad stood so quickly his buddies couldn't hold him. His chair clat-tered to the floor, and he tried barging past the customer tables to the stage. By that time, the bouncer had reached Chad. He used some moves that I hadn't seen since I left South Chicago. Chad was doubled over and out the door in under a minute.

The bouncer's speed and ability subdued Chad's buddies. When a server suggested they settle their tab and join their friend outside, one of them pulled a fistful of bills from his pocket and laid them on the table without counting or even looking at the check. All four left as quickly as they could.

The owner, a tall woman about my age, climbed onto the small stage. In her own way, she was as striking as the Body Artist. Her hair was black except for a streak of white that fell artistically over her forehead, and she was wearing a big white satin shirt, tucked into skintight black pants. She introduced herself as Olympia Koilada.

"We all owe a big round of applause to our Body Artist. Have fun, but be safe, use protection." She flashed a peace sign, and walked back to the bar.

Canned music began to throb and whine through the room, and the noise in the audience grew loud with relief. Jake and his friends decided to take the Raven out for a late dinner. He was good-natured enough to include Petra, but she announced that she was staying on to talk to the manager.

"I heard them say at the bar that they're shorthanded, and I need more work," Petra said. "You know, my nine-to-five, we're kind of going day to day on whether we'll even have jobs at Christmas, so this would be great."

"A club job would be great?" I said. "It would be even more unreliable than your day gig." Petra was working for a Web-based design firm.

"Have you seen the way people are tipping?" Petra's eyes sparkled. "I used to work as a hostess, you know, in the summers, at my folks' country club. The waitstaff *never* pulled this kind of change, and we still had some pretty good tips."

I wondered if I should try to do more to stop her. Petra was only twenty-three, and, in some ways, I felt responsible for her. She'd stopped taking money from her parents after learning about a serious crime her father had spent his life covering up, and she wasn't used to looking after herself full-time.

Jake waited, a little impatiently, while I tried to talk Petra out of applying for work at the club.

"Don't be a snob, Vic," he said. "I was a roadie in clubs like this all through my twenties, didn't do me any harm. Let's go. I told the others we'd catch up with them at the restaurant."

I followed him into the bitter night. The backup at the parking lot exit looked as though it might take twenty minutes, but an alley ran behind the club; I turned my Mustang around and eased my way against the flow of the traffic.

"Petra was right, it was awesome," Jake said. "And at the same time disturbing, especially those dancers in their burkas. I suppose anyone doing art is manipulating public emotions. I do it myself, so why does her expression seem to cross a boundary?"

"It's the body," I said. "You can't get away from it. Whether we like it or not, we live in a world where the exposed female body is a turn-on. Music only suggests the erotic or the private self. The Body Artist forces you to see the private."

"Maybe. Bass players, we have a reputation as the crudest of musicians, so if I'm uncomfortable at a public display of nudity it makes me think I'm not a genuine bassist. I will confess, in private and to you alone, that I sat there feeling like I didn't have enough clothes on."

I laughed. "Speaking under cover of darkness, I also confess— Hello, what are they doing?"

I had turned in to the alley. Chad and his friends were hovering outside Club Gouge's back entrance. I stopped the car.

"Vic, please don't get out to fight them. I've had enough excitement for one night."

"I never get to have any fun," I whined, but added, "Of course I'm not going to fight them, but I do think the club's nifty bouncer needs to know these guys are hanging around."

I made sure the car doors were locked and pulled out my cell phone, but when the quintet saw us, they moved on down the alley. Ice packed with dirt made the going treacherous, and one of the gang tripped and fell, which gave me time to trail them while I looked up the club's phone number. By the time I'd bumped through the ice and potholes to the street, the men were circling back along Lake Street, toward the main entrance to the club.

"Vic, not that I'm trying to tell you what to do, but you know I'm not going to risk my fingers if you go after them," Jake said. "And I'm pining for bouillabaisse."

His tone was light, but he wasn't joking—his fingers were his livelihood. I didn't know whether to laugh or feel hurt. "Do you really see me as someone who's so pining to fight that I'd take on five drunks twice my size and half my age? My only weapon right now is my cell phone."

"I've seen you come home covered in burns and bruises; I've never been with you when you got them. How was I to know?" Jake squeezed my shoulder to take the edge off his words.

Of course, when I used to cruise South Chicago in my cousin Boom-Boom's wake, there were plenty of times I found myself fighting for no reason I could ever figure out. I decided not to tell Jake about it. It would be hard to persuade him that I'd matured since then.

Someone finally picked up the club's phone. A late-night L clattered overhead as she answered, and, at her end, the music and crowd noise were just as deafening, but she finally realized I wanted to speak to the owner, Olympia Koilada. By this time, I was back in front of the club in time to see Chad and his friends get into their RAV4.

Olympia didn't seem concerned about the guys. "I don't know who you are or why you think it's your business—you're a private eye?—and you think your nose belongs in my business? I don't think so. Controversy brings people to the club, and the Artist knows it. She also knows how to look after herself. I've got a live show coming on in two minutes. Ciao."

The girders to the Lake Street L, and all the similar SUVs streaming in and out of the club's parking lot, made it hard to keep an eye on the RAV4. I finally gave in to Jake's plea that we get to the restaurant.

3

Brush Attack

The next Monday at breakfast, I was startled to see my name jump off the *Herald-Star*'s "Around Town" page, in a small paragraph about the Body Artist and Club Gouge. "Angry customers, who objected to her nudity, tried to lie in wait to attack her, but local PI V. I. Warshawski quickly sent them about their business."

I called the club owner to find out if she'd leaked the story. "Do you know who used my name to prop up some bogus story?"

"What do you mean, bogus story? You called me yourself to tell me that bunch of guys was hanging around the club. I figured I was a little short with you, so I did you a favor, giving you credit. Next time, hire your own publicist."

"Ms. Koilada, those punks didn't object to your artist's nudity. I don't know what pissed them off, whether it was her mocking them with her cat drawing, or the woman who was painting her when they charged the stage, but—"

"But nothing," she snapped. "You don't know what they objected to. Neither do I. But the idea of a nude artist offends some people—"

"And titillates others," I interrupted in turn. "So this little story will bring more people to Club Gouge. Congratulations."

I hung up, making a face at myself. A phone call like that was a waste of energy, and I should have known better than to make it. I went down to my office and tried to put the club out of my mind—not so easy, since my cousin Petra had taken a job there. I learned this from her texts: She, like, totally loved the club! *tps r aweso cows gr8!* I got the *tps* but didn't understand the *cows*. Petra sent back one impatient word: *coworkers*.

Two weeks after our outing to Club Gouge, Petra bounced in mid-afternoon on Sunday. Mr. Contreras, her honorary "Uncle Sal," so adores her that she was taken aback when he started lecturing her over taking the job at Club Gouge.

"You're a young gal, Petra Warshawski, but not too young to know right from wrong. What are you up to, wanting to work in a degenerate place like that? And that—that woman, that Olympia, who owns it—she's no better than a madam in a brothel. I saw plenty like her in Italy during the war, and I know one when I see one."

"Are you talking about the Body Artist? She is not degenerate! Her performance is totally cutting-edge. You live, like, in a cocoon here. You don't know anything about art or you'd know that just because someone is naked up on a stage it doesn't mean they're a bad person! If some man painted a picture of her naked and hung it in a museum, you'd think, wow, he's a totally great artist. Well, she's a totally great artist, and she doesn't need a man or a museum to make her famous. You saw her, Vic. Explain to Uncle Sal how she's reclaiming her body and how that helps all women reclaim their own bodies."

I eyed her thoughtfully. In the seven months I'd spent around my cousin, this was the first time she'd revealed any awareness of women's issues, in the arts or anywhere else.

"Pretty sophisticated analysis, Petra. The Body Artist tell you this, or did you think about it in the middle of the night and have one of those lightbulb moments?"

Petra flamed crimson and shifted her weight in her high-heeled boots.

"Does she have a name?" I asked.

"Of course she does, but she likes to be called the Body Artist, so we all respect that. So what did you think of her, if you can say it without being a total snot?"

"You're right, I was a snot. Sorry. I found it disquieting to watch her. The way she talks, the way she holds herself, she seems contemptuous of her audience, or at least of people like me. Maybe she's bold and heroic, turning stereotypes on their heads, and I only was uncomfortable because I'm not liberated enough. But maybe—"

"Liberated?" Mr. Contreras exploded. "Sitting stark stone naked in front of an audience? I'm ashamed of the both of you. Victoria, you're a grown woman. You shouldn't sit back while the kid gets into bad company. And Petra, this isn't healthy, watching a woman take off her clothes in public."

He was seriously upset, using our real names like that, instead of "Cookie" and "Peewee." Petra made her pouty face, and went to put her arms around him. She danced him back down the stairs, hoping to coax him back to his more usual good humor, or perhaps to persuade him that the Body Artist wasn't degenerate. As I was shutting the door behind them, I heard her say, "But, really, Uncle Sal, you can't tell me you didn't look at girlie magazines when you were in the Army. Why is someone nude onstage any worse?"

When I was alone, I felt hollow, restless. I didn't want to be with Mr. Contreras and Petra and their argument, I wanted a relaxing evening with good friends. I could hear Jake across the hall playing with a group of students or colleagues, maybe girlfriends, and tried to suppress a sense of jealous exclusion. At the end of January, he was leaving for a European tour. Between rehearsals and the run-up to Christmas—the busiest season for a musician—most of his life was spent away from me these days.

I cleaned the week's dishes out of the kitchen sink, and then, inspired by Jake's group, did a few breathy vocal exercises. Finally, out of nervous irritability, I looked up the Body Artist's website.

It was an odd site. She had a blog, which was mostly a series of ramblings on women in the arts, but the bulk of the site was dedicated to her body painting. You could actually buy "pieces of flesh," as she called them—photographs of the various images we'd seen last night at Club Gouge. Each picture—priced from a hundred to a thousand dollars, depending on size, format, and content—had the number of buyers clocked under it. The most popular were the lilies growing out of her vagina and the winking blue eye.

Looking at her site added to my rumpled feelings. Who was exploiter, who was exploited? I finally went down to Mr. Contreras's place and collected the dogs. Petra was curled up on the couch, Mitch at her side, but she was still arguing her case with my neighbor. I took the dogs and fled before the combatants could drag me back into battle.

The December night was cold but clear. We ran east, all the way to the lakefront. By the time we returned home, Petra had left. I gave the dogs back to Mr. Contreras but refused to let him reopen his grievance over the Body Artist and Club Gouge.

"Pitchers and catchers report to Mesa in two weeks," I said, "Everything will get better after that."

"Except Cubs fans. Don't go trying no fake smiles on me, doll. I'm not in the mood. Spring training means lowlifes getting ready to piss on the grass."

Mr. Contreras was a Sox fan. He'd grown up west of old Comiskey, and he hated being here in Wrigleyville during the baseball season. At least loutish Cubs fans meant a change of grievance for him, but I didn't feel like listening to that, either.

The year was winding down, and my own workload was heavy. Hard times meant a big upswing in fraud. Even though my clients were slower in paying their bills and negotiating reduced fees for big inquiries, I still had more business than I could comfortably handle.

The only times I saw Jake were when I could make it to one of his concerts; now and then, I'd go out for a late supper with him and some of his fellow musicians. We spent Christmas Day together, and then he left to visit his mother and sister in Seattle.

Lotty and Max flew to Morocco over Christmas; Petra went skiing in Utah with her mother and sisters. Even Mr. Contreras left, although it was only to drive to Hoffman Estates, near O'Hare, where he spent a few days with his unhappy daughter and her two sons. I didn't like the feeling of isolation, home alone in Chicago. I put the dogs in a kennel and flew down to Mexico City for a week of art, music, and warmth.

The return to Chicago the day after New Year's felt in some ways like the descent to the Underworld. No sun, bitter cold, sick friends, and a dozen messages from unhappy clients who wanted to know if I really cared about their business or if I was just living it up on their money. Within twenty-four hours, sun and dancing seemed as remote as the end of the galaxy.

The Thursday after I came home, I left a client meeting in the Loop that had run until almost nine. I was walking east, toward the Dearborn L, imagining dinner, a drink, and a bath, when Petra texted me: *rgent biz cll @ 1s—urgent business, call at once.* I felt young and hip when I realized I had translated it effortlessly.

"Vic, you have to come over right now!" she cried when I phoned.

"Over where?" I demanded.

"The club! Someone just tried to kill the Body Artist."

I ducked into a building entrance so I could speak to her away from the street noise and the cold. "When? Have you called the cops?"

"She won't let us. She says it's nothing. Can you *please* come?"

"*Let* you? You don't need her per—"

Petra cut me off with a hasty, "Gotta go, table 11 is screaming for their drinks," and hung up. I thought wistfully of my bath, and my bottle of Johnnie Walker, but hopped around the slushy curbs on Dearborn and continued east to Wabash and the Lake Street L.

This time of night, the L is full, with students getting out of night school and weary late workers like me heading home. Most of my companions had little white wires snaking from pockets to ears, making them look as though their heads were being transfused. A number of them were texting at the same time or listening to their earclips. They looked like the descendants of *Alien Nation* getting commands from the mother ship.

I got off the train at Ashland and hurried to Club Gouge as fast as I could on the icy sidewalk. Even though it was a weeknight, the parking lot was almost full. The people coming and going through the club's doors seemed to be chattering normally, not with the hushed excitement they'd show around a crime scene.

The bouncer was inspecting people's bags and backpacks before letting them in. That was the only sign that something unusual had happened. No one protested—we're all inured these days to being searched. Pretty soon, we'll have to get undressed before we walk into our apartment buildings at night, and we'll probably submit to that without a murmur.

When I reached the front of the line, I showed the bouncer my PI license and explained that Petra had summoned me. The bouncer, Mark, looked me up and down but nodded me into the club.

"I don't know if the Artist'll talk to you," he said, "but she's in the back. Her performance starts in about twenty minutes—I'll get Petra to take you to her."

"What happened?"

Mark shuffled his feet.

"She'll tell you herself. I'm not a hundred percent sure."

I looked at him narrowly, wondering what he didn't want to reveal, but went into the club. Olympia was behind the bar, helping the two bartenders keep up with the orders. As the Body Artist's performance time was drawing near, the club was filling, and drink orders were piling up.

Olympia was striking, with her dyed black hair and the thick streak of white over her left eye. She was dressed in black and white, too, as if she, like the Body Artist, were a canvas on display. Tonight she was wearing a pantsuit that shimmered like oilcloth under the lights. The jacket was open to her breastbone, where you could see the fringed top of a white camisole.

My cousin was easy to find. At five-eleven, with her halo of spiky hair adding another three inches, she towered over most of the room. When I tapped her arm, she finished delivering drinks to four tables without missing an order and then waltzed me behind the stage to the small changing room set aside for performers.

She knocked perfunctorily on the door but opened it without waiting for an answer. The Body Artist was sitting in the lotus position, eyes shut, breathing slowly. She was already naked except for her thong, which was covered with the same kind of cream foundation paint as her body. Close up, she looked more like a mannequin than before, which was somehow more disturbing than her nudity.

Petra cleared her throat uncertainly. "Uh, this is my cousin, the detective, you know. I told you I was calling her when you said you didn't want the police here. Vic, Body Artist. Body Artist, Vic. I've got to get back to my station."

She backed out of the room, the feathery ends of her hair brushing against the top of the door frame.

The Artist looked up at me. "I don't want to be disturbed before my performance. Come back later."

"Nope," I said. "Later, I'm going to be home. I've been working since eight this morning and I'm beat. Who attacked you?"

"I don't know."

"Where did it happen?"

"Here, in my dressing room."

"The first time I was here, some big guy with tattoos tried to attack you. Was it him?"

"It was . . . an indirect assault. Not a mugging."

"Were you attacked at all?" I asked. "Or is this a publicity stunt—will I see a paragraph in tomorrow's paper that I repelled yet another customer infuriated by your nudity?"

The Artist's eyes were hard to read inside the mask of paint. "It was a real assault."

She rose, with the fluid motion of a dancer, and showed me her left leg. Beneath the foundation paint, I could just make out the long line of a cut.

"A piece of glass was hidden in one of my brushes. It's in the garbage now."

I put on my gloves and extracted the brush from the pile of tissues and sponges that was filling the can. It was soft, made of sable, the bristles about an inch wide and two inches long. A glass shard had been attached to the bristle head with a piece of wire painted the same color as the handle. Even so, it was easy to spot.

"How come you didn't see the glass?" I asked.

"I've done this so many times, I don't think about it," she said. "I unroll my brushes, stick them in the paint containers ready to take onstage, and apply my foundation."

"So your brush was rigged before you got here tonight?"

"Maybe. But I dropped everything off here this afternoon so that I could run some errands, and I don't lock the case." She waved a hand at a large metal suitcase under the dressing table.

"You need to give this to the cops. If there's poison on it, or tetanus—"

"I'll get a tetanus shot tomorrow morning. But I don't want the police here." For the first time, she sounded agitated, even angry.

"Why not? Someone injured you."

"I don't want police in here slobbering over me, and I don't want to put clothes on over my foundation. Period, end of story."

Olympia had appeared in the doorway without my noticing. "Who are you? Oh, right, Warshawski, the detective who craves anonymity. The Artist has to go onstage in five minutes, and you're going to hurt her performance, badgering her like this. You need to leave."

I asked Olympia the same question I'd put to the Body Artist about the tattooed guy at the table of drunks who'd tried to jump the Artist the night I came with Jake and his friends. "Chad, I think I heard his pals call him."

"Drunks don't have the subtlety for something like this," the Artist said.

She was staring at Olympia when she spoke. The heavy foundation made it impossible to read her expression, but it flashed through my mind that Olympia had rigged the brush, or at least that the Artist thought she had.

"Get out now, Warshawski," Olympia said. "Go sit at a table in the back—we'll treat you to a drink."

"Thanks, Olympia, but I'm way past my limit tonight."

Over objections from both women, I put the brush into a plastic bag the Body Artist had used to hold cotton balls, wrote down the date and place I'd found it, and tucked it into a pocket of my handbag. On my way out of the club, I scanned the crowd. I didn't see Chad or his friends, but the heavyset man who looked like a cop was there again. He was nursing a drink at a table by himself. Morose, off-duty policeman without friends, the kind who makes headlines by using his weapon in a crowded bar.

Another person, sitting close to the front, also looked familiar. I studied her for a moment and then decided she was the painter whose work had provoked Chad. Her thin shoulders were hunched up around her ears. Her hands were on the table, tensed so tightly that I could see the tendons raised across the back. She, too, seemed to be alone.

4

Individual of Interest

It was a week later that Petra dropped by my office on her way home from her day job. She was drooping. Even her spiky hair had collapsed, and she looked less like a radiant Valkyrie than a houseplant in need of water.

I was in the middle of a complicated transaction with an Ajax Insurance auditor, trying to unravel a fraud committed by one of their claims adjustors, but I gave my cousin an extra-bright smile to show that I loved her and was delighted to see her.

While I talked the accountant through the entries I'd made in my audit software, Petra wandered around my office. She fiddled with stacks of documents, studied her teeth in the glass over my Antonella Mason painting, and then spun a crystal paperweight, a gift from a grateful client, on its edge. She was so distracting that I finally beckoned her over and told her to go across the street for a couple of espressos. By the time she'd returned, her hair damp from the snow that was starting to fall, I'd finished my phone call with Ajax.

I sat her down in the alcove reserved for clients, the sole clutter-free place in my office. "What's up, babe?"

"I, uh, Vic . . . Did you ever find out who put that piece of glass in the Body Artist's paintbrush?"

"No, why? Has it happened again?"

Petra shook her head. "No. I just wondered."

She had taken off her ski jacket. Underneath, she had on a big sweater topped by a fringed buckskin vest. She wasn't taking money from her dad, but her mother had restocked her closet during their Christmas ski trip.

She started braiding and unbraiding the fringes on the vest. I tried to curb my impatience. She was troubled, and like all troubled people who come to that corner alcove it was hard for her to get to the point.

"I sent the brush up to a forensic lab I use," I said. "The glass didn't have any germs or poisons on it, and they couldn't lift any fingerprints from the handle. Do you think you know who did it?"

Petra looked up. "No . . . No, I don't . . . But I sort of wondered . . . The atmosphere at the club, ever since that night—really, ever since after Christmas—it's changed. Olympia is, like . . . I don't know—"

"You're wondering if Olympia spiked the brush?" I cut into her dithering.

She made a face. "It's nothing so concrete. But there's this woman who comes in almost every time the Body Artist is performing—I think her name is Nadia—and she does this same picture over and over. She's really good, compared to all the weirdos and sleazoids who want to paint their names or, you know, something gross, but—"

"Was she there when Jake and I came right after Thanksgiving? She was painting pink hats, and a woman's face, and she got that tattooed guy all wound up."

"That's her. Well, Olympia and the Artist have been arguing about her. It's almost like—well, the way they talk—it's sort of like Olympia and the Artist are lovers, or were lovers—I don't know—something like that. And now this Nadia is coming between them, or something."

"It is tiresome when people bring their love life to work, but unless you feel threatened I wouldn't worry about it. Just stay out of the middle. Or quit if it gets too rocky."

"I'm not a baby, I don't care who sleeps with who, although it is like being back in tenth grade when they flaunt it at you." She leaned forward in her earnestness, her hands on her knees. "Vic, I know you and Uncle Sal both were kind of down on me working at a club, but when I started there I loved it, I loved everything about it. The energy, my coworkers, the acts. Olympia, she's amazing. Her music is so cutting-edge, she's so bold. She's only a few years younger than my gran—my mom's mom—but she's so together! I loved working for her. Now, though, she doesn't seem the same. And it's not just the stuff with Nadia and the Artist."

Her voice trailed away, and she started pulling at a loose thread in her jeans, hiding her face from me.

"What's going on, Petra? What aren't you telling me? Drugs?" I added sharply when she didn't answer.

She looked up at me, her mascaraed lashes brushing her brows. "I don't know. I mean, I know people there are using—you're running around, waiting tables, you see who's putting stuff up their noses or into their drinks or whatever—but I never saw any sign that Olympia was using or even dealing. I did ask Mark—Mark Alexander, her bouncer—and he says Olympia doesn't tolerate drugs in the club . . . at least, not staff bringing them in."

I nodded but took Mark's assurances with a grain of salt. If people were doing drugs in the club, it was because Olympia was turning a blind eye.

"It's really Nadia and the Artist that seem to cause—well, they don't cause it—but whenever Nadia shows up, even though all she does is paint on the Artist, everyone is out of whack. Like those guys, the tattooed guy and his friends. The one guy, Chad, he gets so furious I think he might have a heart attack on the spot. I don't know why he keeps coming back, but it's, like, he can't leave the club alone. And Olympia, she's, like, Let him come in, as long as he isn't violent, because his gang runs up these huge tabs."

She grinned briefly. "And then his buddies leave these humungous tips because they feel embarrassed. So, of course, in a way we all welcome them on the nights they show up."

She started tearing pieces from her coffee cup. "The problem is, this guy has been hitting on me, and when I put him down, Olympia behaved really oddly."

"What guy?" I demanded. "Chad?"

"No. Chad only cares about Nadia. I mean, she's the person who winds him up, or maybe it's the Artist—it's hard to be sure. This older guy, he's kind of crude, and he can't keep his hands to himself. So first I kidded him, you know, going, 'Whoa, buster, seems like your fingers kind of forgot curfew. Better tell 'em to stay home where they belong.' Well, that was like slapping a whale with a goldfish—totally useless. So next time I kicked him good on the shin, and he talked to Olympia, and she came to me and said I couldn't go around kicking customers. So I explained what happened, and she said, Are you sure? And I said, I know what a hand feels like when it's inside my pants, and she said, If I overlooked it, there'd be something extra in my pay envelope. But—"

"Quit." I said flatly. "If Olympia is running drugs—and a bar is a perfect Laundromat for drug money—you don't want to be there when the cops shut her down. And if she's pimping for some sleazoid, you need to run for the exit."

"I will if I have to. But, Vic, it's almost four hundred a week in tips I'm getting there, pretty much tax-free. And my day job, I don't know how much longer they'll keep me on. Would you—I know it's a lot to ask—but could you—"

"What, shoot him?" I asked when she broke off.

That made her laugh.

"If you could do it and not get caught, I'd be your slave for life! No, but could you check him out, do you think, see who he is, see if there's something you could do to make him stop?"

"Do you have his name?" I asked.

"Olympia calls him Rodney. I'm not sure what his last name is—Stranger-Danger, maybe." She scrolled through her cell phone and held it out to me. "This is what he looks like."

She'd taken his picture from above, when she was passing his table. It wasn't a good likeness, but it didn't surprise me to see it was the guy I'd pegged as an off-duty cop. Petra wasn't working tonight, but she said she'd be at the club the next night. I promised to stop in, although it bugged me that my cousin insisted on staying on at the joint.

Petra zipped up her ski jacket, her face brighter now that she'd unburdened herself and gotten a promise of help. Even her hair, matted down by her ear warmer, seemed to be springing up.

"Vic—don't tell Uncle Sal, okay? He's already on me about the club being so degenerate and all, and—"

"Sweet Pea, I'm not so sure he's wrong. If I see coke or ecstasy or some damned thing passing between Olympia and Mr. Stranger-Danger, you are quitting on the spot, you hear?"

"Sure, Vic, I promise." She held up three fingers in the Girl Scout salute and danced out the door.

I finished my number crunching for Ajax Insurance. The claims manager seemed to have the intelligence of an eggplant. He should have been able to generate the report himself, but a hundred fifty an hour—I wouldn't complain.

5

What on Earth Is Going On?

I returned to the club the following night. The Body Artist was appearing, and the joint was alive, practically shaking with twenty- and thirtysomethings. Rodney was there, and so were Chad and his friends. I didn't see Nadia.

I took a table near the back, but Olympia swept over as I was pulling out a chair at one of the rear tables. Tonight she was wearing a black sweater with a deep cleavage over black velvet pants; her touch of white was a corsage of feathers that brushed the swell of her breasts.

"That table's reserved, Warshawski. I don't have a free seat in the house. You'll have to stand."

"Not a problem, Olympia."

I got up and moved to the railing that created a kind of foyer between the audience space and the club entrance. I wasn't going to give her an excuse to throw me out by losing my temper.

"And there's a twenty-dollar cover on the night the Body Artist appears. All drinks are six dollars, more for name brands."

I stuck a hand inside my sweater and pretended to be fumbling with my bra. "Want the money now?"

She frowned. "A private eye is bad for business, Warshawski. If you interrupt the show or harass the Artist, I'll see that you're thrown out."

"I'll tell you what's bad for business, Ms. Koilada: you dealing drugs, or laundering money, or whatever you and Rodney are up to. I want you to know that my cousin Petra's safety is very important to me."

She flicked her eyes across the room again. "Petra is safe here. No one will hurt her. She's popular with my customers and with the staff. She has the kind of good-natured high spirits that make a server popular. Some of our customers may get overenthusiastic in their reaction to her, but she seems levelheaded. I'd be surprised to know she was blowing up something trivial into something major."

"Me, too. That's why I took her reaction seriously. Olympia, even if I'm not a good-natured, high-spirited kind of gal, you could do worse than trust me with your problems. If this guy Rodney is posing a threat—"

"Maybe being a detective makes you think you can pry into people's affairs, whether they want it or not, but my club is my business, not yours."

"Who is Rodney?" I asked. "Is he a cop?"

"Are you deaf? I told you to mind your own business."

She turned on her heel. The club needed too much supervising on a packed night like tonight for her to waste more time arguing with me.

I didn't see her stop to talk to Rodney, but she must have because he got up from his table and came over to me.

"Girlie, you put one foot wrong here, and I'll personally stuff your body in a snowbank."

"'Girlie'? You sound like a bad movie script, Rodney."

His lips curved into something like a sneer. "Maybe, but you could look like part of a bad movie yourself if you try to mess with me. Got it?"

I leaned against the railing and yawned. "Go put on a sheet and dance around a cross if you want to scare people. That how you got Olympia so rattled?"

He pulled his hand back as if he were going to hit me but thought better of it in the nick of time.

"No one messes with me, girlie. Not you, and not that smart-mouthed cousin of yours, either."

"People who mess with me or my cousin tend to spend a lot of years in Stateville, Rodney, when they aren't picking themselves out of gutters—or snowbanks. Ask around, anyone will tell you the same. Now, go back to your chair. The band is packing up, the Artist will be onstage soon, and the rest of the audience will be peevish if you block their view."

His face scrunched together in ugly lines like a thwarted toddler's. He flipped his coat open so I could see the outsize gun in his shoulder holster, but I pretended to be looking at the stage.

He finally hissed, "Just watch yourself, girlie," and swaggered back to his seat a few seconds before the houselights went down.

I made a face in the dark. Maybe I hadn't changed so much from those days of trailing around South Chicago with Boom-Boom, looking for fights.

The lights came back up, and the routine followed its usual course, with the Artist appearing magically on her stool. The audience reacted in their usual way, gasping with amazement at the intricacy of the work on the plasma screens, shifting nervously with sexual excitement at the more graphic imagery.

Rodney, at his central table, was staring moodily at his sixth bottle of beer. He didn't seem to be in the mood to paint tonight. Nadia had appeared without my noticing, perhaps when the lights were down, or maybe when Rodney was threatening me. She was at a table near the front, twirling her hair around her fingers. She didn't wait, as she had the first time I'd seen her, for the rest of the room to paint. I studied Chad while Nadia painted, but he seemed to have himself under control. Maybe he was getting used to her. Or maybe his friends had persuaded him to stay calm. He seemed to be more intent on Nadia's drawings than on Nadia herself—he was watching the screens onstage where the webcams were broadcasting her work.

Again, she was creating her intricate design. I'd remembered them as pink hats, but they were pink-and-gray scrolls. When she finished covering the Artist's back with them, she began drawing a woman's face, a beautiful young woman with dark curly hair, and then she took a palette knife and slashed it.

I looked over at Chad. He was sweating, and his tattooed arms were shaking. His buddies were holding him, but he didn't make any effort to get out of his chair.

As soon as Nadia had finished, she went back to her table and gathered her coat and backpack from the floor. She skirted the back of the stage and disappeared. Chad suddenly broke away from his friends and followed her.

Most of the club, including the waitstaff, was focused on the Artist, who was stretching and preening to make Nadia's work as visible as possible. Those who saw Chad might have assumed he was heading for the men's room, since the toilets were along a narrow corridor that also led backstage. I pushed my way through the crowd at the back as fast as I could.

A young man in a worn Army windbreaker hurried after me. He'd been with Chad at their table. His face, pitted and craggy despite his youth, was unmistakable. We got backstage just in time to see the alley door shut behind Chad.

"Man! Don't be doing something stupid now."

The guy seemed to be talking to himself more than me, but we sprinted together to the door.

So many cars filled the area that we couldn't see Chad or Nadia at first, but we heard Chad shouting, "Why are you doing this? Who sent you here?" as we slipped and stumbled along the icy gravel of the parking lot toward his voice.

Chad, under one of the streetlamps, was standing over Nadia. He wasn't touching her, but he was leaning down so his face was close to hers. He'd left his coat in the bar, and the lamp picked up the tattoos along his bare forearms. He was holding a black object, something that looked like an outsize oven mitt, under her face. Even in her bulky parka, Nadia looked frail next to him.

We reached them in time to hear Nadia say, "Who sent you? Are you spying on me?" while Chad was yelling, "Don't pretend you don't know what this is! Why are you doing this to me?"

Chad's friend sprinted to his side and wrapped an arm across his neck, affection and restraint in one gesture. "You don't want to be out here in the cold, man. Come on. Let's go back inside, warm up, get another beer."

I pulled Nadia away, leading her across the parking lot toward Lake Street. "Nadia, what's going on here? Why is Chad so upset by your painting?"

"Who are you?" She blinked at me.

"My name's V. I. Warshawski. I'm a private investigator, and if there's something—"

"A detective? Go to hell!" She wrenched free of my hand. "I'm sick and tired of people spying on me. Tell them that!"

"Tell who that? I'm not spying on you. I just want to know—"

"I've seen you in the club. I know what you're doing there. No one is going to stop me from painting—"

"I don't want to stop you. Please, Nadia, can we talk where it's warmer? It's brutal out here."

"We can't talk at all. If you come near me again, I'll . . . I'll spray pepper in your eyes."

She broke away from me, stomped down Lake Street to the L stop.

I watched as she climbed up to the platform, puzzled by the whole exchange. Chad's and Nadia's accusations of spy versus spy made them seem like a married couple in the middle of a bad divorce. But what was the black oblong Chad had held under her nose?

When I returned to the club, the Body Artist was finishing her act. No one had painted over Nadia's work, but the Artist's front and arms were covered with crude drawings, stripes, a tic-tac-toe board, and a few sunflowers.

"All of you are amazing, amazing artists. Feel good about who you are in the world, how creative you are, and come see your work on my website, at embodiedart.com. Remember, it's a cold, cruel world out there, but art can keep you warm even if it can't keep you safe."

She held up her hands in a peace sign, and left the stage. Olympia kept the images running on the screens while she turned canned music back on, and the audience relaxed into explosions of laughter. The release of sexual tension made everyone order drinks, and my cousin and the rest of the waitstaff were running around madly for the next twenty minutes.

I'd had enough of everyone at Club Gouge, but I went back to the Body Artist's dressing room thinking I should at least talk to her. Olympia's bouncer was standing outside her door.

"Sorry, but she doesn't want to be disturbed after her performance. It takes a long time for her to clean up, and she's exhausted."

"I know just how she feels."

I smiled and ducked under his arm and was in the dressing room before he could grab me. He followed me as the Artist started squawking in outrage.

I'd wondered if she wanted privacy to do drugs after her act, but she was, in fact, putting some kind of paint-removing cream on her arms and legs, then wiping it off with hand towels. The floor around her was littered with paint-smeared towels. I wondered if she was a big enough star that someone cleaned up after her or if she had to do her own laundry.

"Ms. Artist, did you tell Nadia I was in the club to spy on her?"

The Artist kept wiping herself off with towels and refused to say anything, but her flat, almost transparent eyes studied me in the mirror.

"She's sure she's being spied on," I said. "Is she paranoid or is someone really after her?"

"You'd have to ask her, wouldn't you?" the Artist said.

"Nadia waits in here, doesn't she, while the band plays? She gets special treatment from you, and that annoys Olympia. But it makes me think she's told you why she's so nervous. Are she and Chad in the middle of a bad divorce?"

The Artist smiled for the first time. With contempt, not good humor.

"I'm not going to help you build a dossier on anyone," she said. "Now it's time for you to leave. Unless you want to clean my cunt for me."

She used the shocking word deliberately, as if to goad me into blushing or flinching. I looked at her steadily until she bit her lips in discomfort and turned away.

"Mark, get her out of here. Or call the cops."

Mark took my shoulder. "You heard her. Don't make me break your arm or something."

"Or your hand," I said, "or the mirrors in here. I'm not going to fight you, Mark, at least not tonight."

I let him escort me out of the room, feeling grumpy with everyone including myself. I had been an ineffectual cousin with Petra and a lousy detective. I felt even worse the following night. That was when Nadia was murdered. That was when I was up past two a.m. talking with Terry Finchley and his team.

6

Blood, Blood, Blood

By the time I finally finished talking to Terry Finchley, to lesser cops, saw my cousin safely into her Pathfinder, and argued with Olympia, it was almost three. None of us got much out of our night together.

I learned from Finchley that Nadia's last name was Guaman. I learned she had been a graphic designer—hence, her skill with the paintbrush—and that she had turned twenty-eight this past fall. I learned that she had died from the massive bleeding caused by two bullets entering her chest, and that she had been shot at a range of about fifteen feet—the distance from the back door of the club to the alley, where the shooters had waited.

While I was talking to Terry, one of his team came over with a report about Chad and his friends. No one could provide a last name for any of them, but Finchley took their descriptions and put out an alert. They hadn't been in the club tonight, but that didn't mean Chad hadn't been lying in wait for Nadia.

When Terry asked me what I knew about Chad and his friends, I only shrugged. I don't know why I didn't tell him about the heated exchange I'd heard between Chad and Nadia the previous night. Maybe it was Nadia's vulnerability, or the fact that I'd cradled her in my arms as she died. Or the discomfort I'd felt when she accused me of spying on her. She thought someone was after her, and I'd thought she might be paranoid. Now she was dead. I didn't feel like discussing it with the police.

I told Finchley most of the rest of what I knew, including finding the glass in the Body Artist's paintbrush. He demanded that I retrieve it from the Cheviot labs, but he also revealed that he'd been able to pry the Body Artist's name out of her.

"Karen Buckley. Not a very jazzy name for a stripper. Maybe that's why she wouldn't let anyone around here know it," Finchley added.

"She's not a stripper," I said. "She's an artist, and a fine one."

"A woman who takes off her clothes on a stage for men to drool over is a stripper, in my book."

"Bobby's right," I said. "You've been breathing the rare air on South Michigan way too long. You need to buy yourself a new book. What about this guy Rodney? You find anything out about him?"

"What guy Rodney?" Finchley demanded.

"Didn't anyone here mention him? Big guy with a gut, looks like an off-duty cop, with a big old nine-millimeter under his jacket. It looked like an HK when he shoved his armpit in my face."

"And why did he do that, Vic?" Finchley said. "You weren't in *his* face, by any chance, were you?"

"I was telling him to stop sticking his hand into my cousin's pants when she's waiting tables. Does that constitute being in his face to you? And whether it does or not, does that mean he gets to wave a gun at me?"

Finchley pressed his lips together. He's a good cop, and a good detective, but he's close to a police sergeant I used to date. He still holds it against me that Conrad Rawlings got shot while he was involved with me. The human heart, or thyroid gland, or whatever it is that controls our emotions, is too tangled for me to understand. Conrad survived, but our affair didn't, and I've never been sure which the Finch blames me for more—the breakup or the shooting.

Finchley sent an underling to fetch Olympia to the small stage, where the police were conducting interrogations. She looked briefly frightened, or maybe angry, when he asked her about Rodney, but then gave him her brightest smile and said, "I'm sure I know who Vic means. He's a regular, he loves Karen's show, but— are you sure his name is Rodney, Vic? I thought it might be Roger, or Sydney."

I gasped at the brazenness of her lies, but before I could speak, Finchley was asking if she had had any complaints from her staff or from other customers.

"I gave one of Vic's cousins a job here, and Vic is a mite over-protective, maybe jumps too fast to conclusions. If Petra can't handle a little good-natured kidding with the customers, then I'm afraid she shouldn't work in a club."

"Is that why you comp his drinks, Olympia?" I asked. "To encourage the good-natured kidding? And why you offered Petra a bonus if she'd overlook His Gropiness?"

Olympia's eyes seemed to glitter, but that might just have been the bright lights on the stage. "Your cousin needs to get a handle on her imagination. I don't comp drinks here. I know she's young, but this is a bad economy. I can take my pick of waitstaff—I don't need Petra Warshawski."

She turned back to Finchley, leaning so close that the white feathers of her corsage almost tickled his nose. "Detective, I'm sorry Vic is try-ing to involve you in her cousin's problems when everyone knows it was that disturbed guy who must have shot poor Nadia."

"Chad, you mean. Yes, we've heard about him. We'll keep our eyes open. A last name would help."

Olympia gave her best imitation of a silly, ignorant female, spreading her hands with a little hiccup of a laugh. "We don't seem to go in for last names here. I only learned poor Nadia's from you tonight. I don't know Roger's—or Rodney's, if Vic insists—and I don't know Chad's, either."

While Officer Milkova took Olympia back to her office, the Finch looked at me. "You may be telling the truth, Vic. Guy may be Rodney, not Roger. He may have wandering hands, and she may comp his drinks. But I don't have the resources to check all that out unless it turns out that Nadia Guaman was shot with a nine-millimeter HK . . . She's very good, Ms. Olympia Koilada."

"I guess. Depending on what good means to you." Smooth as silk lingerie—good like that, I guess. "There's some relationship between Olympia and Rodney, more than customer and patron. I don't know if he's selling drugs here, or is blackmailing her, but it's important to her that he be kept happy."

"I'll keep that in mind, Vic," Finchley said, his voice tight. "Right now, the most likely person of interest is this guy Chad. Once we've found him, we'll see if we need to look for Rodney, if your guy's name is Rodney."

I got to my feet. "Good night, Terry. Let me know how it all turns out."

"You have to sign a statement, Warshawski, like everyone else."

"When you have something for me to sign, you know where to find me."

I climbed off the shallow stage and started toward the exit, but before I could get out the front door Olympia hustled me into a cubby-hole behind the bar that served as her office. There was just room for her computer table and a stool. She stood so close to me that I could smell the mix of sweat, cigarettes, and Opium in her body stocking.

"Why can't you mind your own business? The cops are on the trail of this guy Chad. Why did you have to drag one of my best customers out for them to sniff at?"

"Because he's a violent guy. Sports a weapon, isn't afraid to show it in an effort to intimidate. Not that I really care, but what hold does he have on you?"

"You're the one who's a problem in my club. Ever since you started coming here, I've had nothing but trouble."

"Save your femmy ignorance for Rodney. It won't work on Terry Finchley, and it definitely won't work on me. You're the one who said controversy was great for your business. For all I know, you're the person who put glass in the Artist's paintbrush."

"How dare you make an accusation like that against me in my own club!"

I leaned against the thin plywood wall. "Olympia," I said. "I'm so tired I'm about to fall over. I don't care what you're hiding or doing as long as it's not something criminal that might hurt my cousin. But don't try to jack me around. I don't have the patience or the time for it."

I pried open the door, but Olympia grabbed my arm. "I'm sorry. I'm beside myself, I—Nadia getting shot like that—it's so horrible."

"Okay. Try to think clearly. Tell me what's really on your mind. Why are you protecting Rodney but sacrificing Chad, who also seems to be a good customer, one who pays for his own drinks?"

"If I thought Rodney had killed Nadia—"

"So you agree that's his first name. What about his last name? Or have you paid for protection you're not willing to sacrifice?"

The color drained from her face. "What do you know about him?"

I tried to push my tired brain into sorting out what she was revealing. "Not enough, apparently. But, believe me, I have the resources to help me find out more."

I ignored her bleating and stomped through the club to the rear exit. I picked my way across the ruts in the club's parking lot, my path well lighted by the blue strobes on the squad cars. It was a disconcerting juxtaposition, the strobes outside the club and the strobes inside, as if there were two performance spaces. It worried me that both looked artificial, as if a woman shot at close range were no more real than a naked woman on a stool painting her body.

As soon as I got home, I ran inside to turn on the shower. While I waited for the water to heat, I inspected myself in the mirror. I did have blood in my hair.

I stripped and dropped my clothes in the tub. I didn't know if it would ruin the sweater to get it wet like this, but I wasn't sure I'd ever feel able to wear it again, anyway.

I climbed into the shower and shampooed my hair twice. I used a coarse brush to scrub my fingernails. I climbed out and put my sodden clothes onto the radiator, but I felt a trickle on my spine and shuddered. It was only water—I was sure it was only water—but I couldn't stop myself. I climbed back under the shower. I understood Lady Macbeth's fetish now: every time I got out, I would feel blood on my scalp again. It was only when the hot water ran out that I finally dried off and went to bed.

Nadia and Karen Buckley, the Body Artist, filled my unquiet dreams. Buckley was in the parking lot, painting the ice-packed ruts under the blue strobes of the cop cars. When I bent to see her work, the ruts filled with blood. Olympia was trying to scoop it out with her hands before I could see it, and as she paddled it between her legs, it covered my cousin. I tried to call a warning to Petra but couldn't speak. In the next instant, Rodney had grabbed Petra and was forcing her face down in the blood.

"Alley," Nadia cried, as she had in my arms. "Alley."

I woke, soaked in sweat and shivering. Nadia should have had a mother or a lover with her at her end. She should have died in her great old age, surrounded by her grandchildren. Her last thought shouldn't have been that she was dying in an alley with a stranger.

I got out of bed, pulling the comforter around me, and went into the kitchen. It was six-thirty Saturday morning, the winter sky still black as midnight. I sat cross-legged at the table, staring sightlessly out the window. The air gradually lightened to a ghostly gray-white, but I couldn't see anything: another snowstorm was slamming the city. I went to the window, searching for signs of life but couldn't see even across the alley to the apartments beyond. Finally, hoping Mr. Contreras would look after the dogs, I went back to bed and slept until noon.

By Sunday, the storm had passed, leaving eight inches of new snow and a bright, bitter day in its wake. After taking the dogs for a long, exhausting walk, I spent the afternoon with Jake. We watched *Some Like It Hot,* which inspired him to rummage through his storage closet for a ukulele. He put on one of my sunhats and a skirt and preened around like Marilyn Monroe, so effectively that I laughed away some of the horrors of Friday night.

We were walking up Racine for a late supper when Olympia called me. "Have you seen the news?"

"What, Club Gouge is doubling its space in the wake of Friday's homicide?"

"You have a weird sense of humor, Warshawski. No, the police found Nadia's killer. That huge tattooed guy who kept tearing up the club. They picked him up with the gun used to shoot Nadia. Such a relief. They'll let us open on Tuesday!"

"That is a relief, Olympia. And wonderful that you could keep such a focused perspective on Nadia's death."

I hung up on her demand to know "Just what do you mean by that?"

7

No-Smoking Zone

Olympia's call effectually ended my brief sense of well-being. When we returned from dinner, while Jake practiced I looked up the news of Nadia's killer. Web news sites can be as obnoxious as any tabloid—maybe more so, since it's so easy to play with images.

"From War Hero to Club Killer" screamed the *Herald-Star*'s blog.

An anonymous tip led police to an apartment on a quiet street in Lakeview, where the troubled vet who allegedly murdered Nadia Guaman was living. Chad Vishneski, awarded the Bronze Star for valor in Iraq, couldn't take civilian life. He returned with a ferocious anger that moved him from random acts of vandalism to the sinister, when he began stalking and finally murdered a young graphic artist at Club Gouge on Friday.

The Chicago native was a Lane Tech football star, who went to Grand Valley State on a scholarship, but dropped out to join the Army, where he served four tours before his discharge last summer.

I clicked on a link to a video report and saw footage of a woman, her face swollen with fury.

"The police broke down the door," she said.

The video showed a door with the wood splintered behind a yellow crime scene banner.

"When I heard the noise, I thought it was Chad. He was so angry all the time since he got home, so I went in the hall to look. Only it was the police come to arrest him. Mona, that's his mother, she's out of town. She let him sleep there, even though everyone knows how unstable he is. The condo board is going to have to take action, maybe evict her—we could all have been murdered."

The video footage shifted to Terry Finchley, standing solemn-faced in the lobby of the police headquarters building, holding a gun in the approved fashion—suspended from a stick passed through the trigger guard.

"We found the perpetrator passed out in bed with this Baby Glock next to him on the floor. Our forensics tests prove that this was the weapon that was used to kill Nadia Guaman."

Someone asked if it was true that Chad had been brought in drunk. Terry said Chad had apparently taken a drug overdose. He was in the intensive care ward at Cermak Hospital, on the grounds of the Cook County Jail complex, over at Twenty-sixth and California.

I skimmed the rest of the story. Childhood friends recalled Chad as a lighthearted, fun-loving guy. He hadn't been a football standout, but he'd been big enough to get a Division II scholarship. Back then, "his life was, like, girls, beer, games. The war, it gave him a reason to quit school and serve his country," one high school buddy said. "When he got home, he was so different, just angry all the time. The war really messed with his head. You couldn't be in the same room with him."

The county had assigned him a public defender, although right now it was an open question as to whether Chad would regain consciousness, let alone have enough brain function to stand trial. Still, the PD gallantly told the press that his client was innocent, that this was all a terrible mistake. He didn't add that the county public defender's office didn't have the resources to sort out mistakes, even if Chad's arrest turned out to be one.

Poor Nadia, crossing paths with a distraught veteran. Poor Chad, another casualty of the endless Iraq war. Poor public defender, and poor Mona Vishneski, Chad's mother. She'd been spending the winter in Arizona, looking after her own mother, but was flying back to Chicago to be with her son.

Mona Vishneski responded to the *Herald-Star*'s invasive questions with the age-old litany of mothers: "Chad is innocent. He's a good boy. He never would have killed a girl at a nightclub."

Of course, the maniacs in the blogosphere were out in full force, some braying that Nadia Guaman "had been asking for it," since only an evil woman would frequent a place like Club Gouge. Others claimed that soldiers in Iraq got a taste for blood because of all the Iraqi civilians they'd been encouraged to torture and murder, and vets were bound to take out their bloodlust on innocent civilians, once they returned home.

Still others cried out against liberals who hated America and wanted to ban guns. "Obama used one of his Constitution-hating liberal stooges to commit the murder so he'd have an excuse to take away our guns," warned one hysteric.

I switched off the computer. Chad's life, Nadia's death, weren't my business, except for the way her face haunted me, asleep and awake. "Alley," she'd whispered, her expression arrested, almost happy, as if this were a pleasant surprise, to be dying in an icy parking lot.

I went to put my arms around Jake. He smiled but didn't stop playing. His fingers dancing up and down the strings were sinuous, erotic.

My grip on him tightened. Finally, torn between desire and annoyance, he put his bow down and went to bed with me.

In the morning, I left while he was still asleep. It was dark, but I drove to the lakefront with the dogs and ran almost to the Evanston border and back, seven miles, in the thin January air, hoping to sweat nightmares of Nadia's blood out of my pores.

By the time we returned home, the sky had lightened to a dull pewter. When I'd showered and changed, I accepted Mr. Contreras's offer of French toast. He'd been a little hurt that I'd spent Sunday with Jake—it's his job to fuss over me when I've been involved in violent crime—but, this time, his fussing had included ragging on me for getting Petra involved with Club Gouge. We'd had a fight about it Saturday night, but after a twenty-four-hour cooling off, we were both prepared to let bygones be bygones, more or less.

When I reached my office, a car was parked in front, engine running. My first thought was the cops, but this was a grime-crusted Corolla with a lot of years under its hood. As I typed in the code on my door keypad, the driver turned off the engine and climbed out of the car. All he had on against the cold was a worn khaki field jacket, unzipped.

"You the detective?" He pitched a cigarette butt into the gutter as he limped across the sidewalk.

"I'm V. I. Warshawski. And, yes, I'm a detective. What can I do for you, Mr.—?"

"Vishneski. I'm John Vishneski." His face was lined and scarred, and his voice was a soft, tired rumble.

I paused, with my hand on the doorknob. "You're related to Chad Vishneski?"

"His dad." He shook his head, as if the relationship were new, or surprising to him. "Yes, I'm his dad."

I shoved the door open—it always sticks more in the winter—and held it for Chad's father. When he got inside, Vishneski carefully wiped his boots on the hallway mat three or four times, the gesture of a man who wasn't sure he was welcome and wanted to minimize any evidence he'd been there.

I directed Vishneski to the couch in the client alcove and switched on the coffee machine in the back. While I turned on lights and put my coat and case away, Vishneski sat completely still, looking at nothing in particular. The cold didn't seem to bother him, even though my office was barely sixty degrees. It's such a barn of a place, I keep the thermostat turned low on weekends. I brought a space heater over from my desk, and sat down myself.

"I'm sorry for the trouble you're going through, Mr. Vishneski."

"Yep. It's a hard time." He made it a statement, not a complaint.

A minute or so went by when he didn't say anything else. A lot of people have trouble getting to the point when they're in the detective's office. Like visiting the doctor: you have this lump in your breast, but now you're in the office, you don't want to ask, you don't want to be told.

"Is Chad your only child?" I asked, just as a way to prod him into speaking.

"My only one, and I didn't even know he was in trouble, not until one of the gals in the office called me Saturday night. My own boy, and I didn't know. That's what that I-raq war did, turned him into a boy who couldn't call his old man when he was in trouble."

"Would he have, before the war?"

He nodded. "We used to talk every day, even when he was off at Grand Valley State. Even when he first deployed. But then the war got to him. The violence. He saw his whole unit die around him during his third deployment, and that did him in. It was like he blamed me, in a way."

"Blamed you?"

"I thought a lot about this," he said. "I think he felt I should have protected him. I was his dad, see, and he always, oh, looked up to me. At least when he was small. I worked construction my whole life, although I'm a project manager now, for Mercurio. I was stronger than most guys, and Chad, he thought I could always take care of trouble around him, or me, and I always thought so, too. Until he went off to I-raq, where no one could protect him. It's in my dreams all the time, that I should have saved him from seeing what he had to see. I couldn't save him, and he couldn't talk to me anymore."

He stuck a hand reflexively inside his jacket pocket, then looked a question.

"You're right," I said. "This is a no-smoking zone."

"Smoking in the cold outdoors—don't know why pneumonia hasn't carried me off by now." He ran his fingers through his graying hair. "They're holding my boy in a prison hospital ward. Do you know it?"

"Cermak Hospital. I've been there."

"Terrible place. Terrible, terrible place. Just getting in to see my own boy, they searched me. I had to take off all my clothes just to see my son."

Strip searching, it's so humiliating. When you're worried about your child, the violation is even more acute.

"My boy is in intensive care," Vishneski was continuing. "He's unconscious, but they got him chained to the bed. How can anyone get well if they're chained to the bed like that? I begged them, Let me move him to a real hospital where he can get real care, but the judge, he set the bail at seven hundred and fifty thousand dollars. If I can't pay the bail, Chad has to stay there in the jail hospital."

I could hear my office phone begin to ring behind the partition. Monday morning: everyone wanted me faster than yesterday.

"Why did you come to me, Mr. Vishneski?"

He rubbed his bloodshot eyes. "They told me you were at this nightclub, this Club Gouge. They told me maybe you saw what happened. Maybe you can explain what that dead gal did to Chad to get him so upset."

"Who's 'they,' Mr. Vishneski?"

"Oh. Secretary in the office, the gal who called to tell me about Chad. She read the whole story, going back to before Christmas, she came up with your name. She says you were in the club the first time Chad, well, started carrying on. She looked you up on the computer, read about your work. She told me you have a good reputation, you're honest, you do a good job."

"I do my best, but I'm not sure I can explain what happened between your son and Nadia Guaman. Was there something specific you wanted to know?" I sat quietly, hands easy at my sides, letting the calls roll over to my answering service.

"The woman who owns the club, she's kind of a hard case, isn't she? She says Chad kept attacking this Nadia whenever she showed up. Is this true?"

"You talked to Olympia?" I was puzzled. Surely she wouldn't have been in bond court or at the prison hospital.

"I went over to her club yesterday afternoon after I went to see Chad. I wanted to see what kind of a place it was. The cops shut it down while they did their investigating, if that's what you call it, but she was there, working on accounts or something. Like I said, I'm a project manager, at least I was until this economy destroyed the construction industry. You meet tough women in construction—well, they have to be to survive in that world—but this Olympia, she'd chew up my crew chief for dinner and spit him out and not think twice about it! She claims Chad tried to assault the dead gal. She says after someone broke it up, Chad must've lain in wait so he could shoot her. Is any of that true?"

I hate it when people ask questions for which there's no happy answer. "I was at the club two times when both Chad and Nadia were there, and I'm afraid that both times Chad boiled over when Nadia did her drawings. The first time, he tried to jump her onstage, and the bouncer did throw him out. I'm not going to lie to you, Mr. Vishneski: I heard a snippet of a conversation between your son and Nadia in the parking lot. Each was accusing the other of spying. My first reaction was that it was an ugly divorce case. But if they weren't lovers, if they hadn't met outside the club, what was that about?"

"I don't know." He stuck his hand inside his jacket pocket again and then remembered we weren't smoking in here. "One of his buddies called me, says at the time that gal was being murdered, Chad and them were all in a bar watching a Hawks game, and when it ended, Chad announced he didn't feel well, he was going home. Going back to my ex's, that meant."

"Did any of them actually see him go home?"

Vishneski hunched a shoulder. "This one friend, he dropped Chad off. But when I told the cops that, they said even if Chad watched the game, it ended an hour before that woman was shot, plenty of time for him to pretend to be sick and get over to the club to lie in wait for her."

The office phone had continued to ring while we talked. Now my cell phone chirped out a few bars of Mozart, my signal that one of a handful of key callers wanted me. I looked at the screen: my answering service was texting me that the cops, the media, and my clients were all getting restless over my inaccessibility.

"What is it you want from me, Mr. Vishneski?" I tried to mask my impatience.

"I want to know what really happened. I—my boy, he came back from I-raq in a bad way, I'll be the first to admit that. He bounced off the walls, you couldn't talk to him without getting your head bit off. He ran around with his Army buddies, got drunk, got in fights, couldn't hang on to a job. But it's hard for me to see him shooting a helpless young lady like that. I just don't believe it. The cops, they're happy to write 'Case Closed' on their file. And that public defender the county gave Chad . . . If he can remember Chad's name when he gets into court, I'll be surprised."

"If he's guilty, I can't prove he's innocent, Mr. Vishneski," I said quietly.

"I wouldn't want you to. But I need to know— What is it they always say on those law-and-order shows? 'Beyond a reasonable doubt.'" He smiled, a painful crack in his lined face.

"What about the gun? The news reports say the cops found the murder weapon next to Chad when they went to arrest him."

"It's not his, I'm sure it's not. Maybe he found it in the street and picked it up."

I didn't even try to respond to that parental fantasy. I rubbed my eyes with the heels of my hands, and Nadia's face appeared behind my lids. Death chasing away anger, catching her by surprise.

"You said you weren't sure you could afford bail for Chad, Mr. Vishneski, but I can't take on a case like this pro bono."

"I'm not asking you to. I've been running the numbers every which way all weekend. I'm still working three-quarter time, job-sharing with some other guys at Mercurio, although who knows how long that will last. Sorry, getting sidetracked. Mona's getting into town tonight. I'll talk to her. But if she agrees—she's retired, took early retirement last year, was an office manager with Mercurio, one of their buildings— anyway, I think we can afford to hire a detective and still have something for a good defense lawyer, if we're careful. If you can work without running up the bills on us. If you can recommend a good lawyer who'll give us a bit of a break."

8

The Hind at Bay

After we'd signed a contract and Vishneski left for work, I did a background check on him just to see if he really could pay his bills. He was, indeed, on Mercurio's payroll, and his credit history had no more hiccups than any other person who'd lived as long as he had. For the present, he could pay my bill and maybe that of my own defense lawyer, Freeman Carter.

I put away Vishneski's file and started returning the phone calls that had come in during our meeting. It wasn't until the end of the afternoon that I had time to get back to Chad Vishneski's problems.

John Vishneski wanted to believe Chad was innocent, but he had confirmed the picture of a young man whose anger was close to the surface at all times. "He never was like that as a boy. He had such a happy disposition, even after Mona and I split up. We got two places, Mona and me, sold the house and got two condos pretty near each other so the boy could be both places and not feel he was in the middle of our problems. He always had a bunch of friends, boys, girls, always in and out of both apartments, all having fun. Clean fun. No drugs, no drunks. Mona and I set the same rules."

According to Vishneski, Iraq had changed Chad's personality. Jekyll and Hyde and which was the mean one? He could never remember. As he talked, Vishneski finally pulled a cigarette from his breast pocket. He played with it, tapping it on the tabletop, running it between his fingers, a prop to help him get through his story.

"He didn't tell me he was joining up. I knew he wasn't one for the books, but he just wandered into an Army recruitment office on Addison Street during spring break. Next thing I knew, he was off to basic training."

"That must have startled you," I said.

"I was pissed off, him doing it without even talking to me, throwing away his college scholarship. But then I saw how much the Army suited him, and I thought, well, maybe he knew best after all, he needed that discipline. That and the activity. He used to send us these pictures of him and his unit, they'd be laughing, Chad teaching Iraqi boys how to play American football. 'That soccer, that's for sissies,' he says he told them."

Vishneski rubbed his face. I wasn't supposed to see the unexpected spurt of tears as he thought of his son's happy-go-lucky past.

"But those endless deployments, they put the big hurt on all the kids out there. And they saw stuff no person ought to have to see, grown women fighting over a piece of bread, babies with their arms blown off, other things Chad wouldn't even talk about. It was too much for him."

I went back to the murder weapon that the police supposedly found next to Chad when they picked him up. "What kind of guns did Chad have?"

"He was a soldier. They don't get handguns. Chad, he likes—liked—to shoot, but Mona wouldn't let him keep a gun in her place any more'n I would in mine."

Anymore than they allowed drugs or alcohol, which is to say parents often see what they hope will be in front of them.

"But did he own a gun? Guns?"

John claimed Chad didn't. And certainly not the Baby Glock that the police had found in bed with Chad.

"So whose gun was that?" I asked.

"If you're going to clear his name, you'll have to find that out, won't you?" He gave me a ferocious glare, as if anger with me could keep grief and uncertainty at bay.

"You're not hiring me to clear his name but to find out what happened," I reminded him.

He argued with me a bit about that but in an unfocused way, not sure what he believed about his son. I asked him for names of Chad's friends, those boys and girls who used to have good clean fun with him.

Vishneski said, "The kids he hung out with before he deployed, they couldn't understand why Chad was so angry all the time when he got home, so he kind of lost touch with them. The guys he sees now, they're Army buddies he picked up after he got home last summer. Most of 'em I don't know, but Tim Radke, he's the one who called me after he heard about Chad. He's the one said they'd been at a bar."

Vishneski didn't know Radke's number, but maybe Mona would. I asked if there were any women in Chad's life, not counting Nadia Guaman, whose connection to Chad we were tiptoeing around.

"He dated a sweet gal in high school, but she married someone else while he was overseas. Since he got home, I don't think he's been meeting any women. But his ma would know. You ask Mona when you talk to her."

Women are the repository of personal details in the lives of all who intersect their worlds. Even my own brief husband had expected me to know his clients' and his parents' birthdays.

Back in my office that afternoon, I typed up all my notes from the day and entered them into everyone's separate case files—which I religiously backed up on a portable drive as well as the office backup drive.

Oh, the computer age. It's been good for me, in a way. I used to write my notes on scraps of paper and lose them in the landfill on my work-table. Now everything's tidily laid out in my Investigator's Casebook spreadsheets, which automatically updates my handheld. Something's missing, though: the personal touch on archives. You see things when you're handling documents that you miss on the World Wide Web.

The winter evening had closed in on the city hours ago. I felt cold and lonely in my office, although my leasemate was still hard at it with a blowtorch across the hall. If we still lived in caves, we'd be asleep, not driving ourselves to work in the dark.

I logged on to the Body Artist's website, embodiedart.com. It opened to the slide show I'd seen on the screens at Club Gouge—the eye wink-ing down at her vulva, the jungle scenes up her spine. The Middle Eastern music twanged with the changing screens.

The text, which was also disquieting, changed along with the pictures:

What, is thy servant a dog that she should do this thing?
My eye winks at my muff, my beaver, my little animal
The Female of the Species is Deadlier than the Male

The bashful audience member, drawing a few squiggly lines, a few people attempting actual figurative work with varying degrees of suc-cess, were staples of the shows. And so was Rodney. You didn't actually see him stride up to the stage, his paunch swaying slightly with his rolling gait, but you almost always saw the crude sets of letters and numbers on the Body Artist's buttocks.

I found one of Nadia's drawings, the pink-and-gray scrolls, the woman with a slash down the middle of her face, and tried to print out a copy of that, and of Rodney's crude work. Unfortunately, the Artist had a slick print-protection feature built into her site: all you got was the text around the edge of the page, not the picture itself. You had to pay fifty dollars to print your own version; seventy-five would get you a signed print from the Artist. Two hundred, and it would arrive framed.

I copied down Rodney's contributions. "C-I," he wrote on one occasion. "3521986 !397844125" on another. "L-O 6221983 !4903612." I looked at five different examples of Rodney's work. Each entry had a set of numbers separated by an exclamation point, but, other than that, I couldn't see what they shared. The strings of numbers weren't the same length from entry to entry.

I wondered if they might be phone numbers, perhaps for disposable phones in an overseas market. Europe doesn't share our fixation with the ten-digit phone number. Or perhaps Rodney was a spy for a burglary ring and used the Body Artist to broadcast safe combinations. Or he'd picked pockets at the club and was relaying credit card numbers. No matter what he was transmitting, why do it like that at all? In an era of instantaneous communication, this was incredibly cumbersome. The only thing he really seemed to gain was a sense of power over the Body Artist, and over Olympia.

Before I left embodiedart.com, I looked again at the changing images and captions on the home page, stopping each slide to study it more closely. Many of the pictures were overtly cruel: *The Hind at Bay*, for instance, showed dogs mauling a deer that had a woman's face. *Crucifixus Est* depicted a woman on a cross, a spike hammered through her vulva. Her face was divided in two, one side expressing bliss, the other agony.

As I went through the exhibit, I realized I'd misread one of the captions: "Deader than the Male," it said, not "Deadlier than the Male." And the face was the one Nadia had been painting on the Body Artist, a young woman with curly dark hair, her face cut in two where Nadia had sliced it with the palette knife.

I found myself shivering. Women savaged by dogs. Women crucified through the vagina. Women with their faces slashed. It was horrible and horrifying. If a man had done these paintings, I'd say he hated women. What was going on with Karen, that she hated other women, or hated herself so much she had to dismember her female body? And Nadia Guaman—was that what had drawn the two women together? Slasher art?

I rubbed my arms and got up to walk around the room, trying to dispel the images, or at least push them far enough away that I could think. I needed human company. I crossed the hall to see if my lease-mate was willing to be interrupted, at least for five minutes. Tessa was hovering over a steel bar with a blowtorch, her dark face wet with sweat underneath her protective eyewear. She looked up at me briefly, continued her work until she'd finished the cut to her satisfaction, then turned off the flame and came over to me.

"I need someone alive and wholesome for a minute before I go back into my computer." I explained what I'd been looking at.

Tessa was interested enough to wipe her face and neck dry and come across to look at the Body Artist's slide show. She went through it twice, pausing at several of the images, before she said anything.

"She's a skilled representational painter, no doubt about it, and she knows her art history. *The Hind at Bay,* it's constructed like *The Stag at Bay,* even if Landseer's dogs were more genteel and not actively attacking the stag. And the crucifixion, that's modeled on one Michelangelo painted." She brought up a new window and found reproductions of both paintings so I could see how similar they were to Karen Buckley's work.

"I see why you find them disturbing," she continued. "There's no life here. There's a kind of rage under these, and a kind of exhibitionism, but not vitality. I'd rather see something like these uncertain lines." She pointed at one of the slides of customer art from a Club Gouge night. "The person who held that brush was willing to take a risk."

"You don't think it's a risk being naked on a stage, letting strangers put paint on you?"

"I think it's an extreme form of self-indulgence," Tessa said. "Every time you put paint on canvas, or flesh, you're taking a risk, but your Body Artist isn't doing that. Come to think of it, I'm surprised she isn't cutting herself onstage. I don't like the performance art of people like Lucia Balinoff, but she works along the same themes: the savaging of the female body. Your performance artist isn't doing anything new and she's not taking any risks. She's exposing herself, but not her *self*."

Tessa left on that stern note. A moment later, I heard her blowtorch fire up again.

9

The Dead—Before They Got That Way

I tried to map out a course of action. The most important thing seemed to me to get the client's son better care. That meant I needed sophisticated medical as well as first-class legal help. I started with Freeman Carter. He had been in court all day and wanted to get away; he had tickets to the opera and wasn't going to miss the curtain on my account. I gave him a thirty-second rundown and told him I wanted a court order ASAP so we could move Chad—I hoped to Beth Israel, Lotty's hospital.

"I'll get a doctor over to Cermak tomorrow morning if you can organize the legal side."

"Are you being Donna Quixote," Freeman asked, "or do you really have evidence that the wrong person is in custody? From everything I've read, this was a PTSD vet who lost control. Not that it matters, you understand. I'm used to the odd alignment you make between the law and facts."

"Vishneski is a PTSD vet, but I'm beginning to think he was framed. I'll tell you why when you have more time."

"And is this on your tab, or can your client pay?"

Freeman's bill is one of the things that keeps me from ever getting ahead of the game financially. But the alignment between the law and me is such that I need the best defense lawyer in town. Even though my outstanding balance right now was close to sixty thousand, I assured Freeman that if the client couldn't pay him, I'd take care of it. I hung up knowing that the phone consult itself had just added a hundred dollars to my bill.

I called Lotty, who was also going to the opera, but who gave me a little more attention.

"Eve Rafael is a very fine surgeon, new to our practice, but she has a lot of experience with head trauma and coma. I'll see if she's free. But the billing is going to be complicated, you know. And it would help if I could tell her what your young friend had ingested."

"I won't know that for a few days, but Chad's been at Cermak since Saturday morning. I hope it's not too late for a world-class neurosurgeon to rescue his brain."

"Medicine, Victoria—not a science, not an art, somewhere in between. How badly Chad Vishneski wants to recover will also play a role in this. But I'll talk to Eve on my way to the opera."

"As long as someone else is driving, Lotty!"

Lotty's driving, on a sunny day and with no one else on the road, was still a fine test of anyone's nerve endings. In the snow, with a cell phone in her ear, I wouldn't want my life to depend on her.

"You worry too much about trivialities, Victoria: that will shorten your life as much as fried food."

As she hung up on that crisp note, I realized I should have talked to the client first before making all these arrangements for his son. Fortunately, when I reached John Vishneski, he was so grateful for my arrangements that he didn't question my protocol. I gave him Freeman's number.

"Call him first thing in the morning. He's going to get a court order to allow him to move your son, and either Dr. Herschel or Dr. Rafael will be on hand to oversee his care."

"I have to be at a jobsite at seven," Vishneski said.

"It'll be best if you let someone else take care of that. You told me yesterday that Chad depended on you to look after him, and this is one place where you can do that. Even if he's unconscious, your voice in his ear will reassure him."

He agreed after a moment of rambling talk—how he'd have to talk to someone named Derek, how Mona needed to know—should he call her or would I? Before we hung up, I told him I was sending him a form to sign that would give his and his ex-wife's consent to my talking to Chad's doctors, and he agreed to that as well.

As a courtesy, I called Terry Finchley to let him know what I was doing. Like most sensible people, he'd gone home for the day, so I left a detailed message with the officer who answered his phone. By now, I was too hungry to think clearly: I hadn't eaten since grabbing a sandwich in the Loop at two, and it was after eight now. I drove back downtown, to the south Loop, and went into the Golden Glow, Sal Barthele's bar in the financial district.

Right after the closing bell, the Glow is packed with hysterical traders. This time of night, the atmosphere is mellower. Business travelers mingle with regulars from the high-rises and converted lofts along Printers Row, and everyone relaxes more in the light of Sal's Tiffany table lamps.

Sal stood inside the mahogany horseshoe bar where most of her clients like to sit. Sal is tall, majestic in build, and her wardrobe doubles her impact. Like Olympia, Sal knows her business depends on showmanship. Showwomanship. Tonight she was eye-stopping in a shimmery black sweater and pants topped by a silver vest that hung to her calves. Her Afro was cropped close to her head, and earrings the size of chandeliers swept her shoulders.

She patted the hand of the man she'd been talking to and moved across the horseshoe to the empty side where I was sitting. "That was quite a to-do at Olympia's place. I saw on the news that some stressed-out vet went off the rails and killed a woman."

"That's the word on the street."

Sal brought out the Black Label bottle. "And you don't agree?"

I shrugged. "The evidence, such as it is, points to the guy. His father says PTSD had seriously damaged him, but that it wasn't in his nature to lie in wait for a woman he barely knew just to shoot her."

"So you think he didn't do it?"

She cocked her head, catching the earring on her left ear in her sweater. I reached over and untangled the metal from the threads.

"You should wear football pads with these. I am committed to a client who believes Chad didn't do it. He hired me just to get the facts, but, underneath it all, he wants the facts to prove Chad's innocent. So I'm working on that assumption."

"You practice for half an hour a day, like the White Queen, so you can learn to believe in the impossible? What's Olympia saying?"

"Olympia is behaving oddly. Do you know her?"

Sal shook her head. "We're not old pals, or even lovers, if that's what you want to know. I know her because we belong to an organization of women restaurateurs, and that's a small group in Chicago. Olympia can be good fun, but she's definitely pushed herself to the top by having the sharpest elbows in the heap. I mean, so have we all, in a way, but some of us, we put on velvet elbow pads so the suckers along the way don't realize they've been hit until they get home and study their bruises."

"Ain't that the truth," I said, thinking of the pushing I'd had to do to get taken seriously as a detective.

I gave Sal a précis of my nights at the Club Gouge, my encounters with Nadia and Karen Buckley, and Olympia's insistence that nothing was going on. Sal left me several times to check on other customers, but she sent a minion to the restaurant across the foyer—she supplies their liquor, they feed her customers—to get me some broiled halibut. When I'd finished the story, she shook her head.

"If Petra were working here and she brought you in without my permission, I'd be seeing red, white, and blue. I'd fire her ass and probably shoot yours, if I could get you in my sights. Your cousin is lucky Olympia hasn't let her go."

"But if someone in here were injured the way Karen Buckley was when she cut herself with that glass in her paintbrush, would you refuse to bring in the cops?"

"Devil's advocate, Vic, but—Olympia's got a naked woman onstage. Cops could get her written up for a million violations if they thought it was a dyke scene and they wanted to be ugly."

I thought of Detective Finchley's reaction to the Body Artist's act and pulled a face. "When you put it that way, it's hard to argue with you. But there are other things. This guy Rodney: Olympia pretended she didn't know his name when Detective Finchley was talking to us. But he is there most nights. And he threatened me with violence. I'm wondering if the club is a front for him to run drugs."

Sal's brows contracted. "If—and that's a mighty big if—Olympia is doing or dealing, get your cousin out of there ASAP. It's a big chance to take, though. I wouldn't think Olympia would risk her license and her property by letting a dealer operate so blatantly."

"Maybe so, but there's something going on there. You stop by one of these nights and you'll see what I mean." I picked at a loose corner of the label on the Scotch bottle. "You said you and Olympia weren't old lovers, but what about her and Nadia Guaman? Or her and Karen Buckley? Were Nadia and Karen around the club scene, at least as far as you know?"

"I never heard of this Nadia, Vic. Karen Buckley, I've caught her act. It's a startling piece of performance art for this town, the kind of thing you expect in San Francisco or New York, but not conservative Chi-town. Gal like that could sleep with anyone for any reason. I mean, maybe she's having an affair with Olympia, maybe she slept with the dead woman, but I'm guessing Buckley's not a dyke. I wouldn't even say she was bisexual. She just does what she wants when she wants with whoever she wants."

An omnisexual. I wondered what that felt like, to do what you wanted when you wanted. Buckley hadn't struck me as a very contented person, despite her yoga poses and deep breathing.

"That paintbrush with the glass—at the time, I wondered if the Artist or Olympia did it as a publicity stunt. I'm still not convinced they didn't. But Nadia could have sabotaged it, or even Chad, I suppose."

"Could be. Olympia's been hurting along with the rest of the economy. If she thought it would bring in business, she'd cut her own wrists in front of a webcam."

"Would you?"

Sal laughed. "Hell, no. I'm quite attached to my own good looks, thank you very much."

I looked at her seriously. "You're tough, Sal, and one of the strongest people I know. But you're sane. What you just said about Olympia, you may have meant it as a joke but the very fact that such an image came to your mind means you feel what I'm talking about, that edgy, danger-daring quality."

"You'd be the expert on that particular bit of human nature, Warshawski. You going to drink that whisky or just play spin the bottle all night?"

"Neither." I handed Sal my AmEx card. She used to run a tab for me when she and I first opened our businesses twenty years ago, but those days have disappeared with the rest of the economy.

I took side streets going home. I was tired, and whisky at the end of a long day hadn't been the smartest move before getting behind the wheel. Sal's response to my questions about Olympia hadn't done anything to dampen my enthusiasm for my case. That was because my enthusiasm level had been low to begin with. Chad with a Glock on the pillow next to him was a high hill to climb over, and I didn't think I'd find an easy path on the other side.

I hadn't actually seen any ballistic or forensic evidence in the case. In the morning, I'd check with the ME on that. In the meantime, before going to bed, I turned on my laptop and logged on to my subscription databases; they could spend the night hunting for information about Nadia Guaman. For good measure, I also asked about Olympia, Karen Buckley, and Chad Vishneski.

When the alarm woke me at six, I wanted to shoot it or scream, or something. I've never been much for early mornings, and when it is pitch-black, with the kind of cold that makes you feel your head is strapped inside iron bands, it takes every ounce of will not to pull the covers over your head and wait for spring.

"Bunter!" I cried. "Bunter, get that cappuccino machine fired up. And look smart about it!"

What a strange fantasy, to imagine someone who was dressed and ready to do your bidding at whatever hour it pleased you to bid him. So very obviously politically and socially incorrect, and yet how much I longed for my own Bunter. I flung the covers back and ran across the cold floor to the kitchen, where I put on my espresso maker, before tiptoeing to the bathroom.

I turned the thermostat up to sixty-eight before collecting the dogs from Mr. Contreras.

When I got home and thawed out, I sat at my laptop with my second espresso. LifeStory, an innocuous-sounding outfit, for whose detailed searches into everyone's lives I pay eight grand a year, had sent me a profile of Nadia Guaman.

Guaman had gone to Columbia College in the south Loop after a childhood in Pilsen and high school at St. Teresa of Avila. Her father, Lazar, worked as a baggage handler up at O'Hare; her mother, Cristina, was a cashier at a Pilsen hardware store. They still lived in the bungalow on Twenty-first Place where Nadia had grown up.

Nadia had been the oldest of Lazar and Cristina's three surviving children; another daughter, Alexandra, had died three years ago. The youngest, Clara, a high school senior, was also at St. Teresa. Their only son, Ernest, had been training as an electrical engineer when his motorcycle flipped him onto Cermak Road two years ago. His brain injuries left him unable to work.

I squeezed my eyes shut. The pain the Guamans lived with every day, one child already dead, their son terribly disabled, and now a daughter murdered—I couldn't imagine how you survived such losses and kept any vestige of your sanity or humanity.

I returned to the screen and studied the financial details another of my subscription databases, the Monitor Project, had dredged up. Nadia's bank account was modest; she had earned about forty thousand in a good year. Her rent on the one-bedroom on the fringe of Humboldt Park—the part where gangs and gentrifiers lived in uneasy proximity—ran just under nine hundred a month. She didn't own a car. The computer hadn't come upon any financial instruments, if such things still existed, in her name.

Nadia hadn't been party to any lawsuits. LifeStory and the Monitor Project aren't a substitute for routine surveillance. They didn't give me any details on Nadia's private life—who she dated, how well she'd known Chad Vishneski, if she and Karen Buckley or Olympia had been lovers. All I could tell was that she'd never filed an order of protection or complained of stalking or harassment.

The reports did give other, more intimate information, the kind you assume is private to you alone. I felt filthy, exploring Nadia's medical history, but I wanted to know if she'd had any treatment that might imply an abusive relationship. No recent broken bones, no STDs. By the time I'd been through the whole file, I just had time to shower and change for my first appointment of the morning. I'd look at the reports on Chad, Olympia, and Karen Buckley later.

Now that the police had identified her killer, they'd released Nadia's body to her family. The funeral was scheduled for this afternoon at Ayuda de Cristianos, in Pilsen. I put on my tailored black suit so that I could go directly to the church from my downtown meeting.

10

A Kiss in the Coffin

Nadia's family was gathered around her open coffin, the parents in black, the surviving daughter defiantly flaunting turquoise eye shadow and a pink jersey minidress. Their son, Ernest, was wearing a black suit and tie, but he was twitching and shaking his arms and occasionally letting out little yipping noises. An older woman, perhaps a grandmother, was scolding him.

I joined the obligatory parade up to the family. Lazar Guaman stood like a statue, unable to respond to anyone who spoke to him, seemingly unaware of his son. For Cristina Guaman, Ernest seemed to provide a welcome distraction. Rubbing his neck, or taking his hands when he started sticking them down his trouser front, or hushing his shriek of a laugh seemed to calm her, to give her a kind of purpose.

I murmured condolences, and Ms. Guaman directed me to the coffin.

"Our Nadia looks like the angel in heaven she's become."

I moved reluctantly to the open coffin. I'd last seen their daughter in Club Gouge's parking lot, in pain and covered in blood, but here she lay as calm as if she were in a tranquil sleep. Her face, stripped of the tormenting anger I'd witnessed at Club Gouge, looked heartbreakingly young in death, almost a child's face. The effect was heightened by the lacy white pillow on which she lay.

The funeral people had covered her torn-up chest with a pale blue frock, a girlie outfit very different from the jeans and outsize shirt she'd worn for her Body Artist painting. Was it good, was it bad, to turn the dead into dolls like this?

Someone who seemed to know the family was speaking to Ms. Guaman, when Ernest shouted, so abruptly that I jumped, "Nadia flew, she flew to Jesus! Allie is a dove, flying around and around and around!" and he started to laugh.

The outburst didn't startle his family. "Your sister is an angel, not a dove," scolded the woman who'd been speaking to Ms. Guaman, while the daughter said, "Not in church, Ernie, don't yell in here."

Ayuda de Cristianos was one of those cavernous old churches that dated to the time when Czech immigrants settled this part of Chicago. Back then it was known as St. Ludmila's, and the grim details of the saint's life still filled the narrow stained-glass windows. The nave was made of concrete, with a vaulted ceiling that must have stretched a good hundred feet above us. Everyone's footfalls echoed and re-echoed; each time the street door slammed, Ernest roared with laughter and imitated the noise.

As more people came up to the coffin, I retreated to a pew near the back of the church. The building was bone-chillingly cold. We should have all huddled together in a few pews.

I didn't see anyone I knew among the few dozen mourners who dotted the space. No one from Club Gouge, for instance, and none of Chad's Army buddies. Nor Rodney, the heavy from the club. Most of the people looked like relatives or perhaps coworkers of the Guamans. A man in a black cashmere coat, his hair cut strand by strand, the way they do in those Oak Street salons, stood to one side until he could speak to the family alone. Their doctor, perhaps, or someone from the

airline where Lazar worked as a baggage handler. I built a fantasy for
the family that the airline, saddened by all the Guamans' losses, was
setting up a college fund for the remaining daughter.

The priest appeared from a side door, and the family moved to the
front row.

"Eternal rest grant unto them, O Lord," the priest began.

In my childhood, although I wasn't a Catholic, I attended a lot of
funeral masses for classmates—one of the by-products of growing up
in a rough neighborhood. The mass was said in Latin then, and I'm still
disconcerted to hear it in English.

I joined the congregation in a mumbled response to the prayers, our
voices swallowed by the building before they could travel to the altar.
We had reached the homily, where the priest was explaining what a
devoted daughter and sister Nadia had been, when a door slammed and
footfalls echoed hollowly through the nave. Everyone turned to look,
and Ernest once again jumped excitedly and shouted an imitation of
the sound.

I didn't recognize the woman at first. In a navy wool coat and furry
boots, she looked like every other cold person in the church. Her brown
hair hung below her coat collar; a lock fell across her eyes, and she
pushed it aside as she marched up the aisle. It was only when she passed
me that I realized who it was: Karen Buckley, the Body Artist. For her
act, she pinned her hair up on her head, and her heavy foundation
drained all expression from her face. Now I saw the muscles around her
mouth and eyes quiver.

She paid no attention to the priest, or even to Ernest, but walked
up to the coffin and stared down at Nadia. The priest interrupted himself to demand that she sit down, that she not disrespect the service.
Karen treated him as if he were a heckler at her body art act: he didn't
exist. After a moment, while we all watched in silence, Karen bent to
kiss Nadia. The people closest to the coffin gasped, and Ms. Guaman

half rose in her pew, but Karen turned and left, her furry boots squeaking slightly on the stone floor. When the street door shut behind her, the sound vibrated through the building like thunder.

I got up from my pew and hurried out after her, while Ernest shrieked, "They're shooting. All the girls are dying. You're next, Clara. Better get down. You're next."

The great door shut behind me as Ms. Guaman and one of the older women tried to hush Ernest. Karen Buckley was already opening the door to her car, a Subaru with the Zipcar logo painted on the side. I sprinted to the curb, skidding in my dress boots, calling her name.

"Ms. Buckley! I'm V. I. War—"

"I remember. You're the detective."

She had a lot of practice keeping her face neutral, and her eyes gave nothing away. They were a blue so pale that they seemed transparent in the winter light.

"I want to talk to you about Nadia. Where can I meet you?"

"Nowhere. I don't want to talk to you."

She started to get into her car. I moved quickly and braced myself against the open door.

"You knew her well, I gather, and I need to find out more about her. Did she ever talk to you about Chad Vishneski?"

"Chad Vishneski? Oh, the crazy vet who shot her. I hardly knew her."

She tried to pull the door shut, but I'd wedged myself into the opening.

"Then why are you here? And why did you kiss her so dramatically?"

"I came for the same reason you did: to pay my respects to the dead. Perhaps my respects take a more dramatic form than yours."

I shook my head. "If you came for the same reason I did, it's because you have unanswered questions about her murder. It's not at all clear that Chad was her killer or even that he's crazy."

She turned her head so that her long hair brushed the steering wheel.

Her voice, when she again spoke, was barely audible. "I feel responsible for her death, that's all. Something about the painting she did on my body stirred up Chad, and I came here to ask her forgiveness."

She shot me a sidelong glance. "Does that satisfy you?"

"I almost believed you," I said, "until you put in the coda. I'm in the phone book when you start feeling like telling me the truth."

She flushed and bit her lip, but she wasn't going to give herself away any further. I slammed her door shut and headed back to the church, but it wasn't until I reached the big bronze doors that I heard her start her car.

When I got inside, communion was being distributed. I stood in the rear until the mass ended and the coffin was finally sealed. I moved to the side while the pallbearers carried the coffin down the aisle, the family in its wake. The rest of the mourners straggled to the exits. The subdued chatter, the relief of still being counted among the living, began to grow as the coffin left the building.

I stood on the steps and watched the undertakers bend over the family. One man helped Cristina Guaman settle Ernest into the backseat; a second gently shepherded the numb and gray Lazar through a door on the other side. Clara, the surviving daughter, was standing by herself, scowling. Despite the cold, she wasn't wearing a coat over her pink jersey minidress.

I walked over to her. "I was with your sister when she died. I'm sorry for your loss."

Under the outrageous makeup, Clara's eyes were wet, but she held her head defiantly.

"How come?"

I was briefly confused.

"It's a hard loss—"

"No, no." She gave me the look of withering contempt that only adolescents seem able to produce. "How come you were with her?"

"The woman who came into the funeral to kiss your sister good-bye, her name is Karen Buckley, she performs at Club Gouge. Karen Buckley's safety had been threatened. I'm a detective. I was trying to see that she didn't get hurt."

"You did a good job, didn't you? It was my sister who got killed."

I smiled painfully but held out my card. "Would you talk to me if I came to your school or your home?"

Clara's eyes slid past me to someone behind me. The man in the black cashmere coat appeared next to me.

"Clara." He took one of her bare hands between his two gloved ones. "This is no time to be standing around without a coat!"

She pulled her hand away and gave him the same angry stare she'd turned on me a minute earlier, but didn't say anything.

"This is a hard time for your whole family," the man said. "Your mother needs to be able to count on you. So get into the car before you add to her worries by catching cold, okay?"

He put a hand on her neck to shepherd her to the car, but she twisted away from him. She climbed into the limo, and the man in black cashmere leaned in over her head to say something to the Guamans. He spoke so softly I couldn't hear him, but Cristina replied loudly, "I do understand. You don't need to repeat yourself."

He shut the door and slapped the car's top a couple of times, I guess as a signal to the driver to take off.

"Clara's a tough kid to talk to." He had a light, pleasant baritone.

"All kids that age are. Or can be."

"You a family friend?"

"I was close to Nadia at one time." I didn't feel like explaining my connection as a private investigator. "And you?"

"I'm sort of an honorary uncle to all of them, especially since poor Ernie had his accident." He stuck a hand inside his coat and pulled out a card: Rainier Cowles, Attorney.

"They seem dogged by misfortune; they're lucky to have an honorary uncle who's a lawyer." I didn't give him a card of my own; a La Salle

Street lawyer like him probably wouldn't take kindly to a PI sniffing around the Guamans. "I don't know the family well. Can Ernest be left alone?"

"Not really. It's not that he's dangerous, but his impulses are out of whack. Cristina worries about him leaving the stove on, that kind of thing. Lazar's mother lives with them, helps keep an eye on Ernest."

"So how do they manage?"

I tried to imagine what home life must be like for Clara and her parents: hard work for the parents, but painful for a teenager who had to put her own life on hold.

"Are you a social worker looking for a customer?" His eyebrows were raised.

I smiled. "Like you, I was worrying about the Guamans' welfare, wondering how they cope. And I gather there was another sister who also died—Alexandra."

"They don't like to talk about her." His voice was bland, but all the muscles in his face tightened.

"How did she die?"

One of Ernie's outbursts came back to me: *Allie Allie is a dove.* When Nadia lay in my arms, her last word had been "Allie." Not bitterness at ending her life in an alley—she thought my face bending over hers was that of her dead sister. My insides twisted in an involuntary spasm of grief.

"You don't know?" Cowles said. "It doesn't sound to me as though you ever knew Nadia at all."

"We were close once," I repeated, "but not for long. She let me know Allie was very important to her, but she didn't spell out why."

His face relaxed again. "I'd let that dead dog lay, then. It's too painful to Cristina and Lazar—you'll never hear them talk about Alexandra. By the way, who was the woman who interrupted the service? She knocked poor Father Ogden off balance."

I shrugged. "Her name is Karen Buckley."

"And what was she to Nadia?"

I shook my head. "Anybody's guess."

"What's yours?"

I smiled again. "Not enough data to begin to guess."

"So you're a careful woman, are you? Not a risk taker, hmm?"

For some reason, the time I'd swung from a gantry and landed in the Sanitary Canal flashed through my head, and I laughed but didn't say anything.

He eyed me narrowly, annoyed at my frivolity but smart enough not to expose himself to possible ridicule. He looked at his watch: the conversation was over. He asked perfunctorily if I was heading to the cemetery, and when I said no, he strode briskly down the street to his car. It was a BMW sedan, which looked a bit like him—expensive cut, shiny black exterior, sleek lines.

I moved slowly to my Mustang. This was its third winter in Chicago, and it didn't look sleek at all. It looked like me, tired and even confused, since the front and rear axles seemed to be pointing in opposite directions.

11

The Mama and the Papa, in Concert

Back in my office, I found messages from Lotty and Freeman Carter. Lotty had called to say that her neurosurgeon, Dr. Rafael, had visited Chad at Cermak Hospital. Rafael had insisted on his removal to Beth Israel. Freeman's message let me know he'd provided the court order to expedite Chad's move—he should be at Beth Israel already.

I called Freeman to thank him, and tried to reach Lotty, both to thank her and to try to get an idea about Chad's health. Unfortunately, she wasn't available, and the charge nurse had a scrupulous sense of protocol: I wasn't part of the family or one of the lawyers; I didn't get any news. John Vishneski's phone was turned off; that probably meant he was with his son in the ICU. I asked him to call me and opened the case file I'd started on Chad.

I added Rainier Cowles's name to the Vishneski file, but the name sounded so bogus I did a LexisNexis check on him. He was a partner at Palmer & Statten, one of the globe's megafirms whose Chicago presence occupied eight floors of a Wacker Drive high-rise.

Cowles had grown up in the northwest suburbs and was respectably educated, with a BA from Michigan and his JD/MBA from Penn. He'd joined Palmer & Statten right after passing the bar, and during the next twenty years had moved steadily up the path to partner. The Palmer & Statten website listed his particular expertise as corporate litigation, with a specialty in multinationals.

I didn't find a record of a name change, but it still seemed incredible that parents had burdened their child with such a name. "Prince Rainier," I murmured to the computer. He'd probably been called that a ton in his subdivision growing up. Maybe it's why he'd put on the carapace of corporate success. Imposing trial presence, important car. But he must have a soft center, or he wouldn't be involved with the hard-luck Guamans. Or maybe he'd represented them in litigation over Ernie's injuries.

None of this speculation was helping me look at Chad's relationship with Nadia.

"The client is the boss. His son is innocent. Get to work proving it," I said aloud in my sternest voice and phoned Mona Vishneski.

Mona had left her mother's as soon as she learned of her son's arrest, and was now back in Chicago. She was staying with her ex-husband in Wrigleyville, which John hadn't bothered to tell me. She agreed to meet me for a cup of tea at Lilith's, a little café on Southport near John's apartment, around five.

The snow had started again. Lilith's was six blocks from my apartment. With the ice and snow packed along the curbs making street parking a challenge, it was better to put my car in my building's alley garage and walk. I carried my laptop with me in a waterproof case.

It was already dark by the time I got to the café. The warmth and lights inside seemed feeble against the wind whipping snow pellets against the windows. I ordered a double macchiato and found a table as far from the door as possible.

While I waited for Mona, I started to download the reports LifeStory and the Monitor Project had given me on Olympia, Karen Buckley, and on Chad himself. I was especially curious about Karen, after her performance at Nadia's funeral.

The most important question—who had known whom and how—wasn't one the computer could answer reliably, although I took a stab at the question through MySpace and Facebook. Olympia had a Facebook page, but you had to have her permission to see any details, such as her cyberfriends. Chad had a MySpace page, but none of the women were among his "friends." I couldn't find Karen Buckley on any of the social networks.

Fishing around to see where Karen's and Nadia's lives might have intersected, I checked to see if they had gone to art school together. I already had looked up Nadia's details—her training at Columbia College in the south Loop, her job at a big design firm, followed by precarious freelancing after she was laid off—but I couldn't find any information on Karen Buckley. A quick search revealed hundreds of Karen Buckleys—singers, quilters, doctors, lawyers —across the country, but only four dozen Karen Buckleys or K. Buckleys in our four-state area. About six of those seemed to match the Body Artist's race and age. None of them had a findable history as an artist.

Unlike most artists, who are at pains to tell you where they've trained, where they've held shows, what museums own their work, Karen's history wasn't just sketchy, it was missing altogether. She didn't list her education or her shows on the embodiedart.com website. She didn't offer any personal information at all.

I needed her Social Security number, but I couldn't find a home address for her, let alone a credit history that might yield information on her background. I went back to embodiedart.com. If you had to pay her for her work, she must have a bank account or a credit card somewhere, but she took payment only through PayPal, which meant she could be collecting the money under another name, maybe even in another state.

I sat back in my chair. Here was a woman who was aggressive in exposing herself before audiences and yet she'd left no trail in our hyper-documented age. I could imagine a fear of stalkers might require total anonymity in her life these days, but it was strange that someone so purposefully self-exposing left no public trace of her private life.

I transferred addresses for the handful of K. Buckleys who might be the Body Artist. I could do old-fashioned legwork, see if any of them had a home studio, but I wasn't expecting to find her.

I was so lost in thought, and files, that I didn't notice Mona Vishneski until she appeared at my table and hesitantly said my name.

"Ms. Vishneski!" I sprang to my feet.

She was a lost-looking woman around my age, her clothes hanging on her, as if worry over her son had made her lose a dress size overnight. Close up, I could see how rough her skin was; she didn't seem to have washed her face or combed her hair since Chad's arrest. She took off her gloves and then looked at them puzzled, trying to figure out what they were. She was carrying a scuffed leather handbag, big enough to hold a computer and a change of clothes. She finally stuck her gloves into one of its side pockets.

"John told me he hired you to clear Chad's name. I used to work with detectives back when I was managing a building for Mercurio. We'd hire them to find out where people had skipped off to without paying their rent, but I don't remember we ever hired you."

I agreed that I'd never worked for Mercurio. Companies that size tend to use big agencies, not solo ops like me.

"But, Ms. Vishneski, your husband—ex-husband—hired me to find out what happened Friday night at Club Gouge. You both need to understand, however painful it is to think about, that the evidence points to your son having shot Nadia Guaman."

"If you think he's guilty, then I don't think we should be working with you." Her eyes were bright with emotion.

I kept my voice level. "I'm committed to approaching this situation with an open mind. But I can't ignore evidence, and the evidence is that the murder weapon was found next to Chad. Another thing: I was present myself for two extremely angry encounters between your son and Nadia Guaman. I plan to look into their relationship, to see what lay behind his rage. But if you'd be more comfortable working with one of the detectives you used to know at Mercurio, I can respect that. If Mr. Vishneski agrees, then we'll void the contract he signed yesterday and return his retainer. I would ask you to pay the fee my lawyer is charging for providing the court order we needed to move Chad from the prison hospital to Beth Israel."

Mona Vishneski shifted her weight from foot to foot, uncomfortable at being put on the spot.

"Do you want to think about it overnight?" I suggested.

"Oh, I guess we should go ahead, if we're going to do anything at all." Her shoulders sagged again as the anger went out of her. "John said you've done criminal work and that you come highly recommended. It's not that I'm not grateful for you getting a real hospital and good doctors for Chad. Just don't expect me to agree that my son shot a woman, when I know he never could have."

Clients who blow hot and cold, they're always the most annoying to work with. One day they want evidence at any cost, the next, they don't think you're up to the job. Maybe a smart detective would have voided the contract just to keep from being squeezed between a divorced couple. Instead, I bought Mona Vishneski a drink—ginseng peppermint tea—and ordered another macchiato for myself.

"Tell me about Chad's guns," I said when we were finally both sitting. "John says you wouldn't let him keep them in your apartment, but he did, anyway, didn't he?"

For a moment, her anger spurted up again, but then she made a little fluttery gesture like a butterfly settling down. "I didn't like it, but where else could he keep them? He had two, which I hated, even though everyone in construction carries, even John. But you look at guns and you think of death. I asked Chad how he could stand having a gun anywhere near him after all the death he'd seen in Iraq, and he'd just say, 'No one's ever going to sneak up on me again.' Like the way suicide attackers and them sneak up on our troops in Iraq. Chad lost so many buddies there. It was just a miracle he didn't get killed himself that time his whole unit died around him." Like her ex-husband, she pronounced the country *I*-raq.

"I used to go to mass every week, thanking God for sparing me what so many other mothers had to bear, their sons dead or missing arms and legs. But watching how Chad's been since he got home—and now this—maybe I'm not so lucky. Maybe we'd all be better off if he had lost his legs instead of his mind."

"Mona!" a voice said. "How can you talk like that?"

It was John Vishneski. Mona and I had been so intent on each other that we hadn't noticed him come into the café.

"John!" Mona cried. "I told you I wanted to see this detective of yours for myself."

John gave the smile that seemed to crack his cheeks. I looked away, it was so painful to watch.

"I got too lonely sitting around the hospital," he said, "looking at Chad hooked up to all those machines. That Dr. Herschel, she's something, isn't she? The way she made those county so-and-sos stand up and salute, it's the one good thing I've seen this week. Mona, you want more tea? Do I order at the counter?"

"The Glock," I said to Mona while John was ordering drinks. "Was that one of Chad's guns?"

"How should I know? I told you, I hate them, I don't know one from another. You should ask those Army friends of his. They probably know."

"Ask his Army buddies what?" John Vishneski said, pulling up a chair. "About his guns? Chad didn't own—"

"John, what's the point in lying?" Mona asked. "When it's you who used to take him to target practice?"

"It's not a crime, is it, to teach your own son how to handle a gun?" Vishneski cried.

"You know the Glock is his, and you can't bring yourself to acknowledge it," I said in a flat voice.

Vishneski reached for his cigarettes, as he seemed to do any time he didn't want to talk about something. Studying the pack, not me, he said, "Not know, not for sure. Before he shipped out, he had two, a Beretta and a Smith and Wesson. I kept them while he was overseas, but when he came home and I saw how . . . how . . . well, how he was, I worried he might hurt himself, so I told him there'd been a break-in, someone had stole those guns out of my place. But I'm pretty sure he went down to Indiana, picked up something down there. You can, you know—no one even wants to see your driver's license. So maybe he does own a Baby Glock, how do I know?"

The hair at the nape of my neck prickled. "Mr. Vishneski, everything you're saying makes Chad sound unstable. Why do you think he didn't kill Nadia Guaman?"

Vishneski sucked in a breath as if it were a lungful of smoke. "Shit, Ms. Warshawski—sorry, ladies—you have to know Chad. He might have put a bullet through his own self to put an end to his nightmares, but he wouldn't go out killing some girl in an alley. Or anywhere else. He just wouldn't. He wasn't that kind of boy."

Mona nodded vigorously: Chad wasn't that kind of boy.

None of us spoke. I listened to the espresso machine hiss and to the snow sting the window. The bad weather, the awful economy, they had already pushed my spirits low without adding an unstable Iraq vet to the mix. I wanted to get up and walk away, but the Vishneskis were both looking at me as if I were all that tethered them to the planet.

"Okay," I finally summoned the energy to speak. "Chad's friends that he hung around with since getting home, how do I get in touch with them? Mr. Vishneski said there's one called Marty, another one named Tim something."

"Tim Radke," Mona said. "Marty, I don't know what his last name is. Probably they're on the speed dial on Chad's phone."

Chad's phone was still at her apartment. When the cops rushed him to the hospital Saturday morning, they'd left everything behind—phone, wallet—everything but his Army dog tags and his field jacket. He'd been wearing those.

"That's why I went to stay at John's," Mona said. "It got me down too much, all his stuff, and then the police, they broke down the door when they came to get him. Why did they have to do that? And it's me that has to pay to repair it. The city sure won't! I should have been here instead of in Arizona. My ma, she's got nurses around her, she only made me come down so she could run me around. I should have been here taking care of Chad. Shouldn't have expected that John would know how to keep him out of trouble."

"Mona!" Vishneski expostulated.

I interrupted before they could get into the kind of argument that probably led to their divorce all those years ago: she said, he didn't do, back and forth. We agreed, all three of us, to go to her apartment, where I could collect the phone and study Chad's habitat to see if he'd left any clues about his life that could prove his innocence.

We gathered up our things and walked out into the storm. The wind drove fine snow between my muffler and my sweater, and seemed to be scouring my face down to the bone. By the time we'd reached John's Honda, a block from Lilith's, even he was panting. Mona sat in front, staring at the snow. I dozed in the backseat while John crept the two miles to her apartment.

12

Shooting Up

Mona lived in an old building that had probably been rather grand when it went up in the 1920s. Back then, each of the six floors held only two apartments, those big ten-room jobs with a cubicle behind the kitchen for the maid. In the nineties, some developer had gutted the place, converting grandeur into shoe boxes.

The elevator itself was a small box, barely big enough to hold the three of us. Husband and wife—ex-husband, ex-wife—moved together unconsciously as we rode to the fourth floor.

When we got off, Mona's apartment was obvious at once: wooden slats were nailed across the hole left by the cops and a padlock had been screwed into the wall to keep the door shut. The sight was ugly and shocking. Mona's hand shook as she burrowed in her giant bag for her keys. John silently accepted the scarf, the book, the billfold, the wad of tissues she pulled out as she hunted.

I had that prickly feeling that makes you think someone is watching you. When I turned to look, I didn't see anyone, but down the hall there was a soft thud as a door was quickly shut. Some neighbor cared that we were here. I wondered if it was the woman who'd been screaming on television that she'd sue the condo board, that Mona Vishneski ought to be thrown out.

At last, Mona located her key ring, a plait of twisted metal, as laden with keys as a medieval jailer's. It seemed to take her forever to go through them as she muttered, "No, that's Ma's storage locker . . . Oh, I think that's Chad's bike lock." I resisted the desire to push her aside and work my picks into the lock.

When she finally had her door open and had stretched an arm around the corner for a light switch, I peered over her shoulder into the long rectangle that made up her living space. It had probably been an attractive shoe box a week ago, before the police tracked mud and salt across the newly sanded wooden floors and the area rugs that dotted them. One wall was lined with blond built-in shelves and cupboards.

Craning my head, still staying near the front door, I saw a stereo and a flat-screen TV. Mona didn't have many books, but the shelves around the TV held pottery and treen, those small wooden objects whose original purpose always baffles me. The pieces were unexpected, and I looked at Mona again. What other unexpected depths might lie beneath that flat surface?

The kitchen stood at the far end, separated from the main room only by a kind of work island or maybe peninsula, since it was attached to the wall at one end.

Mona and John started into the room, but I put out an arm to hold them back.

"What all have you handled in here since you came home?"

Mona was startled. "I don't know! How can I remember? The phone. I called an emergency service to put up the board and the padlock, like you saw just now, a place I used to use when I was at Mercurio. They remembered me and came right away, and while I was waiting, I'm sure I had a glass of water.

"I went into the bathroom. It was such a mess in there, Chad probably hadn't even washed the tub while I was gone. I wondered if he'd taken his toothbrush." She gave a hiccup which was half sob. "I stood looking at the sink and shaking my head over his messy ways like he wasn't in a coma. They don't know if he'll recover, but you think these things automatically after twenty-five years: have you washed your hands, have you brushed your teeth."

John put a hand on her shoulder and squeezed.

"I cleaned the sink. It . . . I don't know, cleaning . . . When I'm upset, I clean."

When I'm upset, I add to the landfill in my apartment. And then I'm more upset because the apartment is squalid. I wondered if there were drugs that could turn you into a neat freak.

"Then I went to my closet; I needed to get some sweaters. It wasn't this cold in Phoenix, of course, and I knew I'd freeze to death at John's, he doesn't pay for heat, and—"

"Do you have to go through every detail of every sweet minute of your life?" John asked, his moment of empathy passing.

"Okay, okay," I said. "You touched everything."

"Is that bad?"

"If someone came in while Chad was asleep and planted the gun on him, it will be harder to find that someone's traces, that's all."

"So you do believe he didn't shoot that woman?" she said eagerly.

"Oh, Mona, why'd you have to go destroying evidence?" John said.

"How was I to know?" she defended herself hotly. "It's not like you were doing—"

"Please." I put my hands up traffic cop style. "Don't argue, least not on my dime. It doesn't help the investigation. And before you get too carried away blaming Mona for her glass of water, look at the mud and scratches the cops left behind. If someone else was here ahead of them, the police did a good job of wiping out all signs of them. Let me see the bedroom."

Mona took me across the big room to her bedroom. Parting the blinds, I looked out at an enclosed courtyard, big enough for a bit of garden and some tables and chairs. The skeleton of a swing set rose out of the snow.

The building had been carved up in a way that created small alcoves in the bedroom. One held a desk, where Chad had left a partly eaten chicken dinner on top of a heap of bills and papers. While I inspected the bed, I heard Mona clucking over the bills under her breath.

Chad promised to pay the phone bill and the car insurance, but here are the envelopes not even opened! And Chad's MasterCard . . . Who let him have a credit card when he didn't have any income?

"And these holes in the wall!" she cried out so loudly that John came into to the room.

We both went to look at the wall. Three ovals that cut deep into the drywall made a little triangle over the desk. The paint had come away in a lip around each hole.

"They weren't here before you left for Arizona?"

"My goodness, no. You notice a thing like that. Was he trying to put up a picture?"

"I think he was using your wall for target practice."

"Shooting at a wall? Chad? But that's just ridiculous!"

I took a letter opener from the desktop and dug around in the lath behind the drywall. I was able to recover one bullet, which I showed the Vishneskis. Both of them were shocked; Mona suggested in a feeble voice that one of Chad's friends had come home drunk with him and shot at the wall.

"It's possible, of course," I agreed, but I thought about the way Chad had behaved when I'd seen him in Club Gouge. He was angry enough, and drunk enough, to do just about anything. A disheartening thought, if I was the lead member of the defense team.

John shouted, "So what if he shot up the wall? It doesn't mean he shot that gal at the nightclub. Means he knew to take his anger out on a wall, not a person."

I smiled and patted his arm. "Right you are. I'm going to finish searching in here. You go find me some clean garbage bags for things I want to show to my forensic lab."

Vishneski left the room, relieved to get away from the empty beer cans, the moldy chicken dinner. Mona continued to hover behind me, talking worriedly under her breath.

The bed was unmade, of course. The cops had come in, guns drawn. Everyone knew Chad was big and angry, so they'd tossed the duvet aside, grabbed him as he lay there, cuffed him. Maybe it was then they realized he was unconscious, not asleep. And the Glock that had killed Nadia Guaman, where had it been? I sniffed tentatively at the pillow and detected a hint of sour vomit but not of gunpowder.

I didn't think the cops had searched the room, but, even if they had, I would bet they'd overlooked something. I started with Chad's Army duffel bag, which sat open on the far side of Mona's bed. It was like a mountain spring, with clothes spilling out into a small stream that eddied around the bed and the floor. I photographed the bag and the room with my cell phone before touching anything.

"Why are you doing this?" Mona asked. "What good does it do to see Chad's mess?"

"We'll know what it looks like today so if someone comes in and rummages, we'll be able to tell."

The chaos seemed overwhelming. I poked through the clothes Chad had dropped on the floor, not sure if it was worth taking any of them to the lab for forensic analysis. Most of his wardrobe seemed to be left over from his Army service—fatigues; a second, summer-weight field jacket. He had a handful of civilian T-shirts, including one with Bart Simpson copping an attitude. I felt in the pockets of the field jacket and the jeans and found the usual detritus of modern life: ATM receipts, a stick of gum, the earpiece for his iPod. None of it seemed particularly meaningful.

My shoulders drooped as I looked around at the rest of the room. Empty beer cans littered the place; two were buried in the duvet. I photographed them *in situ* with my cell phone, then picked them up, using a corner of a sheet to hold them. I laid them next to the pillow-case, ready to pack into a bag.

Mona clicked her teeth. "Chad never was really tidy, but when he got back from the war it all got worse. I knew he was drinking. You don't like to think that about your child, but if I called after six or so I could tell by his voice. We tried to get him to go to a counselor, John and me both, and he did see this lady at the VA for a bit. But then he said she was just a waste of time, and he wouldn't go back—"

"You said his phone was still here," I cut in, "but I don't see it."

"Oh. Yes. It was on the kitchen counter. I'll go get it."

I searched through the pile of clothes spilling from Chad's duffel bag and looked into the bag itself. I didn't see the black object Chad had been waving under Nadia's nose the night before she was killed.

I stuck a hand between the mattress and box springs and found two guns, a Magnum Baby Eagle and a Beretta. I smelled them. Both had been fired and not cleaned, but it was hard to say how long ago that had been. Maybe Chad had lain in bed one night, shooting at the wall, and tucked the guns back under the mattress. I laid the guns under the pillowcase so his parents wouldn't see them and start fussing over them. I'd get the Cheviot labs to give me an idea how long it had been since they'd been fired.

A further search under the mattress turned up a copy of *Fortune* magazine. Tucked inside were a couple of steamy publications: *Mags4Lads*, from Britain, filled with giant-breasted women committing extraordinary athletic feats; the other, in Arabic, had similar pictures. Both English and Arabic readers favored blondes, with a sprinkling of redheads. Someone who read only ancient Sanskrit would have no trouble accessing the content of either.

I heard Mona's nervous murmuring as she came back to the room and slipped the athletic blondes back into *Fortune,* then put the magazines into my briefcase. Chad's mother didn't need to see his reading material.

"I thought I saw his phone yesterday, but it's not there now."

"You probably just thought you saw it." John had appeared behind her, holding a couple of black plastic bags. "You were tired and flustered, you know how you get. I've looked all over your living room, and it's not there."

"It was on the kitchen counter," she fussed. "I saw it when I got my glass of water."

I put all my specimens into the bags, conscientiously writing down labels on some scrap paper from Mona's desk, and sealed them with her packing tape.

"If Chad's phone turns up, give me a call. I've seen everything I need for now. It's late, we all need some rest. If you want to talk to a criminal defense lawyer, Freeman Carter is good. He's the person who got the court order that let you move Chad this morning. He has a new associate in his office who seems very capable to me, a woman named Deb Steppe whose fees won't be as steep as Freeman's."

I wrote Freeman's details down for them while Mona took the chicken dinner her son had left in the bedroom to the garbage. When she'd turned out the lights, she couldn't find her keys. While she hunted through her purse, I picked them up from the chair where she'd dropped them on her way into the apartment. I had a feeling Chad's phone was in that big shoulder bag of hers, but I was getting impatient to take off. If I couldn't find a phone number for Tim Radke, the one friend whose name John and Mona knew, maybe I'd mug her and search her bag.

The door at the far end of the hall opened again as we waited for the elevator. If I'd actually believed in Chad's innocence at this point, I would have talked to the watchful neighbor. The trouble was, I thought he was guilty. I was sloppy. It came back later to haunt me.

The storm had stopped when we finally got back downstairs. The building super was running a snowblower around the walks, and strewing salt, but beyond the building perimeter the snow was ankle-deep. I didn't want to trudge through it carrying all the souvenirs I'd collected—Chad's guns, his beer cans, his porn collection—so I waited at the curb while John and Mona went off to fetch the car.

When they dropped me at home, it was past eight. I knew I had to do something about the dogs. And now that I was away from the mess and tension in Mona's apartment, I realized I was hungry as well. I was about to call Jake, to see if he wanted to walk up to Belmont for a snack, when my cousin phoned.

"Vic! Didn't you get my messages?"

I'd turned my phone off when I was meeting with Mona and had forgotten to turn it back on. Petra had been trying to call all afternoon to say that Olympia was reopening the club tonight. Karen Buckley was going to do a special tribute performance in Nadia's honor.

"I thought—I know they arrested that guy, that vet—but do you think you could come? Everyone's so totally on edge, and Olympia is behaving strangely. It's, like, something else is going to happen. I'd like you to be there—if you can, of course."

I looked wistfully at my cozy living room and my dogs, who were panting hopefully in the doorway. "Petra, darling, on Friday I gave you my best advice and you ignored it. But let me repeat: You don't have to keep working at Club Gouge."

"Oh, Vic, I know, I know. I'm a pest. But you will come tonight, won't you?"

Maybe I could talk to Karen Buckley. Maybe she would be more forthcoming after her performance than she had been at Nadia Guaman's funeral this afternoon. I wasn't too hopeful, but I told Petra I'd come down to the club after I'd run the dogs and eaten something.

"Oh, Vic, thank you, thank you. You're the best!"

The best chump, she meant. I was more annoyed with myself than Petra. Why did I cave so easily to her demands?

I was worn out. When I finished taking care of the dogs, I lay down for almost an hour before heading back out into the cold.

13

A Show for the Dead

Despite the storm, the Club Gouge parking lot was crowded. Olympia's marquee announced that the Body Artist was back for a special memorial performance in honor of Nadia Guaman, killed so tragically five days earlier. Olympia had put it out on Twitter, MySpace, YouTube, wherever the Millennium Gen gathers, and they'd responded in force. Oh, the dead do us so much good from the other side of the grave!

The room was almost full when I got inside. Rodney was planted in his usual spot, two-thirds of the way back from the stage. I squeezed into a spare seat at a crowded table near the back of the room where I could watch people as they came in. I didn't see any of Chad's Army buddies, which was a pity. I'd hoped they might show up to save me the trouble of trying to find them online.

Tonight, perhaps because of the short notice, there wasn't a live act as a warm-up. The sound system was turned up loud, but we were listening to Enya's *Shepherd Moons*, whose haunting melodies conveyed a suitable sense of mourning.

My cousin, working the far side of the room, caught sight of me. She hurried over with a glass of whisky. "Johnnie Walker Black, Vic, it's on me. Thank you so much for coming."

Olympia, standing next to the bar like a captain on the bridge of a ship, saw me then and swept over to my table. "What are you doing here?"

"I thought the object of a club was to invite customers, not drive them away."

"You're not a customer. You're a detective, and detectives are bad for business."

"Now, that very much depends on the kind of business you're conducting, doesn't it?" I watched her face, but she played poker with bigger gamblers than me; she showed no signs of any emotion besides impatience, so I added, "I went to Nadia's funeral this afternoon. Karen came, but I guess you were too busy setting up here."

"Karen went to the funeral?" Olympia lost some of her commanding poise. "Why?"

"Better ask her. I was trying to figure out why she kissed Nadia on the lips in front of the altar. I couldn't decide if they had been lovers or if Karen was asking forgiveness of the dead."

"What would she need forgiveness for?"

"Creating the situation in which Nadia became the target for a shooter. Or maybe someone shot Nadia by mistake. Maybe the person who put glass in Karen's paintbrush a few weeks back was trying to do the job right this time and missed a second time. You got any security in place here besides your bouncer? And that guy?" I nodded toward Rodney.

"My insecurity, you mean." Olympia gave a laugh with an edge to it. "Besides, the police caught Nadia's murderer, as you know very well."

"The police made an arrest," I acknowledged, "but that isn't the same thing as catching Nadia's murderer."

"Are you saying that the vet isn't guilty?" Her eyes widened with alarm, dismay, or even pretense—hard to read in the dimly lit room.

"The setup calls for further exploration," I said primly. "Chad Vishneski was asleep in his mother's apartment with the murder weapon—the *alleged* murder weapon—on the pillow next to his head when the cops picked him up. Who phoned them? Why was the gun there? If it was, in fact, his gun, why didn't he stow it with his other weapons? How did he know Nadia? That's a raftful of unanswered questions. Come to think of it, Olympia, that wasn't you or Rodney here who phoned the cops, was it?"

She sucked in a sharp, harsh breath and looked involuntarily at Rodney. In another moment, she'd taken off. She stopped at the bar to check on her staff, paused at Rodney's table with a glance at me, and then worked her way through the crowd, stopping to banter with regulars or to check on people's orders, just the good host, making sure her guests were happy.

I sipped my whisky and pretended not to be watching her. In a moment, she slipped across the small stage and disappeared behind the curtain that led to the changing rooms. I waited thirty seconds, then snaked my own way through the crowd to the back of the stage.

Olympia was standing in the dressing-room doorway, hands on hips, talking through the half-open door. My hiking boots made it hard to tiptoe, but I moved as close as I could.

"Your contract requires that the audience be able to put their art on your body." That was Olympia. "If people walk away disappointed, they won't come back. And we'll both suffer."

"I'm not the person who got into debt, and I don't care about your suffering any more than you care about mine. For once, you and your precious *investor* will have to appreciate real art instead of kindergarten doodles. I spent four days on these stencils. It took Rivka six hours to paint me. I'm not wiping all this off so you can titillate people with death. Or save your club."

"Damn you, Karen, you know damned well you have to do something. And not just to save—" Olympia spun around to bare her teeth at me. "What the fuck are you doing here?"

In my effort to eavesdrop, I'd kicked a screw so that it banged against the dressing-room wall. "I wanted to make sure Karen was all right."

"She's not. Or she won't be if she doesn't remember that we're here to please our public, not ourselves," Olympia said. "Get back to the theater, Detective, or I'll have Mark throw you out."

She went into the dressing room and shut the door before I could follow her. I heard a bolt snap into place. I put my ear shamelessly against the door but could only make out the angry rise and fall of Olympia's voice.

The door to a smaller neighboring room opened, and I saw two slim young men peer into the hall. I realized with a jolt that these were the dancers who gyrated in burkas during Karen's performance.

"Is Olympia murdering Karen?" one of them asked.

"Or Karen killing Olympia?" Both laughed.

"I'm V. I. Warshawski," I said. "I'm a detective, and I'm investigating Nadia Guaman's murder. What did you see the night that Nadia Guaman was killed?"

"Nothing," the first one said. "Kevin and I were long gone."

"We don't do makeup for this gig. As soon as the Artist finishes, back we come, dump the rags, hit the road."

"Did you leave through the back door here? Did you notice anyone in the alley?"

"We steer clear of the alley. Drunks, smokers, druggies, not our scene. Time to stretch, Lee."

The two disappeared, shutting the door firmly in my face. I hate it when people do that. I made a ferocious face—that would teach them a lesson—and went onto the stage. The crowd noise dipped for a moment as people thought I might be the start of the act, but when they saw I was just inspecting the equipment the babble rose again.

I touched the mike and didn't get electrocuted. I inspected the webcam and wasn't sprayed with noxious gases when I pressed the ON button. I turned it off and moved to my position at the back of the room.

Petra zipped by with a trayful of drinks. She shot me an anxious look.

"I haven't killed Olympia," I assured her. "Yet."

A moment later, Olympia herself appeared onstage carrying a tray of paint cans and brushes. The crowd noise grew more intense again. Catcalls began rising, demands for the Artist to get onstage at once.

The lights dimmed, went out for the usual thirty seconds. When they came back up, the Body Artist was on the stage. She was, as always, nude, but I joined in the gasps and applause from the audience at the artwork covering her. No wonder it had taken the unknown Rivka six hours to paint her. A lily stem grew from the Artist's vulva, but instead of a flower it sprouted Nadia Guaman's head, which covered Karen's breasts. Karen's left arm was painted black, the right arm white: colors of mourning in the West and the East. A cypress branch drooped along her white shoulder; on the black shoulder a field of poppies grew.

The Artist stood and turned around. An angel covered her back, its wings spread across her shoulder blades. Its head was bent in grief; in one hand it held a pomegranate, but the other carried a sword.

I looked at Rodney, who was scowling. He snapped his fingers in Olympia's direction. She went to his table and bent so that the feathers at her cleavage brushed his ear—an erotic gesture that seemed wasted on both of them. He was angry; the club's owner was trying to placate him.

On the stage, the Body Artist stood with her back to us, her head lowered. She must have had a mike in her upswept hair because her voice carried easily through the room.

"A beautiful, tormented spirit went home today. To Jesus, if you believe He's the Resurrection and the Life. To the great goddess, if that's how you think of life beyond these frail coverings of skin and bones. Nadia Guaman, who briefly honored my body with her art, was slaughtered last Friday night. Tonight, I offer up my body in tribute to her."

The Artist held her arms wide. The angel's wings lifted, their feathers flowing down her arms. The young men, now anonymous, feminine, in their burkas, each took one of her outstretched hands.

No one in the audience moved or spoke until Rodney pushed his way to the stage. He grabbed the paint cans and with large strokes began to put his usual work, letters and numbers, on Karen's buttocks. His gestures were so aggressive that his painting looked like an assault.

"S-O," he wrote. "1154967 !352990681 B-I 50133928! 405893021195."

I copied the codes into my handheld, even though I didn't expect to decipher them. As Rodney painted, Karen said, "In today's news, the Taliban in Pakistan publicly flogged a seventeen-year-old girl. Her brother was among the floggers. She was accused of using her body as she chose, not as the men around her wished. In other news, two hundred twenty thousand girls under the age of eleven were raped in America last year. If Nadia is in heaven now, or someplace like it, we know she will intercede on behalf of all assault victims."

The audience began to stir restively, and some people booed. It wasn't clear whether they were booing the Artist or Rodney. When Rodney finished his work, he threw down his brush.

Karen came to the lip of the stage. "For those of you who come regularly, you know that I don't interfere with your art. I respect all sincere efforts at self-expression through painting. Tonight is different. Rivka is going to clean the canvas and re-create our work."

"Just as long as you broadcast my painting first, bitch." Rodney grabbed the Artist and dragged her across the stage to the webcams.

Rodney couldn't hold her and operate the cameras at the same time, and the two dancers refused to move when he commanded them to photograph his work. Olympia pushed through her audience to the stage and held Karen while Rodney operated the camera.

Rodney nodded in satisfaction and left the stage. Karen wrenched herself free of Olympia. She grabbed a brush and painted a long red stripe that ran from Olympia's nose, down her cleavage, and onto the black leather jacket that opened below Olympia's breastbone. The Artist dropped the brush on the floor and strode to the back of the stage, where she disappeared behind the curtains.

The crowd cheered and yelled, so Olympia pretended to take it in good humor. She signaled to someone behind the bar to turn up the houselights.

"We never know what the Body Artist will produce for us when she appears, but we all know by now it will be entertainment we won't see anywhere else in Chicago. We here at Club Gouge respect art and artists, and we're contributing tonight's profits to a scholarship that Columbia College has set up in Nadia Guaman's honor."

The images of death and innocence disappeared from the plasma screens on the stage. They were replaced by blue-and-white shadowy dancers, as a hot beat began pounding through the speakers. As always, the end of the Artist's performance signaled a frenzy of drinking. For ten minutes or so, the waitstaff were moving like crazed ballerinas from table to bar to table. Several couples hopped on the stage and began to dance. Olympia quickly directed her staff to move the paints and webcams out of the way. Whatever kept the customers happy . . .

I scanned the room, hoping to spot some of Chad's buddies in the mob. As far as I could tell, none of them had come. Rodney was still at his solitary table, working on what looked like his seventh beer. Although the room was so crowded that thirty or forty people were standing along the perimeter or even on the stage looking for seats, Rodney's sullenness created a force field that no one wanted to cross.

Beyond him was a table of men who looked incongruous in this club setting—four men in their forties, in well-cut business suits. As I stared, I realized one of them looked vaguely familiar. And he was watching me in turn. Of course: Prince Rainier Cowles, the lawyer who'd been at Nadia's funeral—had it been this afternoon? It felt like a hundred years had passed. I squirmed through the bodies around me to his side.

"Mr. Cowles! V. I. Warshawski. We met at Nadia Guaman's funeral this afternoon."

His brows contracted. "What are you doing here?"

I smiled down at him. "It's a cold night, on top of a cold and stressful day. I thought an evening at an art club would cheer me up. How about you?"

A man at his table laughed. "Is that what you call this place? I would have said skin joint. I thought about sticking a twenty up that girl's sunshine, but no one else was doing it."

"That would have been artistic and creative of you," I said. "And a bold statement of leadership."

The speaker frowned at me, but before he could fire back, one of his tablemates said, "That'd be good for the annual report, Mac. We go into danger zones that no one else dares enter."

"We should buy a piece of her tail." Mac looked at me as if to emphasize that he was directing his crudeness at me. "Did you write down the Web address, Cowles? I'd like her tits where I could look at them from time to time."

This caused not just another outburst of laughter but some congratulatory high fives. I dug my hands into my pockets to keep from flinging their drinks in their faces.

I grinned down at Cowles. "This is the kind of evening that the

Guamans would enjoy, isn't it? Witty banter about women's bodies right after burying their daughter."

He got to his feet. "Anyone who comes into a place like this can expect to hear that kind of comment and more besides. If you can't handle it, then you shouldn't be here."

"Are you saying that Nadia deserved to be shot?"

He made an angry gesture. "Of course not. But this is a rough place. I don't want to cause the Guamans more pain than they feel already, so I'm going to whitewash my report of what goes on in here. But you know as well as I do that it's a strip joint going under a classier name. Look at that guy there—" He pointed at Rodney. "You can't tell me he's the kind of person a woman who respects herself would hang around."

"You've got me there, Mr. Cowles," I admitted. "He looks like a Class X felony waiting to happen."

"What was all that about, his painting on that woman's ass?"

"Don't tell me you didn't want to join him, Cowles," one of his friends said.

"What would you have put there?" the man they'd called Mac said.

"Maybe the same numbers," the first man said. "They'd be his billable hours for the last month."

The three who were sitting down all laughed, and Cowles, after a brief hesitation, joined in, but he said to me, "If you're here because of Nadia Guaman, I'd advise you to leave her and her family strictly alone."

"Whoa, Mr. Cowles! You told me you were their honorary uncle. You didn't say you were their legal guardian or their mouthpiece. If they want to talk to me, they have a right to. And vice versa."

"Just who are you, anyway?"

I smiled again. "I am V. I. Warshawski. Good night, Mr. Cowles."

I returned to my own chair, which had been taken over by a couple who were sharing the small seat. As I extracted my coat from beneath them, I saw Cowles flag down a server and point at me. The server smiled and gestured. Within a few minutes, Cowles probably knew I was a private eye. There wasn't any real point in my keeping my identity a secret, after all.

14

And Besides, the Wench Is Dead

As I handed two twenties to Petra for my drinks, Rodney got to his feet and swaggered to the exit. I told Petra I'd be back for my change and hurried behind the stage, down the corridor that led past the toilets and dressing rooms to the rear exit. I reached the alley just in time to see Rodney climb into a Mercedes sedan. I squatted behind another car and managed to copy his license plate before he bounced out of the lot.

When I'd corralled Petra and gotten my change—fifteen dollars, more than I wanted to leave her, or anyone, on a twenty-five-dollar tab—I went backstage again, this time to the star's dressing room. Two women were with Karen. One, very young and white, was sponging the angel from the Artist's back. The second, an African-American with a soft short Afro, was perched on a stool, playing with the paintbrushes.

The Artist looked at me and said to her companions, "The detective I was telling you about."

I smiled at the women. "My name is V. I. Warshawski. I'm sad to see you destroy the angel. It was stunning. And amazing that you could create all these images in one day."

"It's ephemeral art. Like Goldsworthy, only even more ephemeral than leaves along a lakeshore." Karen spoke gruffly, but she turned away from me, as if to hide any pleasure in my compliment. "This is Rivka, who did the tedious work of painting the designs on me and now is doing the equally hard part of removing them again. She's my most reliable aide-de-camp when I'm doing serious work of my own."

The younger woman flushed, and said, "You have to take them off, even though they're so beautiful, because it's hard on the Artist's skin if she sleeps in the paint."

"That's Vesta on the stool." The Artist didn't pay any attention to Rivka's interjection. "She's a third-degree black belt."

"Did you bring her to protect you from overeager fans, or from Rodney?" I asked.

"I think she was just trying to impress you," Vesta said. "I'm not a bodyguard."

She sat easily on her stool, with a kind of confidence in her bearing that I'd seen in other experienced martial artists—no need to be aggressive in the world. I'd learned to fight the hard way, on the streets of South Chicago, and it made me too pugnacious, too willing to believe the worst in the people I met. Although someone like Rainier Cowles and his friends demanded that one think the worst. I asked the Body Artist if Nadia had ever talked about him.

"I hardly knew her," she said, her back still turned to me.

Rivka said, "I thought you said she came to you because—"

"Rivka, darling, don't think so much. It will put wrinkles in your forehead."

The younger woman's neck turned pink at the crude put-down. When the Artist realized Vesta and I were both looking at her in disapproval, she turned and kissed Rivka on the mouth.

"I just mean," the Artist added, "you must have misunderstood something I said."

"Why did Nadia seek you out?" I asked, as if the interruption hadn't taken place.

"She didn't," the Artist said. "Rivka mis—"

"Girl, enough of the lies," Vesta said. "Nadia is dead. Allie is dead. Who else is going to die?"

"You knew Allie?" I asked. "Tell me about her."

"There's nothing to tell," the Artist said. "We met at a music festival. She was deep in the closet, and wouldn't see me back in Chicago because she was afraid someone would tell her parents. She'd only go to remote places, like festivals, to pick up women, and then she'd hop home like a frightened rabbit, back to mass, back to being a good hetero girl. End of story."

"Not quite. How did you find Nadia?"

"Shoe's on the other foot. Rivka, I'm freezing. Can you start cleaning and stop looking as if your dog just died?"

Rivka flushed again and resumed her scrubbing, working on the Artist's vertebrae with the intensity of a sailor sanding a ship's deck.

"How did Nadia find you?" I asked.

"Don't know. She never said. Just showed up and started painting her designs. I was surprised—it's not very often that someone with actual ability paints me. I was even more surprised when she asked me about Allie."

"What did you tell her?"

"I didn't remember Allie's name. That pissed off Nadia, but what was I supposed to do? Keep track of every fucked-up woman who crawled into bed with me? It got her more pissed off to know I hadn't kept track of Allie. I didn't know the woman was dead. It was like the whole world was supposed to worship at Alexandra Guaman's shrine, and, when I didn't, it made me a cold bitch in Nadia's eyes."

In the mirror, I saw tears spilling down Rivka's face. When she realized I was watching her, she started scouring even harder, which led the

Artist to utter a sharp complaint. The Artist turned inside Rivka's grip, took the sponge from her, and brushed her hair out of her eyes.

"Take a break, Rivulet. It's been a long, hard day. I'll work on my front while you get yourself some juice or a glass of wine."

Rivka rubbed her eyes with the back of her hand, smearing paint across her face. She opened a small refrigerator tucked under a ledge and pulled out a bottled smoothie.

Karen spread cream over her breasts and started removing Nadia's face. "It's almost like a metaphor for life, isn't it. One minute you're here, the next minute you're not." Her voice was toneless. It was impossible to tell if she had any strong feelings about Nadia or Rivka, or even herself.

"Did she ever mention Rainier Cowles to you?"

Vesta flipped the brushes she'd been playing with onto the counter and looked at me. "Who is Rainier Cowles?"

"A lawyer," I said. "He claims a special interest in the Guaman family. He may still be out front—he came here tonight with a tableful of corporate types. He said he wanted to examine the strip joint where his protégé's daughter spent her last night."

"The Body Artist isn't a stripper," Rivka cried. "How could you say such a thing? And then to pretend you admired the angel—"

"Whoa, there," I interrupted. "I'm just reporting what he said, not my own beliefs."

"Vesta doesn't need to be my bodyguard while I have Rivka," the Artist said.

The younger woman flushed again. Her slender neck, with little tendrils of hair curling from sweat, made her look as vulnerable as a daylily.

Vesta had slipped out of the room during Rivka's outcry. She came back in now to report that the house was still rocking. "I think your corporate guys are there. Near the back of the room, left side? Go take a look, Buckley. Maybe it'll refresh your memory."

Murray Ryerson phoned just as I returned from floundering through the drifts with the dogs.

"You lead an exciting life, Warshawski, but you're too selfish to include your friends in your adventures."

"Yep, it's a round of nonstop thrills. You want to walk the dogs for me? Eat dinner with Mr. Contreras?"

"I take it back, I take it back," he said hastily. "You're not selfish; you're noble. But you still could've called me after Nadia Guaman died. Now I'm picking up third-hand that the perp's mom hired you."

Murray is an investigative reporter for the *Herald-Star*, which used to be a great newspaper until, like papers all over America, they began cutting staff and pages to keep Wall Street happy. These days, the paper looks more like *My Weekly Reader* than a serious daily.

Murray is still a good reporter, but he has less and less incentive to keep digging since so many of his stories get killed. He has a TV gig through the *Star's* Global Entertainment news channel, so I never worry about his starving to death, but he's depressed a lot of the time and turns to me way too much for news.

"Your sources are as lazy as you are these days, Murray." I was too tired to be tactful. "A: Chad Vishneski is not the perp. And B: It was his father who hired me."

"I know I'm late to the party, but I hear you held the dying woman outside a strip club. Doesn't seem like your kind of venue."

"Go there yourself," I said. "It's a great show. I'm surprised you haven't caught it yet."

"Truth is, I've been on vacation. Buenos Aires in January beats Chicago to hell. I got home last night and saw that the Girl Detective had been super-busy in my absence. Can I buy you a drink tonight and hear all about it?"

"Golden Glow at eight, Murray, if you'll do one little thing for me first."

"Not the dogs or the old man . . ."

"You still have friends in the DMV and I don't. If I give you a license plate, will you tell me who owns it?" I read off the number from the sedan that Rodney had driven last night.

It was a relief to off-load even one of my chores. When I finished changing for work and went back outside, I wished I'd given him something more challenging, like cleaning off my car and shoveling a path for it. It took twenty minutes to dig it out, but there wasn't an easy way to take public transit to Nadia Guaman's apartment. And if Nadia had managed to track down her dead sister's lovers, then I needed to go through her apartment to see who else she might have been targeting.

Nadia had lived about a mile from my office. In the snow, it was a quiet neighborhood, but the telltale gang graffiti were present on the bus stops and overpasses.

Nadia's apartment was in a well-kept courtyard building on one of the side streets just north of North Avenue. People were leaving for work, and I didn't have to stand on the sidewalk long before a woman emerged. She held the door for me, her eyes on the weather outside, not on the face of a stranger entering.

In the entryway, away from the wind and blowing snow, the quiet fell on me like a blessing. I brushed the snow from my pant legs, stomped my feet clean, and climbed up to the third floor. Nadia had respectable locks but nothing out of the ordinary; even with my hands stiff from cold, I worked the tumblers in under ten minutes. I was lucky: I was just opening the door when a man came out of the apartment across the landing.

"Who are you?" he asked. "Miss Nadia isn't at home, and she doesn't live with anyone."

"I'm a detective. You know Miss Nadia is dead—her family buried her yesterday. I want to look for evidence in her apartment."

He shook his head. "You're too late. Someone else was in here yesterday, and they said the same thing, that they were detectives looking for evidence. I saw them going in, and when I asked them for identification, they showed me their guns instead."

"Did you call 911?"

"Why, when everyone knows the police themselves are operating burglary rings in this neighborhood? And you? Are you also a detective whose identification is a gun?"

I fished my wallet out of my briefcase and showed him the laminated copy of my PI license. "I'm a private investigator. I've been hired to uncover the reason for Miss Nadia's murder."

"They made an arrest. I saw it was some lovers' quarrel."

"They make wrongful arrests every day," I said.

The neighbor nodded, and started an involved story about his sister's second son. I went into Nadia's place and found a light switch. The neighbor, still talking, followed me in, but he fell silent when he saw the chaos created by yesterday's "detectives." Whoever had been searching, whatever they'd been looking for, they'd done a thorough job of tossing books from shelves and DVDs from their cases.

Like every artist I've known, Nadia covered her walls with pictures, masks, unusual found objects. Most of these had been flung to the floor, the hooks and the dust outlines on the walls showing where they'd once hung.

"Have you been in here before?" I asked the neighbor.

"I didn't take anything," he said. "You can't accuse me of that."

I looked at him closely. "So you have been in here. That was you in here yesterday, not people pretending to be detectives."

"That isn't true!" he cried. "They really came. I only wondered why. And they hadn't locked the door when they left."

"So you locked up behind them? How did you have a key to Ms. Guaman's dead bolt?"

"She gave it to me. In case there was an emergency. Or to feed her cat when she was out of town."

I had a hard time picturing the shy, intense Nadia with a life that took her out of town. Although maybe she'd gone around the country hunting for her dead sister's lovers. People do odd things when they're gripped by an obsession.

I walked through the apartment's three rooms. In the bedroom, I found the one piece of art left on the walls: a crucifix, where the head of Jesus had been replaced by the head of a girl taken from an old doll. The hair had been pulled from the doll's head and wrapped around the hands of the crucified Christ. The image was profoundly disturbing, not what I would want to wake to.

I realized there were no signs of a cat, no litter box, no food or water dishes. "Where is the cat?"

"In my home. When I learned Miss Nadia was dead, I took in the cat. She called it Ixcuina, after some old goddess. A strange name for an animal, but it is a strange animal."

I looked from the dismantled apartment to his flushed face. I didn't believe that he hadn't been here yesterday, but I also didn't think he would have destroyed the apartment if he'd been inside surreptitiously.

"So, Mr.—?"

"Urbanke," he muttered, defensive.

"So, Mr. Urbanke, as a frequent visitor to Ms. Guaman's, can you tell me what yesterday's fake detectives might have taken with them? Can you tell if any of her art is missing?"

He looked around slowly but shook his head. "It— I can't tell, with everything on the floor like this. Maybe if I put the pictures back on the wall . . ."

We spent the next hour or so matching artwork to dim outlines. We worked our way through the apartment's three rooms, but at the end, even though there were still some gaps on the walls, Urbanke couldn't tell what was gone.

"Besides," he added, "she was always bringing in something new, taking down something she was tired of. It was like a museum, her private museum, where the exhibits were always changing. The one thing I don't see is her computer. She kept it here."

He pointed at a worktable in the corner of the apartment's big front room. The table was built for artists or drafters; one half could be lifted up and down at different angles, depending on how the person liked to work, while the other half remained flat. The flat space, Nadia's office worktop, held bills and a scattered pile of sketches. The charger for the computer was still plugged into the wall, but of the computer itself there was no trace.

Urbanke stood next to me looking through Nadia's sketches. "Who knows if this artwork is valuable. Those detectives didn't take it, but her computer, definitely you could sell it for drugs."

We walked out together. I left Mr. Urbanke to lock Nadia's door since he had a key, no matter how he'd gotten hold of it. I wanted to know what he'd taken besides the cat Ixcuina. I wondered, too, why Lazar and Cristina Guaman hadn't come, but maybe collecting their daughter's belongings was too much for them right now. In the entryway, I stopped to look at the mailboxes. Urbanke's first name was Julian.

I bumped across the slush-packed roads to my office. My leasemate and I contribute to a service that shovels the walks on our street, along with the parking area that we share with the other two buildings abutting it. I thankfully abandoned my car in the small lot and went into my office to catch up with my messages.

Now I felt bewildered, almost split in half, by the two lives I was looking at. Did Chad Vishneski and Nadia Guaman have anything at all in common? Had her killer trashed her apartment? And if her killer wasn't Chad, why was he being brought into her story at all?

All I could do was plod forward with what little I had to go on. The beer cans, pillowcase, and guns I'd collected from Mona Vishneski's were still in my car, and I had Chad's girlie magazines in my briefcase.

I had taken these things yesterday for no good reason except trying to put on a show for the client and his ex-wife—the ghost of Sherlock Holmes dictates that the detective sees something in the detritus of everyday life overlooked by ordinary mortals.

I packed up the guns and the empties and pillowcase and called a messenger to carry them to Cheviot labs. "There may be nothing here," I wrote in my cover letter, "but please check to see whether anything besides beer was in these cans. And see if you can trace the purchase history on these guns."

I didn't include the magazines—I didn't think I needed a comparative analysis of Arabic and British porn directed at U.S. servicemen. I put them into the Vishneski case file, to keep until the matter was resolved.

Once the messenger had left, I leaned back in my desk chair and studied my mother's engraving of the Uffizi. Someone had gone through Nadia Guaman's apartment. I didn't trust her neighbor; he had Nadia's keys, he'd helped himself to her cat. But he hadn't needed to point out that her computer was missing. And he could have searched her place at his leisure, no need to turn it upside down. It was possible that she'd stiffed advances from him and that he'd murdered her himself and then trashed her apartment to finish off his fury—but even that meant Chad Vishneski wasn't the killer.

The story was too complicated for me to follow without a chart. I drew one up on a big piece of newsprint and taped it to my wall. Rodney, the thug who had the run of Club Gouge, I needed his last name. I needed to know who he was, what hold he had on Olympia.

Then there were all the murky sleeping arrangements among the Body Artist, Nadia's dead sister, Olympia, and the two women I'd met last night, Rivka and Vesta, whose last names I'd also need to get. Vesta, a black belt, had once been one of Karen Buckley's lovers. When we'd spoken last night, she'd seemed calm, dispassionate even, in discussing the Body Artist. It was hard to believe she might have killed Nadia in a jealous frenzy.

Besides, according to the Artist, there'd been nothing in her relations with Nadia to make anyone jealous. I didn't believe much of what Karen Buckley said, but her account of Nadia's advances and retreats had a ring of truth to it.

The younger woman, Rivka, was a different story. She didn't have much skin between her feelings and the world. Judging by last night's behavior, she was jealous of everyone who captured the Artist's attention. She could have believed there was more between Nadia and the Artist than ever really took place. And what about Alexandra? I needed more information about her, that was clear. If Nadia had known about the Artist's private life, would the youngest sister, Clara, have known as well? Or would the two older girls have protected the baby of the family? I toyed with a fantasy in which the Guamans murdered their daughter so that her sexuality would remain a deeply buried secret.

Speculation is the detective's enemy. Facts. I needed facts about the Guamans and about the Body Artist.

I tried to put together a list of questions about the Artist. Vesta and Rivka believed she'd run away from home as a teen. Maybe she'd changed her name to protect herself from a violent father/brother/lover. I looked for legal name changes to Karen Buckley during the past decade but drew another blank.

She seemed to think that her performances gave her power: *You can get this close, as close as my skin, but you can't get inside me. I control the boundaries.* I imagined standing naked in front of an audience, and my skin crawled. It felt like a horrible kind of exposure. I flung my pen down. I couldn't find anything out about Karen's past, so I needed to concentrate on what I knew about her in the present.

Her relationship with Olympia, who had financial woes, that bore more exploration. Somehow, Olympia had established a modicum of control over the Body Artist. And the Artist was a woman who definitely liked to be in control of her relationships.

The biggest questions had to do with the outbursts Nadia, or Nadia's paintings, had provoked in Chad Vishneski. And neither the Artist nor Nadia's family was giving me any insight into what that was about. Maybe Chad had written his buddies or his parents explaining why Nadia's paintings had gotten so deeply under his skin.

I called the client. John Vishneski was in the Mercurio office on Huron going over drawings; no one was out on a building in this weather, of course. I asked if Chad had said anything to him about Nadia or the Body Artist.

"I never heard of those two women until they came and arrested Chad. I guess he thought the idea of a club like that would shock me, or disgust me. Kids have such funny ideas about parents, don't they? Like, we don't have basic human feelings or needs or something. I expect I was the same way about my old man."

I thought of my own mother, how painful I'd found it to think she might have the sexual impulses common to us all. Parents aren't supposed to operate in the world of desire. Perhaps that's the only way children can grow up feeling safe.

"What did Chad do for e-mail? His phone? A computer?"

"Computer, I guess. His phone—he's like all the kids his age—mostly he texts. He has a Lenovo ThinkPad; I bought it for him when he first shipped out. He took it all over Iraq with him. He even kept a blog, the way so many folks do these days."

"The computer isn't at your wife's place . . . your ex-wife's. Do you have it?"

I knew the answer would be no before he gave it. Mona hadn't imagined seeing her son's cell phone; someone had been in the apartment ahead of us the previous afternoon. Someone had helped themselves to Chad's phone and his laptop.

I hung up. I was starting to feel as if I were in one of those dreams

16

Nada About Nadia

I had to go downtown for a meeting, a routine inquiry where I'd been able to do all the work without any shadowy menaces blocking my path. I pulled my documents together, put on some makeup and my dressy boots, and went back out into the bracing winter air. The snow had stopped after a mere four inches—nothing, really, to a third-degree street fighter.

As I rode the L down to the Loop, I knew I needed to talk to the Guamans. I'd only been on the case for two days, but it had been five days since Nadia had died. It was strange that they hadn't sought me out, the woman who'd been with their daughter when she died. I decided to go over to Pilsen to try to speak with Cristina Guaman at the hardware store where LifeStory told me she worked.

As soon as my Loop meeting ended, I took the L west and south to Damen and Cermak and walked the three blocks to the hardware store (*¡Sopladores de nieve! ¡Palas! ¡Todo para el invierno! ¡Se habla inglés!*).

The placard in the window had advertised "Everything for Winter," but the store really had everything period. Snow shovels, ice melt, mittens, space heaters, fans, kitchen utensils, TVs, microwaves, coloring where you are running from some menace you can't see and the whole time the menace is shutting every door you turn to. Someone with a lot of organizational talent was running faster than me, cutting in ahead of me at every exit.

I looked at my hands. "I am a street fighter," I said. "No one can stop me." Trouble was, I didn't really believe it.

books. It was a small space, but not only was every surface covered, long hooks dangling from the ceiling held dried tomatoes and garlic, DVDs, dog collars, trusses.

The place wasn't well lit, and I didn't see Cristina Guaman at first, but after stumbling against a rack full of hard hats I found her near the back at a computer. Someone was talking to her in Spanish, but the conversation was apparently desultory because Cristina only nodded her head while she typed.

I stood next to the woman who was speaking to her, waiting for a lull, but the woman saw I was a stranger, perhaps a customer, and asked in Spanish if I needed help.

"I need a word with Ms. Guaman," I said, hoping she really did know English. My Spanish is pretty rudimentary.

The woman moved away from the counter, and Cristina Guaman stopped typing to look at me. "Yes?" she said. "What do you need?"

I pulled one of my cards out of my bag.

"I'm sorry to interrupt you at work, Ms. Guaman, but I'm the woman who was with your daughter when she died. Is there a place where we could talk?"

"We can talk here."

She folded her hands on top of the keyboard, not the gesture of a woman at ease, but to create a barrier between herself and me.

"I don't want to broadcast your family's business to the whole store. Isn't there someplace private?"

"My family has no business that the whole world cannot attend to. Are you the owner of that terrible place, that club where women take off their clothes so men can draw nasty pictures on their bodies?"

I wondered if family ties would make her unbend, so I explained my role as Petra's cousin, my desire to protect her, my observation of Nadia and Nadia's anguish or anger. "She kept drawing a face, the face of a beautiful young woman with short curly hair, and then she would slash a line through it. I'm wondering if that might have been her sister."

"Clara's hair is long and it is almost blond." Cristina Guaman's eyes were wary.

"Alexandra. Do you have a photograph of her? It was her name Nadia was calling as she died."

At that, Cristina sucked in a breath. "Alexandra has been dead a long time. Nadia couldn't let her rest in peace."

"So she was painting Alexandra's face?"

"I have no desire to know what pictures Nadia might be painting on a woman's body. She knew how strongly I felt—her father, too—about her going to that place."

"When did you last talk to her?"

Cristina Guaman looked around to see if anyone was in earshot. "Many months went by. Nadia was angry, always, for the last two years, so angry she would not speak to her father or me. My heart is broken at her death, but she cut herself away from her family. She moved into that apartment in a dangerous neighborhood, she stayed away from mass. Even though I knew she would pay no attention to my words, I had to call her when she started making a spectacle of herself in that degenerate club."

I asked how she had learned Nadia was painting on the Body Artist, but of course people had been using their phones to take video footage of the performances. These inevitably ended up skipping around the World Wide Web, where more than one neighbor had shown them to the Guamans.

"The picture was poor, the light was bad, but everyone could see that woman sitting there naked, showing off her breasts, and people could easily see Nadia's face. Can you imagine how you would feel when your daughter has flaunted herself in public for the whole world to see? I had to call her. I had to try to tell her how very worried I was to see her in such a corrupt place."

"And was it Alexandra's face she was painting?"

Cristina's nose twitched as if she were smelling something bad.

"It was enough to see Nadia together with a naked woman. If she was involving her sainted sister, then I am thankful to God that I was spared that sight."

"How did Alexandra die?"

Cristina backed away from me. "In a painful, hard way that I prefer not to discuss."

"Did she have a boyfriend, a girlfriend, anyone I could talk to?"

"What are you trying to ask?" Cristina hissed.

So she knew her daughter had women as lovers. Alexandra wouldn't come out of the closet for fear her mother would learn, and her mother had known all along. Had Alexandra committed suicide because of the pressure? Had Nadia known and moved out after fighting with her mother over Allie's sexuality?

I couldn't think of any good way to ask these questions, so I asked in a bad way. "Who told you that Alexandra was sleeping with women?"

Cristina gasped. "If you came here to slander my saint, my angel, I will call the police. Leave!"

"I'm not trying to upset you, Ms. Guaman, just to figure out who killed your beloved daughter Nadia."

"They arrested a man. It's enough, enough that we're dragged through the dirt by Nadia, without you coming to me and pouring it over me."

"I went to Nadia's apartment this morning," I said. "Someone had broken in, had stolen her computer and all her discs. All her artwork is missing."

At that, she became very quiet. She shook her head slowly as if unhappy at whatever she was thinking, but even though I tried several different gambits, she wouldn't share her private thoughts with me. I told her about Nadia's conviction that someone was spying on her.

"Who would that have been, do you think?" I asked. "The person who murdered her?"

Cristina shook her head again. "Nadia had many unhappy ideas, and not very many of them are—were—true. Was it she who told you those filthy lies about Alexandra? Nadia believed them and wouldn't accept my word that her sister was pure, a good Christian, not capable of such acts. But enough anger. Nadia is with her sister now, in the arms of the Blessed Mother. I thank God that she has no more pain on this earth."

That was all I was going to learn from her: Nada about Nadia. I walked unhappily from the store, wondering just what it was Cristina Guaman didn't want me to know about her daughter. Daughters.

I stopped in a taquería across the street for a bowl of rice and beans. Ernie couldn't tell me anything. Even if I could get past security at O'Hare to reach Lazar Guaman, it was hard to convince myself that such a gray and beaten man would talk to me. That left the surviving daughter, poor young Clara. It was two-thirty—with luck, I'd make it to her school before she left.

17

Vow of Silence

I rode the Green Line to Halsted and walked the few blocks to St. Teresa of Avila Prep. School got out at three, and the city buses were already lined up. Unless the Guamans' self-appointed protector could leave his La Salle Street practice to collect Clara, the easiest route home for her was on the Number 60 bus down Blue Island Avenue.

I reached the school about ten minutes ahead of the exodus. I shivered in the bus stop catty-corner to the school until the tall doors opened and the students poured out.

They seemed to arrive in one giant wave of screaming, jostling teens, but as they passed me they broke into little clots—groups of high-spirited boys, or girls laughing and kidding together, or couples in that adolescent embrace that doesn't allow a single molecule of air between their bodies. A number were walking alone, shoulders hunched to avoid the glances of a pitying world. Most were bent under their giant backpacks, looking much as their peasant forebears must have, lugging cotton or corn or wood. And all, it seemed, were madly reconnecting to their cell phones and music players after a day of forced withdrawal.

My dressy boots were elegant, but they weren't very warm. I was beginning to think I'd have to amputate my toes if I stood outside much longer, when Clara Guaman appeared in the middle of a knot of other girls. Unlike yesterday, when she'd gone bare-armed to her sister's funeral, she was dressed sensibly in a parka, although she hadn't bothered to zip it shut. She also had foresworn the gaudy eye shadow she'd sported at the funeral. When she and her friends had boarded their bus, I followed them and swiped my CTA card through the machine.

The driver, a thickset woman in her forties, nodded at the kids as they climbed up the steps. She looked at me in surprise—adults don't usually ride the school routes—but she didn't say anything. When the bus was packed from stem to stern, she rolled away from the curb. The shrieks and shouts of sixty or so kids, moaning over tests, over boyfriends or girlfriends, hotly arguing who'd said what to whom, made my head drum, but the driver just smiled to herself, focusing on the potholes that littered Blue Island Avenue. Like the rest of the world, she had her own little soundstage plugged into her ears.

I worked my way to the back, where Clara and her friends had found seats. She was talking animatedly, but her skin was gray, and there were dark circles under her eyes.

"V. I. Warshawski," I said when she looked up at me. "We met yesterday at your sister's funeral."

Her face shut down into the arrogant angry lines I'd seen at the church.

"Are you here to apologize some more? Don't bother."

"I want to know when I can talk to you—"

"You're doing it right now. I guess I can't make you shut up."

Her friends stared at us with frank curiosity.

"Privately."

"You can't. If there's something you want to say to me, do it right here. And then get out of my life."

We had both been bellowing to be heard over the ruckus around us, but the noise began dying down as kids nearby caught what we were saying. One of them asked if Clara wanted him to call 911.

"She's harmless," Clara said roughly.

I didn't want to say too much in front of this texting, Tweeting audience, but I needed some way of getting her to talk to me.

"When I heard the shots, I ran to your sister's side. I held her as she died. Her last word was a call to Allie."

The silence around us became absolute. Clara sucked in a breath, her face as shocked as if I'd slapped her. Her friends gazed at her with vampire-like avidity.

When Clara didn't say anything, I said, "Could we go someplace to talk about Nadia and your other sister?"

"You can't talk about Allie!" Clara cried.

"Why not?"

She looked around wildly, and then said, "Her name is sacred! You can't use it. No one is allowed to talk about her!"

The kids around us began murmuring excitedly among themselves. Even if I hadn't been tired and cold, the chatter made it hard to think. It certainly made the bus a stupid place to try to talk, but I plowed ahead.

"When did you last talk to Nadia?"

"I don't remember, and it's none of your business, anyway."

The lurching of the bus meant I couldn't keep my eyes on her face, but I thought Clara looked more scared than angry despite her defiant words.

"Your mother says she called Nadia when your sister was seen on YouTube painting on the Body Artist. How did Nadia respond?"

"Have you been talking to my mother? She has enough to worry about without someone like you butting in."

"Karen Buckley put on a special program in your sister's honor last night. Karen's the Body Artist who came to your sister's funeral."

"I remember who came to my own sister's funeral."

"What did Nadia tell you about Alexandra's death?"

At that question, Clara definitely looked more frightened than angry.

"I told you we can't talk about Allie, so butt out!"

"All right, if we can't talk about Allie, let's talk about the Body Artist. How did Nadia find her?"

Clara looked at me but didn't speak. One of the boys near her left the bus. I took his place.

"The club was full last night for the Artist's program in your sister's memory. Rainier Cowles brought a party; one of the men—"

Clara bounced to her feet and bent to stick her head in my face. "If you're a pal of Rainier's, you can leave me alone. Go back to Prince Rainier and suck his dick."

The raw language was meant to shock. She stared at me for a few seconds, hoping for some sign that she'd hit home. When I only smiled sadly because her youth and pain were so poignant, she marched to the front of the bus, deliberately shoving people, as if vicariously punching me.

Her friends gave me the kind of frigid looks I remembered from my own adolescence. They sniffed as if smelling garbage and pointedly turned away from me, then started giggling loudly.

"It would be more to the point if you'd help Clara," I said. "She's frightened and lonely."

This made them laugh more loudly.

The bus was stopped for the light at Nineteenth Street. I pulled out one of my business cards and scribbled on the back, "Rainier Cowles is not a friend or business associate of mine, and I would never repeat anything you told me. Call or text me when you feel up to talking."

Enough kids had left the bus that it was easy for me to walk to the front and stand next to Clara. Her rigid posture, despite the weight of her backpack, told me she was very aware of my presence. I tucked the card into her parka pocket, but she refused to turn her head. I got off at the next stop and crossed the street to pick up a northbound bus.

As the winter twilight closed in on me, I rode buses and trains back to my office. My leasemate Tessa was hard at work, her half of the building flooded with spotlights and the flame of her blowtorch.

My own half was dark. I didn't bother turning on a light, just took off my boots and sat with my feet curled up under me on the sofa to warm them, trying to decode Clara Guaman's response to my questions.

Allie's name is sacred.

Clara had been told never to discuss her sister. But why? Because the family was afraid Alexandra's sexuality would leak out? It was hard to accept that a parent still thought of homosexuality as so shameful, but of course many people do.

Clara thought, or feared, I was connected to Rainier Cowles. Last night at Club Gouge, he had claimed he was there to make sure the club respected Nadia, but he and his friends had definitely felt they were on a boys' night out and not at a wake.

Nor did I place any credence in Cowles's casting himself as an honorary uncle; lawyers like him bill themselves at five hundred dollars an hour or more. They don't waste their time on the families of baggage handlers. But if he wasn't protecting the Guamans, what was he doing hanging around their lives? He was certainly protecting something, and that something had to be himself, or possibly a high-flying client.

Allie, Nadia had cried. She wanted her sister, not her mother, as she was dying. Or she knew she was dying and hoped Alexandra would be there to greet her in the country of the dead.

At length, I turned on a light and walked over to my computer. "Find me Alexandra Guaman. Fetch, boy!"

The floor was numbingly cold underneath my panty hose. I rummaged in my back storeroom and found an old pair of running shoes to wear as slippers.

While LifeStory was searching out Alexandra Guaman's details, I logged on to embodiedart.com, the Body Artist's website. I wanted to look again at the paintings Nadia Guaman had made on the Artist to see if I could understand why they had roused Chad Vishneski so thoroughly.

Instead of the slide show I'd found on my previous visit to the site, the screen was blank except for the message "Out of respect for the dead, we have temporarily taken the site off-line." I somehow had not expected so much sensitivity on Karen Buckley's part. It forced me to think of her as less completely self-centered than she'd seemed.

I made myself a coffee and opened the report I'd ordered on Olympia, which had been sitting in my computer's pending folder since the previous afternoon. The details of Olympia's life were sketchy, as were her financials. She owned a loft apartment on the near North Side, in the stretch made newly hot by the destruction of the old Cabrini Green high-rises. She didn't actually own it; she was paying a mortgage on it, as she was on a summer place near Michigan City. The debt on the two properties was around half a million.

Olympia didn't own the building where she ran the club; that was held by a blind consortium managed through the Fort Dearborn Trust. I whistled through my teeth, trying to pick apart what I could of the club's finances.

Olympia had been running Club Gouge for almost three years. Her background had been in restaurants and entertainment; she'd managed a restaurant at one of the metro-area casinos, then opened a nightclub of her own in west suburban Aurora. The Aurora Borealis proved so successful that she'd apparently decided she was ready for the big city. Three years ago, she'd sold her Aurora place and opened Club Gouge.

Olympia's first two years at Club Gouge, even during the boom economy, had been disastrous. She'd run through almost a million dollars, maxed out her credit cards, and overdrawn her line of credit. And then, as the bottom fell out of the economy, just as everyone else in the country was losing their jobs and their homes, Olympia's bills were wiped clean. There was no way of seeing who her godfather had been, but someone had put a million dollars in cash into her account.

Santa Claus. Rodney Claus. He was the person Olympia was trying to keep happy. He was the one she'd called her "insecurity." But he wasn't Olympia's savior; he was the foot soldier sent to keep an eye on the investment.

Nadia had sought out the Body Artist because Buckley had known Allie. I couldn't get away from that. But how had Nadia found out that her sister had known the Artist? If murder happened because of the Guaman family's sensitivity over Allie's sexuality, why was Nadia dead and not Karen Buckley?

I was making myself crazy with all these unprovable scenarios. It was close to five p.m. now. I'd planned on going home to walk the dogs and eat a bowl of pasta before meeting Murray, but I was too exhausted from my day in the snow. I called Mr. Contreras and asked him to let the dogs out. I was heading to the daybed in my back room, when my computer pinged to tell me one of my requested reports had arrived.

Alexandra Guaman. The file on her wasn't very big, but when I opened it the first thing I saw was her high school yearbook picture. Her face, framed by curly dark hair, didn't have a knife slash across the middle. Other than that, she looked like the portrait Nadia had drawn on the Body Artist's back. That didn't particularly startle me; I'd been expecting it. What jumped out at me was where she died. Alexandra Guaman had been working for a private security firm in Iraq. She'd been driving a truck on a supposedly safe route when an IED exploded and killed her.

18

And the Wheel Goes Round and Round

I printed out the files on Alexandra Guaman and took them with me into the back room to read while I stretched out on my daybed. An hour later when I came to, the pages were strewn across me and the floor like dead leaves.

I struggled upright, washing the sleep out of my eyes under Tessa's shower, making myself coffee in our kitchenette. I had an hour before I had to meet Murray, and I was feeling so tense about my lack of headway that I wanted to get through as many documents as I could.

What I had on Alexandra Guaman didn't tell me much. So many people have died in Iraq since we invaded that journalists now dump them all into a journalistic mass grave: fifteen killed in an explosion outside Basra, seven dead in a Baghdad market, thirty obliterated in a bombing run on Fallujah.

Alexandra's bio was correspondingly slim: the oldest of the Guaman daughters, the first to attend St. Teresa of Avila Prep, followed by college at DePaul here in Chicago, a degree in communications, then a job at Tintrey, the big security contractor. Tintrey's headquarters were in Chicago, or at least the suburbs, in the corporate corridor along the north leg of the Tri-State.

Alexandra had gone to Iraq for Tintrey four years ago. Tintrey had contracts for everything from over-the-road trucking to providing field first-aid kits. Alexandra's job title, a level 8 employee in communications, could have meant anything: creating PR, monitoring computer networks, getting real-time information to field personnel.

Chicago's Latino paper had an obituary, showing the smiling yearbook picture I was getting to know by heart. I squinted at the page, picking my way through the Spanish: the anguish of the parents, the long wait for news, the sad realization when Alexandra's boss wrote a letter of condolence to the family: an IED had exploded when she was heroically driving a truck as part of a convoy to the Baghdad airport.

Nothing in the story, or in any of my skimpy reports, about her sex life. Or about the Body Artist. Maybe Alexandra had been a lesbian, but she'd been in Iraq at the same time as Chad Vishneski. It was her face on the Body Artist that roused him to fury.

Had she turned Chad down in Baghdad? Had an affair with him that she'd regretted? Or maybe Chad had attacked Alexandra. His service record was clean—certainly no assault charges—but that didn't mean the two didn't have a history together. And then when he saw her face pop up out of the blue, he'd gone after Nadia. I knew I was committed to Chad's innocence, but these connections did not look innocent. Maybe Terry Finchley was right after all. Maybe Chad had doped his own beer out of guilt over murdering Nadia. If that was the case, though, who had broken into her apartment yesterday?

The ideas spun round and round, uselessly, like wheels unable to find traction in a snowbank. Frustrated, I looked up reports on Tintrey.

If I couldn't find enough about Alexandra, I had the opposite problem with the company that took her to Iraq. I started with their website, which showed heroic warriors defending America from terrorists in the Middle East and Africa but also stressed that "Tintrey is more than just a group of highly skilled fighting men and women. We're there when you need us . . . whether it's at the PX or the RX."

Tintrey provided base security, they had a division that produced protective gear, they built base housing, they bodyguarded visiting VIPs, and they helped staff the post exchanges.

The website flashed me through the PXs, which looked like giant shopping malls: electronics warehouses, clothes, fast-food restaurants, banks, even car dealerships. You might be twelve thousand miles from home, but you couldn't escape McDonald's or multiplexes. I was astonished. Somehow, when people talked about base PXs, I'd thought of small general stores, the kind they show in old Westerns. But if the U.S. needs to get everyone on board our far-flung military operations, of course ordinary vendors need a piece of the pie, too: it can't all go to Lockheed Martin.

The news reports were more tempered and more mixed. As one of some hundred thirty private security contractors working in tandem with U.S. military bases, Tintrey had made their share of missteps: billing the Department of Defense for phantom supplies, building a bridge that collapsed the first time a tank rolled across it

Everyone agreed, though, that Tintrey owner Jarvis MacLean had a classic rags-to-riches story. Or, at least, jeans-to-riches. The most enthusiastic report came from *Wired Into: The North Shore,* a webzine that covered news in the metro area.

GLENBROOK GRAD HITS THE JACKPOT

Jarvis MacLean was flipping burgers while he went to Glenbrook High School, but those days are long behind him. He's traded his deep-fat fryer for a Ferrari and has a home chef who's more likely to serve him Burgundy than burgers.

MacLean, home from his eighth trip to Baghdad, talked to us about

life in a war zone and the dangerous but rewarding work his nine
thousand Iraq-based employees do.

While he was in high school flipping those burgers, MacLean started
a firm that provided security at suburban functions. The company grew
and branched out, and he made some smart acquisitions, including the
purchase of Tri-State Health, which had turned into Tintrey's medical
division, and Achilles, which made protective gear.

"Will Jarvis MacLean's golden touch change Achilles' fortunes?"
asked an article in *Fortune*.

Making a fresh start from the ground up and the top down, MacLean
has also replaced Achilles' advertising firm with the high-flying Dashiell-
Parker company. Perhaps Dashiell-Parker can improve morale in a firm
plagued by cost overruns as it ramps up production of its patented
nanoparticles for shielding both Tintrey employees and U.S. soldiers
in Iraq.

Another story, in the *Financial Times,* gave a thumbnail sketch of
Tintrey's rise. The company was still relatively small when MacLean
tied his fortunes to W's coattails in 1999. After the invasion of Iraq,
MacLean was rewarded with one of the many lucrative security and
rebuilding contracts the U.S. handed out to private companies. Between 2001 and 2005, Jarvis MacLean's annual revenues bloomed from
under a hundred million to over a billion.

Mazel tov, I snarled under my breath. *You got rich while Alexandra
Guaman got dead and barely merited a line of type.*

My phone dinged to let me know I needed to leave to meet Murray.
I'd been so wrapped up in my reading I hadn't even noticed my feet
getting cold. I was just logging off when I did a double take on Jarvis
MacLean's name. Mac. The happy boys at Rainier Cowles's table last
night had called one of their party Mac.

I went back to Tintrey's corporate site and looked for photos of MacLean. Sure enough, he was the guy who'd said he wanted to look at Karen's breasts—tits, he'd called them—from time to time. The report showed him accepting an award from President Bush in one picture; solemn-faced in battle fatigues in another and flanked by Rainier Cowles. What was Cowles to them? Their outside counsel?

Another person in the photo had also been with Cowles at Club Gouge last night. According to the caption, this was Gilbert Scalia, head of Tintrey's Enduring Freedom Division, which oversaw their Iraqi operations. How cute to call the division after the official name for the invasion. I logged off in disgust.

While I laced up my work boots, I looked up the phone number for Tim Radke, the only one of Chad's friends whose name John and Mona Vishneski remembered. Radke responded to the news I was investigating Chad's death unenthusiastically, but he did agree to see me.

"I haven't known Chad all that long," Radke warned me. "But he's not a bad guy. I'd like to help him out."

That was not exactly a ringing character endorsement, but we set a date at a Division Street bar for the next evening. Radke repaired computer setups for a local cable company; he'd be finishing around six and reckoned he could meet me by seven.

Before finally packing up for the night, I called Terry Finchley over at CPD headquarters. A detective at his level, being groomed for a major promotion, didn't keep regular hours any more than I did. He was still at his desk.

"Warshawski. You were next on my list to call."

I'd known Finchley long enough to hear the tightly reined fury in his thickened voice. I could picture the pulses throbbing at his temples, turning his ebony skin a deeper black.

"I take it you got the message I left last night?"

"Just what were you doing moving a murder suspect out of county custody? I just got the report. You had this guy lawyered up so fast, we didn't have a chance—"

"'Lawyered up'?" I repeated coldly. "That is a disgusting phrase. By which you mean, I saw Chad Vishneski had access to some basic, constitutionally protected rights. Aside from the fact that he's in a coma, so it's hard to believe he's a flight risk. And aside from the fact that you arrested him based on no more than a phone tip, which came from where exactly?"

"I do not have to reveal anything to you, Warshawski, crime hotlines least of all. But I will remind you that the gun used to murder Nadia Guaman was found in bed next to Vishneski—"

"Who was unconscious and unable to answer any questions. When your crew picked up the murder weapon, what did they do with Vishneski's cell phone and his laptop? A Lenovo ThinkPad, it was."

"That, again, is none of your damned business unless you are representing the perp, in which case you can present the usual subpoenas for evidence."

"His parents hired me, John and Mona Vishneski. When I saw that Chad's computer and his cell phone were missing, I assumed you had booked them in. But, if not, it supports our hypothesis that someone was in the apartment with Chad the night Guaman was murdered. And that whoever was there thought it prudent not to leave his electronics lying around where someone like you, or even me, could read his files."

Finchley was silent for a minute. I heard the clicking of his fingers on his keyboard, and then a swearword, under his breath but unmistakable.

"*If* the electronics are missing—and I'm not relying on your word for that or anything in this case, Warshawski—it doesn't prove squat about Vishneski's innocence."

"Not in and of itself," I said. "But I went over to Nadia Guaman's apartment this morning, which the CPD didn't seem to think was worth searching. Here's something strange: Her place had been tossed. Her computer was gone. Some of her artwork."

He tapped more keys. "She lived in Humboldt Park. Plenty of drug-happy housebreakers there."

"If it was just Guaman, or just Vishneski, whose computer was gone, I'd agree. But both? Come on, Terry."

He let out a sigh, deliberately loud to signal that I was annoying him. "We have a solid case against Vishneski. He assaulted the dead woman twice in the weeks before he shot her. He's a textbook stalker. And the murder weapon was in bed with him."

"You've tested the weapon?"

"I know you think we're too inept to tie our shoes without you hold-ing the laces for us, but, yes, it did occur to me to get the weapon tested. The Glock on the pillow next to Chad Vishneski fired the bul-let that killed Nadia Guaman."

"And residue? You did an atomic absorption test on Chad's hands?" I persisted despite his annoyance.

"Of co—" He broke off mid-word. "I'll get back to you on that as well."

I was aching to know what Finchley was reading on the computer. Had someone screwed up and forgotten to test Chad? Or was there some anomaly in the result itself that gave him pause?

"By the way," I said, "it would help Chad's treatment if the doctors knew what drugs they found in his system. Did they test him over at Cermak?"

"Freeman Carter can get a court order, if you need to know."

That raised my hackles. I hadn't planned on riding him about sloppy work at the crime scene, but I added, "You might like to know that Chad vomited on his pillowcase. I sent that, and the empty beer cans by the bed, out to a private forensic lab for analysis."

"Damn you, Warshawski, couldn't you have called me first?"

"It was four days after Guaman's murder. I figured if your team had wanted to collect evidence, they had plenty of time."

I thought I could hear Finchley gnash his teeth, but all he said was, "If someone jumps you tonight, or breaks into your place, don't call 911, Vic. Even if we caught the perp red-handed, you wouldn't think we knew what we were doing."

I opened my mouth to apologize, then stopped. I would not apologize for letting Terry Finchley know his team had missed evidence. And I would not apologize for getting Chad Vishneski good medical care—assuming it wasn't too late.

19

The Grumpy Cousin

The client called moments after Finchley had slammed the phone in my ear to ask if I'd found anything.

"It's more what I haven't found, Mr. Vishneski." I explained what my search at Nadia Guaman's had turned up—or actually, hadn't turned up.

"So you're saying you can't prove anything," he cried, frustrated. "And I still have to come up with money for your bill. If I promised someone a building would go up and he came around and found an empty hole in the ground, he'd be within his rights to sue me. Especially if I'd taken his money."

"Detecting isn't like putting up a building. It's like hide-and-seek. They're hiding, I'm seeking, and right now the hiders are ahead of me. They're very good. If you think you can find a better seeker, I can understand that. I will say that I have not failed a client yet, but I'm sure that's how you feel about your buildings, too."

He wasn't ready to fire me, we both knew that. He just needed to vent his fears about his son. His son, who Iraq had changed from happy boy to angry man. His son, who was lying in a coma. His son, who might have killed a young woman.

Outside, I dusted the residue of the snow from my car. My cousin had been texting me when I'd been on the phone with Terry, her messages increasing in urgency. While the engine warmed up, I phoned her, wondering what new crisis had occurred at Club Gouge.

"Vic, I got fired," she blurted as soon as she heard my voice.

"I'm not sure that's such a bad thing," I said. "Club Gouge is looking more and more unstable—"

"You don't understand! From my day job. That's why I'm calling. I desperately need the club job now. And when I called in this afternoon, to see if they could add to my hours, Olympia told me she'd only do it if you stopped hanging around the club. She says you're bad for her business and she can't keep me on if you keep showing up."

I massaged my forehead with my gloved hand—a mistake, because I rubbed melted snow into my face. How typical of Olympia to blackmail one of her waitstaff like this.

"You need to look for a real job, pronto. Olympia is way too erratic for you to count on her for your rent money. Besides which, I need to be at the club as I work on Nadia Guaman's murder. If I have to come back, I'll figure out a disguise, but—"

"You can't!" Petra cried. "I just told you—"

"Petra, turn off the temper tantrum and listen to me. I just said that I'll do my best not to jeopardize your job. I need to talk to Karen Buckley, and I don't know where she lives. Tell me the next time she'll be at the club, and I'll wait for her outside."

"Vic, no, don't." Not even the bad connection could mask the panic in her voice. "You don't understand. I need this job."

"Petra, we seem to keep having a version of this conversation. Surely, under the circumstances, you could take some money from your mother while you find work."

"She's totally wound up with my dad's trial right now. I'm not going to bother her about stuff I can handle on my own."

I wondered if Petra was unconsciously hoping to get into enough trouble at Club Gouge to force her mother to start paying more attention to her. I started to say something, then decided my armchair psychology would further raise my cousin's hackles.

"Petra, even in this economy money isn't everything. It isn't worth a jail term, or worse. This guy Rodney, Olympia both fears him and protects him. And he and Olympia are involved in something rotten. You came to me last week because she was essentially demanding that you let him feel you up. Now it's—"

"You got that to stop, everything's been okay lately."

"'Okay'?" I squawked. "A murder is okay? Your boss threatened your job if I show up, which means she's got something going on she's afraid I'll uncover. That is not okay. That's a recipe for disaster. If Olympia is providing cover for a money-laundering scheme, you could end up in front of the grand jury. You could even be implicated!"

"Then my big grumpy cousin will come to my rescue, won't she?"

I could picture Petra's face, the self-mocking pout she puts on when she knows she's being a brat. The trouble was, of course, I would come to her rescue. And she was banking on that. Growing up the way I did, my mother dying when I was in high school, my father forced to turn the house and meals over to me, I felt as though I'd been born old. I was tired of my own knee-jerk reaction. *You're in trouble? Say no more. V.I., the grumpy cousin, will bail you out!* I wished I knew how to turn off that particular switch.

I wondered for a moment if my whole detective practice was built on my private history of being an adolescent caretaker. The thought upset me so much that I couldn't keep an edge of fury out of my voice when I spoke.

"Petra, call me the next time the Body Artist is going to appear. It's not a lot to ask considering how much hot water you're willing to get me in."

"Uh, well, actually, it's tomorrow night." Petra spoke in a kind of mumble that made it hard to understand her. "She's doing a special show because Olympia got so pissed off about her erasing Rodney's stuff last night."

Petra cut the connection. I put the car into gear and started down Milwaukee Avenue. The bitter winter was acting like a wrecking ball on the city streets, as if a band of hyper-energetic gnomes were hacking their way to the surface, choosing new spots every night. I was almost half an hour late to the Golden Glow, but I did find an open space across the street. Parking had also become a source of bitterness in the city—the mayor suddenly sold street parking to a private firm, which had quadrupled the rates overnight. We all had to carry bags of quarters everywhere we went, as if we were heading for slot machines, which I guess the pay stations had become. Slot machines completely and permanently skewed in the house's favor.

Murray was already in the Glow when I got there, drinking a Holstein. The nasty weather had kept all but a handful of hard-core drinkers at home, so Sal had pulled up a stool next to his. Murray lifted the bottle in a token greeting but didn't get to his feet.

"Beer in this weather!" I said. "It makes me feel colder just watching you drink it."

"Warms me up." He grinned. "I imagine the seat behind third base, the July sun as hot as your temper, the Cubs—"

"Trailing hopelessly, Lou Pinella's iron jaw shooting sparks. I get the picture."

Sal reached across the mahogany countertop for the Black Label bottle. "How much does Murray know?"

"Try me," Murray said. "Who had the worst ERA for the 1987 Cubs? Who died first, Leopold or Loeb?"

"I don't think we can trust Murray," I said to Sal. "He's too desperate for a story."

Murray snatched the Black Label bottle from Sal before she could pour me a drink. "Deliver, you two feminazis, or you'll never see this bottle alive again."

"Do we go quietly or break his arms?" Sal said.

A lifted glass sent her to a corner table with a bottle of wine. When she came back, she said to me, "You know, I told you the other night that your friend was a good manager, but that was old news, dating back to the Aurora Borealis."

"Olympia, Club Gouge." Murray's smile was smug. "I can still do research even if no one wants to print my stories."

"She got in over her head. And then a benefactor pulled her to shore," I said.

I told Murray and Sal about Rodney, and asked Murray if he'd tracked the license plate from the sedan Rodney had been driving the night before. "Did you get his last name or an address?"

"The sedan belongs to a guy named Owen Widermayer, who's a CPA with an office in Deerfield and a home in Winnetka," Murray said. "Owen does not have a criminal record, and no one named Rodney works for him."

"They're lovers, then." I copied Widermayer's address into my handheld. "I don't understand what Rodney is trying to communicate through Karen Buckley's body. But maybe Widermayer will talk to me and it will suddenly make sense."

While Sal went over to check on her other customers, I showed Murray the numbers I'd found on the Body Artist's site. He puzzled over them with me but couldn't offer any suggestions. And he had the same objection I did: If it was a code of some kind, why rely on such crude transmission. Why not use a cell phone or the Net, where you knew you'd reach your target. Or if you were afraid of eavesdroppers and hackers, why not write a letter?

Sal came back and offered me another drink, but it was getting close to ten; despite my nap earlier, I was beat. Once again, I took the side streets home. A few lazy snowflakes were falling, just enough to cover my windshield from time to time. The blurry view just about matched what was going on in my head.

Before getting ready for bed, I went to the safe I'd built into my bedroom closet. It's where I keep my mother's few valuable bits of jewelry and my handgun. I pulled out the Smith & Wesson and looked it over to make sure it was clean. I put in the clip, double-checked the safety, and laid it on the nightstand next to my bed. It was starting to feel like that kind of case.

20

An Egghead Enters the Scene

In the morning, I drove to the northwest suburbs under a sun that dazzled and blinded. I brought along Mitch and Peppy; before going to Owen Widermayer's offices near the Tollway, I stopped at the Forest Preserve in Winnetka. We ran down to the lagoons, which were frozen solid enough to hold my weight, and covered with a dusting of snow that provided traction.

None of us had had much exercise the last few days, and I was glad for the chance to run. The dogs rolled in the snow and chased after balls, which bounced high on the ice. We passed people on cross-country skis who cheered us on—everyone's spirits were better for this rare day of bright sunshine.

As we moved on, I sang "Un bel di" just because the beautiful day brought the words to mind. Yet a sense of menace underlies that aria, and menace seemed to rise up and greet me when I reached Widermayer's building. The address board listed two tenants for the second floor: Owen Widermayer, CPA, and the Rest EZ company.

I don't know every sleazy operation in Illinois, but Rest EZ was hard to overlook. About eight months ago, the owner, Anton Kystarnik, had been in the middle of a messy divorce when his wife conveniently died in a small-plane crash. Investigators came to the reluctant conclusion that it had been a genuine accident. I'd followed the story with the same enthusiasm as every other conspiracy theorist, learning along the way that Kystarnik's wealth came from payday loans, which, in my book, are just juice loans that aren't conducted in alleys.

Say you get caught short near the end of the month. No problem: you sign over your upcoming paycheck to Rest EZ as surety, they advance you cash. At up to 400 percent interest, if you repay it in 120 days, 700, or even 1,000 percent interest if you go over the limit. See? It's juice and it's legal.

I stared at the tenant list. Rodney drove Owen Widermayer's car. Widermayer shared a floor with Kystarnik. Surely Kystarnik wasn't the guy who'd bailed out Olympia. She was supposed to be a savvy businessperson. No one would sign up for a million-dollar bailout at 700 percent. But why did she give Rodney the run of her club if she didn't owe Kystarnik some big kind of favor? Or were she and Rodney, or even she and Anton Kystarnik, lovers? There was a disgusting thought.

Nothing in the building supported the reports of Kystarnik's wealth, estimated at eight hundred million at the time of his wife's death. The cheapest gray matting covered the hall floor, the doors were that pale faux wood that fools no one, and the hall lights had been chosen to save every watt possible—not, presumably, because Kystarnik was green, but because all his money went to his lavish homes here and abroad. I didn't remember the reports that clearly, but I seemed to recall something in the south of France or Switzerland or Italy, or maybe all three, besides a two-swimming-pool affair in nearby suburban Roehampton.

The only money the tenants had spent on their public space went to the security cameras above the doors. These were small, discreet, and high-quality.

Rest EZ's offices were at one end of the second floor, Owen Wider-mayer, CPA's at the other. The doors in between weren't numbered or labeled, so who knew where the CPA began and the juice lender left off?

I was pretending I didn't know about the juiceman, so I pressed the buzzer next to the CPA's door. There was a pause while someone looked at my honest, friendly face in the camera and then buzzed me in.

Widermayer's office was as drab as the hallway. There wasn't any art on the walls. The only decoration was a tired philodendron that wasn't exactly dead but didn't seem to be growing, either. A beverage stand in one corner held some Styrofoam cups and a shaker of fake powdered milk. The coffee in the carafe was so overheated that a sickly caramel smell filled the room.

The woman who sat behind the cheap metal desk looked as tired as the plant. She was going through pieces of paper—the little receipts you get from taxis or from restaurants, as far as I could tell—and typing from them into her computer. She didn't look up until she'd finished the stack under her left hand.

"I'm V. I. Warshawski," I said in the overly bright voice one uses around depressed people. "I'd like to talk to Owen Widermayer."

"You don't have an appointment." She wasn't hostile, just stating the facts.

"No, ma'am. Is he in?"

She was tired, not ineffectual: no one could see him without an appointment. If I told her what I wanted, she'd see if he could fit me in.

I held out a business card. "I'm a detective. I'm investigating a murder, and Mr. Widermayer's car was found at the scene."

That did get her attention. She started to dial, then got up and went to a door behind her desk. She shut it behind herself so quickly that I didn't get a look inside.

I moved around so that I was standing next to her desk, half facing the shut door. She hadn't bothered to exit her computer spreadsheet.

My mother had brought me up with very strict rules. Only *una feccia*, a fecal kind of lowlife, ever looked at other people's private papers or opened their mail.

Sorry, Gabriella, I murmured, leaning over to look at the screen. As I'd thought, she had been logging in expense receipts. For someone named Bettina Lyzhneska. One eye on the door, I scrolled across the spreadsheet. Konstantin Feder, Michael Durante, Ludwig Nastase, and, at the end, Rodney Treffer.

I scrolled back to Bettina's column just as the door opened behind me. I was holding my hands over the radiator next to the desk as the assistant reappeared. She frowned, looking from me to the computer, as if wondering what I'd seen, but I merely made a bright comment on the miserable winter.

"Mr. Widermayer can see you for ten minutes, so I hope you have your facts organized. He likes people to come to the point."

"Excellent," I beamed. "I like pointy people, myself."

Her frown tightened, but she motioned me to the door behind her, which she'd left half open.

Widermayer, like his assistant, was communing with his computers. He held up a hand, like a trainer ordering a dog to sit, without looking up from his three monitors. I sat in a chair that would have dug into my bones if I hadn't had on so many layers of clothes.

Widermayer, as much as I could see of him, was built like an egg—not exactly overweight, but definitely rounder in the middle, narrower at the top. His head, bald except for a fringe of gray hair, looked egglike, too. I began to feel hungry, longing for a fluffy omelet.

The boss's office was just as spartan as the front room. Widermayer's desk was handsomer, being made of some kind of wood instead of metal, but the blinds blocking the winter sun were bent and dusty, and nothing hung on the walls except a clock, which showed seconds slipping past us into eternity.

Widermayer kept his eyes on his monitors. I was getting bored.

"You have ten minutes for me, Mr. Widermayer," I said, "so why don't you let me know why Rodney Treffer is using your car to stalk artists in Chicago."

Widermayer held up one of his pudgy white hands again. I got up and circled around his desk to look at the monitor he was studying. There I was on the screen, my profile in LifeStory, my own favorite subscription search engine.

"I don't think you'll find anything on Rodney Treffer in there," I said. "Nor about your Mercedes sedan."

"But it's telling me you don't have any legal standing to ask me questions." His voice was deep and booming, unexpected from his flaccid body.

"You agreed to see me, Mr. Widermayer, and my business card explains that I'm a private investigator. I've been hired to discover who murdered Nadia Guaman. Rodney is a key suspect."

"The police made an arrest. Rodney had nothing to do with it."

"No one's been convicted yet. And there's compelling evidence that the guy in custody didn't shoot Ms. Guaman."

I leaned over his shoulder to read the details about me. Funny how I'd never bothered to test LifeStory's accuracy by checking my own records. They had my outstanding mortgage correct, but they showed me still driving my old car.

I tapped the screen. "They show me owning an old TransAm, which was totaled a few years back. I signed over the title when I sold it for scrap. Makes you wonder how reliable their research is, doesn't it?"

He clicked a key to bring up his screen saver and leaned back in his chair to look at me.

"What evidence?"

"I just told you, they're listing the TransAm among my assets, when—"

"What evidence that Chad Vishneski didn't murder that Mexican gal?"

"You're sort of following this story, aren't you? You know the name of the guy who's been arrested, but, like LifeStory, you're relying on poor sources. No Mexicans were killed."

He opened a new window on his computer and called up the news reports on the shooting. "Nadia Guaman. Mexican gal. Killed outside some nightclub."

"Nadia Guaman, woman, American. And you know darned well where she was killed because Rodney was there, so surely he told you about it. And a few nights ago he drove one of your cars to the club. If anything happens to Rivka Darling or Karen Buckley, or even me, Rodney will definitely be the first person the police will question. And then they'll talk to you because you own the car he drives, and then they'll talk to Anton Kystarnik because you lease your office from him."

I was making up the last item—it just seemed like a reasonable assumption. Since Widermayer actually looked as startled as possible for a boiled egg, it must have been accurate.

"Tell me about the evidence. Then I'll know whether it's worth talking to Rodney."

"My clients pay for confidentiality."

"In other words, you've got a big fat zero."

"I've been around too long to let someone goad me into revealing confidential information. I'll tell you, in exchange for another fat zero, that the police are taking my results very seriously." No one ever said it was wrong to lie to Anton Kystarnik's accountant.

Widermayer pretended to yawn. I sat on the cheap deal credenza that held his tax and law books. It wobbled a bit, and I wondered if it might give way beneath me, but I liked the way it distracted his attention.

"Olympia Koilada," I said. "Anton Kystarnik bailed her out, and now she lets Rodney run tame around her club. If—"

"Who told you that?"

I smiled. "Sources. Nadia Guaman was getting Chad Vishneski all wound up. When he started attacking her in the club, it created a stir, and the club got in the news. Anton can't afford to have a spotlight on him these days. The feds are already paying too much attention to him. So he gets Rodney to shoot Nadia and frame Chad, and two problems are solved at the same time."

Widermayer gave a derisive snort. "I thought you were a detective, not a fairy-tale writer."

"It doesn't matter if it's a fairy tale as long as the state's attorney and a jury believe it."

I drew my feet up under me, despite the bulk of my boots, and the credenza gave kind of a squawk.

"Get off that," Widermayer said sharply. "If you break it, you replace it."

"Fifty bucks at Walmart. Not worth worrying about."

"Olympia Koilada doesn't figure in your fairy tale, I notice, but if she's your client I'd advise her to be very, very careful."

"Yeah," I said, "why's that?"

"She hasn't kept her side of a bargain she made, and that means she's not trustworthy."

The credenza wobbled under my weight. Widermayer watched it and me with as much alarm as his large plate of a face could express. I hopped off: I didn't want to impale my spine on a tax book.

"If Olympia shows up dead or beaten, or something, you and Anton will definitely be the first ports of call for the cops. Not to mention your boy Rodney."

"Nothing to do with me," Widermayer said.

I leaned over the desk and smiled into his face. "He's using your car. The law tends to hold you responsible for little things like that."

"If you're threatening me, you're wasting your breath."

I straightened up. "I wouldn't call it a threat, Mr. Widermayer. More like information."

As I left his office, I looked back to smile at him. Not even his eggy face could conceal his expression this time, and it wasn't one that proclaimed eternal love and devotion.

21

The Super-Rich and Their Fascinating Lives

When I got back to my car, I wrote down the names I'd seen on Widermayer's assistant's computer while they were still fresh in my mind: Bettina Lyzhneska, Konstantin Feder, Michael Durante, Ludwig Nastase. An Eastern European crew, except for Durante and Rodney.

There were only a dozen or so cars in the lot, mostly the nondescript Fords and Toyotas that people like Widermayer's assistant might drive. I copied down their license plates, anyway. Maybe I could push on my relationship with Murray and find out who they were registered to.

The Mercedes sedan Rodney had been using was parked there. I sat up straighter. Rodney drove a car registered to Widermayer, but I had a feeling that anything Widermayer owned really belonged to Kystarnik, or at least was available to him. Which probably included Rodney himself. He was exactly the kind of muscle Kystarnik might use.

I dug my maps out from under Mitch. Roehampton, where Kystarnik had his Chicago-area home, was only a few miles up the road. While I was this far north, I might as well see what eight hundred million dollars bought you. I started to query one of my subscription databases for Kystarnik's home address, then realized how exposed I was sitting there.

I drove back down Dundee Road and pulled into a strip mall. Wireless service in the northern suburbs was golden: before I could leave the car for a sandwich, LifeStory was flashing Kystarnik's address and a few biographical details on my tiny screen.

I squinted at the text, but finally had to enlarge it and read it a few words at a time. I hated to think that glasses lay in my future, that my eyesight was dimming as my body was slowing down. Weren't there any compensations for turning fifty?

Kystarnik had bought a house on seven acres almost twenty years ago. There were two pools, stables, tennis courts, three kitchens, nine bathrooms, and bedrooms enough to entertain all his visiting thugs at once, along with their partners and children. I assumed there were flunkies to look after the stables and kitchens and so on, but my little screen didn't tell me that.

Kystarnik had been born in Odessa, but he'd lived in America since his late teens. He'd been married only once, to the woman who died eight months ago. Melanie Kystarnik, born Melanie Frisk, had been a native of Eagle River, Wisconsin. How had they met, I wondered, where had they met? Of course, Eagle River was notorious as the vacation refuge for members of the Chicago mob. Maybe as Kystarnik cut his teeth on the extortion racket, someone like the Outfit's late, lamented CPA, Allen Dorfman, took Kystarnik under his wing. I pictured Anton and Melanie meeting at a Friday fish boil.

Melanie and Kystarnik had one child together, a daughter named Zina, who had died almost fifteen years ago, of unspecified causes. Even juice lenders suffer pain.

I drove up Telegraph Road to Argos Lane and found the gates to the Kystarnik place. Seven acres is a lot of ground; even though the bare trees and shrubs let me peer through the gates I couldn't really see the house, although I did see little red lights that told me my pausing at the perimeter was being recorded.

In the city, I would have canvassed the neighbors, but out here it was hard to imagine a neighbor close enough to see what the Kystarniks were doing, even if I could weasel my way past their gates to talk to someone. And what plausible reason could I provide for asking?

I'd passed an indie coffee bar just before turning onto Argos Lane, so I turned around and went back. I needed a bathroom stop, anyway, and some kind of snack. The coffee itself smelled rich, fresh-roasted, unexpected in this exclusive, retail-lacking little enclave.

A utility service truck was in the lot, and a couple of cars. It was lunch hour; some eight or nine people, who looked as though they might work on the surrounding estates, were perched at the little tables with drinks and sandwiches. The two people behind the counter—young, fresh-faced—kidded with the regulars, but they treated me with an impersonal briskness.

When I'd ordered my cappuccino and a toasted cheese panino, I pulled out my map. "I'm looking for Argos Lane—how close am I?"

One of the men waiting for his coffee laughed. "You're just about standing on top of it. You looking for anyone in particular?"

I flashed a grateful smile. "Melanie Kystarnik and I went to school together, and I thought, while I was in the area, I'd see if I could pay my respects to Anton."

The people in line at the counter shifted a bit, as if trying to back away from me.

I spread my hands. "I know it's been a while since she died, but I wasn't able to get back for the funeral. We'd lost touch after she married—she was living in such a different world than what I knew—but we used to go canoeing together in Eagle River when we were kids. I know it was quite a blow when Zina died."

There was a wordless communication going on among the regulars, and then a heavyset woman about my age said, "You really have been out of touch if you think Zina's death was a blow to Mrs. Kystarnik. She was off to Gstaad for skiing six weeks later. Maybe the mister felt it harder. Everybody said Zina was more his child than hers."

Someone tried to shush her, but the woman continued, "If this lady . . . What did you say your name was?"

"Gabriella. Gabriella Sestieri." I brought out my mother's birth name glibly.

"If you really were a friend of Melanie's, it would have broke your heart to see how much trouble that girl of hers got into by the time she died."

"That's so sad!" I exclaimed. "No wonder Melanie didn't answer my Christmas cards. I wondered at the time, but then I decided it was because her life had gotten so glamorous, those ski vacations, the private yacht and everything. But if Zina was doing drugs—"

"Doing drugs!" a man chimed in. "They say she was running the ring that supplied all the kids in the northwest suburbs, her and Pindero's kid."

"Clive!" another woman said. "You can't know that. And this lady doesn't need to hear that kind of talk when Mrs. Kystarnik is dead. And the girl, too. What has it been, fifteen years now? Let the dead bury the dead."

"Yeah, but Steve Pindero was a good guy, and he suffered as much as Kystarnik when his Frannie OD'd. More, probably." Clive's jaw jutted out, the grievance as fresh as if it had happened yesterday. "And then to find out his girl had been using his own rec room as a drugstore!"

Two men at a table in a corner had been watching me. They had hard hats sitting on the window ledge behind them, but their fingernails were carefully cut and buffed. Not the kind of manicures that would last long if they had to handle heavy equipment.

I finished my coffee and wrapped my sandwich in a napkin. "It's like my granny used to say: the rich get richer, the poor get trouble. Maybe I won't call on Anton after all. Sounds like he wouldn't want to be reminded of Melanie."

"Forgot about her already," Clive said, "If you go by the blonde who's—"

"Clive," the heavyset woman warned.

This time, he subsided, but as I opened the door to leave I heard the others pick up the gossip. One woman, who worked at a neighboring estate, had heard the doctor say the new girlfriend was already five months pregnant. Another had seen her wearing a necklace that used to belong to Melanie. Diamonds and emeralds, worth a hundred grand, easy.

As I got into my car, the two men who'd been watching me left the coffee bar and climbed into the utility truck. They followed me when I turned onto Argos Lane. I didn't slow for the Kystarnik estate, but the truck stayed with me as the road wound around a golf course and bent south. When I connected with a major artery, I stood on the brakes and jumped out.

The passenger got out of the utility truck and came over to me, no hurry. "You're just visiting the area, but you drive a car registered to a local person, hmm?"

"And you drive a truck, but you've got computer access to the Illinois DMV in it," I said. "You handling the feds' stakeout on Kystarnik?"

Hands on hips, he gave me a Clint Eastwood stare that made him think he looked tough. "Maybe you should get back to the city where you belong."

"Maybe, indeed," I agreed. "Any reason to think my old friend Melanie was killed to make way for the new pregnant blonde?"

"We've entered your plate number into our database," he said by way of reply.

"Now I am impressed. Or I would be if I didn't already have a federal file. By the way, if you want anyone to believe your work really requires a hard hat, nix the weekly manicures."

When he pulled off one of his gloves to look at his nails, I took a picture of the utility truck's license plate with my cell phone. He ran to my side, dropping his glove, and tried to grab my phone.

"Off-limits," he said.

I shook my head. "I have no idea who you are. I thought you were with the feds, but now I'm thinking you work for Kystarnik. The Chicago cops need to see who's tied to his operation."

The other guy got out of the truck. "What's the problem here?"

"Problem is, she took a picture of our plate."

"Problem is," I said, "you guys are hanging out around a thug. If you're on his payroll—"

"Oh, Chrissake, Troy, show her your badge."

The first guy scowled but pulled out his ID. Troy Murano was with the Secret Service, not the FBI after all. In a spirit of generous reciprocity, I showed them my PI license.

Besides guarding the President, the Secret Service investigates large-scale fraud, but when I tried to ask Troy and his partner what they thought Kystarnik was up to, they told me to mind my own business.

"So why is a Chicago PI sniffing around him?" the partner asked.

"Just minding my own business," I said in the spirit of reciprocity. I tucked my cell phone into my pocket before getting back into my car.

The utility truck didn't follow me when I turned onto the main road. I pulled into another strip mall and shared my sandwich with the dogs, who were getting restless after spending several hours in the car.

If the Secret Service was tagging around after Kystarnik, they weren't being too secretive about it—those security cameras dotting Kystarnik's fence would have spotted the utility truck long ago. Maybe the feds were hoping to pressure him into a misstep. If he was laundering money, maybe they thought he'd reveal his bank accounts to their electronic scanners. Maybe I should have suggested they look at Club Gouge, but, for all I knew, they already had a lead on Rodney and the club. More than ever, I wanted to get my cousin out of the place.

I guess it had been instructive to drive up here, although it was hard to say what I'd gained besides seeing my tax dollars at work.

I turned to my voice mail, which had been beeping at me in some indignation. "You have eleven new messages," it cried in my ear.

One of the calls was from Sanford Rieff at the Cheviot labs, saying he'd found something interesting. Since I was in their neck of the woods, I drove on west to Cheviot's complex.

Rieff came out to the lobby to see me. "Vic! I don't have anything so dramatic or definite that you needed to make a trip out here."

"I was in the area," I explained. "What's up?"

"We're still waiting for a report back from a national ballistics clearing center to see if the two guns are involved in any other shootings, but we've done an analysis of the beer cans. Mass spectrometry shows a high concentration of Rohypnol. Roofie, you probably call it. In beer like that—whoever drank it is probably very sick."

Roofie. The date rape drug.

"He's in a coma," I said slowly. "Is there any way to tell if he put it in the beer himself?"

Rieff smiled. "That's the interesting piece of your little puzzle. If this comes to court, it's going to be tricky, very tricky. Lawyers and expert witnesses will battle for days, and defendants will watch their bank accounts vanish before their startled eyes."

"Thanks, Sandy, but why?"

He led me back to his office and brought my report up on his computer screen so I could see the graphics.

"The fingerprints on the cans are odd, at least to Louis Arata, who's our expert. If you pick up a can or a glass yourself, you press only one finger, usually the middle, full against it. Besides your thumb, of course. You touch the can with the tips of the other fingers. Here, face on, we have prints for all five fingers."

He tapped the screen with a soft pointer to show me what he meant. "The can is clean except for those five fingers. Usually, you pick a can up, put it down, pick it up. Your prints soon overlay one another. I'm betting—or Louis Arata is betting—that a third party held the drinker's fingers on the can. I'll put it all in writing for you."

I stared at the screen while Rieff rotated the image for me. Who would have gone to so much trouble to frame Chad Vishneski? Rodney and Olympia? Karen Buckley? Anton Kystarnik? And why? That was the even more urgent question.

I got up to go.

"I'd say this is pretty darn dramatic, Sandy. Guard those beer cans and so on in your deepest vault."

Back in my car, I talked with Lotty's clinic nurse, Jewel Kim, and told her about the Rohypnol. "Can you make sure that Lotty and her pet neurosurgeon know ASAP? I don't know if it can help with Chad's treatment this many days out, but that's probably what put him in the coma."

Jewel looked at Lotty's notes on Chad. "She's ordered a broad-spectrum search for drugs, but I will let her know that she can narrow it down to Rohypnol. Thanks, Vic."

I stared out the windshield for a long time, thinking over Rieff's report. I e-mailed the gist of it to Freeman Carter, and then, even though I knew Freeman would advise against it, I called Terry Finchley. He answered the line himself, but when I announced myself his voice grew cold. He was still angry, which prompted me to become super-perky.

"Guess where I am right now."

"If you said sunning yourself on a Florida beach, now that would cheer me up."

"Almost. I'm on the banks of the Skokie Lagoon. At the Cheviot labs, where they did some nifty forensic work on the beer cans that had been in Chad Vishneski's bed. Guess what they found?"

"I'm not in the mood, V.I. Just tell me."

"Roofies."

"So the perp tried to off himself. Make my day."

"The fingerprint analysis suggests a third party was present."

The dogs had been cooped up in the car too long. They were whining at me, making it hard to hear Finchley. Cheviot's building sat in a cul-de-sac that backed into one of the lagoons that dot the area. I let Mitch and Peppy out.

"Why are you doing this?" Finchley demanded.

"Doing what?"

"Trying to show me up over the Guaman homicide. I know you and I have had our differences, but—"

"Terry, I've always liked you, and I respect you as a cop. I'm not trying to show you up. If I were, I'd be giving my news to Murray Ryerson to broadcast wholesale instead of telling you."

Mitch had found something to roll in. Peppy was barking at him, demanding her turn. I pretended I didn't know them.

"I told you yesterday that Nadia Guaman's and Chad Vishneski's computers were both missing. This makes me think that one or both of them knew something a third party wants to keep hidden. I just learned there's a story about Vishneski's beer cans: not only did someone mix Rohypnol in his beer, they wiped the cans clean and then placed his fingers on them to make prints once he'd passed out."

"You'd be hard-pressed to argue fingerprint pressure in court," Finchley said.

"That may be true, although Freeman Carter has persuaded juries of more implausible things. But I don't think we'll get to a courtroom. I started this investigation prejudiced against my client's son, but the more I learn, the more I think he was framed, poor stressed-out vet. Someone's covering their tracks exceptionally well, but somewhere, somehow, they're sure to have slipped up. When I find whatever mistake the real perp made, I'm counting on you to release Chad Vishneski. Assuming he's still alive."

"Oh, damn you, anyway, Warshawski."

He cut the connection. The dogs had moved down to the lagoon. I trailed after them, stopping where they'd been rolling. A dead raccoon. When I'd persuaded them to get back in the car, I was annoyed with myself for my stupidity in letting them run free. They stank, and it was too cold to ride the Tollway with the windows open.

I drove along Dundee Road until I came to a groomer's. I had to wait almost an hour until they could fit in Mitch and Peppy, but the wait allowed me to catch up on the rest of my calls. Even the expense of two shampoos beat wrestling the dogs into my own bathtub at home.

22

The Road to Kufah

I stopped at my apartment just long enough to leave the dogs with Mr. Contreras. At my office, I found a little pot of tulips heavily wrapped in newspaper on the doorstep and a note from the client.

We got Chad moved to Beth Israel, and now Mona's sitting with him. I like your doc. She said to bring along some of his music to play when we can't be there, so Mona's got his iPod running and I'll play my clarinet for him tonight. I guess you know what you're doing.

J.V.

The candy-cane-striped tulips made a bright circle of color on my desk. Heartened by the flowers, and the client's goodwill, I wrote up my notes for the day. I synced my handheld with my machine so that the names I'd seen in Widermayer's assistant's spreadsheet got uploaded into my case file software. Ludwig Nastase, Michael Durante, Konstantin Feder. There'd been a woman as well, a Bettina Lyzhneska. A truly diverse, international crew, rounded out by Rodney Treffer.

I went back to Rodney's cryptic jottings, wondering if any of the letters he'd written on the Body Artist corresponded to his teammates' names. There'd been several *I*'s and *O*'s, along with *C, L,* and *S.* Except for Lyzhneska and Ludwig, I couldn't see a match.

I wrestled with the numbers. I've never been a fan of codes and ciphers, and these looked so random that you probably needed a key to uncode them. Maybe they were page numbers, where you counted lines and letters, but you'd have to know the book first.

Still, I'd had a bit of a break today, getting Rodney's last name. I did a little rooting around on him, and on Owen Widermayer as well. Rodney had been a cop with the Milwaukee PD. Now LifeStory claimed he was an independent security contractor. I remembered Olympia's brittle laugh, her referring to him as her "insecurity." He'd been divorced—twice—and both his ex-wives had entered orders of protection against him. Big surprise there.

Widermayer's profile was blander. He lived in Winnetka, he was on the board of his temple, serving as their accountant. Other than that, I couldn't get a client list out of my databases, but that didn't really surprise me. I kind of thought Kystarnik might be Widermayer's only client; looking after a mob thug could be a full-time job.

At six-thirty, I left for my meeting with Tim Radke. Plotzky's, the bar he'd chosen, was on the western end of Division Street where Nelson Algren used to hang out. Algren probably wouldn't recognize the street anymore. West of Ashland, the newest Yuppie invasion had turned the cold-water flats and honky-tonk joints into expensive lofts and restaurants with names like Suivi and Arrêt. Instead of a shot and a beer, you got martinis with funny names and weird ingredients.

Plotzky's was one of the last surviving blue-collar joints. With an upscale sushi place on one side and a wine bar on the other, I didn't give them much chance.

It was a few minutes before seven when I got there. A handful of men in their forties or fifties were sitting at the bar, their parkas unzipped to reveal dirty work clothes. Unlike my federal friends in Roe-hampton this afternoon, these men had earned their hard hats.

The Black Hawks pregame show was on the TV over the bar. No one was watching it. They were rehashing their own lives with each other and with the bartender, a middle-aged woman with bleached hair and thick pancake makeup. Like Sal at the Golden Glow, she kept an eye on the whole room while nodding empathically at the men talking to her.

I looked around but didn't see anyone who seemed to be waiting for me. I perched on a stool near the street door. The bartender put her hand on the arm of one of the men.

"Be right back, Phil. What'll yours be, honey? Scotch? We got Dewar's, White Horse, Johnnie Red."

I chose Dewar's. The regulars eyed me with a frank, impersonal curiosity, then went back to their own conversations. After twenty minutes, when I was beginning to wonder if Radke had gotten cold feet, a guy in a worn Army parka came in. I recognized his pitted, craggy face. He was the man who'd run after Chad when he'd confronted Nadia in the parking lot.

I got to my feet and sketched a wave. Radke came over to me at once, but nodded along the way at the other men at the bar, who called out greetings when they saw him.

"Gerri, don't go bringing him no beer without seeing his ID first. Kid's too young to drink in public, even if he's trying to impress his date."

"Don't pay them any mind, honey. They're just jealous that they have to drink alone," Gerri said to Tim. "Bud?" She slapped down a bottle on the bar in front of him.

"You were at the club, weren't you?" Radke said to me once the men stopped razzing him.

"Yes—you and I almost ran over each other backstage when Chad was chasing after Nadia Guaman that time. I told you on the phone that Chad's father hired me to find out what was going on, how Chad got involved with Nadia Guaman."

Radke nodded cautiously over the neck of the bottle.

"I'm having trouble getting any information about either Chad or Nadia," I said, "so anything you can tell me would be a help."

"I didn't know him that well," Radke warned me.

"I thought you were in Iraq together."

"Iraq's a big country, and we were in a big Army. Chad, he was in a rifle company. Me? I was in Network Support."

"Network Support? Computers in the field, you mean?"

"The whole Army runs on computers these days. I came to be pretty good, but I don't have a college degree or anything, so when I got out I could only get me a job installing electronics. Maybe something better'll come along when the economy picks up, if I haven't forgotten everything the Army taught me."

He gave a tired smile. "Anyway, Chad, him and me, we never met until we got home. We were part of the same post-deployment group at the VA. How is he? On the news, they said he tried to commit suicide and was unconscious, but when I tried to go see him, they had him in prison, not in a hospital."

He smacked his bottle down on the countertop. "I couldn't get permission to go see him. Him and me, we fought for our country, and some two-bit county employee gets to tell me whether I can see my own buddy or not. If it was even a cop, I wouldn't take it so hard— they're like every soldier I ever met, putting their lives on the line every damned day of the week. But these county assholes, getting jobs just because they raised so much money for some politician, and then lording it over . . ."

Gerri moved within range in case I needed to be thrown out for annoying one of her regulars. Radke subsided but twisted his beer bottle so ferociously, I thought the glass might break in his hands.

"I got the police to let us move Chad from the prison hospital to

Beth Israel," I told him. "I haven't been able to speak to the doctor in charge, so I can't tell you how he's doing, but I'm sure his folks would let you go see him now that he's in a regular hospital."

Radke asked me to write down the address, and the name of the doctor, and promised he'd stop by as soon as he had time. "It'd be better if he was at the VA on account of the insurance, but I know you went out of your way getting him out of that hellhole. Well, you didn't ask me here to rant and rave. What did you want to know?"

"When Chad and Nadia were arguing, it sounded like a couple in the middle of an angry divorce. But John Vishneski says Chad didn't know Nadia."

"I don't think he did."

Radke drained his bottle and signaled to Gerri for a second. She had it on the counter almost before his hand went down.

"So what were they fighting about?"

"Her drawings. He told Marty and me they gave him flashbacks." Radke drank most of the second bottle in one big gulp. "It was something to do with what went wrong when his unit was on the road to Kufah."

"What was that?" I prompted when he fell silent.

"You ever been in a war? It's nothing like what they show on TV or video games. You're tired all the time. You're scared, you don't know who's a friend, who's an enemy. If fighting starts, it's not organized. You don't always know where the shots are coming from and, if you shoot back, will you hit your own guys? Maybe it was different in World War Two, but in Iraq—even me, I was in Support, but I still got caught in a couple of gun battles because there aren't any lines, yours or the enemy's."

He shredded his napkin and started laying pieces out on the counter as if he were trying to establish some real battle lines. I shook my head at Gerri as she started toward us.

"Is that what happened on the road to Kufah?" I asked.

"Chad couldn't say, even at the VA when we were with one of those counselors. We got five sessions! Five sessions to undo five years of war!" Radke snorted in derision. "Chad lost his whole squad. That's all he ever said, not any details about how it happened. You know what that's like? Guys you been eating and sleeping with, suddenly they're lying dead all around you. They sent him home after that for four months, then he had to redeploy. And he was fine, he said, as long as he was over there. But once he got discharged, once he got home, he couldn't take being around civilians. No one here gives a rat's ass about what we went through. It's hell to be there, to be going through it. But it's a hundred—no, a million—times worse to be here where no one cares.

"'I lost my whole squad on the road to Kufah,'" he mimicked in a savage voice. "'Bummer, man. But what about *American Idol*?' And the women are worse!"

"How'd you end up at Club Gouge?"

He gave me a sidelong look, checking me for signs of shockability or maybe prudery. "We heard this gal sits naked on a stage. And the drawings . . . It was something to do."

I'd printed out a copy of Alexandra Guaman's yearbook photo. I pulled it out and showed it to Radke.

"She was Nadia Guaman's sister and she was killed in Iraq. She wasn't with the Army, though—she worked for one of the private security firms. Hers is the face that Nadia kept painting on the Body Artist. I wondered if Chad knew Alexandra Guaman in Iraq."

Radke shook his head. "He never said. It's like I told you, it's a big country. And it's not just we're a big Army, but the contractors . . . You know they have more contractors than Uncle Sam's soldiers over there? Some guy, he said, 'Iraq isn't the war of the willing, it's the war of the billing.' And until you've seen it, you don't get it! The contractors, they're everywhere, building crappy housing for us, good shit for themselves. They're hustling a buck at the PX; they're taking convoys around. We're busting our asses for base pay, and we have to protect the contractors, who are drawing double overtime doing less work than we are!"

His voice was starting to rise again so I broke in. "What would Chad say after you left Club Gouge if he never said whether he knew Alexandra or Nadia Guaman?"

"We'd come here—here to Plotzky's, I mean—a lot of times. Like, the night that gal got shot, we were here, right on these stools, watching the Hawks. Marty, one of our crowd who we met at the VA, you know, he'd say to Chad, 'Why are you letting that broad get under your skin? Did she ditch you or something?' But Chad, he'd just say, 'She's rubbing my face in it.'"

"Rubbing his face in what happened on the road to Kufah or in a busted relationship?"

Tim started peeling the label from one of his empties. "If I had to guess, I'd guess the road to Kufah just because—if some girl is riding you, she can make you madder than hell but she's not what's giving you flashbacks. Maybe Chad wrote about her on his blog. He kept one—a lot of guys did . . . do—where they write pretty much everything. It's not just that it passes the time, but it makes you think that somewhere someone cares if you live or die."

Chad's blog, of course, I should have been reading that already. Maybe John Vishneski had been right to suggest I was incompetent. Despite my brave words, I was being a slow-footed, clumsy seeker, something like a two-toed sloth crashing through a jungle. I was making it easy for a skilled hider to stay twenty steps ahead of me.

"The night before Nadia died, when Chad confronted her in the parking lot, you came out and brought him back to the club. He had some kind of dark object, looked like a cloth about yea big." I sketched the shape in the air. "Did he show you that? Do you have any idea what it could be?"

Tim shook his head. "A dark cloth about eight or ten inches wide?

Could it have been, like, a scarf folded into a square? Maybe he thought she'd knitted it for him."

That hadn't occurred to me. *Don't pretend you don't know what this is,* Chad had yelled. Maybe it had been something some woman mailed him. Maybe he thought Nadia had been a secret correspondent sending him presents while he was in the desert. Yet another unprovable idea. It seemed impossible to get real information about anything or anyone connected with Nadia and Chad.

I tried not to let the weight of impossibility drag me down. I thanked Tim and signaled Gerri for the check. Tim gave me the names and numbers of the three other guys in his and Chad's band of post-Iraq brothers, as well as the name of their counselor at the VA. Chad might have told her something privately that he hadn't felt able to say in front of the group.

23

What's in a Blog?

Eleven American soldiers were killed Tuesday on the road to Kufah
when they were trapped in an ambush and insurgents burned their
Hummers with incendiary devices, the Army reported today. Convoys
had been traveling that route with relative safety since May. Insurgents
loyal to Amir Harith al-Hassan, a dissident Shia mullah, claimed
responsibility.

That was all I could find about any incidents on the road to Kufah.
Only three of the dead were mentioned by name, because they were
from New York, and the story had been carried in the *New York Times*.
I didn't find any mention of it in the Chicago papers, which surprised
me since a Chicago youth had been the sole survivor of the attack.
No wonder Tim was bitter about the American response to him and
his comrades.

I was curled up on my living-room couch with the dogs and my
laptop. The dogs still smelled faintly of lavender, and they were still
tired enough from their morning run that they'd been content to chase
tennis balls in the backyard while I made a pot of spaghetti. Mr.

Contreras had shared it with me, even though I only put in mushrooms and peas instead of the tomato sauce he preferred. After dinner, he'd gone out to spend an evening with some of his remaining pals from his old local.

I turned to Chad's blog. As John Vishneski had reported when he hired me, the early entries were filled with a kind of happy zest, as if Chad were writing up a road trip with his buddies. When he reached Iraq and was reporting in the blistering heat, you still got a sense of underlying good humor and a serious commitment to his country.

> A few months ago I was playing football and going nowhere. Now, even though I know it's hard on my folks and my friends, I feel like I'm serving my country and doing the right thing. So, naming no names, you guys back home think all I can do is drink beer. Let me tell you, here in Iraq I STILL drink beer, plus carry a hundred pounds of equipment into the desert. And do a hundred push-ups. Of course, football training didn't hurt my conditioning, but I'd like to see the Bears forward line go through the workout we get here!

Even after his first year in Iraq, when he'd been under fire a number of times, he managed to keep his spirits up in his posts.

> I keep thinking of that Tommy Lee Jones flick *Men in Black*. When we see men in black here, we know we're in trouble, and I wish to God some alien would rise up out of the desert and put a big old tentacle around their necks. Or just one of our local little pets.

> Vipers are a big deal here, something they never talked about during Basic. We have a snake guy here. His name is Herb, which is so right because a snake man is a herpetologist when he's at home, so we call him Herbie the Herpes. But you'd better believe it's in good fun because old Herpes is the go-to guy if you find one of his little friends

crawling around your tent. He tries to get us to love them like they are our brothers in nature, but nothing doing for this infantryman!

Anyway, men in black came up on us in the middle of the night. We fought for three hours. I can't tell you how scared I was, RPGs exploding around us, IEDs, the whole nine yards. How we didn't lose anyone I don't know, but we had five guys with big-time wounds, including Jesse Laredo. You've read about him if you've been with me from the get-go, great joker, littlest guy in the unit, but the strongest. Jesse would give his right arm for a buddy, and that's just what he did tonight. So all of you reading this blog send a prayer Jesse's way, and for his mom and dad in Albuquerque.

We love you, Jess, we're praying for you. And a big thank-you prayer to our medics, too, in here with their choppers in no time, getting Jess and the rest of them off to the hospital ship out in the Gulf.

Chad wrote about collecting food and toys for Iraqi orphans during Ramadan, and setting up a football squad at his forward operating base. He wrote about warm showers on hot days, cold showers on cold rainy days, but it wasn't until his third deployment that his tone turned bitter.

Maybe if I had a wife back home, I'd love my time Stateside the way the other guys do, but there's no one who can really relate to what I'm going through here. My mom and dad read my posts, they send me care packages, but it's not like having a wife or a buddy who stays up nights hoping I'll make it through another day. I spent four months in Chicago, and every day got me longing more and more for the desert and the vipers. Everyone's got their own life to live, I understand that, mortgages, dental bills, trips to the mall, but does anyone remember we're fighting a war over here?

The blog entries ended there, a week before the news report of the incident on the road to Kufah. I couldn't figure it out. The archive list down the right-hand column showed thirteen more weeks of posts, but when I clicked on them, only a blank page came up.

I did as many searches as I had the skills to figure out, but I couldn't come up with Chad's post about the battle he'd survived.

It was going on ten p.m., but I called the client, anyway, to ask him if he remembered Chad's blogs.

"I'm trying to read about the battle where he lost all the men in his unit, but all his posts after October second that year have disappeared from his website. Did you or Mona print them out? Or do you remember what he wrote in them?"

"Why does it matter?" John Vishneski asked. "That was almost two years ago now. What does that have to do with this dead gal?"

"Maybe nothing. But Tim Radke says Nadia's paintings were giving Chad flashbacks to the road to Kufah. The dead woman's sister also died in Iraq when an IED exploded. I'm wondering if the sister was present at the battle for some reason."

Vishneski sighed heavily. "I read his blog, of course I did, but I never printed them out. You think, with a computer, it'll always be there. So, no, I don't remember, except he was trying to give first aid to these guys who had phosphorus burns on them. And I think that's when he really started to fall apart, he felt so helpless. Helpless! I felt so goddamn helpless myself."

His voice suddenly cracked. "I called him every day. I could tell he was hurting and I couldn't get anywhere near him to help. That's why that prison hospital just about did me in. At least now I can sit with him. Believe me, I am real grateful to you for making that happen even if you can't figure out why someone framed my boy for killing that woman. I went over and played my clarinet for Chad for an hour, even though I expect the other patients thought they were hearing a cat being tortured."

It was a gallant effort on his part not to break down on the phone.

"Bet if you played like Larry Combs, Chad wouldn't know it was you, would he?"

He gave a little laugh. I thanked him for the tulips before he hung up. Another gallant gesture on his part.

I lacked the computer skills to figure out what had happened to Chad's more recent blog postings, and I haven't found a reliable computer forensic expert yet. I used to turn to Darraugh Graham's son, MacKenzie, but he's working in Africa these days.

I wandered restlessly around my living room. I dug through my old LPs until I found Edwin Starr's 1972 album with "War" on it. *It ain't nothing but a heartbreaker / Friend only to the undertaker.* I didn't realize how loudly I was playing the cut until my phone rang. Jake Thibaut was calling to say he'd tried knocking on my door, but I hadn't heard him over the music.

"How come you're having a party and didn't invite me?" he demanded. "This sounds like sex, drugs, and rock 'n' roll."

I lifted the phonograph arm from the turntable.

"Rock 'n' roll. You could come over and add the sex and drugs, if you'd like."

When he came to my door holding a bottle of wine, I tried to keep up a light tone, but Chad's blog postings and John Vishneski's anguish lay heavy on my mind.

"Web pages are disappearing all around me," I said. "I wanted to look again at the Body Artist's site, but she's taken it down. And now I can't read Chad's blogs, either."

Jake Thibaut read the postings over my shoulder.

"Maybe you can track down this guy Jesse Laredo that he mentions. It sounds as though they were close. They might have kept in touch."

"Now, that gets you the biggest smooch in Chicago," I said. "First good idea I've had all day, and I didn't even think of it myself."

I put Starr's *Involved* back on the turntable while Jake poured some wine. It made me feel young again, the wine, the black vinyl spinning on the turntable, though I have to admit Jake's cabernet was better than what I drank in college. And adult sex was so much better than teenage fumblings that it almost made up for growing older.

In the morning, after Jake left for his first student of the day, I lost some of my optimism. I tracked Jesse Laredo down at his mother's home in Albuquerque, but Jesse had died five months ago. His wounds had taken too great a toll on his heart, his mother said.

I commiserated with her, and told her some of the details of the trouble Chad was in.

"Jess loved Chad. I sure am sorry to know he's having problems," she said after I explained why I was calling, "but you'll never make me believe he murdered anyone."

"When Chad lost his unit on the road to Kufah, did he call or e-mail anything to Jesse?" I asked. "I'm trying to find the blog postings he put up then. And the ones he's done this year. Maybe Jesse printed them out."

She promised to look, although she said that Chad always tried for a light tone when he wrote or phoned her son. "He knew Jess was hurting bad, and he knew Jess felt like he was letting his unit down, not being in Iraq with them. But I'll see what I can find."

I thanked her, but my hopes weren't high. Nothing was coming easy in this case. The thought of all the dead and walking wounded from that pointless war was heartbreaking.

You've got nothing to complain about, V.I. Get back in the trenches!

I made another cup of coffee and called the people whose names Tim Radke had given me last night, but none of them could tell me anything. The guys had all been part of their post-deployment counseling sessions at the VA, but none of them ever remembered Chad opening up about what happened on the road to Kufah. The therapist actually took my call on the first try, but she didn't even remember Chad's name until she'd looked him up in her files. She told me she needed to see his parents' signed release before she could talk to me, but she waited while I faxed it to her.

"I see so many men that I can't keep track of them all," she apologized. "A lot of them are angry. I'm sorry to hear that Chad Vishneski got in trouble with the law, but frankly, we're seeing it more and more."

After looking through her file, she said Chad had never shown up for the one private meeting he'd scheduled.

I rubbed my forehead, frustrated, trying to come up with anyone who could talk to me about Chad or Nadia or Alexandra. Finally, I decided to put on my business clothes and return to the northwest suburbs.

24

Inside Fortress Tintrey

Tintrey's corporate offices were only a quarter mile from Glenbrook High, as if Jarvis MacLean wanted to remind his alma mater how successful he'd become. MacLean had built his complex in the middle of a landscaped industrial park. Rustic bridges crossed the obligatory water feature, bits of shrubbery poked through the snow, and the walkways that surrounded the building and led into the parkland had all been shoveled and salted.

I parked in the lot in the same row where senior staff seemed to park, judging by the array of BMWs, Mercedeses, and Land Rovers. Nothing as cheap as a Buick. I paused behind a green E-Type Jaguar. Even in this weather, its body was clean and polished, not a mark on it. If Warshawski Enterprises ever got to be as successful as Tintrey, I was getting me one of those. Right after my corporate jet and all those other goodies.

I sighed wistfully but squared my shoulders and walked into a lobby that made no secret of Tintrey's success. Unlike Anton Kystarnik, whose dingy building seemed designed to show the IRS that he had no assets, Jarvis MacLean had built to proclaim success to his prospective customers. Well-kept plants were potted around the entryway, along with a couple of sculptures of the kind my leasemate created—big abstract pieces of twisting steel and high-gloss wood.

A pair of receptionists, so highly polished I could almost see my face in their cheekbones, staffed a high rosewood counter. They were dressed in powder-blue blazers with TINTREY embroidered on the breast pockets. Behind them, electronic gates blocked access to the building's interior.

On the far side of the gates, open glass-and-metal staircases invited you to walk to the upper floors. The elevators were along a far wall, but their doors were drab. A green architect clearly had been involved in putting the building together.

"May I help you?" one of the gleaming receptionists asked.

I produced a business card and asked to speak with someone in Human Resources. "I'm doing a background check on a woman who says she used to work here."

The receptionist murmured into her telephone and then asked who was "the subject of my inquiry." We fenced for a minute—me explaining that it was a confidential inquiry, she explaining that she was trying to save me time. In the end, she directed me to the third floor, where Belinda would see me. We smiled widely at each other, which made me very aware of my caffeine-stained teeth, and she pressed a switch that let me through the magic gates.

As I climbed to the third floor, I saw that MacLean was an unrepentant supporter of the Iraq war. The walls held some interesting art photographs, but these were overwhelmed by outsize pictures of Donald Rumsfeld and MacLean getting out of a Stryker together, of MacLean with Dick Cheney at an undisclosed location, and a blowup of the photograph I'd seen of MacLean online accepting some kind of award from Bush.

The personnel office was in the middle of the floor. Three people sat at computers in the outer room. The one nearest the door took my

name, checked it against her computer log, and directed me to an alcove with the assurance that Belinda would be with me shortly. The
alcove reminded me of a doctor's waiting room. It was crammed with
worried souls who were filling out forms on clipboards, each looking
up hopefully when one of the receptionists came to call a name. They
looked at me suspiciously. Each newcomer was a potential competitor.
Suspicion turned to hostility when a receptionist came to get me after
a mere ten minutes had passed.

"I was here long before her," one man called out.

The receptionist just smiled, and said his turn would come soon.

Belinda turned out to be a stocky woman in her early forties. She
was the first Tintrey employee I'd seen who didn't look as though she
were preparing for a photo shoot. Her nails were cut bluntly, close to
the fingertips, and her clothes had been chosen for comfort, not glam-
our. She led me into an office behind the reception area that held four
cubicles. In the other three, job supplicants sat trying to look earnest,
eager, productive—whatever would get them a foot in the door. Belinda
took me to her desk in one of the two middle cubes.

"They told me downstairs that you're a detective who wants information about one of our employees. They should have known better
than to send you up here. We don't give out confidential employee
information. Too many competitors in this business."

"The message got garbled in translation," I said. "I'm doing a background check on a woman who claims she used to work for you. Her
résumé has two years that I can't verify, so I'm wondering if she lied
about her employment history with you."

I pulled a folder out of my briefcase. I'd stopped at my office before
heading for the Tollway and produced a résumé for Alexandra Guaman,
inserting her yearbook photo at the top of the page. I'd used the information I'd found online for Alexandra, including her Social Security
number, her educational background, and her employment history at
Tintrey. I'd beefed up her credentials—I made her a cyberfraud expert

working for Tintrey in Baghdad's Green Zone. I showed her leaving Iraq two weeks after her reported death, working for a credit-card holding company I'd invented in Cleveland, and looking for "new challenges" back in the Chicago area.

I handed the résumé to Belinda. "It's impossible for me to get any information out of Lackawanna Systems. They seem to have disappeared in the economic tsunami of the last few months, and I can't find anyone who can vouch for Guaman in Cleveland."

"Did you go to Cleveland in person?" Belinda asked.

"I do what the job requires."

I kept my smile pasted on my face. She was shrewd; she knew I could have handled my query with her by phone or e-mail.

"Guaman's résumé arrived online with a lot of fancy podcasts and video bits, but it boiled down to this history. If you'd just verify the dates with Tintrey and let me know if she really can set up the kind of cybersecurity she's claiming, I'll get out of your hair. I can see you're swamped."

While I'd been speaking, the lights on Belinda's phone had been flashing, and her computer kept dinging to let her know she had IM messages piling up. These prods from the ether made her decide it was easier to cooperate than argue. She started typing and brought up Alexandra Guaman's file without any trouble.

Her monitor was at an angle so that I could see a bit of the screen but not enough to read the text. Belinda frowned over what she was reading, then scrolled down until she was at the end of the file. Her mouth dropped open in shock, and she looked from her screen to me with growing suspicion.

"Who are you really?"

"Really, I am V. I. Warshawski."

"That's not what I mean. How did you get this woman's résumé? What is it you're really after? Who hired you?"

I started to move around her desk to look at her screen, but she held up a hand, traffic cop style and hit a key that brought up her screen saver, a collection of family photos.

"I am a confidential investigator, and I don't betray my clients' identities, so I'm afraid I can't tell you that. Is there something wrong? I'd like to know so that I can remove Ms. Guaman from consideration for the job they want to hire her to do."

Belinda bit her lips and looked again at her screen, perhaps hoping her toddler could help her decide what to do. She finally picked up her phone and tapped in a four-digit number with her pencil.

"It's Belinda here, Mr. Vijay. We have a situation, a QL file that someone's asking about."

She listened for a moment, then spelled Alexandra's last name. I could hear Mr. Vijay barking with excitement, and then, apparently, he put her on hold. After another wait, while I kept prodding Belinda in my role as baffled visitor, a stocky man in a gray jacket and sporting a pale pink tie strode into Belinda's cubicle.

"I'll take over from here, Belinda. You go on with your other assignments. I'll call you when I'm through with this person."

He took Alexandra Guaman's résumé from Belinda.

"What did you say your name was?"

I handed him a card.

"V. I. Warshawski. What's the problem with Ms. Guaman's file?"

He refused to answer but led me down the hall to a door with his name on it. It was a small office, but it was private.

"What are you up to?" he asked without preamble.

"I am trying to verify Alexandra Guaman's work history," I said. "It's a simple query, so I'd appreciate it if Tintrey would stop acting as though I wanted the design specs for the cruise missile."

His mouth tightened, and he consulted the computer in front of him. I kept a look of honest bewilderment on my face, which wasn't a complete act. Why couldn't they just tell me that Alexandra had died in Iraq? Vijay typed an e-mail, and then sat with his hands folded in

front of him. I asked him about Alexandra's assignment in Iraq, but he
didn't speak. I asked him if he thought Indianapolis would make it to
the Super Bowl again, and he looked nettled, so I expanded on that
theme.

"Manning is the kind of quarterback a championship team needs:
reckless, and convinced he's invincible. Teams believe in leaders like
that. Remember—"

"I'm not interested in football," Vijay snapped before I could dwell
nostalgically on Jim McMahon, the old Bears quarterback.

"Then let's talk about Alexandra Guaman," I said. "What did she do
that warrants this kind of reaction?"

Vijay's door opened, and another man came in wearing the kind of
hand-cut wool you can afford only if your stock options survived the
market meltdown. I recognized him from Rainier Cowles's table at
Club Gouge and from the Tintrey website. It was Gilbert Scalia, head
of Tintrey's Iraqi operations.

"I'll take over from here, Vijay. What does she know?"

"I didn't ask. The policy on QL files—"

"Right. Well done."

Scalia looked at me narrowly.

"Haven't I met you before? Oh, yes. At that strip joint the other
night. You're a detective, that's what the owner told us. A detective
who's unpleasantly obsessed with Nadia Guaman. And now you're up
here trying to blackmail us about her sister."

"What an extraordinary accusation," I said. "And, by the way, an ac-
tionable one, as your friend Prince Rainier would be glad to tell you."

"Don't try to play word games with me. You're way out of your
league. You're in my building under false pretenses, and, believe me,
any legal action will be directed against you. By us. Not the other way
around."

He looked at Vijay. "What was she asking?"

"She has a résumé that she pretends came from the Guaman woman. She's been trying to find out what Guaman did for us in Iraq."

Scalia shook his head. "Her activities are classified."

"Whoa, there, Mr. Scalia. You're a private contractor, not the Department of Defense."

"When we're doing DOD's work, their security clearances extend to our employees. We all regret the death of Alexandra Guaman, but we're not at liberty to discuss it. Especially not with an ambulance chaser. Time for you to get out, before I bring along a team to throw you out."

"A whole team?" I said. "That's flattering, but I'm afraid someone— Olympia, maybe—exaggerated my fighting skills. One person would probably be enough if she knows what she's doing. Two, if she doesn't."

Scalia's lips tightened. "Before you leave, you'll hand over whatever document you brought with you."

"Wrong again. It's a private document, and you don't have the necessary security clearance to read it."

"Where is it?" Scalia asked Vijay.

"She put it into her briefcase."

"Then call security. We need someone up here to take her case and get the document."

Scalia had me backed up where he wanted me, which I hated, but I opened my case and took out the spurious résumé. Scalia held out a hand for it, but I ducked under his arm and stuck it into Vijay's shredder, which gulped it down with a satisfying growl.

Scalia grabbed my case and dumped the contents on Vijay's desk, his face swollen with rage. My field notebooks that I use in client meetings and off-line research, a tampon that was coming unraveled, and a small makeup kit bounced out. I crossed my arms and leaned against the door while he looked through the papers.

Scalia suddenly ripped a page out of the center of one of the notebooks and fed it through Vijay's shredder, then dropped the notebook on Vijay's desk and dusted his hands with a satisfied smirk. I fought back the tide of rage that swept through me. I had just enough self-control to know that if I slugged him, I'd spend the next week either in jail or a hospital.

"What a he-man," I said, my voice high and bright. "Able to rip a piece of paper with your bare hands. No wonder they put you in charge of war operations."

"Pick up your shit and get out of my building," Scalia roared, his face swelling again in anger.

I put the notebooks and the makeup back into my case. As soon as I had the door open, I turned back and stuck the tampon into Scalia's jacket pocket.

"A souvenir," I said. "Something to put on your wall along with all those pictures of you in uniform inside the war zone."

I moved briskly to the stairs. A couple of guys in heavy security costumes appeared as I reached the front doors, but no one shot me, or even tripped me, as I crossed the walk to the visitor's spot where I'd left my car.

25

Surviving Guaman Daughter

I drove east until I found a forest preserve where I could take time to pull myself together again. I dug through my case for the notebook that Scalia had mutilated. He'd pulled three pages out of a section where I'd been researching title changes last year. The case was coming to trial next month. I'd been deposed, I'd written the report. It was just the violation of having my papers attacked that I minded.

You might say I had provoked him by shredding the bogus résumé, but his reaction had been designed to humiliate, and, unfortunately, it had worked. My own response, with the tampon, had been briefly satisfying but not too bright. Someone who had as much need to be in power over others as Scalia did would feel it as real indignity, especially since a subordinate had witnessed it. Who knew what he might do next.

I opened one of my notebooks and started doodling. What had I learned? That despite the twenty thousand or so employees Tintrey had worldwide, and the nine thousand in Iraq, there was something about Alexandra Guaman that kept her in the foreground of the company consciousness—so much so that a senior officer had to be summoned when someone asked questions about her. I wished I knew what QL stood for—that was what Vijay had called Alexandra's file. Maybe "quit living."

I stared at the bare trees. Even if Alexandra had known Chad in Iraq, why would that be important to Tintrey? Unless Chad had been on some mission that involved Tintrey and he'd learned a discreditable secret about them? If Alexandra had died as part of a truck convoy, maybe Chad had been in one of the trucks. That black oblong he'd waved in front of Nadia, was that something he'd picked up from the detritus around her exploded truck? But a piece of black fabric, something that might be a scarf, as Tim Radke had suggested? I slapped my notebook shut. All this speculation, it led nowhere.

Gilbert Scalia had come to Club Gouge with the head of Tintrey, Jarvis MacLean. If Alexandra Guaman was this big a hot button at Tintrey, I had to believe they'd gone down there to see if the Body Artist's tribute to Nadia included anything about Alexandra.

More speculation.

I would have to move fast to get some answers before Gilbert Scalia closed every door I knocked at. Rainier Cowles was already hovering over the Guaman family, but maybe if I drove down there now I could find out something from Ernest or the grandmother. That didn't seem likely, but I didn't know what else to do. And I felt an urgency to be doing something.

I pulled onto the road and turned back to the Tollway, covering the thirty miles south as fast as I could. Giant tractor trailers roared around me all the way down as the open land bordering the Tollway changed to the bungalows lining the Kennedy and then to the scrap-metal piles and grocery warehouses that bordered Pilsen where the Guamans lived. It was a relief to get away from the noise and into a residential neighborhood, although parking was a challenge. People who'd shoveled out spaces had blocked them off with garbage cans or broken-down furniture, a Chicago tradition. I found a half-legal space around the corner, not quite blocking a fire hydrant.

Bungalows and two-flats stood on lots so small that the buildings almost touched. Many were decorated with ceramic tiles; one even had a mosaic of a jaguar worked all the way across the front. Nativity scenes and Santas still stood in front of some of the houses. The Guamans didn't have tile or a crèche, only a statue of Our Lady of Guadalupe. She was knee-deep in snow, a black ribbon around her neck serving as a heart-troubling reminder of loss.

A woman came out of a nearby house. She had a wagon, a toddler, and a drawstring bag filled with laundry that she was carrying down the stairs. I hurried over and took the wagon and bag from her. She thanked me but looked me up and down frankly. In my Lario boots and tailored coat, I wasn't dressed for the neighborhood.

"Is that the Guaman home?" I pointed at the black-ribboned Lady of Guadalupe, just trying to get the woman talking.

"Are you from the lawyer?"

"The lawyer? No, I was a friend of Nadia's. That was terrible, how she died."

The woman nodded solemnly. "But why was she in such a place as that nightclub to begin with? It's very hard on Cristina to have her daughter in the news that way."

"Nadia told me she and her mother had quarreled. That must be hard, too, on Cristina, to know her daughter was killed while they were estranged."

"They're a strange family. Ever since the oldest girl died—"

"I know. In Iraq."

"Alexandra's death deranged them all," the woman said. "Next thing you know, the boy turns into an idiot from a motorcycle accident, then Nadia fights with her mother and moves away!"

The toddler began to fuss. I pulled a sheet of paper from my case and folded it into a cocked hat while I spoke. The child stopped whining to watch me.

"Poor Nadia was angry and upset all the time," I said. "She took Alexandra's death very hard."

"Cristina will never talk about Alexandra to anyone. Maybe to the priest, although he's not a man who inspires confidences."

I handed the cocked hat to the child. "I guess I'll try to pay a condolence call, anyway."

"Cristina works during the day. Only Ernest is there, with Lazar's mother. They take him for therapy, they hope he'll learn to live on his own one day. Of course, he can walk, he can dress himself, he can talk, but in many ways he acts like a child. Almost like Fausto." She pointed at the toddler. "How they can bring back his memory, that I don't understand. They're lucky they got a little extra money."

"Extra money?" I blurted. "Nadia never mentioned that."

"Oh, everyone knows it's why she fought with her mother. They got some money, I think from Ernest's accident, and Nadia, she thought her mother shouldn't take it. Although, why not? What are you supposed to do, live on air and water?"

"What, the person who caused the accident paid them something?"

The settlement hadn't shown up in any of my databases, but if it had been done through mediation it wouldn't be part of the public record.

The neighbor shrugged—the money was old news, not interesting anymore. "Wherever it came from, they need every penny of it. His therapy, all the extra care. Why couldn't Nadia stay at home and help instead of fighting with her mother and leaving?"

"It must be hard on Clara," I suggested. "Two sisters dead, her brother seriously injured."

"Everyone's life is hard." The woman settled Fausto into the wagon and started down the street. "My husband, he left me when I was pregnant with Fausto. But I keep going, and the Guamans do, too. And maybe the therapy will help Ernest. Two days a week, off he goes with his *abuela* to see if he can learn to behave normally around others. He can't work unless he knows how to control himself."

It was far too cold to stand around talking. I walked with her, pausing at the Guaman home.

My acquaintance shook her head. "I'm sure it's hard on Cristina, seeing her son like he is. He used to be such a great boy, wonderful brother, good son. Shoveled the walks in the winter, took his sisters shopping. Whatever you wanted, he would do. And to see him like this—" She shook her head again, pitying.

"And they're safe living here even though they have more money now?"

"Everyone knows them. No one wants to bring them any more sorrow. Punks did try to break in twice—we have gangs here, same as everywhere—but Lazar, he put in all this new security—wires, new glass, everything. One of the punks cut himself so badly, he lost the use of his right hand. And then, a few days later, someone shot another of the gangbangers, killed him as he was going into a drug house over on Nineteenth Street. We were all just as happy."

We'd reached the Laundromat. I held the door for my acquaintance while she wrestled the wagon inside. The child had been chewing on the cocked hat, and it was pretty much a pulpy mess now, but the woman didn't seem to mind.

I returned to my car and backed into the intersection so I could drive east, past the Guaman house. I don't know what I was hoping to see, but just as I was about to turn north, the front door opened. I stopped at the corner and watched in my wing mirror while Ernest and his grandmother came down the stairs. She had a firm grip on his left arm, but his right arm gesticulated wildly.

They walked down the street away from me. A couple of left turns caught me up with them. I drove past them and turned again. After a number of similar maneuvers, I watched them turn north on Western

Avenue. The grandmother's head only reached Ernest's shoulder, but she was definitely in charge of the expedition, propelling him along whenever he wanted to stop.

One storefront completely engaged him, and she had a hard time moving him on. When I passed a few minutes later, I saw it was a pet store. Puppies in cages—the kind of thing that makes you want to join an animal liberation army to set them free—but utterly entrancing for children. Propped in the window was a glossy picture of a puppy licking the face of an ecstatic child. On impulse, I went inside and got a flyer.

After a few blocks, the grandmother stopped and seemed to be forcing Ernest to decide where to go. He turned right, and she shook her head. He waved his arms and shouted, loudly enough that I caught the echo down in my own car, but finally he turned around and headed west.

Lotty's hospital, Beth Israel, runs a rehab place down here, one of the ten or fifteen health-care centers that fill up Chicago's near South Side. I figured my quarry was heading there. I drove past them and found street parking where I could keep an eye on the entrance. Sure enough, in another few minutes Ernest and his grandmother turned up the walk and went through the revolving doors.

I followed them in, not sure what I was hoping to accomplish. Women with infants, women with boyfriends on crutches or in wheel-chairs, women looking after aging parents, old women like Señora Guaman taking care of grandchildren, filled the lobby. One television was blaring in Spanish, another in English. Children were crying, mothers stared ahead in stolid resignation.

Ernest and his grandmother were standing in line to check in. The grandmother had found someone she knew sitting nearby; the two women were talking in Spanish. I bent over, pretending to pick up something from the floor, and held out the flyer with the puppy's picture to Ernest.

"Did you drop this?"

He looked at me, not understanding what I was saying, but then his eye fell on the picture of the puppy, and he snatched it from me.

"My dog! Nana, my dog!"

His grandmother turned. She sighed with fatigue when she saw the picture, and I felt ashamed for exciting him—looking after her grandson must be a hard enough job without a private eye rousing him.

"Your dog, Ernest?" she said. "You don't have a dog. This is a picture of a dog." Her English was fluent but heavily accented.

"I'm sorry," I smiled at her. "I found this next to him on the floor and thought maybe he'd dropped it."

"He wants a dog, and maybe we should get him one, but I don't want to care for a dog as well as for Ernest. Anyway, his sister is allergic."

"He's here for therapy?" I asked.

"I don't know how much they can do for him, but we come two times every week. After all, if you give up hope, you have nothing left."

"It's hard," I said. "One of my cousins was shot in the head. He can still walk and talk, but he's lost his impulse control. He behaves so wildly in public we don't know if he can ever live on his own again."

Lies. The detective's stock-in-trade was really making me squirm today.

"With Ernie, it was a motorcycle," she said. "We kept him out of the gangs. He was a good boy, always, but not a scholar like his sisters, They all are brilliant students. *Were* brilliant students." Her face creased in sorrow. "Two of them are dead now."

"I'm so sorry! Was it in the same accident where he was injured?"

It seemed disrespectful to talk about Ernest as if he wasn't there, but, in a way, he wasn't. He was crooning over the picture of the puppy. My guilt mounted.

"The oldest, she died in Iraq. These two were close. Her death hit him in the heart. I think that's why he was careless with his motorcycle. Six months after Allie's death, he ran off the expressway. Somehow, the motorcycle climbed over the railing. I don't understand how, I wasn't here. And my son couldn't explain it to me."

"Allie!" Ernest heard his sister's name and dropped the picture. "Allie is a dove. She flies around with Jesus! Now Nadia is a dove. Men are shooting my sisters. They'll get Clara next! Bam, bam! Poor Clara."

"What, Allie was shot in battle?" I asked the grandmother.

"They shot Allie, bam, bam!"

"No, Ernesto, poor Allie was killed by a bomb."

"They shot her, Nana, bam, bam! They shot Nadia, bam! Next, Clara, bam, bam!"

He was getting more and more agitated. I picked up the picture of the puppy.

"The puppy will kiss Clara and make her all better," I suggested, holding it out to him.

"Yes! Nana, we need to get Clara a puppy. No one can shoot her if she has a puppy."

In another minute, he was crooning happily over the picture again. I apologized to his grandmother for stirring him up.

"How could you know?" she said. "The death of his sister, he still can't understand what really happened to her. And his mother, she won't allow us to mention Alexandra's name. So he never has a chance to talk. Maybe one day his poor brain will clear, and he will understand what happened to her."

"The third sister isn't really in danger, is she?"

The grandmother's eyes clouded. "I pray night and day for her safety. When you have lost two—three, really"—she nodded toward her grandson—"you are frightened all the time."

The clerk called her by name. "Daydreaming, Mrs. Guaman? It's your turn! Ernie, your friends are waiting for you."

I slipped away as the grandmother began to chat in Spanish with the clerk and drove to my office in a sober mood.

26

A Show in the Dark

Back in my office, I wrote up my conversation with Scalia and the odd reaction of everyone I'd met at Tintrey to Alexandra's name. I left out the tampon—why include that in a document that might get subpoenaed for a trial?—and threw out the notebook that Scalia had damaged. The last column in my investigator spreadsheet was labeled "Dead Ends." Jesse Laredo, Chad's buddy from Iraq, was dead. Jesse's mother had called while I was out to say she couldn't find any trace of Chad's blogs or e-mails among her son's things. The message wasn't a surprise—it would surprise me if I learned one reliable thing in this wretched case—but it did depress me further.

I looked up embodiedart.com again to see if there were any new postings, but the site was still down "out of respect for the dead." I took out my notes where I'd copied some of Rodney's code. There were several *L*'s but no *Q*'s. I rubbed my eyes. Kystarnik had to know he was under surveillance. He had to realize he needed multiple avenues to communicate with his thugs. So it seemed reasonable to assume that Rodney's scribbles were some means of communication. Even so, the feds could also be watching the Body Artist, so it wasn't exactly a secret code. So why was he doing it?

Maybe Rodney's mission was simply to taunt Olympia about the money she owed Rest EZ. When she'd been so angry with Karen Buckley the other night for refusing to let Rodney write on her buttocks, Olympia had told her they were in the same boat together. But Karen said it wasn't any of her business if Club Gouge went under. I turned the argument this way and that in my mind, but couldn't come up with any compelling reason Karen had for doing what Olympia and Rodney wanted.

I looked at the column I called "Key Players" and added Gilbert Scalia. I couldn't see any place that Tintrey and Rest EZ intersected except at Olympia's club. Rodney, Rainier Cowles, Scalia, and Tintrey owner Jarvis MacLean had all been there on the same night. But what did that prove?

Olympia knew things she wasn't telling. So did the Body Artist. All I needed was for one of them to open up, and the whole house of cards would fall neatly around me.

I dug deeper into Rainier Cowles's biography and found that he had handled litigation for Tintrey. As I'd suspected, Palmer & Statten was Tintrey's outside counsel. But so what?

I flung a pencil at the wall in frustration. As if on cue, John Vishneski called to say that Mona hadn't printed out any of Chad's blog postings, either.

"The docs say he's holding his own still," he said. "What have you found out?"

"I'm trying to see where his life and Nadia Guaman's intersected, and I'm assuming it had to be in Iraq, where Nadia's sister died, so that's the lead I'm working right now. I'll call you when I know something definite. Or if Chad regains consciousness and can talk, let me know. Meanwhile, keep playing your clarinet for him."

I hung up before he could criticize my lack of progress or pry more deeply into what I was or wasn't doing. Because I couldn't think of anything else to do, I looked up Ernest Guaman's motorcycle accident. Of course, injuries like his are routine in a city like Chicago. Like Chad Vishneski's squad—eight men dead and only three mentioned by name—there so many accidents in Chicago that you'd have to be in a spectacular one for anyone to care.

Finally, in the Hispanic newspaper, I found a brief paragraph on Ernest Guaman. That gave me the date—seven months after Allie's death—but no details. "He was alone on his Honda at two in the afternoon, but no one has come forward to say how the accident took place," I translated laboriously. I guess I'd been imagining someone forcing him off the road to try to silence him. I'd wanted said the article to say, "Ernest Guaman, crusading for justice for his sister Alexandra, was forced off the road today by _____," and the blank would be filled in with the name of the person who'd gone on to shoot Nadia for drawing her sister's portrait on Karen Buckley's back.

It was Friday night, and I'd had a long week. Jake had decreed a moratorium on rehearsals. I declared a similar moratorium on the Vishneskis. I put on makeup and a formfitting sweater, and we went to an old-fashioned night club, one where everyone kept their clothes on. Jake knew the bass player, so we got a table up front. We stayed until the club closed at three, dancing and drinking. We spent Saturday catching up on sleep, taking a lazy walk along the lakefront with the dogs, watching an old Alec Guinness movie.

On Sunday, the brief honeymoon was over. Jake's early music group came by at four for a rehearsal. I headed back to Club Gouge, in the hope of finding a way to get the Body Artist or Olympia to talk to me.

I'm not much for disguises, not like Sherlock Holmes or Aimée Leduc, but I did put on makeup using a heavy hand with the eyeliner and mascara and dug through the junk in my hall closet for a pink plastic wig I'd worn at Halloween. With that and the Smith & Wesson in my tuck holster, if I didn't fool anyone with my getup, at least I could shoot my way past Olympia's bouncer.

It was just after nine when I reached the club, and excitement was building as the Body Artist's performance time drew near. I parked down the street and attached myself to a high-spirited group waiting in line. Everyone had to show IDs to make sure the drinking age limit was met. The crowd was large enough that one of the bartenders was helping the bouncer. The two were shining flashlights on the birth dates only, not bothering to check pictures against faces, so I held my driver's license out to the bartender, thumb casually covering my photo, and slipped inside.

It felt like old times. Rodney at his spot, glowering at a bottle of beer. My cousin swooping around with drinks, laughing and flirting equally with men and women. Olympia, tonight wearing skintight white leather with a trailing black scarf, behind the bar, captain on the bridge, surveying the deck.

Finally, the lights went down, then came up on Karen Buckley naked on her stool. The two figures in burkas appeared at the edge of the stage, miming longing and fear.

I couldn't take another show. I worked my way through the crowd to the edge of the room and went into the corridor where the toilets were. I'd planned on going through the door between the public space and the dressing rooms to wait for Karen there, but Olympia, or perhaps Karen, had posted a guard at the door, a stocky, scowling man in black. In my role as Pink Plastic Bubble Hair, I smiled and waggled my fingers at him. He scowled even more thoroughly.

I went into the women's toilets, where I amused myself by answering e-mails, and finally heard the eruption of laughter that announced the end of the show. In a few minutes, the bathroom was full of women, laughing with embarrassment or chattering excitedly about Karen's performance. I went back into the corridor, where a long line was waiting to use the facilities. A much shorter line, naturally, stood outside the men's room.

The lights suddenly went out again. People screamed, pulled out cell phones to light up the hallway, jabbered in confusion. A man's voice, heavily accented, boomed through the sound system. "We're experiencing electrical problems. I'll have to ask everyone to leave, guests and staff. We have a crew with flashlights to help you find your coats and personal belongings. If you haven't paid your bill yet, the last round was on the house. See you Friday, and our apologies for the inconvenience."

I flattened myself against the wall as the crowd pushed toward the exits. Panic seemed to infect people in the dark. No one seemed to wonder how the electricity could be out while the mike onstage worked perfectly.

Inside the club's main room, powerful flashlights played around. I couldn't see who was wielding them, but a man appeared next to a table where a couple was still seated and urged them to their feet—and not in any gentle way. As the lights shone on the bar, on the tables, on the exit, I saw another man in black outside Olympia's cube of an office.

I thought Olympia would stick around to go down with her ship but couldn't locate her in the crowd. I did see my cousin's feathery halo of hair heading toward the exit and breathed a sigh of relief. Whatever was going on, I didn't want Petra to be part of it.

While the flashlights were focused on the middle of the room, I slipped behind the curtain at the back of the stage. A door behind the stage that led to the corridor was partly open. I stood flat against the wall and peered between the door's hinges.

Karen's dressing room was directly across the hall. A man in black, wearing a black ski mask, stood there making sure everyone moved down the corridor to the rear exit. And making sure no one could leave Karen's dressing room.

I dropped to the floor so that my silhouette wouldn't show. I felt a draft and realized that the stage back here was raised, that there was a gap of about a foot between it and the floor. I wriggled underneath, dislodging my pink wig. Any noise I was making was masked by the tromping of feet toward the exit. That wouldn't go on for long. I took my gun out of its holster and felt for the safety. I didn't want to shoot it by mistake in the dark.

In a surprisingly short time, the room was cleared. Voices called to each other, male and female, affirming that everyone had left. The lights came back up.

"Bring them out." It was the sound of authority, a man speaking with the rumbling *r* of a Slavic accent.

I heard someone open the dressing room door. I couldn't see anything, only heard a cry of pain suppressed and footfalls overhead. One set was heavy, boots, the other almost noiseless, perhaps the Body Artist's bare feet.

From the other end of the room, I heard Olympia snap, "Let go of me, damn you!" Then the horrible sound of hand on skin, a noisy slap, and a woman, also with a rumbling Slavic accent, saying, "You speak when we ask questions. Otherwise, you are quiet."

"You've no right—"

Slap. "This is not an American courtroom. You are not having rights. You are having only responsibilities, and these you are not meeting."

I fumbled in my pocket for my cell phone and typed a text to Petra, begging her to call the police and get them to the club. I didn't know Terry Finchley's number by heart, so I put in the number for his friend Conrad Rawlings, who works now in South Chicago. *tell Conrad 2 call Terry. thugs r beating Olympia.*

Above me, I heard another slap, and a man's voice saying, "Go to the computer, bitch, and turn your gallery back on."

That was Rodney.

The Body Artist said, "I didn't shut the site down. I thought you did. I can't get access to it." Her voice was a little wobbly, but she was maintaining an admirable level of control.

The thugs hit her again, and then I heard a crash, cascading metal, amplified by the wooden floorboards. Loud cursing in a language not

English. A paint can rolled across the stage and bounced to the floor near me. A scuffle, more metal flying about, and then another smack of hand on flesh and a high-pitched yelp.

"Hold that stupid bitch." The master voice, maybe even Anton Ky-starnik himself. "You know our agreement, Olympia. I don't want to burn your pretty little club down. So no more little-girl lies. And you, you no-good whore, no more little-girl tricks from you, either. Fix your website. Then we all can go home happy."

"But I don't know why my site is—"

Again someone hit her, harder this time.

I slid out from my hiding place. The man who'd been guarding the door to the corridor was gone—they figured they had control of the premises. I moved to his spot behind the curtain and peered through the gap.

The thick wires connecting the plasma screens to the mains came through here and went under the door to a wall outlet in the corridor. I stepped carefully so I wouldn't trip and betray myself.

The stage was covered with paint. I saw now what the noise had been: Karen had hurled the contents of her cart at her attackers. Brushes and palette knives were scattered wholesale. One knife had landed near me. I slid a hand through the gap in the curtain and picked it up. Its blade was too pliable for use as a weapon.

The thugs all had on those black ski masks so popular with bullies. I thought I could tell Rodney by his beer belly, but the others were indistinguishable. One figure had a gun trained on Olympia, another on the Body Artist, who was still covered in her performance paint. Someone with red paint all down the front of his jacket forced Karen to sit, smacking her hard, and brought the laptop she used with her slide show over to her.

"Open the website," he growled.

Karen, her fingers shaking, typed in the URL. Lights shifted and flicked in the house, and I realized the computer was still attached to the plasma screens on the stage. By craning my neck, I could see the same message I'd been getting: *Out of respect for the dead, we have temporarily taken the site off-line.*

"Now you put online," he said.

"Someone got into my system and changed the password," Karen said. "I can't open it."

"Liar," the head man growled. "Log on."

Karen typed something, and, on the screen, we could all see the message come back.

"Invalid password. Try again."

She tried again and got the same message.

The man giving the orders nodded and the thug holding Karen slugged her jaw. I couldn't stand and watch, and I couldn't take them all on, either. I knelt and gouged at the insulation around the thickest of the wires snaking through my feet, peeled it back. My hands were trembling in my panicky haste. I finally loosened a strip, pulled it away from the wires, and stuck the palette knife in between them.

A crack like thunder, an arc of lightning, and the theater went dark again. The knife blade splintered in my hand, and the shock knocked me backward. Sparks sizzled and spat from the exposed wires. I scrambled under the curtains onto the stage on my hands and knees.

The room was briefly quiet: no one knew what had happened. Then shouting and cursing began, in Russian or perhaps Ukrainian. People crashed across the room, scattering tables, falling. Someone fired a shot, and I could see the spurt of flame. The master voice bellowed in Russian or Ukrainian, and no one else fired. I ran onto the stage and tried to grab Karen, but she swung a fist at me and started kicking.

"It's V. I. Warshawski," I panted. "Come along, damn it!"

She flailed at me even harder. I pulled her from the stool, tried to orient myself to the back of the stage. One of the thugs had found a flashlight and pointed it at the stage. Another gun went off, this time aiming at us. I let go of Karen's arm and dropped to the floor. I rolled over and fired back, but my shot went wide.

"Karen! Karen, where are you? We need to get out of here!"

The curtain dropped against the fused wires. I could smell charring. If the curtain caught, the wooden floor and chairs would feed a fire in no time.

I pushed through the curtains, looked down the corridor, saw movement in the dressing room. Karen had put on her coat and boots and had her jeans in her hand. I slung my left arm under her armpits and hefted her over my shoulder before she realized what I was doing.

"Put me down, damn you!"

She drubbed on my back as I jogged down the hall to the back exit. Pushed open the door while she kicked at me. I was panting now from the load and from her fighting me, and I still had to circle the building to get to my car out on Lake Street. Before I'd gone more than a few steps, she managed to break free.

She ran to an SUV parked near us and opened the door. She was in luck: the keys were in the ignition. She got the engine going as I ran to her side. I yanked the door wide, but she punched at my head.

"You interfering, ignorant, stupid bitch, now you've really fucked me over. Get out of my way or I'll run you down!"

She roared out of the lot, the still-open door swinging on its hinges. I just had time to read the plate number before she turned onto Lake Street.

27

Thank God for the Boys in Blue!

I don't know who was angrier, me or Finchley. We were sitting on stools at the Club Gouge bar, and Olympia, her cheeks pale but her lips smiling, was telling Terry that nothing had happened.

"It's a club, we do performance art. I don't think Ms. Warshawski understood that we had a special rehearsal tonight after the club closed. She took it too seriously. Really, Ms. Warshawski, you need to get out more, see what's happening in theater these days."

"And the fire?" Terry asked.

When he and his team arrived, the back curtains were in flames. The cops had pulled them down and managed to stamp out the fire, but the stage was a mess. Parts of the floor were scorched, and the whole surface was covered in paint from the cans the Body Artist had hurled at her assailants.

Five squad cars pulled up as I was getting into my Mustang to follow the Artist. The cops pinned me in. They wouldn't listen to my frantic cries about going after the SUV—"I'm the one who sent for you. A key witness is taking off!"—and forced me to come back into the club with them. Most of the thugs had fled, but the patrol units grabbed the few who'd stayed behind, including Rodney, and cuffed them.

The fire department showed up a few minutes after the cops. A middle-aged firefighter dealt with the wires I'd fused. He had sad eyes and a drooping mustache, but his thick fingers moved skillfully among the wires, and he restored power to the building—a mercy, because the furnace had shut down in the outage.

Finchley walked in a moment or two later. "You know, Vic, I'm going to suggest to the captain that we pay to relocate you to New York, because I swear Chicago's crime rate would drop fifty percent if you weren't here. Conrad relayed your message. Now, tell me why we've all left our beds to do your bidding."

"It's not that I'm not grateful," I said, "because, believe me, I am. These goons are the remnant of a whole swarm of creeps who took over the club and started beating up the Body Artist and Olympia. But the Body Artist took off in a borrowed SUV, and I was hoping to follow her when your crew hustled me back in here, not listening to my suggestion that they go after the Artist."

Terry sighed, exasperated either with me or his crew, I couldn't tell which, but he asked me for the plate number and phoned in a bulletin asking patrol units to look out for the SUV.

That was when Olympia started her little-girl act, pretending that it was all just a "giant but unfortunately truly dangerous" misunderstanding on my part. The thugs whom the cops had cuffed began to smirk. Even Rodney, who'd been trying to start Owen Widermayer's Mercedes when the police pulled him out of it, looked as though he might break into song. I wanted to shoot holes in all of them just to wipe the smiles off their faces. They knew they were going to beat any rap I might be able to hand out.

The fire crew chief joined us in the front of the club.

"You the owner, miss?" he asked me. "You were way over code

there with the load you were carrying. This was an accident waiting to happen."

"Thank you, Officer," Olympia surged between him and me. "This is my building. I'll get this taken care of first thing tomorrow—today, really, isn't it? But you know what I mean—when the rest of the world is awake and going to work, you and I are in bed."

She blinked from the fire chief and his drooping mustache to Terry in what was meant to be a helpless, appealing way. "I'm sorry the Warshawski woman was such an alarmist that she roused everyone, but we're grateful for the quick response. Let me give you gift vouchers. You and your friends are welcome to come here on your nights off as my guests." She reached over the bar and fumbled in a drawer for the vouchers.

"No." Terry's quiet voice carried authority, and both his team and the fire crew looked stolidly ahead. "Tell me about the fire."

"The fire on the stage, you mean?"

"Was there another?" A pulse was starting to throb on Terry's forehead.

"Sorry to be so silly, Detective, but this Warshawski woman's wild behavior has me so rattled that I—"

"Vic, tell me about the fire."

I repeated what I'd said earlier, about thugs taking over the theater. "Going by the voices, at least one was a woman, maybe more. They forced the staff and customers to leave, but I hid under the stage. The whole point of the attack seemed to be connected with the Artist's website—it's been down for several days, and they wanted her to bring it back up. When she either wouldn't or couldn't, they started beating up Olympia and the Body Artist both. I couldn't take on the whole lot—I wanted to create a diversion while I hustled the Artist off the stage. I didn't know my intervention would produce such drastic results."

"So you set the fire?" Finchley said.

"I fused the wires. The open wire set the curtains on fire."

"Ms. Warshawski, I expect you to pay for the damage you caused here," Olympia said.

"Were you born stupid, or did you work hard to get like this?" It was all I could do not to grab her and shake her. "You take this to a court of law and you will—"

"I will have witnesses that you did malicious damage to my building." Olympia's triumphant tone was startling. "Karen won't testify for you, and neither will these men here." She waved an arm toward the handcuffed thugs.

My mouth opened and shut several times, but I couldn't get any words out.

"Where does this Body Artist live?" Terry asked. "We looked in the dressing room. She'd left her keys, but we didn't find any ID. We need to talk to her, get her version of what happened here tonight."

Olympia bit her lips in momentary indecision, then told Terry she'd get it from her computer. I tagged along with them to her tiny office. She tried to keep us from looking at the screen, but Terry pushed her aside and scribbled the address into his notebook. Back in the main room of the club, he ordered one of his squad cars over to the address on Superior that Olympia had given him and ordered another unit to take the thugs to the station for booking.

"You can't arrest them just on Warshawski's say-so." Olympia had given up her little-girl act. "I'm not pressing charges."

One of the men in cuffs winked at her and said, "Not to be worrying like this, Olympia. Lawyer will come. All will be well."

There were a few minutes of bustle, with Terry's minions shoving the punks out the door, followed by the fire crew and the rest of the cops.

"You need to go, too, Warshawski." Olympia's smile disappeared with the disappearing lawmen. "I warned you to stay away from my club, but you came back, you set a fire—"

"If you keep saying that, Koilada, you are going to be facing such a big lawsuit that even your sugar daddy won't bail you out."

Olympia gave an exaggerated yawn. "Good night, Vic. Get out and don't come back, not unless you're bringing a check to cover the damages. And tell Petra she's got to find a new job."

"No, Olympia, darling. I'm not your manager. You want to fire one of your staff, you spit it out in person, to her face. And if you think you can do a deal with Anton Kystarnik, in or out of bed, do remember that his wife died in a plane crash so well orchestrated that everyone agreed it was an accident."

"It *was* an accident."

I gave a tight parody of a smile. "And so was the fire on your stage. Good night, Olympia. Angels guide you to your rest, and all that."

An unmarked car, bristling with antennas, was in the lot. I felt for my gun, but it was Terry, waiting for a private word with me. He got out of the backseat and followed me to my car.

"Vic, you know there's not a lot we can do if Koilada insists on her story. Not unless the—uh—Artist backs up your statement. But just for my own curiosity, what was going on in there?"

"I don't know, Terry. Olympia owes a bundle to someone. It could be as much as a million dollars, and it could be to Anton Kystarnik. Rodney Treffer, the heavy you picked up tonight, works for Kystarnik, and the boys and girls who took over the place tonight were speaking some Slavic language. Connect the dots your own way, but to me it looks as though Olympia lets them use the club as some kind of way of getting information to each other without going through any wires. That's why they're so furious that they can't get access to the pictures on her site. My opinion only, of course."

I started my engine.

"What were you doing here tonight?"

For a moment I couldn't remember, the evening had been so full of drama.

"Nadia Guaman's older sister died in Iraq," I finally said. "I'm thinking Nadia's murder is connected to that, to the fact that Chad Vishneski was over there when Alexandra Guaman died."

Terry slapped the roof of my car in frustration.

"I don't know who gets my goat more: that piece of work in there"—he gestured toward the club—"pretending a bunch of lowlifes were rehearsing a show, or you, thinking you can skate right over evidence of murder because it doesn't fit some damned theory of yours."

"Listen to me . . . Oh, forget it. Do what you want." I fumbled in my bag for a dollar bill. "This picture of Washington bets that when your team gets to the address Olympia gave you, you'll find a vacant lot. Or maybe an abandoned warehouse. You won't find Karen Buckley."

He was starting to answer me when his phone rang. He had a short, biting conversation with someone and then squatted to look me in the eye.

"How did you know?" he asked. "Have you been over there?"

"That was your officer out on West Superior?"

"It's a warehouse, but it's empty. How did you know, Warshawski? Are you involved in some con of your own?"

"It was a guess. I've been around these women awhile now and they are the original shell shufflers."

"Oh, *hell*!" he swore uncharacteristically. "That explains—"

"What?" I asked, when he bit off the sentence.

"Just that an alert squad car found the SUV your Artist boosted. She'd dumped it on Irving near the Blue Line, which means she could have jumped the L to anywhere in town or even the airport. We put an alert out at O'Hare, but TSA can't find the bathroom with both hands most days. If you know where the Buckley woman lives and you're not saying—"

"Terry, on my mother's name, I do not know word one about the Body Artist—not even whether Karen Buckley is her real name or not."

He shut my door, none too gently, and stomped to his waiting car.

As I drove down Lake Street, my right hand hurt so badly I couldn't hold the steering wheel. I stopped at the light on Ashland and took off my glove. A fragment of the palette knife was lodged in my index finger near the palm. I hadn't noticed it during the heat of battle.

I wasn't about to go to an emergency room and sit for the rest of the night. Nursing my hand in my lap, I went north to Ukrainian Village, to Rivka Darling's home. If Karen Buckley had ridden the L back down here, Kystarnik would have found her easily.

A Hummer was parked in front of Rivka's building, engine running. The driver flicked up the brights as I went passed, looking to see who was on the street. I pretended not to notice, although they probably had my license plate in their files.

I called Rivka on my cell phone. We had a short, annoying conversation. She wouldn't say one way or another if Karen was there, even when I said that the Artist's life was at risk.

"You weren't in the club tonight," I said, "but a gang of serious thugs attacked her at the end of the performance. She managed to get away, but if she's with you, you need to call the cops. One of the creeps is in front of your building, so if she's there, don't let her leave without a police escort. If she doesn't want the cops, call me. Do you hear?"

"Karen can look after herself. She doesn't need you."

I guessed from the quiver in Rivka's voice that the Artist hadn't shown up. I drove to my own home, where I looked at my right hand under my piano light. The fragment was just visible below the skin. I found a bottle of peroxide in my pantry cupboard and poured it into a mixing bowl. Tweezers and a needle, which took a little more finding— I don't often mend clothes or dig out splinters. When I had my kit assembled, I went back to the living room and stuck my hand in the peroxide.

"Courage, Victoria," I said.

I'm right-handed, and digging around for metal splinters with my left was a challenge that brought me close to the screaming point. I was beginning to think an emergency room was the answer when Jake knocked at my front door.

"We just finished rehearsing, and I saw your light," he said. "You interested in a nightcap?"

"I'm interested in someone with long, delicate fingers and a surgeon's deft touch."

I held out my hand, which was bleeding pretty heavily from my bungled probing.

"Vic! Blood makes me throw up."

I thought he was joking, but his face actually did have a greenish sheen.

"I'll rinse it off," I said, "if you'll take this splinter out for me. Please! I'll even open my last bottle of Torgiano for you."

He made a face but took the tweezers from me.

"You go rinse this off until it's not bleeding," he said, "or you'll be removing lasagna from it along with the blood."

When I got myself cleaned up, he clamped my hand between his knees as if it were a cello. He was sweating, but he had the chip out fairly fast. He turned his head while I wrapped the hand in a towel.

"What is this?" He held the chip under the light.

"A metal fragment. A palette knife exploded in my hand."

"A palette . . . No, don't explain. I'm happier not knowing. And I don't know about you, but I need something stronger than red wine right now."

I got out a bottle of Longrow. It was a small-batch single malt that my most important client, Darraugh Graham, had brought me from Edinburgh. It went down like liquid gold. By the time I'd had my second glass and followed Jake into my bedroom, I'd almost forgotten the throbbing in my hand.

28

Mourning Coffee

When my cell phone rang four hours later, at first I incorporated it into my sleep. I was in Kiev, and the Body Artist, painted like a Russian Easter egg, was madly pulling ropes to ring church bells all across the city. The ringing stopped, then started again almost at once.

"I know the Bottesini," Jake muttered. "I don't have to rehearse it."

"Neither do I," I said, but I got up and found my phone, in the pocket of the jeans I'd dropped on the floor last night.

My call log showed the same person had called three times. The phone was chirruping to tell me I had new voice mail, new text messages. *r u there? ansir!*

My head was too blurry from a short night on top of a gun battle to call back. I stumbled, shivering, down the hall to the bathroom. Seven in the morning, still dark. I didn't think winter would ever end.

I stood under the shower, washing sleep out of my face, while my phone rang again from the towel shelf. On the caller's fifth try, I answered before it rolled over to voice mail.

"Who is this?" It was a husky whisper.

My least favorite conversational gambit. "V. I. Warshawski. Who is this?"

"I . . . Clara. I'm supposed to be at mass in fifteen minutes. I need to see you. There's a coffee shop on Blue Island a block from the school."

A truck or bus roaring by made it hard to hear her; I shouted over the noise that I'd be there in twenty minutes. Jake didn't wake up as I banged drawers and doors open and shut, pulling on sweaters, jeans, my practical heavy boots. For a perverse moment, I wanted to yank the blankets off, freeze his toes, force him to wake up, but he'd done surgery on me that turned him green, he'd spent the night, he'd made me feel less alone and more beautiful than I usually do.

My right hand was swollen, the palm a purply brown. When I couldn't get a glove over it, I stuffed it into an oven mitt, grabbed my coat and gun, and ran down the back stairs to the alley, where I'd parked last night. Once I was in the car, I put the Smith & Wesson on the seat, under my coat, wondering how well I'd aim if I had to shoot left-handed.

Lake Shore Drive is a parking lot this time of day, but the side streets weren't much better—parents dropping kids off at school blocked most of the roads. It took half an hour to reach the coffee shop, a franchise of one of the big chains, on Blue Island. I didn't see Clara Guaman at first and thought she'd gotten fed up with waiting. However, while I stood in line for the espresso I urgently needed, Clara emerged from the shadows at the back.

"I thought you'd never get here. I have to get to class before they miss me."

"I'll walk up with you. We can talk on the way."

"No! I don't want anyone to see you with me. Come over here where it's dark."

She headed toward the back, to an alcove near the doors to the toilets. I collected my drink and joined her. This was the only coffee shop close to her school, and it was filled with kids on their way to class, so I didn't think she'd be particularly anonymous. At least so far no one had called out to her.

Once we were in the alcove, she couldn't seem to get to the point. She fiddled with her phone and kept peering around the corner to see who was standing in line.

"What's going on, Clara?" I tried to keep irritability out of my voice, but my short night made me not only foggy but grumpy.

"Did you go to—did you ask—were you talking about Allie with Prince Rainier?"

"No," I said. "I went up to Tintrey's headquarters in Northfield yesterday. Did Rainier come around?"

Like so many chains, this place had overheated the milk for the cappuccino, which ruins the taste. Caffeine is caffeine, though. I poured some into the lid to cool and swallowed it, wincing at the bitterness.

"Did you go up there to spy on Allie? Why can't you let her and Nadia rest in peace?"

"The soldier who's accused of shooting Nadia lost his whole unit in Iraq. I was trying to find out if Alexandra had died in the same attack."

"Why do you care?" she said in a fierce whisper.

"I'm trying to understand where Nadia and Chad Vishneski's lives connected. It seemed to me that Iraq was a place—"

"Leave Allie alone. What don't you understand about that?"

"Everything. Why can't I talk about Alexandra?"

"Because we're not supposed to." Clara peered around again. "She did something awful in Iraq. The company won't publish it as long as we don't talk about her. But if we do, they'll put it online. They'll put it everywhere."

"The company? Tintrey?" When she nodded, I asked, "What did she do?"

"I don't know! Mamá and Papi won't tell me. Ernest, he knew, but look at him now. He doesn't remember, he just starts waving his arms and saying Allie is a dove with Jesus when I ask him."

"This doesn't make sense." I tried to force my sleep-deprived brain to work. "What difference does it make if anyone knows?"

"The company paid us her insurance," Clara muttered. "Even though they shouldn't have—at least, that's what Mamá says—because Allie had gone off on her own. Whatever she was doing when she got killed, it wasn't part of her job."

"That shouldn't affect her life insurance. Maybe it was workers' comp?"

"What difference does it make?" Clara cried, and then looked around again, afraid her outburst had attracted attention.

Someone asked if we were waiting for the bathroom and pushed past us to use it. We moved deeper into the alcove, farther from the noise at the front of the shop.

"It doesn't. You're right, it doesn't matter. At least, from a legal stand-point. The insurance company could demand their money back if they thought they'd paid a fraudulent claim. Is that how Rainier Cowles got involved?"

"I hate him." Clara's voice was savage. "Mamá and Papi were beside themselves when Allie died. They wanted to sue. They said the company was to blame for not taking care of Allie, but then *he* started showing up."

"Cowles?"

She nodded.

"And what did he tell your folks?"

She grimaced. "I didn't really know what they were talking about. These horrible arguments started, round and round, I wasn't sure who was on whose side, but Ernie, he'd just been in his accident, and finally Papi said we'd better take the money or we'd never be able to take care of him. Nadia, she was furious. She said Allie's life shouldn't be for sale.

In the end, she promised Mamá not to talk about Allie, not to talk about how Allie died. But Nadia never stopped being angry. So she moved out. And then we just went on and pretended like it was all normal, Ernie flapping his arms around, Nadia never coming home, me going to St. Teresa of Avila's."

"It sounds like your home life is a nightmare."

"It is!" she burst out. "You don't even know, you can't imagine. But it's worse now because of Nadia dying. And what if Mamá finds out—"

She cut herself short.

"What if Mamá finds out what?" I asked.

"Nothing. Nothing!"

"That Allie was a lesbian?" I suggested.

"She wasn't. She wasn't, you can't be saying things like that. She was so beautiful, every boy who ever saw her fell in love with her, but she never dated. She was saving herself for marriage!"

I sighed. "Oh, Clara, it's not a sin, let alone a scandal, for a woman to love another woman. How did you find out? Did Allie tell you herself?"

"Nadia," she muttered after a pause. "Right before she died, she told me that Allie was—that Allie, that she'd met this woman, this Artist, who—who, I guess she seduced Allie and made her do—"

"Clara, the Artist didn't seduce your sister. Or, if she did, your sister was a willing partner. The only sad and shocking thing is that Alexandra felt she had to keep her life a secret from her family. When did she tell Nadia?"

Clara looked around the alcove, seeking inspiration. "I don't know how Nadia knew."

I bit back a sharp retort. "Clara, you trusted me enough to get me out of bed and down here. Can you trust me enough to tell me the truth?"

She scowled, not so much in anger, perhaps, as some way of holding back her fears.

"It wasn't Rainier Cowles who told Nadia, was it?"

"No, although I guess he knows somehow. Someone in Iraq, they knew. They—I don't know—they wrote Nadia because she was the one Allie was close to."

"Someone in Iraq wrote Nadia about the Body Artist and the women's music festival?" This time, I couldn't keep the scorn out of my voice.

"Believe me or not, I don't care. But Prince Rainier came over last night—it was awful how he talked to Mamá and Papi! He knows you were asking questions up at Tintrey. You have to stop! He thinks we told you to ask questions, and if you don't stop, he'll . . . he'll—"

"He'll what?"

There was another long pause, and then she mumbled, "I'm not sure."

"What hold does he have over your family? If it's Alexandra's sexuality, that means your parents already know about her."

"They don't! They don't!"

I couldn't budge her, and I tried for several fruitless minutes. I couldn't put together a plausible story about why Tintrey was giving money to the Guamans in such a secretive way. If it was some kind of compensation for Alexandra's death, that would be a straightforward workers' comp payment.

Maybe Tintrey had done what so many companies do these days, namely, taken out a life insurance policy on a high-risk employee, with the company, not the family, as beneficiary. Maybe the Guamans had threatened to go public with that information. Or maybe Tintrey was splitting the insurance payout with them but threatening to reveal Alexandra's sexuality if the Guamans said anything.

"It's my fault that Allie died," Clara burst in on my convoluted thoughts.

I was too tired to deal with an adolescent's wild mood swings—one moment attacking me for ruining Alexandra's reputation, the next drowning in fear and remorse over crimes she hadn't committed. I took a breath and tried to speak in a warm and compassionate voice.

"What can possibly make you say that? You just said you were a kid. I don't believe you were in Iraq putting your sister in harm's way."

"Allie, she wanted me to go away to college, someplace special. That's why she took the job in Iraq, because Tintrey pays people in war zones, like, four times what they pay here. Allie wanted me to go someplace grand, Yale, or somewhere like that. If it hadn't been for me, she wouldn't have gone off to war. And now? With Nadia gone and Ernie hurt, I have to do something big with my life or they'll all be dead for nothing!"

"That sounds like a terrible burden to carry around."

"I have these dreams," she whispered, "where Nadia and Allie push me off a cliff, and Mamá and Papi are holding out their arms like they're going to catch me, only they disappear, and I'm still falling. I wake up just before I hit the ground."

Her shoulders began to shake, and she was suddenly sobbing—those heaving, gut-wrenching sobs that make you feel your whole body will rip apart. That's what it means to cry your heart out. I put an arm around Clara.

"Tough road you're on, kid, tough road," I murmured into her hair.

People kept coming to the back of the shop to use the toilets. They stared at us, and one of them started to call Clara's name but backed away when Clara glowered at her. Eventually, her sobs died down. I made her swallow some of my cold, overboiled coffee and handed her a napkin to blow her nose.

"What did Nadia tell you about Chad?"

"Just that he scared her. She thought first he was from Prince Rainier and that he was going to beat her up for drawing Allie's picture. But Chad thought she was making fun of him, that's why he was so angry. It doesn't make any sense, does it?"

"None of this makes any sense. Not the insurance money. Or why a lawyer like Cowles cares. Although Chad has PTSD, and things set him off that might not seem logical."

"I have to get to school," Clara said. "I left before mass, but now I'm late for first period. What are you going to do?"

I made a face. "I don't understand anything right now. But, I promise, I will act with your safety in mind. If you do start feeling scared"—I pulled out one of my cards and wrote my home address on it—"go to this address, ring the first-floor bell. An old man named Mr. Contreras will let you in and look after you. He's my neighbor. I've known him for years. Believe me, there's no one more trustworthy in this city."

The pen pressed against my swollen palm and made it hard to write clearly, but I added CONTRERAS in block letters under my address on Racine and handed it to her along with a twenty.

"That's for a cab if you need to run fast. Don't spend it on eye shadow or coffee drinks. It's your bolt-hole money."

29

Stale Act

When I got to my office, Petra was sitting in the lot in her silver Nissan, the motor running. She climbed out as soon as she saw me pull up and started talking before I was out of my car.

"What happened last night? Olympia just called to tell me I'm fired! She said it's because you burned down her club, and I couldn't be trusted as long as you were in my life. You didn't really, did you?"

"And the top of the morning to you, too, my little chickadee."

Lack of sleep was making me dizzy. I forgot about my sore palm and picked my gun up from where I'd left it on the car seat. Cold metal on open wound made me cry out involuntarily.

"Don't snarl at me—thanks to you, I'm unemployed."

"Thanks to *Olympia,* you are unemployed," I snarled. "I haven't had breakfast. Olympia kept me up late, and another crisis got me up early. You can come to the diner with me or wait in my office."

Petra trudged down the street with me, everything in her body, from the jut of her lower lip to her hunched shoulders, designed to tell me how big a burden I was in her life. I didn't even try to make conversation. Let her sulk.

At the diner, I thought about the healthy option—oatmeal, fruit, yogurt—but I needed protein. And I was craving grease. Fried eggs and hash browns. Petra petulantly told the waitress that she wasn't hungry.

"What did you do to Olympia and why is she taking it out on me?"

I shut my eyes and leaned back in the booth. "Not until I get food."

As soon as my breakfast arrived, Petra repeated her plaint. She, un-hungry cousin, also helped herself to my hash browns. I ate the eggs, trying to pretend I was alone, or with Jake, perhaps in a luxury suite at the Four Seasons. Finally, though, I told Petra what had gone on last night after the thugs had sent her and the rest of the staff away.

"Olympia is playing a very dangerous game if she's playing with Anton Kystarnik," I said. "Frankly, since you wouldn't quit, I'm glad she fired you."

Petra took a piece of my toast and spread jam on it. "But you said you weren't sure who those guys were."

"I'm not sure what makes the sky blue, but that doesn't mean I don't believe it is."

"But—"

"Rodney, the guy who stuck his hand in your pants, works for Ky-starnik. Olympia gives him the run of the club. She forced Karen to let him put his cryptic messages on her butt when she was doing her mourning piece for Nadia. Look up Kystarnik. He is one scary dude."

I glared at her and snatched the last piece of toast before she could get it. "Order your own damned breakfast."

"So how come you set the stage on fire?"

"Collateral damage." I explained how it happened and showed her the purple mess in my palm. Not that it was relevant, just that it hurt, and I wanted Petra to see that I'd been wounded in the line of duty.

"Olympia is scared. She's thrashing around, she's blaming me for her troubles, and she's taking it out on you as a way to hurt me."

"But what am I going to live on?" my cousin cried. "I lost my day job. Now this. Don't tell me to beg my folks, that's what my friends are saying, but I just can't, not now that I know how they got their money."

"Petra, I need help." I wondered if I was insane or just too tired to think straight. "You can work for me for a bit. Not anything glamorous, and definitely not anything dangerous, but I'd pay you fifteen an hour to start."

"Really?" Her face instantly lost its sullen pout and came to life. "Oh, Vic, you're the best. I'm sorry I called you names!"

"A few provisos," I said in my driest voice. "Everything I do is confidential. Everything. People who come to a detective have problems that they can't solve any other way. If you text or blog or phone or communicate *anything* about any client without my permission, I will fire you that minute. Got it?"

She looked instinctively at her phone, which had been Tweeting at her while we talked. "Gosh, Vic, there's no need to look like Darth Vader. I know how to keep a secret."

"Good," I said, although I didn't really believe her. "The other thing is, you aren't licensed, you don't have the experience or the credentials for a license, so there's a limit to the kinds of tasks you can undertake. But the state will view everything you do as happening on my orders, so don't, under any circumstances, start imagining a better way to handle a tricky situation. If it backfires, I could lose my license, and then we'd both be in the gutter, living on Peppy's leftover dog food."

"This doesn't sound like fun," Petra grumbled.

I put twelve bucks on the check and got to my feet.

"You don't have to do it. I can get someone from an agency."

"I will, I will," my cousin stood up, too. "Just don't be a bully. I work best when I'm part of a team, not a robot."

"There's a certain amount of robot to the assistant job," I warned her. "You'll have to pretend I'm not your cousin, that this job is as important as, well, as keeping Olympia's customers happy. There's filing, there's keeping track of e-mails, phone messages—a lot of all investigative work is sheer, unmitigated, boring routine."

Petra nodded. "I will be the unbullied gofer to end all unbullied gofers, as long as you don't hog *all* the good stuff."

I smiled at her. "I promise I will let you take the next metal shard to the hand."

As we waited at the long light on Milwaukee, I asked if the Body Artist had ever said anything that suggested she knew Rodney Treffer as more than one of Olympia's customers.

"Why?"

"When I was trying to help her escape last night, she fought me, screaming that I'd totally messed things up. So even though she fought back against the guys who were pounding her on the stage, she didn't want me to save her from them. Which makes me wonder."

Petra shook her head. "She likes being mysterious. And she likes, well, fucking with the waitstaff. That's about all I can tell you."

"Fucking with the waitstaff?"

"Oh, you know, she'll ask for a drink after her show, and you know who she is screwing by who was willing to take it in. It was, like, some kind of initiation rite when I started work there, to answer the call. And then she'd be, like, 'Oh, Petra—is that your name?—just get this makeup off my ass,' and she'd see how far you'd go with her."

I made a sour face but changed the subject. "You know, by the way, that Chad Vishneski's father is my client. And that means the Warshawski Agency is committed to Chad's innocence."

Petra grinned. "I *love* being part of the Warshawski Agency. I renounce all other loyalties. I am one hundred percent behind Chad."

We'd crossed the street and made it to my building, where another surprise visitor waited. Rivka Darling was pacing the sidewalk outside my front door. When she saw me, she burst out, "Where is she?"

"Where's who?" I asked.

"The Artist!"

I typed in the code on the door keypad. "Darling Rivka, Rivka Darling. What makes you think Karen is missing?"

"Because she *is*. You knew she was when you called last night, and she never did come home—"

"Does she live with you?"

Rivka paused. "She's been staying with me. While her life is in danger. And—"

I ushered her and Petra down the hall to my office. I sat Rivka on a couch in the client alcove and turned to my cousin. "Petra, this is a potential client. She also is a potential suspect in a murder inquiry. So we ask questions and take notes, but we won't volunteer information. Although we will tell her what we know about last night."

Rivka gasped as if I'd stuck her headfirst in the icy lake. "What do you mean, I'm a suspect? I came here for help. You have to find Karen. They could have killed her—"

"Who are 'they,' Rivka?"

"The people who attacked her last night." Rivka was shrieking with fury at my refusal to join her in hysteria. "I called over to the club this morning, looking for Karen. Olympia was there. She told me you set the place on fire, and—"

I turned to my cousin. "Petra, your first assignment is to phone Olympia and tell her that we are making a note of every time she says I set her club on fire and that these statements will form the basis of a lawsuit for defamation."

Petra's jaw dropped. "Are you serious?"

"Yep. Don't argue with her, just tell her you're calling to give her information. I'm sure she's scared. But being scared should make you smarter, not stupider. Call from the landline on my desk. The law requires you to tell her you're recording the conversation; you'll see a RECORD button on the phone. Olympia will try to get under your skin. Don't let her."

Petra moved toward my desk but slowly, nervous about making the call. I turned back to Rivka, who'd been shocked into silence.

"I helped your friend escape from the club last night," I said, "which made her furious. It was as if she wanted to sit there and take the beating. Why?"

"You're wrong!" Rivka blazed. "You just hate her because she makes you look stupid."

"I don't have the time or energy for histrionics this morning," I said coldly. "If you know where the Body Artist lives, if you've been there and she's vanished, tell me. Or leave."

Rivka started to storm out, but at the door she changed her mind. "I don't know where she lives. That's what I want you to find out. And to make sure she's not in any danger."

"Do you know who's blocking her website?"

"What does blocking her website have to do with—"

"It's why they were beating her up last night. They need the codes Rodney keeps painting on her. What do you know about those?"

"Nothing! I keep telling her she shouldn't let them desecrate her art. And she just laughs, and says it's all about making art accessible even to cretins so that America becomes an art-friendly country."

I could hear Petra starting to lose her cool, saying that since Olympia had fired her, she didn't have a right to dictate to Petra.

"What does Vesta say?" I asked Rivka.

"She doesn't care! She just says Karen's a big girl, she knows how to land on her feet! It's all part of the jealousy and small-mindedness that surrounds Karen's art. I need to know she's safe. Why can't you do that for me? You're involved even if you didn't set the club on fire. You have to do something."

I squeezed my eyes shut. When I opened them, Rivka was still sitting there, her small face swollen with worry and anger.

"Okay," I said. "Call Vesta. And the burka dancers. You get them here this morning, right now. We'll all talk. We'll figure out where to look for Karen. Until then, you sit here and keep your mouth shut, because I've got a wheelbarrowful of work to do."

Rivka wanted to argue the point, but I told her I wasn't in the mood. "Get your pals or go home. No other choices."

Petra had finished her call with Olympia and came to me, head hanging. "Sorry, Vic, you were right about Olympia. I *did* let her get under my skin."

"Not to worry, it was a tough first assignment. Anyway, the War-shawski Agency is famous for the crankiness of its operatives. I want you to start on some of the backlog of paper until Rivka gets the rest of her gang here."

I showed my cousin where the office essentials were—the bathroom and kitchenette at the end of the hall that I shared with my leasemate—and the importance of cleaning up instantly since it's shared space. Refreshments for clients or ourselves in the little fridge. We have a good-quality coffeemaker and an electric kettle for tea, but I still use the coffee bar across the street for espresso.

By the time we'd finished and I'd shown Petra how to send messages from my computer phone log to my cell phone, Vesta and the burka dancers had arrived. The dancers were well swaddled in sweaters and coats, one with a big fur hat pulled so far over his ears it covered his forehead. I asked Petra to get everyone set up in the client corner while I made one last effort to log on to embodiedart.com.

The site was still down. This time, the message announced, "We're rethinking our site. Come back soon, and thanks for visiting."

When I joined the group, the two dancers were on the couch, with Vesta half sitting on one of its arms. Rivka had pulled up a straight-backed chair; an armchair might make her seem relaxed, and her business was too urgent for that. Petra was prim in the corner of the couch, a notepad open in her lap.

I reminded the dancers that we'd spoken backstage a few weeks ago.

They'd called each other Kevin and Lee then. Their full names were Leander Marvelle and Kevin Piuma. Kevin the Feather. What was on their birth certificates, I wondered.

The dancers shed their coats, but Leander had a heavy sweater-jacket zipped up to his chin while Kevin remained swathed in a long scarf. Even so, I could see they were painfully thin, cheekbones jutting, mouths extra-wide because there was too little flesh along the jawline.

"How did you two hook up with Karen?" I asked.

Leander looked at Kevin. "The Hothouse?"

"No, no, that's where we found Jerome. He told us this chick was trying to put an act together and she was usually at Frida's."

Frida's was a club in the west Loop—not far from Plotzky's where I'd drunk with Tim Radke, but part of the hip wave that was flooding the neighborhood.

"See, we'd just come back from a road run of *Chorus Line*. We needed a gig. The Body Artist dug our act. And it was kind of cool, you know, the disguised, gender-bending thing. But it's old now."

"Yeah," said Leander. "Time to move on."

"You can't!" Rivka cried. "The Body Artist needs you."

Kevin looked at her coldly. "She needs to update her act. It's old. It's stale."

"She's only done it for six months. How can you—"

"Six months!" Leander flung up his arms. "That is beyond stale, it's rotting!"

"Right," I said. "Where does Karen live?"

Kevin's wide mouth gave an exaggerated grimace of contempt. "We weren't *dating* the chick. We worked with her on her act."

"Did you rehearse the act outside the club?"

Leander explained that one of his ballet teachers was on the faculty at Columbia College and let him and Piuma use one of the practice studios when they were in town.

"If you want to call the Body Artist, what number do you use?"

"E-mail. She didn't give us a number."

I looked at Rivka. "What about you?"

She bit her lips. She wanted to claim some special inside knowledge of Karen Buckley but couldn't. The Body Artist always phoned Rivka, but she blocked her own number.

Vesta nodded agreement. "Girlfriend liked her secrets."

Vesta had met Karen at the dojo where she trained. "She wanted to study self-defense. She took about four months of classes. That's when we . . ."

She didn't finish the sentence, but I assumed from Rivka's scowl that Vesta meant when she and Karen had been lovers.

"What about Olympia?" I asked. "How did all that get started, the act at the club and so on?"

"Karen goes to all the clubs," Vesta said. "She studies other people's acts. She had this thing she wanted to do with body art; she pitched it to Olympia, who thought it was enough of a novelty to bring in a crowd. Nothing happened for a few months, and then suddenly, around Thanksgiving, the act took off."

"Why?"

"People realized they had the chance to see an extraordinary artist for free," Rivka said.

Vesta said, "It was more that people took video footage with their cell phones and put it out on the Net."

"When did Rodney start taking part?" I asked.

Leander and Kevin looked at each other again as if they could only think in tandem, but it was Leander who spoke. "Rodney's the big thugly guy, right? We'd been doing the act for about six weeks, maybe two months. At first, it was all about Karen painting on herself and we'd hold mirrors for her, but that was way too hard. Then she started this public art idea. About a week after that, Rodney the Rod Man arrived. Raw sex. Not a nice man."

The last phrase hung in the air for a moment, allowing us all to wonder if he'd had raw sex with Rodney or if that was just his way of describing a brutish person.

"I'm assuming it was Anton Kystarnik who was at the club last night," I said. "If he's not the person blocking her website, who is? And why?"

The four of them looked at one another and then at Petra, obediently quiet in her corner of the couch. None of them had any ideas.

"Rivka," I asked, "do you have a picture of Karen? Do any of you?"

"She hated being photographed except when she had her full body art on," Rivka said. "The one time I took her picture, she grabbed my camera and erased it."

"You're a good artist," I said. "Can you draw her from memory? I'm going to need a picture if I'm going to canvas for her."

"She won't like it if I do." Rivka's face was flushed.

"There's no point to my asking around about her if I don't have a picture. This is the last discussion we'll have on the subject. Either draw a picture of Buckley for me or go home and don't bother me again."

Rivka started another protest, but Vesta shook her head at her. "You're the only one who pulled the detective into this. Do like she says—put Buckley's face onto a piece of paper or go on home."

30

Deserted Home—or Whatever

Vesta and the dancers left while Rivka was working on the Body Artist's portrait. Whatever Rivka's more tiresome qualities, she was a skillful artist. In less than an hour, she put together a couple of sketches that captured the Artist's elusive quality. Working only in ink, Rivka showed the transparent, expressionless eyes and the sternness around the mouth that kept people at a distance.

"Where are you going to search?" Rivka asked.

"Maybe I'll throw a dart at the map." I pointed to a big map of the city that hangs in my main workroom. "They say if you pick stocks that way, they perform as well or better than a financial adviser's portfolio. Maybe it will lead me to the Artist as well."

"I'm staying with you."

"No, you're not. Not unless you've been lying and know where the woman is. Or what name she might be hiding behind."

Rivka started to argue the point, but I shut her up without finesse. "You want to find Karen Buckley, but you're wasting my time. Which I bill at a hundred fifty dollars an hour."

Her jaw dropped. "I don't have that kind of money!"

"Then you'd better get out of my way before I decide to start charging you, hadn't you."

She scurried out the door so fast that Petra burst out laughing.

"But why aren't you charging her?" my cousin asked when I'd made sure Rivka had gone out the front door.

"Because I want to find the Body Artist myself. And these pictures may help us."

"Where are you going to start? At the club?"

"If Vesta and Rivka don't know where she hangs out, no one at the club will, either. Nope. We're going up to Irving and the Kennedy, where Karen abandoned that SUV. I'm going to assume she raced home, picked up what she thought she needed to survive on the run, and hopped on the L."

"Then you won't find her up there," Petra objected.

"If we can discover where she's been living, we may find the name of someone who knows her well enough to tell us where she might go next," I explained. "She is a remarkably invisible person, considering how much she exposes herself. And considering how hard it is to hide your life in the age of the Internet. You make copies of these sketches while I get my maps out."

I've got those apps on my cell phone that guide you around the streets, but I still prefer seeing the big picture— How many blocks did we have to cover? And how long might it take?—although the apps would come in handy when we needed to find a bathroom.

The first challenge was to make sure no one was after us. If Anton was trying to find the Body Artist, he could get Rodney or one of his other minions to stake me out, knowing I might be looking for her, too. I made Petra pull a wool cap over her halo of hair—it was far too recognizable. Her height I couldn't do much about.

We went by L, changing trains and directions four times at less-used stops to make sure the same people weren't getting on or off with us. Finally, we picked up the O'Hare train and rode to Irving Park. The L runs alongside the Kennedy Expressway here, and traffic was heavy.

The Irving Park stop served K-Town, so-called because it's a corridor where all the street names begin with *K*. We would treat the search like all canvassing, going door-to-door, looking at the names on the buzzers if there were any, seeing who was home, showing a picture of Karen, seeing if anyone recognized her.

We started at the L ticket booth. The woman in the booth shook her head over the two sketches: the customers who stood out were the ones who complained or who chatted with the agent on duty.

"I see so many people," she apologized. "I'm real sorry you're having trouble finding your sis. If I see her around here, you want me to call you?"

Our story was that our sister was developmentally disabled and that she'd wandered off. She'd last been seen here two nights ago, and the police said that was too soon to file a missing person report, so if anyone knew who was giving her shelter, we'd be grateful.

We gave the ticket agent Petra's cell phone number and moved on to the local laundries, a deli, a grocery store, a coffee bar. If Karen lived up here, she did so as invisibly as she did everything else. The manager at the Laundromat thought she recognized the picture but wasn't a hundred percent certain. I even asked the homeless guys sleeping under the expressway.

That was the easy or, at least, less hard part. When we'd exhausted the public places, we moved on to the grim business of going door-to-door. I decided arbitrarily to limit the search to a half-mile radius around the L stop. Petra went east, and I took the west stretch.

It was a long, cold day. By the time I'd covered Karlov and Kedvale, I'd found two German shepherds, five terriers, three Labs, two Rottweilers. Petra and I met briefly to warm up at one of the coffee shops near the L. She wasn't as discouraged as I because it was her first real detecting job. And also because she herself has the eager personality of a Labrador.

The area was mostly a collection of houses and two- or three-flats, which at least meant we weren't trying to get into the lobby of big apartment complexes. Even so, we faced a lot of doorbells, with no guarantee that we were even in the right neighborhood.

By midafternoon, as snow began to fall again, I was so tired and so numb that I almost overlooked the name on the bell. It was a work-man's cottage on the west side of Kildare, divided into a two-flat. I was halfway down the walk before the second-floor name registered with me: F. Pindero.

F. Pindero. When I'd been in the coffee shop in Roehampton and the regulars had been talking about Kystarnik's daughter, someone said Steve Pindero had been a good guy and it broke his heart when his Frannie OD'd along with Zina Kystarnik. I'd assumed Frannie was dead, too. But maybe she'd survived, and resurrected herself as the Body Artist.

I called Petra to tell her where I was, and went back up the steps to ring the bell again. A terrier, number nine for the day, began hurling itself at the ground-floor door, but no humans answered either bell. A curtain shifted in the house across the street. I walked over and rang the bell.

A woman about my own age came to the door and opened it the length of a chain. Fortunately, I hadn't worked the east side of Kildare yet, so I could switch my story from the developmentally disabled sister to one who was married to an abusive husband.

"She thought she was safe here," I said, "but he tracked her down somehow, and she called me about two this morning really scared. Have you seen her today?"

"You mean the gal across the street? If she acted as stuck-up around her man as she does to the neighbors on the street, no wonder he hit her. I wanted to myself."

"No woman deserves to be beaten. Surely you believe that! Have you seen her today?"

"I believe a woman's duty is to make a good home for her man. If she acts like a person who says hello to her on the street is dirt beneath her feet, then maybe she earned a black eye or two."

"Are you always this warmhearted or does the cold weather bring out the best in you?"

"I can see how you're related. You're just as stuck-up as her. I hope you've got a man like hers waiting for you at home!"

She slammed the door in my face.

I walked back across the street, seething. So what if my story was fictitious? To believe any woman deserved a beating—I serve on the board of a domestic violence shelter, and it hurt to know there were women in the community who believed their battered sisters got what was coming to them.

My hands were shaking with anger and stiff with cold, so by the time I worked the picklocks into the cylinders and got inside Pindero's house, Petra had joined me. I could feel the woman across the street watching. If she called the cops, I'd—I broke the ugly thought off mid-sentence. I was as bad as she was, thinking of beating her up.

The terrier barked hysterically as Petra and I climbed the stairs to the second floor. The stairwell was dark, but it was warm and out of the wind. I leaned against the wall, rubbing the circulation back into my fingers. Petra also seemed glad of the chance to catch her breath. Finally, as I knelt to pick the lock on Pindero's door, I explained how I'd learned her name.

"Why would Karen use a fake name?" Petra asked.

"I don't know. But if she was Zina Kystarnik's friend, maybe she was scared Anton would be after her for letting Zina OD."

"I guess," Petra said doubtfully. "Karen doesn't do drugs, you know. I mean, she never acted like she was getting high, and she didn't have stuff in her dressing room."

"If she was Frannie Pindero, she OD'd ten or fifteen years ago. Could have been her wake-up call to sobriety. Here, hold my phone so the light shines on the lock. Let's see if we've found the Body Artist before we speculate too much. It will be embarrassing if it turns this place belongs to Felicity Pindero, a sober bookkeeper."

The door opened directly into a small square room. It was impossible to see any details in the gray light coming through the window. When I found a light switch, a spartan industrial fixture with a single bulb gave some meager light. The room was bare except for two large exercise balls.

A cold draft was blowing into the room from our left. We followed it down a short corridor to the kitchen. Karen, or Frannie, or maybe a burglar, had hurled a brick through a window and climbed in over the kitchen sink. Glass and puddles of congealed blood covered the floor. The brick had landed in the sink.

Petra peered over my shoulder. "Gosh! Looks like there was a bar fight in here."

The back door boasted an array of bolts and chains, but it wasn't locked. I walked out onto a narrow platform that served as a back porch. Stairs had been built onto the house when it was converted to a two-flat; they were made of rough, unfinished wood and probably didn't meet city code. Several large Rorschachs of blood stained the ice on the porch and stairs, but the snow, now falling more furiously, was covering the trail.

"She left her keys in the dressing room, Finch said last night," I told Petra. "So she picked up a brick—you can see where they're stacked by the back gate—came up these stairs, came in through the kitchen window. She had on her coat and her boots, but she was probably so wound up she flailed around and cut herself. There's blood in the sink besides what's on the floor and the stairs. She parked in the alley, came here to collect who knows what, and fled again, leaving the door unlocked because she didn't have her keys."

Petra followed me back into the kitchen and solemnly inspected the sink, where blood had pooled around jagged glass fragments. I found a roll of aluminum foil and tore off enough wide pieces to cover the hole in the window. In this weather, the radiator would freeze and burst, and why should P & E Loder, who occupied the ground floor, suffer.

We followed the blood to a bathroom, which lay just beyond the kitchen. Karen, or Frannie, or whoever, had cleaned herself in the shower; a damp towel and the bathmat were both stained reddish brown.

A giant jar of makeup remover and a bag of cotton balls stood on a glass shelf over the sink, but I didn't see a toothbrush or a comb. She had left a tube of shampoo and a bottle of liquid soap in the shower, but no body lotion or moisturizer.

I began to look around, for any evidence that pointed to who Karen or Frannie knew, people she trusted enough that she might flee to them.

It was the barest dwelling I'd seen in a long time. The kitchen held a table and a chair, a coffeemaker and two cups and plates. I looked in the cupboards and found a few odds and ends, plastic salt and pepper shakers, a freezer-to-microwave dish, but no food except a half-empty box of cereal.

The room with the exercise balls didn't hold anything else, no furniture or boxes, not even a philodendron on the windowsill. In the front room, which faced the street, the windows were so heavily curtained that no outside light came in. When I'd groped my way to a light switch, I found myself face-to-face with dark-haired woman in a navy coat. Petra gasped. I reached for my gun—and realized I was about to shoot my own reflection. The walls were lined with mirrors.

"Vic, this is totally creepy! What does she do in here?"

I waited for my heartbeat to steady before I answered. "I guess it's the studio where she practices her art. See—she's got a set of paints, a set of stencils. This looks like part of Nadia's memorial."

I held up a piece of the angel's wing, which had instructions on the colors she wanted to use.

"She must carry her cameras to the club and back," Petra said. "She doesn't have a computer here, either."

Paints, photographs, palette knives, and several slitter blades were tidily arranged on a plastic cart. A black drop cloth in the middle of the floor had dried paint on it, but the rest of the room was clean. Besides the cart, the only thing in the room that might be considered as a kind of furnishing was a DVD player, with a handful of discs scattered around it. When I knelt to inspect them, Petra wandered into the bedroom.

A minute or so later, she called out to me, "Oh my God, Vic, this is *so* amazing!"

I scooped the discs into my bag and went in to join her. Like the rest of the apartment, the bedroom was almost unfurnished: a futon, with the covers tidily arranged, a narrow chest with three drawers, and a bedside stand holding a clock and a book, which was what had grabbed my cousin's attention.

Called (*Re*)*Making the Female Body*, the cover showed a naked anorectic woman with multiple piercings and even, as I saw when I looked closer, stabbings. The material inside was just as disturbing, ranging from Hannah Wilke's efforts to use her body as a canvas for responding to her cancer, to Lucia Balinoff, who slashed herself onstage. Along the way were women who used plastic surgery to add animal features to their faces or bodies, women who pierced their lips and hung fetishes from them.

"What kind of person would watch a woman cut herself open onstage?" Petra asked.

"No one I know, I hope! Maybe the same person who'd go to a dog-fight or bear-baiting." I handed the book back to her. "I have to confess, it makes me queasy."

"The slashing, for sure," Petra said. "But the animal surgery—it's, like, being free to decide about your own body. How it looks, I mean. And how you want people to react. Do you know what it's like to be me? Guys always saying, 'How's the air up there,' and then they laugh like they've made the funniest joke anyone ever heard. And being blond—"

"It's a burden, but you carry it well," I suggested.

"See? That's just it! Even you, mega-feminist, you're laughing at me because I'm young and blond. If I put one of these horns on my head, people would think twice before they treated me like I have the brain of a two-year-old." She flipped through the pages to a picture of a woman who'd had something resembling a rhino horn grafted onto her forehead.

I squeezed her shoulder. "Petra, I apologize, you're right. If I promise to take you seriously, will you promise not to mutilate your face?"

"It'd be worth it just to see Uncle Sal's expression, you know. Or when Daddy is on trial, it could freak out the jury, confuse them into acquitting him." She bit her lip and looked determinedly through the book. "I don't see anything about Karen in here, but you know, her stuff looks pretty tame compared to this."

Petra was right. It made me wonder about the slitter blades in the living room. Had Karen decided she had to up the stakes in her act so she could grab more attention? A woman with a hidden identity and a thirst for attention. Strange combo. Unstable combo.

"She's gone, don't you think?" I said to my cousin. "No toothbrush, and although she's obsessionally tidy, the drawers are open in here—she snatched socks and underwear, and whatever else she needed, on the fly.

I'm guessing she took the discs she wanted and left the others thrown every which way. And there isn't a piece of paper in the place. If she owns a bank card or any document with a name or a picture on it, she's taken them with her."

"To where?" Petra asked.

"I'm hoping she'll go to her father. I'm going to drive up to Roehampton after we get back to the office and see if I can find him."

"All that blood, you don't think she got shot, do you?"

"I think it was from coming through the window. She didn't have her jeans on when she left the club—maybe she was too rattled to put them on before diving into the kitchen. But we'll check with hospitals, see if she might have gone in for an expert patch-up." I grinned at Petra. "I'm so glad to have my high-rise assistant to off-load these tasks to. You're going to have a fun afternoon on the phone."

We walked back to the L stop. The snow wasn't heavy, but we could see the traffic on the Kennedy going about ten miles an hour. Petra wasn't the only one with a fun afternoon in front of her: I was going to have a great time on the Kennedy myself.

"I don't get it," Petra said as we got on the train. "If Frannie Pindero knew Anton Kystarnik, why didn't she say something last night when those guys were beating her up?"

"Hard to say without talking to her. The other big question is, if Kystarnik isn't blocking her website, who is? You any use as a hacker?" I asked my cousin.

"Sheesh, Vic, I'm not a geek!"

"You can be a fashionista and still know how to hack," I objected. "What about your friends or lovers? Did you completely waste your time in college?"

She pulled a face. "You're the crime expert. Don't you know anyone?"

"Tim Radke," I finally said. "He told me he was a systems something in the Army but hasn't been able to find civilian work using his training—right now, he's installing consumer electronics."

I called his cell phone and asked if he'd be interested in a freelance systems job, something that might help prove Chad's innocence.

He was out in the western suburbs again today, but he said he could make it to my office by eight-thirty or so.

31

Searching for an Artist

At my office, I left Petra with a list of five or six hundred Chicago-area hospitals and picked up my car for the drive to Roehampton. It was after five p.m. when I got to the little coffee bar I'd visited the previous week. The couple behind the counter were cleaning their machines while a trio of women sat slumped at a table, drinking coffee. Their clothes and general fatigue suggested they were maids warming themselves before their long bus ride home. The two baristas were exhausted, too, but tried to pretend pleasure at seeing a customer.

"I don't need anything," I said, "and I won't keep you from locking up. I was up here last week, and a guy named Clive was talking about Steve Pindero and his daughter, Frannie. I need to find Steve Pindero. If you don't know him, maybe you can tell me how to reach Clive."

The baristas looked at each other and slowly shook their heads.

"I remember you," the male barista said. "You were asking about Melanie Kystarnik. We can't share information about our customers with you."

I shut my eyes and thought for a longish moment: it was time to put some cards on the table.

"Everyone is tired and wants to go home after a hard day's work," I said. "Including me. My hard day's work yesterday ended at three this morning after I fought a bunch of thugs who were beating up two women in a nightclub. It began again four hours later with a call from a terrified teenager whose family is being harassed by these same thugs."

The three maids were looking alert. Someone else's troubles, danger faced by a remote party, good news all the way round. The young man behind the counter kept rubbing a cloth over the steaming spout for the big cappuccino machine, but he was paying attention. The young woman had stopped rinsing milk pitchers.

"My name is V. I. Warshawski, I'm a private investigator, and I'm trying to find out who shot and killed a young woman outside a nightclub right after New Year's." I took out the laminated copy of my license, and the couple behind the bar gave it a cursory look.

"Oh my, yes," one of the maids said softly. "I read about that shooting. It was some crazy vet, wasn't it, some poor boy who got his mind taken to bits fighting over there in Iraq."

"That's who the police arrested," I agreed, "but I don't believe he killed Nadia Guaman. I had never heard of Steve Pindero before I came in here the other day, but either his daughter, or someone using Frannie's name has been performing as Karen Buckley at the nightclub where Nadia was murdered. Whoever she really is, she vanished last night. I'm hoping you can give me some ideas on how to trace Frannie, or maybe her dad. I looked up Steve Pindero online, but I couldn't find him listed anywhere."

The maids murmured among themselves, and then the oldest of the trio said, "Oh, no, miss, you wouldn't find him. He died years ago. After his girl had the overdose and Zina died, it took the stuffing out of him. He was a cabinetmaker, see, living over in Highwood. His wife died when Frannie was a child, and he loved that girl like he was her mother and father both. Francine, her name was, but they called her Frannie, see. Steve, he used to take her with him in the summer when he was working on a job. She was so cute, tagging after him with her own little hard hat. Hard to remember now what a bright little girl she was after everything that happened later."

"You knew her pretty well, then?" I suggested.

"Not to say I knew her well, but we're a small community up here. Everybody knows everybody else's business, and people talk. I work for a family called Gordon, and, a long time back, maybe twenty years, Steve did a big job for them. Little Miss Frannie, she used to stand on a ladder next to him handing him nails. It was a pretty picture."

She sighed. "Everything changed when the Kystarniks bought that big old mansion. They had a lot of work done, rebuilding the stables, putting in new bathrooms, kitchens, who knows what all. But that was how the two girls got to know each other. Zina and Frannie, they were the same age, same year in school, see.

"I never did know which was the one leading the other into trouble, but by the time they was teenagers trouble was pretty near all they knew. The Kystarnik girl, I heard she had two abortions before she was ever even sixteen. And the drugs! Well, these rich kids with too much money and not enough to do, that's what they do. And, what I heard, Francine and Zina were selling anyone pretty much anything."

"Lela!" one of the other maids protested. "You don't know that, do you?"

"Don't I just? Noel Gordon was in school with Zina and Frannie. And when those girls came over to party, it wasn't Pepsi, let alone beer, they had in their cute little pink makeup kits."

The two baristas had given up any pretense of work. The man went to the door and put the CLOSED sign up.

"And then the girls OD'd?" I asked.

"It was an ugly scene," Lela said. "Zina died, Francine came close. And the cops found all the stuff in Steve Pindero's basement. Why they didn't arrest Frannie as she lay in her hospital bed, I'll never know, but she recovered. And Steve? Oh my, I guess he tried to convince the cops it was him that had bought the drugs. But you didn't have to be Sherlock Holmes to figure out that Steve didn't know word one about what Francine was up to. While he was trying to get himself arrested, Frannie took off. No one ever saw her again. Steve took to drink, and that's what killed him. Drinking on the job. Fell to his death two or three years after his girl disappeared."

We were all silent for a moment, respecting the tragedy of the Pindero story, and then I asked whether young Frannie had shown any gifts as an artist.

"Funny you should say that. I forgot all about that part of her. She could draw pretty much anything. Got the gift from her daddy, I guess. He was always drawing up these designs, these plans for stuff he was building. He was in high demand in all the big houses around here for what he could design and build."

"Would there be anyone Frannie might seek refuge with? An art teacher? What about Noel Gordon?"

Lela shook her head. "I'd be surprised. Noel, he straightened himself out after Zina died, went on to medical school, works at some clinic in Texas, down on the Mexican border, where he treats poor immigrants. I can't think Frannie would know where to find him, even. And I don't know any family up here that wouldn't turn her right over to the authorities if she showed up."

It was my turn to sigh: one dead end after another.

"But you said you found her," another maid ventured. "Where has she been hiding all this time?"

"The times I talked to her, I didn't know her real name. She was calling herself Karen Buckley. And now, as I said, she's disappeared." I looked at the wall clock: long night ahead, with Tim Radke coming to look over the Body Artist's computer. "Thanks for talking to me so frankly," I said. "I'm headed back to the city. Anyone need a lift?"

The two baristas lived in Waukegan to the north, but the maids all lived in the city. They crammed into the Mustang, a tight fit for the two in my small backseat, but better than the three buses they told me they took to get from the far northern suburbs down to their homes on Chicago's West Side.

When I finally returned to my office, Petra was still there, calling hospitals to see if anyone named Karen Buckley or Frannie Pindero had sought care for deep cuts. I was so tired that I just shook my head when she asked me if I'd found Steve Pindero. I went into my back room, where my portable bed is. My jeans and socks were wet from the snow. I took them off and flung them on a radiator and collapsed on the bed.

I was on a freight train, rocking along. The tracks were badly scarred, and the train kept bouncing, jolting me from side to side.

"Vic! Wake up, why can't you? Mr. Vishneski's on the phone."

It wasn't a train, just my cousin shaking my shoulder.

"I said he could leave a message with me, but he wouldn't."

I staggered upright, pulled on my jeans, and padded out to my desk in my bare feet. There was still an inch of cold cappuccino in the cup I'd bought this morning. I swallowed it, trying to clear the thickness of sleep out of my voice.

"Mr. Vishneski. Sorry to keep you waiting."

He was too intent on his story to care. "We have good news. My boy came to for a minute. He'd been restless all night, and the docs said that was a good sign. And then he opened his eyes."

"That's wonderful news," I said. "Did he seem to know you?"

"We couldn't tell, his eyes weren't focusing that great. He said a couple of words, then he passed out again."

"What did the doctor say?"

"She says it's a good sign, and maybe he'll make a full recovery. But it could be days or a week before he really regains consciousness for good."

So we couldn't ask him any questions.

"What did he say? Anything about the shooting? Or if someone came home from Plotzky's bar with him?"

"He wants a vest. Mona and me, we both agreed that that was what he was saying. The nurse, she heard it, too. But we don't feel like we want to leave the hospital right now, so we thought—we hoped—we want you go to Mona's place and bring it here to the hospital for him."

"A vest?" I said blankly. "What does it look like?"

"We don't know," Vishneski said. "Neither Mona nor me gave him one, so we're thinking one of his buddies, or maybe a girlfriend. If you find any vests, bring them all over, and we'll see which one he wants. Could be he left something in a pocket, a good-luck charm or something."

I started to say I'd come to the hospital to collect keys, but then I imagined the drive through snow-packed streets to the hospital, parking, waiting while someone fetched Mona out of the ICU, and her haphazard search through her giant bag for her keys. It would be easier for me to pick the lock, but I didn't share that thought with the client.

Before I left, I went over Petra's work for the hour I'd been sleeping. She'd finished checking hospitals, but no one who sounded like the Body Artist had come in to have cuts treated.

"Peewee, it's been a long day, but I need you to stay here until I get back. Tim Radke is coming to see if he can find out who's blocking the Embodied Art website. He's probably not going to have a computer with him, which means he'll use mine. There's too much confidential data on the Mac Pro—I'll want you to hover to see what files he looks at."

"What should I tell him you want him to do?"

"The Artist said her hosting service told her the site was being blocked from her computer, but she claims not to know who's doing it. I want to know if Tim can verify that one way or another."

Petra looked doubtful, not wanting to be left in charge. "Won't he need her computer?"

"I don't know. If he does, I think she left it at Club Gouge last night. Which means checking at the club, if it's open. While you wait for him, can you start viewing some of these discs I took away from Frannie Pindero's place? I don't know what you might see on them, but I'm curious about Rodney's codes. Pay special attention if you find him in any of her videos."

I hesitated. "Don't let anyone in except Tim Radke, okay? Or the Vishneskis, if they show up for some reason."

"You think we're in danger?"

I bunched up my mouth. "I don't know. But if anyone gets hurt in the line of duty, it's me. Got that?"

Petra saluted. "Yes, ma'am! I want it to be you, too!"

32

Sand in the Pocket

On my way over to Mona's place, I stopped at La Llorona for tortilla-chicken soup, which I ate at traffic lights. Between my bulky clothes and my sore hand, I spilled a lot of it and got to Mona's building looking like a toddler who'd just been introduced to solid food. I dabbed at the spots with a tissue but gave up when I realized I was covering my coat with white pilling. I definitely should join the slow-food movement—this eating on the run is as hard on the wardrobe as it is on the digestion.

Parking on the North Side is always a challenge, and with the improvised territorial markers, as well as the ridges of ice blocking access to curbs, it was impossible. I finally left the car in front of a hydrant and hoped the police had too much else on their minds to bother with ticketing side streets.

Up on the fourth floor, Mona's apartment looked much the same as it had on my first visit. As I worked my picks into the padlock, cumbrously because of my sore hand, a door opened at the far end of the corridor. I glanced down the hall and saw that it was the same unit where someone had peered out when I first came here with Chad's parents. In the dim light I couldn't tell if it was a man or a woman.

"Hello!" I called. "Can you come here and hold a flashlight on the lock for me?"

The figure scuttled back into its own apartment. I laughed softly, but hoped they wouldn't feel compelled to call the cops. The lock finally clicked loose, and I went into Mona's vestibule.

I turned on all the lights. A week had added a film of dust to the room, making the destruction look more wanton and more permanent. No wonder Mona was staying with her ex-husband. The room was so cold, so dreary, that I found myself tiptoeing through it to the bedroom.

Chad's duffel bag was still on the floor, with clothes spilling out of the top like beer foam over the brim of a glass. When I'd been here before, I'd given the bag only a cursory look. Now I pulled everything out, laying each piece on the bed, but I didn't see anything that resembled a vest. I looked in Mona's closets and behind all the doors, where people sometimes drape coats or bathrobes. I found Mona's pink flannel bathrobe, with a fuzzy rabbit stitched to one pocket, and Chad's parka. I searched the parka but discovered only chewing gum, a business card from a tattoo parlor, and half a bagel, rock-hard by now.

I went back into the bedroom to return Chad's clothes to his bag. I ran my hand around the bottom to make sure I hadn't overlooked anything and felt sand. I wondered if Chad had brought back part of the Iraqi desert as a souvenir.

I probably wouldn't have looked at it, except I was frustrated by all the dead ends I'd run into recently. I hunted around the apartment for a newspaper that I could empty it onto, and finally found a roll of butcher paper in the kitchen. I laid a sheet of it on the bed and carefully emptied the bag onto it. The stuff looked like gray sand, or maybe crushed gravel. I stared at it for a long minute, then folded the butcher paper into a tidy oblong. I tucked the ends inside each other to keep the gravelly sand from spilling out, and stuck the little bundle into my red leather bag.

I took the duffel into the bathroom to shake the last grains in the tub.

A black pocket fell out, too. Perhaps it had been caught in the duffel bag's seams—I hadn't felt it when I ran my hand through the interior.

The pocket was made of a thick black cloth, about the size of an oven mitt. There were a number of holes in the heavy fabric, which went all the way through both sides. I guess that was how the sand had leaked out. I stuck my fingers inside the mitt and felt more sand inside. THIS SIDE FACES OUT had been embossed on the outside, although the holes partially obliterated the words.

A black oblong. This was what Chad had been holding out to Nadia in the parking lot the night before she was murdered. *Don't pretend you don't know what this is,* he'd said. But what was it?

I went back to Mona's kitchen for a clean plastic bag. It was when I was putting the black mitt in the bag that I felt the image stamped into the fabric just below one of the holes. I held the mitt under the light. The design, a kind of trefoil, looked familiar, and I frowned trying to remember where I'd seen it. As I turned the mitt sideways to fit into the resealable bag, I suddenly recognized the design—the pink-and-gray scrolls Nadia had painted on the Body Artist looked just like this.

The hair stood up on the back of my neck. This was what connected Nadia to Chad. But what was it? When Chad saw the scrolls, he was sure that Nadia was making fun of him. I stared at the mitt in the plastic bag, then pulled the butcher paper from my purse and put it in the bag with the mitt.

I looked around the apartment. What else had I overlooked when I was here before? I went through the garbage in the bathroom, the bedroom, and the kitchen, but I only found a discarded razor blade, a bunch of tissues, and some fairly ripe banana skins. If I had infinite resources, I'd bag all the garbage and send it up to Cheviot for analysis, but the mitt seemed the one important item. I finally left, putting the hasp back in the padlock.

Just as the elevator doors opened, I decided I needed to be more thorough. I went down the hall to see who had come out to watch me. As nearly as I could tell, it had been the third apartment on the left. I knocked, several times, and finally a woman of eighty or so peered through a crack in the door.

"I'm V. I. Warshawski." I flashed my ID at her. "I'm a detective working on the Vishneski case. You seem like the only observant person on this floor. Have you seen people coming in and out of the Vishneski apartment besides the family?"

"Can I see that ID of yours again, Missy? How do I know it's not a fake?"

"You don't, of course." I held it up to the crack in the door.

The State of Illinois, Division of Professional Regulation, had duly certified that I had completed all required training, and was of good moral character. I could be a licensed private detective. The woman frowned from the card to my face and decided we were the same person, even though it didn't have my picture on it.

I repeated my question. The hall was so dimly lit, I couldn't believe she'd be able to identify anyone even if she'd noticed them.

"I haven't seen anyone. Of course, Mona Vishneski, when she came home Monday, that was a shock for her to find her door broken in like that. I don't know why the cops thought they had to do that. When I heard the noise, well, it woke me up—I'm sure it woke everyone up. Only, you know what people are like, don't get involved, MYOB. That's what gets people killed, too much MYOB—"

"Right," I interrupted. "I could tell you're a concerned citizen. What about the night before the police picked up Chad? When did he come home?"

Her mouth scrunched up in thought.

"I couldn't sleep. I was watching TV in the front room and heard them going down the hall, him and his buddies. He knew they made too much noise, but he isn't careful about it. That one time Mr. Dorrit complained, Chad swore at him in an ugly way, and it really did frighten us. He's so big, you know, and he's a soldier. If he shot us, he'd just tell the judge he was protecting America from terrorists and the judge'd let him go."

I started to wonder how reliable anything she said might be, but she knew where she was heading.

"See, that night, that night he shot that woman in the nightclub, I heard them coming off the elevator. And I just peeked, you know. Turned out my light so they couldn't see me. Like I did this afternoon when you showed up."

"And? Who was with Chad?"

"Not his usual friends. These men, they came out of an office, not off the streets like the bums he usually brings home. They were laughing, slapping him on the back, like they were encouraging him to get louder, and I thought, that's not very responsible of you even if you do work in an office instead of digging sewers. There's Mrs. Lacey, with a new baby, and Mr. Dorrit, he has cancer, you got to be more considerate. But then they went into Mrs. Vishneski's place, and, I will say this, the soundproofing in this building is good enough, once he gets inside, you don't really hear him carrying on."

"When did the other men leave?" I asked.

"I couldn't tell you that, Missy. I'd gone to bed, I was asleep, I didn't hear them. But Mr. Dorrit, he was out walking his dog, he's got that little dachshund. He said they took out Mona Vishneski's garbage with them, put it in the dumpster out in the alley. Those other boys would never have done such a thoughtful thing."

No, indeed. I thanked the woman and backed away from her down the hall. She was ready to keep talking all night; she believed minding your own business got people killed, and, by gum, she was going to keep her whole building safe by reporting every detail that she could.

When I was here last week, I should have followed my first impulse, to canvass the building. Damn it, why hadn't I? It was inexcusably sloppy detective work. I'd assumed Chad came home alone. And even after the people at Cheviot labs found roofies in his beer can, I hadn't tried to see who might have doctored the beer.

While I'd been talking to the woman, Petra had been texting me, *Tim R here, don't no wht u want him 2 do.*

On my way, I texted back. I guessed she was nervous about being left in charge and didn't want to give him instructions on her own.

Before I left, though, I knocked on Mr. Dorrit's door. Maybe I was doing too little, too late, but he might be able to describe Chad's companions. The dachshund barked frenziedly, hurling itself at the door.

After a moment, I heard a slow step on the other side, saw a ghastly eye magnified at the peephole, and finally the sound of locks being turned back.

"No solicitation in this building, young lady."

I've never enjoyed the "young lady" greeting, and as I age I like it less and less, but I put on my best public face: confident, friendly. "No solicitation intended. I'm a detective investigating Chad Vishneski. I hear you saw the men who came home with him last week."

"Where'd you hear that?"

I jerked my head down the hall toward his neighbor.

"Mrs. Murdstone," he sighed. "Always minding everyone else's business but her own."

"What did they look like?"

"How should I know? I barely saw them. I was just trying to keep Wood-E here from going after them. He bites strangers." He had the dachshund in his arms, but the dog was squirming, wanting to get at me.

I tried to look even friendlier. "How many were there?" I asked.

"Two, far as I could tell."

"Were they white? Chinese?"

"White, I guess," he said grudgingly after a moment.

"Tall? Short?"

"About average. Taller than you, but not by much."

"About Chad's age?"

"Maybe some older. More like your age, I reckon. What are you, forty?"

"Lucky guess." In the dim light, anything was possible. "You know how they always have some trick in the detective stories: the guy limped, he had a scar on his face, he wore a ring with a Celtic cross in it. Anything stand out for you?"

"A Celtic cross? I don't think . . . Oh, I get it. You mean, did one of them have anything odd that would make you know him if you saw him again?"

He was definitely going to the head of the class after this. I nodded, my warm, empathic smile beginning to make my cheeks ache.

"Not so I could say," he said. "Real expensive clothes—I thought that at the time. You know, soft overcoat, not a parka like the rest of us put on. That all?"

He closed the door on Wood-E's disappointed whine—my nose apparently had looked like a tasty snack. Dorrit was sliding the dead bolt home when he changed his mind and opened the door again. "One of them, he had this gold pin. It was like a military medal. Sort of like my Vietnam service medal, don't you see. The guy didn't look like a soldier, but I thought at the time that that was how they knew Chad. They'd been in Iraq together."

"Thanks, Mr. Dorrit." I stopped trying to grin and felt embarrassed instead. He really did belong at the head of the class.

I thought it over as I got on the elevator. Expensive clothes, military service medal. Maybe Tim Radke would know. Maybe one of them had been Tim Radke. True, he wasn't anywhere near forty. But his pock-marked face made him look older, especially in a bad light.

The building super was out front salting the walks again. I asked him when garbage was picked up for the building. Tuesdays. Even if I'd talked to the old woman my first time here, I would have been too late to look in the Dumpster. A very minor consolation.

I started to build a frame, an outline, of what had happened the night Nadia was murdered. Two men came home with Chad. Where had they picked him up? Outside Plotzky's bar? Or had they been waiting for him to come home? They took him upstairs, they fed him doctored beer, they put the Baby Glock in his flaccid hand when he'd passed out. And then they'd taken something—the vest Chad wanted?—out to the garbage. They'd waited until morning to call the cops, maybe figuring that Chad would be dead by then. One of them wore an Armed Forces service medal. But who were they?

While I waited at the long light on Broadway, I called Lotty, who was working late at her clinic. "Your Dr. Rafael worked a miracle with Chad Vishneski. He came to and asked for his vest."

"Vic, I have eleven people waiting to see me. Don't bother me with talk about clothes."

"Lotty, before you hang up . . . We shouldn't advertise the fact that he's recovering. I don't want the state's attorney to pronounce him fit enough to move to County Jail. I'd like to see him live until his trial date, if we can't get them to vacate the arrest."

"I'll talk to Eve about it." Lotty's mind wasn't on my problem. "I'm backed up here for another two hours, so if that's all—"

"Lotty, if he goes back to the prison hospital, or to the jail itself, he may be murdered, with his death conveniently blamed on some gangbanger in the jail. I think he was supposed to die of an overdose, and it's only because he's got some superhuman genes that he's still alive now. We can't risk sending—"

"Victoria, I don't care why you think this: it doesn't matter. What matters is my intensive care unit. I cannot have it turned into a war zone.

If someone may attack Chad Vishneski in my hospital, then you must move him somewhere else. Too many other lives are at stake."

"Find out how movable he is. If he doesn't need to be on a ventilator, or whatever, maybe I can park him with Mr. Contreras."

"With those dogs bounding around? Victoria, you have no . . . Oh, never mind. I can't think about it now. I'll call Eve Rafael tomorrow. We'll go over Chad's situation and get back to you."

33

A New Recruit

Petra's voice floated down the hall toward me when I opened my office door.

"And then, she shot one of them in the shoulder and another in the stomach. Meanwhile, I was swimming across the river—I totally needed antibiotics after swallowing that water—have you ever looked at it? It's, like, completely brown and green, with weird stuff floating on it, but, anyway—oh, hi, Vic!"

Petra was beaming. She'd been a hostess at a country club during her summer vacations from college, she'd helped run a U.S. Senate campaign last year, she'd been Olympia's star server at Club Gouge. She knew how to smother clients in youthful charm. Tim Radke, sitting upright in an office chair, was blinking uneasily.

I held out a hand. "Mr. Radke, good of you to come out at the end of a long workday. Do you need coffee? Beer? Whisky?"

"I offered him drinks, Vic," Petra assured me. "He only wanted tea. But we were, like, not a hundred percent sure what you wanted him to do. He logged onto embodiedart.com, and we got the message that the site was shut down—"

"I want to know if you can find out where the blocking originates," I said, "but, before we do that, look at this and tell me if you know what it means."

I pulled the plastic bag out from under my sweater and held it out so that the black mitt with the logo was visible. Radke frowned at it.

"It looks kind of familiar," he said, "but—"

"I know!" Petra had ducked down to stick her head over my shoulder. "That's the design that Nadia was painting, isn't it? It's got the same kind of curlicue at the ends."

I was impressed that Petra spotted it so quickly but said to Radke, "I found this in Chad's kit. Is it something he could have brought back from Iraq?"

Radke turned over the plastic bag. More granules trickled out of the mitt. "You know, this thing, this looks like the shields they give gunners for their body armor. We all wore armor if we went outside the Green Zone, but infantry, gunners, high-risk guys, they had these extra things that supposedly stopped most bullets. I never saw an empty one before. That's why I couldn't tell what it was at first."

He went over to my desk and typed a few lines into the computer. When I went to look, he had pulled up a page about body armor, with a photograph of something that looked like a life jacket.

"See this?" He pointed at a dark line armpit-high in the picture. "It's a slit in the armor—that's where you stick these slabs in. They're heavy, which is why we don't like to wear 'em—really, you can keep these vests on only a couple of hours before you've sweated so much you could pass out."

"They fill the mitts with what? Sand? Gravel?"

"It looks kind of like sand, but really it's some kind of fancy-pants stuff they invented for body armor. Tiny particles, but superstrong when they're packed together. The Israelis thought of them first, I think that's what they told us."

Radke started to open the plastic bag, but I pulled it away. "I want to get it analyzed, and there's already a fair number of other contaminants in it from lying in the bottom of Chad's duffel. Why would he have cut holes into it?"

Radke shrugged. "Guys do weird things when they're bored or stressed. I saw this one guy, he got burned. And he started picking at his skin. And the next thing you know, he's pulled all the skin off his forearm."

"Oh, gross!" Petra's mouth cocked open in disgust. "Why didn't you stop him?"

"He was out of his head in pain, kept holding his rifle on us when we tried to get near him. The chaplain finally talked him down, but it was bad, man. So if Chad was coming unstuck, he could've started cutting up his own armor. Could've been testing the odds after he lost his squad."

Survivor guilt. It made a certain sense. Better that than pulling all the skin off your own forearm.

"I just learned that a couple of older guys in suits were with Chad on Friday night, the night Nadia died. Who could they have been?"

Tim shrugged again. "Like I told you, I don't know Vishneski that well. He grew up here. He could know a ton of guys I never met. Maybe they were friends of his mom's. He was crashing at her place, after all."

"True enough. But one of them had on an Army medal, a service medal, something like that. Do you know all of Chad's Army friends?"

Radke gave a helpless gesture. "I don't know. The five of us who were in counseling together at the VA, we're the ones who hung out, went to bars or Hawks games or whatever. But maybe they were from that college he went to over in Michigan. You know, if they stopped in Chicago to see him he wouldn't necessarily mention it to us."

The difference between cats and dogs—if two women had spent two or three nights a week together for four months, they'd know each other's family histories for four generations back, not to mention their taste in everything from linebackers to lingerie.

"How about the computer problem you actually came over to solve?" I asked. "Think you can find out what computer the command to shut down the site came from?"

"I can try," Radke said, "but I'm no computer genius, just a guy who fiddles around with them some. Do you have the password for the site?"

"Uh, no. I have nothing for the site."

Radke made a face. "I can't climb Mount Rushmore without a rope, you know."

My stomach sank. Everything was just too damned hard right now.

"Does that mean you can't do it?" I said.

"I can download some software, but it's pricey. Or let me talk to the person who owns the site."

"You know her—it's the Body Artist from Club Gouge. And she's skipped." I explained what had happened the previous night. "So is it worth going down to the club on the chance her machine is still there? Anyone could have walked off with it, including the Body Artist herself. But the point is, she says someone took over the system from her and changed the password. I don't know why she would lie about that. But even if she did, would we be able to get the password from her machine?"

Radke fiddled with a pencil, thinking it over.

"Do you know what her ISP is?" he asked.

"The website is run through WordPress," I said, "but I don't know who the service provider is."

"That's what we could get from her computer easier than by me trying to hack, and if I had the ISP, then I could maybe start figuring out who's controlling the site right now."

"So. Once more into the breach, and all that." I tried to sound jaunty about going back into the biting air. My earlier nap had given me a brief second wind, but it was rapidly dying down. "Petra, you want to call it a day?"

"Are you kidding?" My cousin let out a gust of laughter. "This is the fun part, where you show me how you pick locks and everything."

"Youthful high spirits," I murmured to Radke.

We were putting on parkas and lacing up boots when John Vishneski called from the hospital to see if I'd found Chad's vest.

"I didn't see any vests, just a pile of—" I broke off mid-sentence. His body armor. Chad thought of it as a vest.

"Mr. Vishneski, I think Chad may have meant his body armor. It looks as though someone took that, along with his computer and his cell phone, the night Nadia Guaman was killed. The guys who left him to die in Mona's bed dumped something in the garbage behind her building. I can't prove it was the armor, but that's my best guess right now. Chad apparently cut into one of the supplemental shields; I found the pouch and some of the special filler in the bottom of his duffel bag."

"Why would anyone throw out his vest?" Vishneski demanded.

"No idea. Chad might have cut into the shield out of anger or frustration at losing his unit. But I'm wondering if he sewed something valuable into it when he was overseas and cut it open when he—"

"Like what?" Vishneski asked, again demanding.

"I don't know. Something small—a microchip, a diamond. In case it's still in the armor cover, maybe stuck inside to the fabric or lost in the sand or nanochips or whatever this filler is, I'm going to take it up to the forensic lab I use and get them to go over it with one of their scanners. In the meantime, if Chad wakes up and asks again for his vest, tell him it's in a vault, that it will be safe until he gets home. If it's weighing on his mind, we don't want him worrying about it."

I paused, then added, "It would be best not to spread the word that Chad seems to be improving. Whoever framed Chad for Nadia Guaman's murder, we don't want them getting another shot at him."

Vishneski gave a bark of laughter. "I don't know why I'm acting so surprised. We hired you, Mona and me, because we didn't believe our boy could've shot that gal. It's just—you're making it sound like he's in the middle of some big-ass conspiracy, and Chad, he doesn't know any secrets. Are you sure about all this?"

"It's guesswork," I said. "But if, well, if someone came after him again while we were trying to prove my guesses, that would be a very bad way to prove me right. Just to be on the safe side, I'd like to get some bodyguards in place at the ICU. It'll require cooperation from the medical staff, and I'm not sure how willing they'll be, but there are a couple of guys I use when I need muscle. Very reliable."

"I've got friends," Vishneski interrupted. "Construction's slow, and I know plenty of guys who'd be glad to look after my boy."

"You should clear it with the head of the ICU. She'll be more sympathetic if it comes from you than from me. But I'd suggest instead of saying you're bringing in a bodyguard that you tell her you want a friend with Chad at all hours in case he wakes up when you're not around."

"I'll talk to her, but, man, I wish you knew what was going on. This is so frustrating, you not knowing if my boy's in danger or not, or who from. How could he survive Iraq and get caught in some conspiracy here at home? Do you think it's al-Qaeda, stalking an American soldier out of revenge?"

"I don't think Arabs were with your son the night he was drugged." Mona Vishneski's nosy neighbor would have noticed Arabs. "And if al-Qaeda was at work here, the Justice Department or Homeland Security would be tripping over me in this investigation. Does Chad know any older guys who served in Desert Storm, maybe, or even Vietnam?"

"God, I don't know. Maybe he met some guys at the VA, but he never said anything about them to me."

I looked across the room at Tim Radke and Petra and remembered that chunks of Chad's blog had been blocked or deleted.

"I've got to go, Mr. Vishneski. But if you were going to guess at a password your son might have used on his blog, what would it be?"

"Password? What are you talking about now?"

"Some way to try to get at his missing posts. Do you have a hunch about a password for him?"

Vishneski thought a moment, then said, "Probably he'd have the number 54 in it, on account of he's a big Brian Urlacher fan. Maybe something about the Black Hawks. I'd try those."

34

Night Work

We drove down to Club Gouge in Petra's Pathfinder, Tim in the front seat with my cousin, me drowsing in the back. I'd collected my pick-locks from my car's glove compartment and locked my handbag, with Chad's black armor mitt, in my trunk. I planned to drive straight to the Cheviot labs in the morning.

"So is this, like, your first break-in?" Petra asked Tim. "It's my—I don't know—do I count the time you broke into my apartment when I forgot my keys, Vic?" She looked over her shoulder at me as she spoke, and the Pathfinder fishtailed.

"Keep your eyes on the road," I squawked. "I don't want it to be my last."

Petra managed to straighten out, narrowly avoiding a collision with an oncoming bus.

"Do you two gals think because I was a soldier I'm some sort of outlaw?" Tim Radke asked. "I mean, Vic here thinks I'm a hacker. And you, you think I'm a break-in artist."

"I'm the outlaw in this party," I said just as Petra started to say, *Oh, gosh, me and my motormouth.* "Unless you have skills you're keeping to yourself, I'm the one who can pick a padlock in thirty seconds using the lip of a sardine can. Petra, darling Petra, put your damned phone away or let Tim or me drive, okay?"

"Gosh, Vic, I was just—"

Tim took the phone from her. "I didn't survive five years in Iraq to die in a Chicago car crash."

"Okay, okay, you two bullies," Petra said. "I'll get back at you, see if I don't."

Without seeing her face, I knew she was giving her exaggerated pout, the look she assumed when she knew she'd been caught in the wrong. We were taking her car because neither my Mustang nor Tim's old truck handled well on these slush-filled streets, but I was beginning to realize that a good car isn't as important as a focused driver.

When we got to Club Gouge, I had Petra drive slowly past so I could see if Olympia had any security in place. The fire had been confined to the interior, so no boarding alerted you to the damage. Only the empty parking lot told passersby the club was closed. That and a message in the box by the front door used to announce upcoming acts. Tonight it read "Club Gouge is closed for repairs. Stay tuned for our grand reopening next week." Which was clever, because no matter when the repairs were complete, the grand reopening would always be next week.

No one seemed to be watching the club, either from the alley or the L platform. I told Petra to park up the street and stay in the car with Tim while I worked the lock. If I holler, take off, and leave me on my own."

Tim got out of the car with me. "I learned a thing or two about keeping a lookout when I was in the Army. If you're going to become an outlaw to help Chad, at least I can keep watch."

Petra decided that meant she should join us as well. She thought she needed to skulk, lurking behind L girders, then dashing across the open spaces between them. It was Radke who told her she was attracting attention.

"Act normal," he told her. "Act like you've got a right to be here. It's the only way to be if a patrol—a cop, I mean—rides by."

A keypad worked the front lock, but Petra had never been given the combo. The side door, which opened onto the parking lot, had a keyhole that sat flat against the panel. It was tricky but not impossible, although my sore palm enhanced the challenge.

While I worked the lock, Tim disappeared into the shadows behind us. I trusted him. *Of course* I trusted him. Even if he had a combat medal, he didn't own expensive clothes—he wore a faded Army parka, not a "soft overcoat." Still, I was relieved when the tongue of the lock slipped back, and he reappeared, a shadow sliding up to the door.

While I held the tongue flat, he slid a metal strip along the edge of the door and pried it open. When I tried to turn on the hall lights, nothing happened. The building was bitterly cold. Olympia, or perhaps the city, had shut off the power to lessen the risk of the fire restarting— or maybe to save money until reconstruction started.

As we moved deeper into the dark building, the acrid stench of charring began to choke us. Charred and frozen at the same time, what a gruesome end. I pulled my muffler over my nose and mouth. I didn't want to think about what poisons the fire had released—the synthetic fabric in the curtains, the varnish on the stage floor, the polymers in the wire casings—all no doubt Grade A carcinogens when they burn. I imagined my lungs coated with some kind of black grease that would never go away.

"Not all the perfumes of Arabia," I muttered.

"Say, what, Vic?" Petra demanded.

I hadn't realized I'd spoken aloud. Bad sign. I shone my flashlight up and down the corridor. The shadows made ghastly shapes—the wires looked like the tentacles of a giant praying mantis. I shuddered but moved forward. Even Petra was subdued, clutching Tim's arm as we edged our way to the back of the stage.

The Body Artist's computer was still there, still attached to the webcams and the plasma screens. I held the flashlight while Tim unplugged the connectors. We were out of the club and back in Petra's Pathfinder within ten minutes.

Petra turned north onto Ashland, moving at a fast clip, talking in disjoint sentences. The adrenaline rush made her higher than a fistful of speed.

"Stop!" Tim shouted.

"I'm just saying—"

He grabbed the wheel from her and shoved his foot on the brake. We stopped inches from a green SUV that was blocking the intersection at Carroll. I twisted to look behind us and saw a Mercedes sedan pull up. As I looked, Rodney began to work his bulky figure out of the car's passenger side.

"On three, you two get out and run as fast and far as you can. I'm getting into the front seat. No argument. Just go!"

My gun was in my left hand as I spoke, and Tim was already opening his door. On my count, he jumped from the passenger seat while I slid out of the backseat. Petra sat frozen in the driver's seat. I yanked her door open. Tim ran around the back of the Pathfinder and pulled her out.

Men were climbing out of the SUV and heading toward us. I fired over their heads, and Tim and Petra took off down a side street, away from us. Someone shot back at me, but I was crouching behind the Pathfinder's open door. I climbed into driver's seat, put the car into gear, twisted the wheel, and floored the accelerator.

The wheels spun on ice, then grabbed. I crashed into the green SUV's left headlight. The impact knocked me against the steering wheel, but I backed up, gears whining. Someone was firing at my windshield. The glass splintered. I bore down on the shooter, and he fell backwards, away from my mad driving.

I wrenched the wheel around again and managed a U-turn away from the shooter and toward Rodney and his Mercedes sedan. I slithered around him, but just as I thought I was home free, he shot out the Pathfinder's rear tires. I bumped down the road on rims. In the rearview mirror, I saw him get back into the Mercedes and come after me.

Oncoming traffic honked at me or at the sedan blocking the right lane, but no one stopped to see what was going on. Too much MYOB, just like Mrs. Murdstone had said this afternoon.

I jumped from the car at Lake and sprinted toward the L steps. I'd almost made it when a figure in black outran me and pulled me down. I rolled over and away, got in a crouch, gun out, but someone else came from behind and hit me on the side of the head.

35

Send in the Marines

I never really lost consciousness. Someone pinned my arms behind me. I tried to fight free, but I was woozy, moving slowly, a dream figure. Another someone stuck his hands inside my sweater, feeling my skin. I kicked backward, connected with a boot, not a leg, and the groping hand pinched me hard, then flung me to the ground. I twisted to the side, trying to scrabble away.

"Where is it?" Rodney Treffer was looming over me in the dark. His breath stank of too many beers.

"What?" I kicked at his kneecap.

I was sluggish, and he moved away easily, kicking me in the stomach as he came back at me.

"Don't get cute with me, girlie, I know you have it."

Someone came up and seized my feet. Called to another thug. Two or three others were in the background, I couldn't see.

Rodney bent close to my head, grabbed my hair. "Where is it?"

The Body Artist's computer. I couldn't remember if it had still been in the front seat when I got into the Pathfinder.

"AIDS, you mean?" I said. "Swine flu? Is that what you think I have?"

He let go of my hair and punched at my face, but I moved my head in time, and he hit my coat shoulder. Good job, V.I. Not dead yet.

"We know you took it, bitch! Where is it?"

He kicked me in the stomach, and I threw up. The hold on my feet eased, and I bucked and twisted away from Rodney's oncoming boot. He lost his footing, slipped in my vomit, fell hard, head bouncing against the ice.

I rolled over to the L steps, clutched the rail, and tried to hoist myself upright. The thugs grabbed me before I could get to my feet. I dropped to the stairs and kicked out hard with my right leg, smacking one in the midriff. His motorcycle jacket took most of the impact, but he couldn't punch without exposing his stomach to another kick. His companion tried to circle around me from the other side, but the stairwell kept him at bay. I prayed for a train.

"Your kneecaps," a cold voice spoke from behind my attackers. "My gun is trained on them. Get up, come with me, or forget about ever walking again."

It was the rumbly-voiced man who'd been in command at Club Gouge last night. I got up.

"Ludwig, Konstantin, bring her to me."

The two grabbed me and shoved me toward the voice. The gun barrel looked cold and gray under the thin light of the streetlamp. The man holding it was tall, with a fur hat adding another few inches. When he smiled at me, the streetlamp glinted on his gold teeth.

The roar of an oncoming train drowned whatever he started to say. He gestured with his head, and the men holding me shoved me forward into the backseat of the Mercedes sedan. They sat on either side of me, pinning me to the seat, while the commander got into the front next to the driver. Nobody paid any attention to Rodney, who was still lying on the sidewalk near the stairs.

"Tell me where you are hiding it." The rumbler's voice filled the car.

I shook my head. "It's Anton Kystarnik, isn't it? If I knew what you were looking for, it would be easier for me to tell you where it was."

"Don't play games with me, Warshawska. I can make you talk."

The softness of his voice was more frightening than Rodney's loud shouts. "I'm sure you can. Torture can make anyone talk. It just can't make you tell the truth about stuff you never heard of."

"Maybe it can help you remember, though."

I didn't say anything. A third-degree street fighter? I'd been flattering myself. The train pulled in, and four people climbed down the L stairs. I looked at them helplessly through the Mercedes' smoky windows. They stepped around Rodney—I suppose he looked like a drunk they couldn't bear to touch, lying there in my vomit and all.

"What were you doing at Olympia's club tonight?" Anton asked.

"Looking for the Body Artist. Karen Buckley. You know her? She's disappeared."

Anton laughed, an ugly sound. "Don't worry yourself about little Karen. She knows how to look after herself, first and last. Don't imagine her as the scared little girl she pretends to be."

"Yes," I said, "I know you and she go way back, back to when Zina was still alive. Why did she change her name?"

"She was thinking she could hide from me, but no one is that smart or that lucky. When I want to find them, they get found."

"So you know where she is now?"

"I don't care where she is now."

"What about her website? You don't care about that anymore?"

Anton laughed again, this time more loudly, almost like an operatic stage laugh. "I fixed that problem. Now you are my new problem. Why are you caring about these people?"

In the warmth of the car, I was starting to feel the place in my abdomen where Rodney had kicked me.

"Which people?" I tried to sound alert, but I could tell that my voice was thick with fatigue. I tried to imagine how Anton would react if I simply fell asleep. He wouldn't like it, I decided.

"These stupid Mexican girls who get themselves killed, in Iraq, in Chicago."

Konstantin and Ludwig were watching Anton, and Anton had his back to the street. I didn't tell them someone hiding behind the L stairs was stretching an arm out to dig into Rodney's pockets.

"Get themselves killed? Is that like getting yourself pregnant all alone with a turkey baster in the basement? They stand in front of someone like you who's holding a gun and say, 'Shoot me'?"

Anton thought that was funny. "These girls are behaving like that. 'Shoot me. Blow me up,' maybe they should all wear signs, put that message on them. Now, you will tell me where you are hiding the papers."

The figure had disappeared from the L stairs. Through the Mercedes' whisper-proof windows, I could just hear another train roaring in, and then a loud report, right below us. A second shot sounded. The driver floored the accelerator, but halfway down the block, the sedan spun to the right and slammed into an L girder. An oncoming car honked furiously and swerved out of the way.

Konstantin, or maybe Ludwig, opened his door. I put everything I had into my right shoulder, shoved against him hard enough to knock him out of the car. I rolled over on the seat and followed him.

Three people were pounding toward us up the middle of Lake Street. I got to my feet and swung my arms wildly. Behind me, I could hear the front door of the Mercedes open.

"Vic! Vic! Is that you?"

My cousin's voice, high-pitched, terrified, more welcome than an angel just then.

I shouted to her to get out of the road, to get out of the way. "Anton has a gun. They all have guns. Get down!"

I was ducking behind a parked car as I shouted. A door opened in a building behind me. A couple of men in waiter's aprons came outside to smoke. I yelled at my cousin that I was going into the building. A moment later, Petra arrived, with Tim Radke and another man, one I didn't recognize. All three were out of breath.

Inside, a jazz combo was playing an old Coltrane piece, or sawing at it. In the dim reddish light of the room, I saw that only half the tables were occupied and that no one was paying much attention to the music. A young man came up to us and asked if we wanted a table.

"There's a ten-dollar cover whether you sit down or not," he said when we shook our heads.

I stuck a hand into my pocket, fishing for my wallet. My gun was there. The thugs hadn't patted me down, that was how ineffectual I'd looked to them. I found the wallet and took out two twenties, then cracked open the door.

The Mercedes was listing toward its right side, both tires completely flat. As I watched, Anton's driver flagged down a passing cab. He held the door open for Anton and climbed in next to him. Konstantin and Ludwig started to get into the front seat, but apparently Kystarnik didn't want them along—they shut the door and darted looks at the club we'd entered.

"Uh, you guys want to sit, or what?" the manager asked us.

I flashed a smile, or at least tried to. "We're looking for Club Gouge. We wanted to see this Body Artist everybody talks about."

"Oh. They burned down last night. But we have a good act coming on in half an hour, a stand-up comic. Take a seat, you'll see." His heart wasn't in the spiel.

I watched Konstantin and Ludwig kneel behind parked cars as I opened the door all the way.

"Konstantin! Ludwig! We're in here. Come on, the act's going to start in half an hour!" When they didn't stand up, I shouted, "Come on guys, no games tonight—it's too darned cold!"

The two smokers outside the door looked from me to the two thugs. The manager hovered nervously behind me. "If you're drunk, maybe you should come back another night. You're kind of making too much noise."

"You're so right," I said. "Petra, just hold the door here while Tim and your friend and I go tell those two bozos to head for home. If anything happens, well, dial 911."

The three of us ran across the street. Anton's men got to their feet, guns drawn, but Tim hurled himself at one man's knees, knocking him into the path of an oncoming car. The driver slammed on his brakes, stopping inches from the thug's head.

I pressed my own gun against the base of the other man's skull. "Drop your gun. Now!"

The driver of the car had rolled down his window and was yelling at Tim. My thug thought about turning around to slug me, but I had my left leg outside his and slammed him behind the ear with my left hand. It wasn't hard enough to knock him out, but it dazed him, and he dropped his weapon. My anonymous teammate scooped up the gun and put our guy in a choke hold.

I hurried to the car and bent down to talk to the driver. "I'm so sorry," I said. "Our friend is drunk. We were trying to get him to come with us to the L, and he tried to fight us off. You okay?"

"No, I'm not okay. If I'd hit him, it would have been your fault."

"You're absolutely right. We'll get him out of here right now."

The thug in the street was groaning but getting to his feet. "They attacked me," he said blearily to the driver.

"That's right, Ludwig, we attacked you. That's right, that's what we'll tell your wife when we get you home. Upsy-daisy, now. Tim, get him back on his feet and out of the street before someone really gets hurt."

Petra hurried out to join us. "Guys, the manager, he's, like, calling the cops. What are we going to do?"

"I'm parked just over there on Lake Street," our new helper said. "Can we get these lowlifes that far?"

"Marty, we'll cover them," Tim said. "You go get your truck, if that's okay with Vic, here: double-time."

Marty sprinted down the street. The manager and the waiters were crowding the sidewalk outside the club entrance. Tim had taken over the choke hold on Marty's thug. The guy who'd been knocked into the street was too dazed to fight, but I kept my gun on him, anyway. Petra's teeth were chattering, and she kept up a flow of nervous, worried commentary: Where is he? Doesn't he know we have to get out of here? What will we do if the cops get here first?

"Say your prayers, sweetheart," I finally said to her.

A battered pickup bounced to a stop next to us. Marty got down and helped Tim and me shove our captives into the backseat. Tim and I joined them, leaving the front seat to Marty and Petra.

I leaned back in my corner as Marty pulled away from the club. We'd reached the intersection of Racine before blue strobes swept up the street to the club.

36

A Trip South—Alas, Not to Sunshine!

Now what?" Petra said.

The backseat hadn't been designed for four. None of us could maneuver well, and I wasn't happy at the possibilities this gave the thugs when they regained their equilibrium. I told Marty to pull over and let me put Petra into a taxi home. If we had more violence tonight, or the police caught up with us, I didn't want her involved, anyway.

We were just a few blocks from the heart of the restaurant scene, where taxis were plentiful. My abdomen was so sore that it was painful to climb down from the pickup and hard to walk, but I made it to the curb, flagged a cab, got my cousin tucked away. I gave her a twenty and told her to get home to bed, to call me in the morning before she tried to go to the office.

I climbed into the front seat next to Marty. "Who are you, by the way? And how did you guys show up like that?"

"Marty Jepson," Tim said for him. "He was a Marine staff sergeant in Iraq. He's one of the gang who Chad and me met at the VA. I texted Marty as soon as Petra and me left you, and he was at Plotzky's, so he hustled over to help out."

"Bless you, Staff Sergeant. Was that you who shot out the Mercedes' tires?"

"Yes, ma'am. Tim here thought the guy who was passed out back there by the L might have a gun, so I crawled over and found it and shot into the rims—fastest way to deflate tires. What do you want me to do with these bastards, pardon my French?"

"I don't know. I'd like to drive them down to Thirty-fifth and Michigan, give them to Detective Finchley, see what he can pin on them. They must have records for extortion or murder or something."

The men began spewing invectives, curses in two languages. If their English was any guide, they didn't think much of me in Ukrainian, either.

"On the other hand," I said, "if we learned a couple of things from them, like why they thought I had a piece of interesting property, and why Anton Kystarnik is interested in whatever it is, we might let them go off into the night."

"We can't interrogate them here," Tim objected. "There are people all over the place. Besides, the cops might find us."

"Where do you want to go, ma'am?" Jepson asked.

I thought of Mexico City—sunshine, sleep—but I told him to head toward South Chicago, the poverty-stricken corner of the Southeast Side where I grew up. "We can talk on the way."

I turned painfully in the seat to look at the captives in the back. "Which one of you is Ludwig?" I asked.

"Bitch, we don't tell you nothing."

"Want me to hit them?" Tim asked. "They have a few punches coming, judging from how they were roughing you up."

"It doesn't really matter," I said. "We know what they are—creeps who work for Anton Kystarnik—and we know their names are Ludwig and Konstantin. Now, which one of you is which?"

They stared at me, sullen, silent.

"Okay," I said, "just so we can call you something, you, by the window, you're Konstantin, and your pal is Ludwig. We can find you easily enough if we need you again. Go on over to Lake Shore Drive, Marty, and head south."

A cell phone rang in Ludwig's pocket, and he reached for it. Tim knocked his hand away, and we listened to the phone ringing. Konstantin's phone started next, a sound like a buzz saw.

"What does Anton think I have?" I asked over the ringing.

"We tell you nothing . . . You or your boy toys, you dried-up cougar!"

"A dried-up cougar? Is that a step up from a bitch or a step down?" I wondered. "Anyway, so far you and your pal are oh for nothing, so let me explain where we're going."

We had reached Lake Shore Drive and were heading south, passing the enormous exhibition halls that made up McCormick Place. "You know those high-rise projects the city's been tearing down? They were home to old-line gangs like the Vice Lords. The city's relocated a lot of the residents to South Chicago, and the gangs who are coming in have unsettled all the power relationships on the Southeast Side. It's not a good place for strangers, especially white strangers, to wander around after dark."

All the time I was talking, both their cell phones kept sounding. I wondered if Anton was trying to reach them, trying to find out if they'd killed me.

"When we get to Ninety-first Street," I said, "take a right. We'll drop these creeps off at Houston—that's where I grew up. Ludwig and Konstantin can see who will drive them north again. Maybe they can flash a bankroll and hire a ride. But maybe that wouldn't be so smart. Because a bankroll—"

"We don't know." That was Ludwig. "Rodney, he calls us, texts us, tells us we are looking for you. Someone is tracking your GPS in your phone. They—"

"Shut up!" Konstantin cried.

I pulled my cell phone from my pocket and removed the battery. We'd reached the north end of Hyde Park, the toney neighborhood around the University of Chicago where Barack Obama has his home. If someone was tracking my GPS, with any luck they wouldn't have a tail in place already.

"Tim," I said. "Just in case Anton cares enough about these two to track them, pull out their cell phones and remove the batteries."

I covered the pair with my gun, while Tim carefully stuck an arm across each man and found their phones. We were riding close to the lake now, close enough to see the desolate, ice-covered surface stretch to the horizon under the pale starlight.

"You guys were at the nightclub last night," I said. "What did Anton Kystarnik hear me say, or where did he see me go, that has him so interested in me?"

"We not knowing," the talkative thug said. "We following orders only."

"Order followers—the lowest of the low." I turned around to face front. "Let's get this pond scum down to South Chicago and go home. I've had it."

"I can pull over, ma'am," Staff Sergeant Jepson said. "Tim and me, we can beat the truth out of them."

I thought of Anton's threat to me, that he could torture me into talking. "You can beat them into saying something," I said, "but who knows if it will be the truth? Let's just drop them in the middle of Latin Kings turf. Let them get home as best they can."

I switched on the radio and stumbled on Nina Simone covering "Strange Fruit." Her voice, pausing on the beat, cracking, brought a heart-wrenching vividness to the lyrics.

Outside the truck's dirty windows, the lake had disappeared. The expressway had ended; we were on city streets. We passed shabby houses and boarded-over apartment buildings, the ominous empty lots of a neighborhood that had gone past decay into ruin. Jepson hit a hidden pothole, and we bounced so hard that I couldn't hold back a cry of pain as my abdomen shook. In the backseat, our duo conferred in Ukrainian.

Finally, Konstantin said, his voice sullen, "We telling what we are knowing."

Here is fruit for the crows to pluck, Nina Simone was singing.

"And what are you knowing?" I asked. "About the Body Artist, or why Anton doesn't care about her website anymore, or about what he thinks I have?"

"Anton, he says you have special papers, but we not knowing what they are. We knowing only about Body Artist."

Jepson kept driving, following Route 41 as it twisted past the weed-filled land where U.S. Steel used to operate. I turned off the radio.

"So . . . tell me about the Body Artist."

"Everyone is paying attention to Anton. The police, the FBI, everyone. Anton can't move, we can't move, without the police, the FBI, the Secret Service, moving with us.

"How did he manage it tonight?" I asked.

"Oh, there's always a way. With Owen." He pronounced it *O*-ven. "We switch cars—back, forth, back, forth—until we know we're clear. But Anton knows they are also watching computer, e-mail, telephone. So he talks to Rodney. And Rodney paints Anton's words on the Body Artist. And then all our friends overseas can read Anton's wishes."

It took Konstantin a few minutes to explain the system, and he wasn't clear on all the terminology. He was one of Anton's pit bulls, not part of the decision-making inner circle, so he could only repeat what he'd overheard when he'd been bodyguarding Anton and Rodney.

Basically, it seemed that Rodney had been using the Body Artist to signal Anton's offshore money-laundering partners. The letters Rodney painted stood for countries—Lichtenstein, Cayman, sometimes Belize—wherever Anton kept accounts. He opened and closed them frequently, trying to stay a few steps ahead of the Secret Service. From what Ludwig could recount, it sounded as though one string of the numbers painted by Rodney stood for banking sort codes; the other string probably represented the password for a given account. Simple, easy for anyone to pick up on the World Wide Web, and hard to prove what it was or that Anton was masterminding it.

"So then that stupid bitch, she is shutting her site, and Anton is crazy. Team members are calling from Switzerland, from the Caymans, from the Middle East, they're saying the accounts are in a mess. All because of her. And you. We saw you helping her leave the club."

"If you saw that, then you saw her knock me away and tear off into the night. I have no idea where she is."

"Maybe," Konstantin said. "Maybe not. Only suddenly tonight, Anton, he calls us, saying the website isn't important now. Only you, and the papers you are stealing, these, we need to get back."

They had no more idea what papers Anton was hunting than I did. I asked them a dozen different ways, but they were thugs, not thinkers. Anton talked in front of them, but not about what he was looking for.

If it was Karen Buckley's computer they wanted, I wondered why they hadn't taken it last night when they attacked the club. But, of course, the cops had arrived, it hadn't been possible. Maybe Anton had headed to the boarded-up club tonight. Maybe they got there just as we were leaving and followed us. But a computer wasn't paper, and Anton had very specifically been looking for papers.

I was too tired to think clearly. I told Marty to turn around, drop the thugs near McCormick Place, and get the rest of us home for the night.

37

Checkup by Lotty, Ordered by Contreras

I slept around the clock that night, waking up around eleven with my abdomen so sore that I cried out when I tried to get out of bed. I gave up the effort and lay listening to the wind whip against the windows. It didn't seem as though spring would ever come, or that I would ever care enough about anything—clients, baseball, food, sex—to want to get up again.

I wondered what Anton Kystarnik had said when his team reported in. *Miserable losers,* he'd cried in Ukrainian when they finally made their way back to his office. *I will whip you all and send you to bed without supper.* Or would his response have been vengeful? *She has insulted me by embarrassing you. Bring me V. I. Warshawski's head on a platter.*

Staff Sergeant Jepson had dropped the two thugs at Thirty-first Street, a mile south of McCormick Place. If they couldn't find a cab, it was only a mile or so to Printers Row, the Yuppie haven south of the Loop. Konstantin protested when Tim Radke yanked them from the backseat, but I told them I was doing them a favor.

"You're getting soft because you only attack helpless targets. If any muggers are foolish enough to be out on such a bitter night, they'll help you polish your street-fighting skills."

When we were moving again, I asked Jepson to take me to my office so I could pick up my car. In his polite Marine voice, he told me I was in no condition to drive tonight, "ma'am." He and Tim would take me home if I would give him the address.

After that, I dozed my way up to Racine and Belmont. When the vets woke me in front of my building, Tim said he'd get some work done on the Body Artist's website on his lunch break the next day.

"You have the computer?" I was amazed that he'd remembered it in the middle of our street fight.

"I took it with me when Petra and I jumped ship. It's under Jepson's front seat."

He and the staff sergeant helped me up the walk to my building. They made me feel old and frail, supporting my arms. I wasn't a dried-up cougar, I was just dried up.

While I found my keys and unlocked the outer door, Tim asked, "This business tonight anything to do with Chad Vishneski?"

"It's got something to do with it, I just don't know what." I remembered the mitt and sand in the trunk of my car. "I've got to get that out, too—I've got to keep it safe. If that's what Rodney was looking for and he wakes up remembering that he didn't get it, his master may think to look in my car."

"We'll take care of it, ma'am, if you give us your car keys," Jepson said. "Tell me what you want me to do with it."

"Drive it up to Cheviot labs in Northbrook. Take it to Sanford Rieff. I want the mitt and the contents and Chad's duffel bag searched for—anything that may be in it. And I want a priority turnaround, which means paying a fifty percent premium. If you have time in the morning, I would be grateful if you took care of it."

"Nothing but time, ma'am," Jepson said. "I'm job hunting, these days."

The dogs had been whining behind Mr. Contreras's front door while we talked. The old man opened the door and the dogs ran to me, barking eager questions: *Where had I been, What had I been doing, Was I all right, Could they trust these strangers,* they seemed to ask. It was only as I extricated myself and the vets from their onslaught that I saw Petra had followed my neighbor into the hall. She'd needed petting, pulling together, and no one could do that better than her Uncle Sal.

When Petra saw me, she burst into tears. "I've been calling you and calling you," she said. "When you didn't answer, I thought you were dead."

"Told you she had a hundred and nine lives," my neighbor said, but he did come over to inspect me and my escort. "Why do you need to keep sticking your neck out, just so Peewee and I can break our hearts?"

I hugged him, feeling his unshaven chin against my face. "I'm as burned out as last year's firecrackers. These are the heroes of the evening. A couple of Iraq vets, Tim Radke, Marty Jepson. Guys, Mr. Contreras fought at Anzio. Gave him a taste for grappa. Which I'm sure he'll be glad to share with you."

Before I left him and the young people with the dogs and the grappa, I asked Petra about her Pathfinder. As far as she knew, it was still in the middle of the street where I'd abandoned it.

"Tim, Marty, can you pull it to the curb if it's still there when you go back to get Tim's car? We'll deal with towing and repairs when we have more time."

Marty solemnly promised I could count on him, ma'am.

With that comforting thought, I staggered up the stairs to bed. I undressed only because I know that if you sleep in a bra you wake up uncomfortable. I didn't even take time to pull on a nightshirt before falling deep into sleep.

The next day, when I'd finally forced myself out of bed, I called Terry Finchley at the Central District. He wasn't available, so I told the receptionist that my business concerned Club Gouge. After a longish wait, Officer Milkova came to the phone.

When she said that Detective Finchley had warned her I might call about the Vishneski-Guaman case, I remembered her. She'd been one of the officers who'd responded the night Nadia Guaman was killed.

"Do you have any new information on the murder, ma'am?"

I was starting to feel embalmed, the way everyone under thirty was calling me ma'am.

"A lowlife named Rodney Treffer passed out on Lake Street last night, near the Ashland L stop. He's been beating up people around Club Gouge. He and a team of creeps broke into the club two nights ago and attacked the owner. Last night, he attacked me. Can you find out if he's in custody or in a hospital someplace?"

"I can't give you confidential information about any citizen, whether they're in our custody or not." Milkova's voice was severe.

"Ma'am," I added.

"What?"

"You forgot your punctuation mark," I explained. "Whether they're in our custody or not, *ma'am*. So if my lawyer files an order of protection against Treffer, you can't tell us whether he's unconscious or anything?"

She was new to Finchley's team; she didn't know how to respond off the top of her head. "You said he passed out, then you said he attacked you. How could he do both?"

"He did them in the reverse order. First he attacked me, then he passed out. I want to know if he's in a hospital or the morgue or even police custody."

She thought this over. "I think I need to see you in person. Do you know where Detective Finchley's office is?"

"I know where it is, but if you want to see me in person, you'll have to come to me. Rodney hurt me badly enough last night that I'm not hiking down to Thirty-fifth and Michigan in this weather."

"I'll tell Detective Finchley you called."

"He'll be ecstatic at the news. Tell him I cracked the code on what secrets Kystarnik has been sending to his troops. Although maybe I should call the Secret Service—they're the ones who've been playing cat and mouse with Kystarnik."

"I think I'd better just ask Detective Finchley to call you," Milkova said.

When she hung up, I made myself a large espresso and took it with me to drink while I soaked in a hot bath. My abdomen was a mass of purple-black. Jake Thibaut was leaving for Europe tomorrow night. If the blood in my hand had turned him green, what would the sight of my stomach do? Maybe if I wanted to preserve the relationship I should keep out of his way until he got home from his tour.

It was more important that I keep out of Kystarnik's way. Just because I'd managed to wriggle out of his jaws last night didn't mean I was home free—especially once he found out that my pals and I had shanghaied his crew. Although maybe Konstantin and Ludwig wouldn't want Anton to know that a dried-up cougar had outwitted them.

But what papers did Anton think I had? And where had the Body Artist fled? And why had she been so angry when I tried to help her get away from Anton?

Those seemed to be enough questions to keep a fit and lively detective busy for a year or two. How could I handle them with just my cousin's help—my young, inexperienced cousin who'd been badly shaken by last night's assault?

When I was dry and warm, I wrapped my torso in an Ace bandage. By pulling it tight across my abdomen, I could move well enough to make my way downstairs to my neighbor.

His face lit up when he saw me. "I didn't want to come up," he said, "in case you were asleep. You looked like you was on your way to Graceland last night, doll."

By this, my neighbor meant a nearby cemetery where Chicago's most famous citizens are buried, not Elvis's Memphis home.

"Those were a couple of nice boys you brought around last night, real thoughtful," he added. "They drove Peewee home, and the one boy, the Marine, came by a little bit ago. He brought your car keys and a note from that lab you use."

Mr. Contreras pawed through the newspapers on his coffee table and came up with an envelope that had the Cheviot labs logo—two rams going head-to-head—on the corner. Inside were my car keys and a receipt from Sanford Rieff's assistant, listing the duffel bag, the black armor mitt, and the sand, and summarizing the search I'd requested.

Mr. Contreras insisted on cooking for me, scrambled eggs, bacon, toast. When he saw how painful it was for me to sit down, he also insisted that I go see Lotty.

"We'll take a cab, doll. You can't take a chance. If you got a perforated kidney or something, you gotta get it looked at."

"You know darned well how much I hate being in the medical maw," I grumbled. "I can eat, I'm not bleeding when I go to the bathroom."

"Even so, even so . . . I'm calling that service you used for the dogs when you was in Italy last summer; they'll walk them until you're fit again. And I'm going upstairs to get your coat while you finish your eggs."

Lotty was in her clinic today, not at Beth Israel. When Mr. Contreras and I reached the storefront on Damen Avenue, we found a roomful of the usual clientele: streppy kids, overweight adults with diabetes, worried pregnant teens. Mrs. Coltrain, Lotty's receptionist, has handled all of her patients for fifteen years, with the poise of Solti conducting the CSO. When I told her what had happened, she promised to fit me in as soon as she could.

While I waited, I used the clinic landline to call my cousin. Konstantin and Ludwig had told me last night that Anton was tracking me through my cell phone, so I just couldn't take a chance on using it.

Petra was at her apartment, tired, nervous, not sure she was ready for detective work. "Marty Jepson is here, though," she suddenly thought to say. "He came over to see how I was doing. And we're watching some of the Body Artist's DVDs together. So far, it looks like old stuff. Collages, things that she photographed and uploaded later."

Jewel Kim, the advanced practice nurse who ran the clinic while Lotty was at the hospital, interrupted me then and took me into one of the exam rooms. "We can send you for an MRI if you want it, Vic, and I'll have Lotty double-check you, but I don't think you have any organ damage. I know it's miserable outside, but you should put cold packs on your belly until the swelling goes down. Try arnica as well."

Lotty came in a few minutes later. "Victoria, what on earth—no, never mind, I don't have time, what with all these people worried that their colds are swine flu and the ones with swine flu who waited too late to come in. You weren't reckless, no one could *ever* say you were reckless. Simply, you were minding your own business until someone kicked you. That's good enough for me."

"Thank you, Lotty, I knew you would understand." I was bitter at her sarcasm. "In fact, I was minding my own business—at least, I was tending to my detective business. I do not go out of my way to get hurt. If a bully is running the street, do you want me to stay inside with the door locked and hope he hurts someone else?"

Lotty had been probing my abdomen with quick, skillful pressure, pinpointing the sorest spots, but she stopped, fingers over my right ovary. "I don't suppose there's a middle ground? Perhaps with a bully, there never is."

She finished her probing. "So—do as Jewel suggests, a cold compress, arnica. I'll give you prescriptions for a good anti-inflammatory, and an antibiotic, to be on the safe side. In a day or two, with your DNA, the worst will be past. You won't run or let those dogs pull on you for a week."

The last sentence was a command, not an observation, and I took it meekly with me to the waiting room.

38

A Pleasant Chat with Olympia

Mr. Contreras was torn between relief that nothing serious was amiss and disappointment that I couldn't be confined to quarters for a month or two while he looked after me. He rode with me in the taxi down to my office so I could collect my car. When I told him I wasn't going home, he tried to argue with me at first, then decided he should drive me.

"I'm going to pay a surprise visit to Olympia Koilada," I said. "You sure you want to come along? I can't have you breaking her neck, or anything, just because you don't like the way she treated Petra."

"You're the one that likes to run around town getting beat up. I'll be there to protect whichever one of you needs it most."

I laughed, clutching my abdomen, and turned the keys over to him.

Olympia lived in a loft building just northwest of the Gold Coast, one of those conversions that followed the gutting of Chicago's old industrial corridor. According to my computer search, she'd paid almost a million dollars for half of the fourth floor, the side that faced the Chicago River. I wondered what it would fetch if she had to liquidate in the middle of this slump.

When I rang Olympia's bell, she squawked at me through the intercom.

"It's V. I. Warshawski, Olympia."

"Go away," she snapped.

"I don't think so. I think we'll have a lovely conversation about you, Anton, and money laundering."

A couple of minutes passed where the wind made a good substitute for an ice pack on my sore belly, and then a buzzer sounded, unlocking the door. When we got off the elevator at the fourth floor, Olympia's door was cracked open. She waited until we got close enough for her to identify us before she opened it all the way.

I had never seen her away from the club. In blue jeans and a turtleneck, without makeup, she looked younger, even a bit vulnerable, although the large gun in her left hand kind of countered that image.

"Rodney kicked me so hard last night that I'm having trouble getting around today," I said. "My neighbor, Salvatore Contreras, is helping me out. Mr. Contreras, Olympia Koilada."

Mr. Contreras stuck a hand out, but Olympia didn't move. I lifted my sweater and peeled back the Ace bandage to show her my bruises.

She blenched. "Rodney did that?"

"Yes indeed. But it was all for the good because, after he got knocked out, I persuaded two of his cretinous team to confide Anton's code to me."

"You knocked Rodney out? Oh my God."

I didn't tell her the big role luck played in my salvation last night. I wanted her to think that I was as powerful—more powerful, even— than her tormentor. Besides, in a way I had knocked him out—he'd slipped on my vomit, after all.

"Weeks ago, I told you to trust me," I said. "If you had talked to me to begin with, I wouldn't have these bruises today."

Olympia moved away from the door, the gun shaking in her left hand. We followed her in, shutting and bolting the door. I took her gun and sat down on a white couch. My boots were making dirty little puddles on the salt-and-pepper rug, but Olympia didn't seem to notice.

"You know about Anton's code, right? You knew the feds were investigating Kystarnik's mob ties, but you let him have the run of your club, or at least let his chief enforcer have the run, because he'd bailed you out. What other favors are you doing for him?"

"Where is Rodney now?" Olympia didn't seem to have heard me. "Did he follow you here?"

"I don't know, and I don't care, but you apparently do. Don't tell me you're sleeping with him—that's so disgusting, I can't bear to think about it."

"If Anton and Rodney think I'm helping you," she said, "I might as well jump off the roof right now and end everything the easy way." Her words were melodramatic, but her tone was matter-of-fact.

"Hey, that's no way to talk," Mr. Contreras reproved her. "If you've gotten yourself in trouble and you're too scared to talk to the cops, talk to Vic here. She's helped people in worse trouble than you are in."

Olympia flicked a contemptuous glance at him: no one had ever been in worse trouble than she.

"So," I said, "Rodney telegraphed bank codes to Anton's overseas pals via the Body Artist's butt. What else? You slipped Petra extra money to pretend she hadn't noticed him copping a feel. Don't tell me you let him sleep with your staff."

"Not everyone thinks her body is as sacred as you seem to." Olympia shrugged. "If the money was right . . . It's a bad economy . . ."

I thought I might throw up again. My neighbor, as her meaning dawned on him, started a furious protest—directed against me—for letting Petra work in such an environment.

"Later," I said to him. "Rodney had the hots for Petra, so you kept her on, but I was too close to her for his comfort. He told you to give her the ax, right?"

She shook her head. "It wasn't like that."

"What was it like, then?"

I didn't keep the contempt out of my voice. She flinched but didn't speak.

"Let's see," I continued. "You provided Rodney with sex partners and set up Anton's message board. That doesn't seem like enough to offset a million dollars of debt. What else? Could it be—money laundering? Anton paid off your debts, right? So that while you used to bleed money like scarlet, your books are now white as wool. And, in return, for whatever businesses he's involved in where he doesn't want the feds to see his cash flow, he can funnel money through Club Gouge.

"No wonder your business began to take off last fall when the Body Artist appeared on your stage. You suddenly had money to burn. At least, it was Anton's money, but you could advertise in the important places, you could invest in that shiny set of plasma screens and that really cool sound system. What was the Artist's role in all this? Did she sleep with Rodney?"

Olympia made a sour face. "It was all I could do to get her to sit still when he was painting her. That was Anton's idea, when he first heard about her act. He thought it would be a good way to keep the feds from tracking his offshore accounts. Now that you've ruined that, I don't know what I'll do."

"Say it more plaintively," I suggested. "Make me care. Karen Buckley has disappeared, by the way. Any thoughts on where she'd go? On who would take her in?"

"That stupid girl who drools on her, I suppose," Olympia said.

"Rivka Darling? Think harder, dig deeper in your brain."

"I don't care," Olympia shouted. "She was a royal pain to work with, a fucking prima donna! If Anton hadn't told me—"

"Told you what?" I said when she bit the statement off. "What her real name was?"

"I *knew* it couldn't be Karen Buckley! What is it, really?"

"How did you know?"

She looked sulky but said, "You're not the only detective in Chicago. I saw Anton had some kind of hold on Karen, so I hired Brett Taylor to run a background check. He dug deep, but he couldn't find word one about her. And then he charged me a bundle!"

Brett Taylor was another solo op in town. Our paths crossed occasionally.

"What a happy little band you are at Club Gouge," I said. "Anton has you clamped in a vise. You spy on your performers so that you can hold any secrets you uncover over their heads—we won't use such an ugly word as *blackmail*. Who's Anton working for now, by the way?"

A sly smile tilted the corners of her mouth. "I couldn't say, although if I knew Karen Buckley's real name, it might trigger a memory or two."

"Can't tell you that." I got to my feet. "I'll be talking to Terry Finchley, the cop who's spearheading the Guaman murder investigation. I'll be sure to let him know he should look at your books. Not the books the IRS sees—the ones Anton's pet CPA, Owen Widermayer, keeps for you."

"You wouldn't! You can't go to the cops. Not when your own niece—"

"She's my cousin, not my niece. And if you try to smear her, it won't be Anton Kystarnik who puts a bullet through you."

"Yeah, it'll be me." Mr. Contreras startled both of us, he'd been silent so long. "You letting a horror show like that Rodney stick a hand on her and paying her—you're no better than a pimp yourself."

Olympia looked from Mr. Contreras to me. "If I tell you," she said, "if I help you, will you promise not to talk to this cop, this Finchley?"

"Of course not: I'm a licensed investigator. I could lose my license if I covered up a crime, especially one like laundering money for the mob." I moved to the door.

"I'll call Officer Finchley myself," she said boldly. "I'll tell him I just found out that Anton was using my club as a front."

"And he'll believe you because he's such a gullible guy. Especially if you wear that black thing that shows off your cleavage," I suggested.

She held out her hands, beseeching, sister to sister. "You could help me," she pleaded. "You could tell him you discovered the discrepancy when you were investigating this Guaman murder. And when you brought it to my attention—"

"Your cooked books are connected to the Guaman murder? Is that what Chad and Nadia were arguing about?" I stopped with my hand on the knob, my jaw gaping in astonishment. Was that what had been in Chad's black mitt—some microchip with Olympia's accounting data on it?

"What do you mean, my cooked books?" she protested belatedly. "As for Chad and Nadia, they were just a couple of fucked-up people who came to the club. And that's all you'll get from me. Unless you back me up when you talk to your tame cop."

39

Girlie Mags—and *Fortune*

As soon as we were in the elevator, Mr. Contreras tore into me.

"Why didn't you tell me that woman was letting some scumbag put his filthy hands on Peewee? Why didn't she tell me herself? She shoulda known I'd help her out if she got in a jam."

I put an arm around him.

"Darling, the only reason we didn't tell you is because we love you. What good would it do either of us if you were in prison for murder, even if you killed a scumbag who wouldn't be missed?"

He let himself be mollified at the suggestion that I thought he was tough enough to kill someone who bothered Petra. He drove me to the store, helped me push my shopping cart, didn't fight me over the bill even though he'd put a few items of his own in the cart.

"Guess I can call that payment for chauffeuring you, doll."

I needed to be in motion, but I was so exhausted by the outing that I had to lie down when we got home. I let Mr. Contreras put my chicken in the oven to roast, let him make me an ice pack to put on my sore stomach while he settled down in my living room with the dogs.

I tried to relax, but I kept replaying my conversation with Olympia.

She was afraid of Anton, but who wouldn't be? She seemed especially afraid that he would know that I'd been to see her. I felt a grudging sympathy. When I met Anton last night, I hadn't been sure I'd be alive today. In fact, if Tim and Marty hadn't come along, I might well not be.

The ice had melted through my Ace bandage, and my stomach was wet and cold. A counter-irritant to take my mind off the pain. I rolled to a sitting position and unwrapped the bandage.

Nadia had kept painting Allie's face surrounded by the same design that was on Chad's body armor. If Rodney and Anton had been using the Body Artist as a message board, maybe Nadia had been doing the same thing. She was writing about her sister, that was definite. But the rest of the message was obscure. There was a connection to Chad's body armor, but was it to the secret object he might have brought back with him from Iraq? Or was it to Chad himself, or to his massacred squad?

I thought of the porn magazines I'd taken from under Mona Vishneski's bed, the magazines Chad had tucked away so Mom wouldn't see them. Maybe Allie had posed in one of them and Chad was blackmailing the Guaman family. The magazines were at my office.

I got to my feet, put on a dry shirt, pulled on a sweater over it—a big, loose one that didn't require me to wriggle and struggle—and went to the living room. Mr. Contreras was dozing on the couch. I thought about slipping out without waking him on the theory that it was better to apologize than to explain, but we'd had too many skirmishes over the years about my secretive nature. And I was too weak and sore to fight my friends along with my enemies.

When I woke my neighbor, he didn't want to go back out in the cold and snow, and who could blame him? He argued that the magazines could wait until morning, but when I said I'd call Petra, ask her to stop at the office and find what I needed, he grumped to his feet.

"You ain't sticking Peewee's head in another tiger trap."

"There's nothing dangerous about going to my office," I objected.

"Trust me, if you send little Petra there to get a magazine for you, chances are someone's put a bomb in it."

"So you'd rather my head got blown off?" I was half teasing, half hurt.

"Don't give me those puppy-dog eyes," he growled. "All the years I been knowing you, I been begging you to keep yourself safe, and you ain't paid one minute of heed to me. I'm just asking you to take better care of the kid than you do of yourself. Look at you—bruises on your hand, your stomach, would make your own mother faint—"

"You're right." Gabriella used to beg me the same as Mr. Contreras when my cousin Boom-Boom and I ran into danger. *Cuore mio,* spare me more grief than my life has already held.

I bit my lip. But I still wanted to look at those magazines. The old man nodded, grimly pleased that his words had hit home. He started the slow process of pulling on his boots and his coat while I set the oven timer for the chicken. We took the dogs for company—the walker wasn't coming for another couple of hours.

At my office, Tessa was working on some immense steel thing. While I went into my files, Mr. Contreras pulled up a stool to watch her. Tessa doesn't usually tolerate an audience, but Mr. Contreras was a machinist in his working life, and she respects his advice on tools.

Chad had stuffed his girlie pix inside a copy of *Fortune,* and I'd left them bundled together when I put them into the file. The issue dated to before the economy's collapse: there was an article on the high demand for luxury goods and the way you could make the middle class feel they were part of the hyper-wealthy elite. Another teaser claimed that *Fortune* had tested the iPhone against all comers. A third asked, "Will a change of owner change Achilles' fortunes?"

I had removed the girlie magazines and was thumbing through them looking for Alexandra Guaman's face, wondering if I would recognize it floating airbrushed above improbable breasts, when I did a double take on the Achilles headline. I had read it online when I was looking up background on Tintrey.

I went back to *Fortune* to reread the story. Tintrey had acquired Achilles, the maker of body armor, when it became obvious that the war in Iraq was going to last for a long time. Achilles had been developing nanotechnology, using particles I'd never heard of and wasn't sure I could pronounce. Inorganic, fullerene-like nanostructures. They apparently were "gallium-based," whatever that was, and stronger than steel. In a photograph of one of the particles blown up a few hundred times, the stuff looked pretty much like the cement they were pouring into potholes on the Kennedy Expressway.

Achilles had been losing money; R & D doesn't come cheap. *Fortune* had a lot to say about shortsighted corporate policy that let Wall Street's insatiable demand for current-quarter profits block long-term development strategies. Anyway, the long and the short of it was, Tintrey bought Achilles, which was bleeding red ink too fast to fight off a hostile takeover bid.

Jarvis MacLean's first order of business was a campaign to sell Achilles shields to the Department of Defense. Some Achilles staffers, who spoke on condition of anonymity, expressed concern that Tintrey was marketing a product that wasn't ready for full-scale production. Yet the new owners had spent almost ten million dollars on building a PR campaign.

"When you're making a new product, why worry about graphic design? Why not put the money into hiring a good science team?" asked one former member of the R & D staff.

Indeed, Tintrey has been downsizing the R & D division since acquiring Achilles. "They have a great product in place. We need to focus now on getting it into the hands of our troops, not on endlessly refining it," said Gilbert Scalia.

As head of Tintrey's Enduring Freedom Division, it's Scalia's job to outfit the nine thousand Tintrey employees in Iraq and to provide matériel to the U.S. Armed Forces deployed around the world.

A year after acquiring Achilles, Tintrey has already changed the profit picture at the division. Maybe the new publicity did the trick.

The magazine showed some of the PR materials, including the Achilles logo: a pink-and-gray fleur-de-lis. This was the design on the black mitt I'd found in Chad Vishneski's duffel. And it was the design Nadia Guaman had been painting on the Body Artist.

I read the article through carefully twice, curled up on the couch in my client corner with the dogs at my feet. I learned a bit about the structure of fullerene nanoparticles, at least, I learned they were named for Buckminster Fuller, but not much else.

The article had been important to Chad Vishneski, important enough that he kept it alongside his girlie magazines. And he'd cut holes in one of the armor mitts. But why he'd done it would have to wait until he regained consciousness—or Sanford Rieff at Cheviot labs found out a dramatic secret about the shield.

Neither John Vishneski nor Tim Radke had ever heard Chad talk about the armor. But Chad's squad had been killed around him: that was when he lost the equilibrium that carried him through his first deployments. Maybe he blamed Tintrey for the failure of their armor in protecting his men and was savaging their equipment as a way to vent his feelings of helplessness.

I called Vishneski. He'd had to go to a jobsite, a building far enough along that they were working on the interior, but he said Chad's status continued to improve.

"The docs are all pretty optimistic. He hasn't been speaking anymore, at least, he hadn't before I left this morning, but he's restless in a good way, they say. The police have been around some, wanting to know if he's well enough to go back to prison, but that Dr. Herschel, she's a pistol, isn't she? She told them where to get off."

I silently blew Lotty a kiss. "No strangers have come around to try to see him?"

"Not that I know of. But I'll talk to Mona. Of course, we don't know who his friends are, so they'd all be strangers to us. But, like I said, some of my buddies are hanging around. They'll let me know if anyone comes calling."

That was one less worry, at least for now. When he'd hung up, I started looking for Rodney Treffer. He wasn't in the morgue, so I called around to the hospitals on the near North Side. I hadn't heard back from Finchley or Milkova. And I wanted to find out how much time I had before Rodney was fit enough to come after me. I said I was Sunny Treffer, searching for my brother. He was supposed to meet me for breakfast this morning and never showed, and given his history of psychosis, I was worried whether he'd had some breakdown and been brought in.

I was lucky with the third place I called. The ER charge nurse told me Rodney had injured himself in a fall but didn't seem to be having a psychotic episode when he was with them. They'd kept him overnight for observation and discharged him an hour ago. He'd had a concussion and some brain swelling, but they'd done a second CT scan before they released him; the swelling had gone down.

"You're his sister? Make sure he rests for the next several days. He shouldn't be out on this ice where he could slip and fall again."

"I'll do my best to keep him off the streets," I promised. "Did Mr. Kystarnik pay his bill?"

The charge nurse transferred me to the billing department, where a service rep said someone had stopped by with Rodney and paid cash, all twenty-three thousand dollars that were owed for his emergency care.

I gave an embarrassed titter. "I need to know who paid for my brother. He . . . Well, he's not good with bills, and I'm kind of responsible . . ."

The rep misunderstood me. "Don't worry about that, honey. Our cashier looked at the money, it wasn't counterfeit."

"But who paid for him?"

I heard her clicking at her keyboard. "His friend said the receipt should be made out to your brother."

"Did he give his own address?" I asked. "On Bobolink Road in Highland Park?"

She clicked her teeth. "No, he said he was at 1005 North Inscape Drive in Deerfield."

"Oh, dear," I said. "That's his ex-wife's address. Well, it can't be helped. Thanks for looking after him. He probably didn't tell the doctors about his risperidone, either. You should add that to his chart."

The helpful rep said she'd pass a note on to the doctor who'd treated my brother.

The address Rodney had given, on Inscape Drive, belonged to Anton Kystarnik and/or Owen Widermayer at Rest EZ. As his worried sister, I hoped Rodney would stay there, firmly put, for a month, but I was more afraid he might be looking for me and for Karen Buckley's computer.

40

Karen, Revealed

Mr. Contreras and I were climbing into my Mustang when a strange truck pulled into the parking lot. I reached reflexively for my gun, but Petra bounded from the passenger seat, as lively as a new puppy. Mitch broke from me to rush to her side, while Staff Sergeant Jepson climbed down from the driver's seat, followed by Tim Radke, who'd been squeezed into the back.

"Afternoon, ma'am, sir," Jepson called to Mr. Contreras and me. "You on your way out? We spent the day on your gal's computer, and Tim thinks he's got a lot of it sorted out."

I explained that I needed to get the dogs home for the dog walker but invited them to follow us north. Mr. Contreras enthusiastically seconded the motion, mentioning my chicken. "Big enough for five, right, doll, when we make some fettuccine."

At home, Jepson helped me check around the building to make sure Rodney or his minions weren't lurking.

"So, Vic, Tim totally hacked into this computer. He's amazing. You should hire him!" Petra yelled as I made my painful way up the three flights of stairs.

"It wasn't cheap," Tim warned me. "I had to download some pretty expensive software to come up with her password—none of Chad's dad's ideas worked."

"I told him to go for it," Petra sang out cheerily.

"Out of curiosity, little chickadee, how much is expensive?"

"Uh, thirty-two hundred dollars," Tim mumbled.

"Thirty-two hundred, hmm? So—at fifteen dollars an hour—well, rounding up to give you the benefit of the doubt—that would be two hundred free hours of work you can give me, Petra."

"But, Vic," her big eyes opening so wide her lashes brushed her brows, "I knew this was important. And I didn't want to wake you up after you got injured."

"No, Peetie, that was thoughtful. That's why I'm rounding your salary up as a thank-you. You see, you're working for me. I'm paying the bills. And I probably know a vendor who could get me a better deal on software than you can."

Petra glowered at me. "You're not serious. I can't afford—"

"Then you need to learn to think twice, or even three times, before committing me to debt, Petra."

I looked at her seriously for a beat. "I will let you off the hook this time. But if you do such a thing again, I will hold you responsible for paying for it. Clear?"

"I told you I wasn't a robot—"

"Clear?"

"Oh, all right!" She stomped back down the stairs.

Tim Radke, who'd been standing by uncomfortably while we argued, said he thought he should pay for the software, since he was the one who talked Petra into buying it.

"No, we're cool on this. Petra just needs help curbing her magnanimous impulses." I headed on up the stairs and left Radke to follow Petra back to Mr. Contreras's place.

Jake Thibaut was on his way out as I reached the third floor. I hadn't seen him for a couple of days, and he was surprised by my painful progress upward.

"Your hand bothering you?" For a bass player, an injured hand was worrying enough to cause a limp.

"Not so much. I'm just tired. See you before you fly out?"

"Not if it means looking at something gruesome stuck into your body."

To my surprise, I found myself fighting back tears. "I'll wrap myself in gauze, head to foot, so that only my eyes and mouth show."

"Hey, hey, just teasing, V.I., just teasing." He brushed my wet eyes with a callused fingertip. "I'm a bass player, nothing grosses me out. Except blood. Can't explain that one. We have one last rehearsal tonight, and I'm just on my way to buy food for the group. Are you free tomorrow, four-ish? They're not picking me up until six."

He pulled me to him and kissed me, and I tried to translate the pain in my abdomen into passion on my lips. As he held me, I heard the dog walker arrive, the dogs' yelps of pleasure, and then my neighbor start up the stairs with Tim, Staff Sergeant Jepson, and Petra.

Jake murmured that he'd leave me to cope with my circus on my own and went on his way.

Inside my apartment, Tim opened up Karen's computer. He showed me what happened when he logged on to her site. We got the message that the site was down. Then he typed commands onto the screen itself. Lines of equations began to scroll downward.

"Here's the command to block content from the site," he froze the screen and pointed to a line of text. I could see the words "respect," "for," "the," and "dead" separated by strings of code.

"Now, watch this." He typed another set of commands. Green text scrolled down the screen once more. He typed another command line, and suddenly the Body Artist's website was on the computer in front of us.

I forgot my sore belly. "How'd you do that?"

"It's a clone." Tim tried not to grin, tried to be casual—Aramis Ramírez quickly doffing his hat after back-to-back homers. "That way, whoever is blocking the original site doesn't know we can access it."

"But who is blocking it?"

He shrugged. "Can't tell you that. The server is in Olathe, Kansas. When I talked to one of their techies this afternoon, the best he could tell me is that the commands weren't coming from *this* machine. They're coming from Baghdad. But whether they start there or just are being bounced through there, whoever is doing it is pretty sophisticated."

"Your old buddies?" Jepson asked.

"USAC-NOEW?" Radke grimaced. "They could, but why would they? I didn't see anything pertaining to military ops in here."

"USAC-NOEW?" I said. "Sounds like a cat in pain."

Tim laughed.

"U.S. Army Computer Network Operations and Electronic War-fare," he translated. "You know the Army. It's all alphabet soup."

"Of course, they're not the only big outfit in Baghdad," I said. "There's also Tintrey."

"Them and a hundred other jackals." Marty Jepson was suddenly angry. "I'm so sick of those damned contractors, those private armies! I lost two good buddies who had to go out shotgun to protect one of their farking CEOs."

"Yeah, man, they're total scum," Radke agreed. "But why would they care about this stripper's website?"

"She's not a stripper." Petra started to protest, then looked doubtful. "Maybe I shouldn't be sticking up for her if she really is, like, a drug dealer or something."

I scrolled carefully through the images looking for Nadia's paintings. "We know what the codes that Rodney was using mean, but what was Nadia trying to tell us about Alexandra?"

Petra and the other two men crowded around my shoulders as Tim enlarged various parts of Nadia's drawings. The last one she'd painted had shown her sister with flames sprouting out of her head.

"She was killed by an IED," I said. "I suppose the fire symbolizes that."

"Could well be, ma'am," Jepson said, his voice very dry. "Where was this incident?"

"On the way to the Baghdad airport, her boss told me. Tim, are there any other files in here that we can look at?"

"What are you looking for?"

"I don't know. Anything." I flung my hands open in frustration. "Where the Artist might have gone to earth. What she knew about Olympia and Rodney's business. What she thought of Alexandra Guaman—the two had a brief affair the summer before Alexandra deployed."

Tim did some more keyboard work and brought up a list of all Karen's folders. She had virtually no documents except drafts of scripts for the commentary she made during her shows and outlines for possible future shows. Any financial records, or letters, or even e-mails, didn't reside on this machine. We should all be so careful about our privacy, I suppose, but it felt eerily like walking through an empty house—like walking through Karen Buckley's, or Frannie Pindero's, empty apartment. She might carry a vast burden of emotional baggage, but physically she traveled light across the landscape.

"Her videos, then?" I said. "What's in those folders that you didn't see on her DVDs?"

That folder bulged, of course. Movies are very byte hungry, and something only five minutes long might use a megabyte of memory.

Tim got up so that I could sit at the controls. At first, he and the others watched as I browsed through Karen's junk footage, early shots of herself painting her own body, done with mirrors, in what I assumed was the darkened front room Petra and I had found yesterday afternoon.

After a bit, though, the two vets wandered off to join Mr. Contreras and Petra in my kitchen. The dog walker rang my bell. I sent Petra downstairs, with Staff Sergeant Jepson as protection. I kept watching videos as they came back up with the animals.

I saw footage of Leander Marvelle and Kevin Piuma dancing without their burkas. They moved beautifully—a marvel, a feather; they'd named themselves well—in a bare space that I guessed was the Columbia College rehearsal room.

Karen had taped herself with Vesta. They were in bed together. Vesta murmured something, low-voiced, out of mike range, and then sprang to her feet and ordered Karen to leave.

"Take your camera with you, Karen. And your clothes, your toothbrush—all those things. I don't want you back here."

And Karen hadn't argued. She sat up in bed, her face as impassive a mask as when it was covered with paint. I saw her naked torso, her hand stretched out. She wasn't beseeching Vesta but holding a small remote control and turning off the camera.

I looked for footage during the weeks Nadia had been visiting Club Gouge. I found a scene in Rivka's bedroom with Rivka demanding to know what Nadia meant to Karen.

A chance to explore the world of art. She's a tormented soul, little Rivulet. Don't torment your own soul over her. And certainly not over me.

I moved on to other files. And came upon a crucifix with a doll's head, black plastic hair tied around Jesus' hands. That was the cross Nadia had kept over her bed.

Karen said, *You've never done this before, have you?* Her voice held cool amusement, no tenderness.

Wherever she'd placed her camera, it wasn't quite close enough for good focus. I could tell Nadia was naked, but not what her face was registering. Her response to Karen was so soft that the mike didn't pick it up.

Why did you hustle me so hard after the show, then? Karen said. *Just out of curiosity.*

A long tick of silence, except for the rustling of the bedclothes, and then Nadia said, *You knew my sister. Alexandra.*

I meet a lot of people, Nadia.

In Michigan, at a music festival. Maybe she told you to call her Allie; that's her pet name at home.

Oh, yes. Beautiful girl, totally ashamed of herself. Are you the go-between? Is she ready to come out? Or did she tell you to use me for your own sexual experiments? If so, try this.

It wasn't clear what Karen did next, but it hurt. Nadia gave a sharp yelp and sat up, wrapping a sheet around her shoulders.

Alexandra is dead. She was killed in Iraq.

Do you want me to stand at attention and play the "Star-Spangled Banner"? Karen's cool tone didn't change.

Do you have any feelings at all, for anyone besides yourself?

I figure chicks like you, emoting all over the place, have so many exhausting feelings that there isn't room for mine. Karen was being sarcastic, but I thought there was an undercurrent in her tone—anger? bitterness?

If you had a sister like Allie and she was murdered, you might not be so cold.

Karen sat up in bed so fast that the camera recorded only a blur. I heard the slap, hand on face. *Fuck you, bitch. I* had *someone like Allie who was murdered. So stop bleating at me like a sentimental sheep.*

I hit PAUSE, startled. Did she mean Anton's daughter, Zina? Was that a person Karen/Frannie had felt close to? If that was the case, then maybe Zina's overdose had been someone else's deliberate work. Or maybe Karen/Frannie just thought an OD was an act of murder. Impossible to know.

I clicked PLAY, and the recording began again. Nadia was apologizing. *But my sister was tormented, she was hounded, she wrote it in her journal. All because someone where she worked in Baghdad found out that she liked, she preferred—that women—*

That she was a dyke. Why can't you just say it?

Don't use that word about Allie! Who told them? Was it you? Because you were so angry with her for not returning your calls?

Karen sat up and began pulling on clothes—sweater, jeans, boots.

Nadia, you want someone to be at fault because the sister you adored so much is dead. But if she was a lesbian, people in Baghdad would have known. Believe me, I did not say one word to one person about my week with her. She was of no interest to me once she made it clear that I was of no interest to her.

For once, Karen spoke in a real voice, someone who was feeling the words she was saying. Or at least someone who acted as though she felt them.

The clip ended there, abruptly, as had the segment with Vesta. There was no way of knowing whether Nadia, like Vesta, had realized Karen/Frannie was recording her.

41

A Clutch of Apartment Raiders, Plus Dogs

Dinner was a success, at least for my guests. Petra had recovered from last night's trauma, aided by her military escort, and they, in turn, seemed to be thawing in her ebullience. My neighbor was beaming happily. Mr. Contreras wanted to see Petra settle down with "some nice boy," and Marty Jepson and Tim Radke both fit the bill.

I sat at the end of the table, smiling, nodding, wondering where Alexandra Guaman's journal was. I had played the video the Body Artist had recorded with Nadia three times. Alexandra felt so hounded and tormented that she wrote about it in her journal. Nadia had said that. Which meant Nadia had seen the journal. Which meant that whoever ransacked Nadia's apartment might have been looking for it.

"Julian Urbanke," I suddenly said out loud.

Everyone at the table stared at me, until Petra said, "Vic, there's no one with a name like that in my family, unless it's someone on the Warshawski side. Marty was asking who in my mom's family had been in the service."

My aunt's ancestors had mostly been in the Confederate Army. I wondered how the veterans would react to that.

"Sorry," I said. "I was trying to remember the name of the man who lived across the hall from Nadia Guaman. Her apartment was ripped apart, the pictures even taken down from the walls. A couple of days after she died, someone took her computer and all her discs. Urbanke had a key to her apartment. He seemed to have had a crush on Nadia— maybe he helped himself to Alexandra's journal, thinking it was Nadia's, before the home-wrecking crew arrived."

"What would you like us to do, ma'am?" Jepson asked.

"Marty, it's so funny to hear you call Vic 'ma'am.'" Petra laughed. "She may be older than us, but she's not, like, a hundred. Just call her 'Vic,' like everybody else does."

"Darling, I love the staff sergeant's impeccable manners," I said. "Who knows, maybe some of them will rub off on you and me."

I looked at Jepson, who was staring straight ahead, blushing.

"I'd like to go over to Urbanke's place," I continued, "see if he has the diary."

Petra's eyes sparkled. "All of us? A midnight raid—"

She stopped, remembering last night's fight. The muscles in her face tightened. "Vic," she said, "why don't you just call and ask him."

"Too easy to brush people off on the phone," I said.

"You're not going to beat him up, are you?" She was pleating her napkin by now.

"Of course she ain't," Mr. Contreras grumbled. "If she had any sense, she'd stay right here."

He turned to me. "If it wasn't for these boys here riding to your rescue last night, you'd be dead and in the morgue right now."

"I'm going to bring Peppy; if Urbanke tries to attack me, he'll trip over her and fall, and then she'll smooch him into confessing." I stood too quickly for my abdomen and ended up clutching the edge of the table.

"Uh, ma'am?" Jepson said. "I mean, Vic. I'd, uh, it would be a pleasure to visit this man Urbanke with you."

Well, if he was going to put it like that, implying that the Marines had a sense of duty even if no one else understood it, then Mr. Contreras had to join in, which meant Tim Radke and Petra could hardly stay behind.

Petra bent over Mitch, hands on his jowls. "You want to come, too, don't you, Mitch? Just in case."

After Petra and Tim finished the washing up, we laced up our winter boots and zipped up our coats and went back into the night, dogs and all. I wondered if any other detective on the planet had ever traveled with this kind of entourage. Sam Spade, with dogs, cousin, old man, and Marines—kind of like calling on a suspect with a circus parade in tow.

My fellow performers were full of enthusiasm. Jepson took me and the dogs in his truck; Tim Radke followed in my car with Petra and Mr. Contreras.

The heater in Jepson's pickup was as old as the shocks, and my feet turned numb as we bounced over ruts. I grabbed the edges of the seat, trying to minimize the jolts to my sore muscles.

"Sorry about that, ma'am. Vic, I mean. Kind of like the roads in Baghdad, just without the gunfire and the IEDs and so on. Although this part of town, I guess we could get some gunfire," he added as we moved into the grimmer, gang-ridden streets west of Western.

We got to Nadia's building ahead of the others. While we waited, we talked about ways and means.

"I don't want all seven of us barging in on Urbanke," I said. "Why don't we let Mr. Contreras and Petra wait in Nadia's apartment with the dogs while you and I talk to the guy."

It was hard to persuade Mr. Contreras that this was a good idea—he hadn't come along just to sit on the sidelines and cheer for me, thanks very much. In the end, Tim offered to babysit Petra and the dogs while my neighbor and the staff sergeant and I went into Urbanke's.

A bit of good luck: he was home. A bit of bad luck: he remembered me and did not wish to see me.

"You're not a cop," he squawked over the intercom. "You can't make me talk to you."

"Right, Mr. Urbanke," I bellowed at my end. "We don't need to talk. We just want to ask you about Alexandra's journal."

Another bit of good luck: someone came out of the building just as I was debating whether to open the outer door on my own. The man looked at us suspiciously, and I grinned happily.

"We're the new tenants in 3E. Thanks! The key they gave us for the outside door doesn't work."

"No dogs allowed in this building," he said.

"They're not moving in, just helping my friends set up housekeeping. We'll see you."

My parade swept past him and up the stairs to the third floor. I opened the door to Nadia's place with my picklocks, then knocked on Urbanke's. Petra stood in Nadia's doorway, watching. Mitch and Peppy were behind her, trying to push between her legs. When Urbanke didn't answer his door, Jepson began kicking it, and Mitch started to bark. In about thirty seconds, we'd drawn a crowd, people from two of the other apartments on the floor and a woman bending over the railing on the fourth floor.

"No dogs allowed in here." "Who are they? Someone call the cops." "Call the police and let them rob us in our beds? Call the building management." "The building management? Don't be insane—they still haven't fixed my broken window." "Because you're three months behind on—"

"Mr. Urbanke has been really helpful in looking after my niece's home since Nadia was murdered." I cut into the flow. He has a key to her apartment, he took her cat. But he also took some of her other things—I'm sure for safekeeping! Security is terrible in this building, and he didn't want anyone to steal her jewelry. But I need to get it back to give to my sister. Nadia's mother is so overcome with grief, she can't come herself. So she asked me to stop by and collect her jewelry."

"That's a lie!" Urbanke had opened his door just enough that we could see his nose and mouth. "She's no aunt. She was going through Nadia's apartment herself, pretending to be a detective."

"I saw you go into the girl's apartment the day after she died," a woman on the upper landing said to Urbanke, fortunately not to me. "Poor Nadia, you were always looking at her like—like this dog here looking at a bone." She pointed at Mitch, who had pushed past my cousin and was nosing around the crack in Urbanke's door. "And then she's barely dead, and you let yourself into her place. How you even got a key to her door, that's what I want to know."

"She gave it to me," he said.

Mitch suddenly yelped, a piercing shriek of pain. A white ball of fur bolted between his legs, crossed the hall, and ran into Nadia's place. The dog's nose was bleeding.

"What'd you do to my dog?" Mr. Contreras demanded as Urbanke opened the door, shouting, "Ixcuina! Chain up that vicious dog or I'll shoot him. Ixcuina! Ixcuina, kitty, kitty!"

Urbanke ran after the cat, tripping over Peppy, who was standing in Nadia's doorway barking her head off. Petra was doubled over with laughter.

I grabbed her shoulders. "Get those dogs under control! Now! This is an investigation, not Comedy Central."

I didn't wait for her response but took the opportunity to go into Urbanke's apartment. Jepson and Radke followed me. And Mr. Contreras. And two of the people from the building. And Mitch.

Urbanke lived in three shabbily furnished rooms, with a layout similar to Nadia's. Jepson and Radke went through the rooms as if it were a terrorist hideout in Iraq, crouching, peering around the corners. After a moment, Jepson called to me from Urbanke's bedroom. They'd found a shrine to Nadia that he had created inside his closet.

Photographs he'd shot of her when she didn't know he was watching her. A few pieces of her artwork that he'd filched. We didn't find her computer or any of her missing DVDs, but there was a red-covered notebook, propped up inside an open papier-mâché box, with roses and candles around it.

The notebook was open. I bent over to read it.

September 2. Leaving Istanbul for Baghdad. It's so hot that we all sit unmoving, waiting for them to close the plane doors and turn on the air-conditioning so we can breathe again.

"Is that what we were looking for, ma'am?" Jepson asked.

I nodded, breathless, and lifted the notebook carefully as if it might disintegrate with careless handling. The interior of the box was decorated with paintings of Alexandra Guaman—Alexandra in a coffin, arms crossed over her chest, tears like chandelier drops falling from her eyes. Alexandra kneeling in front of the Virgin, who was placing a crown of roses on her head. Alexandra in heaven, reaching her hands down to Nadia, Clara, and Ernest.

"Clara should have this box," I said to Jepson. "She's the surviving sister."

He helped me place the journal back into its papier-mâché container and said he'd carry it for me. Before heading home, I went looking for Urbanke. I found him in Nadia's kitchen, trying to coax Ixcuina, the attack cat, out from behind the refrigerator, where she'd taken refuge.

"I'm taking the diary," I told him. "It wasn't Nadia's, by the way; it was her older sister's."

He looked up at me. "I know. I read it. The sister was perverse. But the diary mattered to Miss Nadia, and I am protecting her memory. Or I was *trying* to protect her from people like you who want to drag her through the mud. I could sue you for breaking into my home. And for having a wild dog."

I smiled. "Your neighbors are worrying now about whether their daughters are safe around you. If I were you, I'd lay low for a bit, not bring any lawsuits where you might need a witness to describe what happened tonight. Their version and yours are likely to be a million or so miles apart."

An ugly expression crossed his face, but before he could speak I added, "Another thing. I wouldn't mention Alexandra Guaman's journal to anyone. To a neighbor, to your children, even to your pastor. We don't know what the people who trashed this apartment were looking for. Maybe it was Nadia's computer. But maybe it was this diary. If they learn that you've read it, you will need the charmed nine lives of this cat here to escape."

He tried to stare me down, but my words had taken the stuffing out of him. He turned back to the cat, looking a little pale. It made me think he'd already told someone about the journal. *The sister, she was perverse*, he would have hissed to a coworker, trying to make himself the center of attention.

I couldn't worry about his problems. I just hoped he was embarrassed enough by his neighbors' reaction to his actions that he wouldn't complain publicly about my taking the journal.

I left him to Ixcuina and rejoined my circus in the hallway. Mr. Contreras had struck up an acquaintance with the woman from the floor above, both of them clicking their teeth over the dangers of living in the city, the dangers of apartment life where you couldn't know what kind of fiend might be renting right next door to you!

"Look after your beautiful granddaughter," she told him, nodding her head toward Petra when she saw we were leaving, which delighted Mr. Contreras so much he repeated it several times on our way down the stairs.

42

A Love Story/A Horror Story

When we got home, the two vets followed us inside. Staff Sergeant Jepson seemed to think I needed extra support on my way up the stairs. I wondered if he saw me as elderly and frail or mature and exciting, and then I remembered Kystarnik's thug calling me a dried-up cougar the previous night and felt myself blushing.

Jake and his friends were still rehearsing. They were working on Berio's *Sequenze,* discordant, not to everyone's taste. Still, I resented it when Tim Radke muttered, "Sounds like that guy Urbanke's cat is dying in there," and Petra burst out laughing.

"Vic, you totally rock! How did you even know he'd *built* a shrine to Nadia?" my cousin demanded when we were inside my place.

I bent over the piano bench and slipped Allie's journal inside my score of *Don Giovanni.* "I didn't. Lucky guess. Even luckier was when the cat ran for cover."

The adrenaline wave I'd been riding began to recede, leaving me so overcome with fatigue that I had to hold on to the piano for support. I guess the answer to my question was "elderly and frail."

"That wasn't lucky!" Mr. Contreras huffed. "I have half a mind to report him to Animal Control, keeping a cat like that. Wild animal, it attacked my dog."

"Just don't let them see the poor, abused victim," I said, collapsing on the piano bench.

Mitch grinned up at me, red tongue lolling, to show he knew he was a con artist—and what was I going to do about it.

I looked at Petra and the two vets. "Thank you all for your help tonight, but I need to get some rest."

"Hey, no way," my cousin said. "We didn't go through all that so you could go to bed. We're reading Allie's journal before we leave."

I pushed myself to my feet and propelled Petra into the kitchen. "You're not a child, and I'm not your nanny, so don't start whining and cajoling. Looking at a piece of evidence in a murder investigation is not the same thing as begging for a new bike."

"I told you when I agreed to work for you, I won't be bullied." Petra scowled.

"And I told you I was running a detective agency. If you want to be part of it, please respect the fact that we are working for people who often are in desperate need. You had one assignment tonight, to hold on to the dogs. You blew that. Mitch roared around Urbanke's apartment and was a major nuisance until Tim grabbed his leash and got him under control."

"If Mitch hadn't gotten away, he wouldn't have freaked out Urbanke's cat and we wouldn't have gotten in to find that creepy shrine. I did you a favor."

"You'll get your Distinguished Service Medal first thing in the morning," I said drily. "In the meantime, if you want to keep working for me you can't be playing games. And you can't ignore your assignments because they're dull, or because you're flirting with Tim Radke."

"I don't believe you," Petra cried. "Is this about you being jealous because I'm young and attractive?"

I was so angry I jammed my hands into my pockets to keep from slapping her. "Weren't you the one who chewed me out yesterday for teasing you about your youthful attractiveness? Your looks are off limits, but my age isn't?"

She glared at me, but asked, "Am I fired?"

"Not tonight. But you are not captain of this expedition."

I went back to the living room, wondering how long it would be before I ended up in the Dwight women's prison for murdering Petra.

Jepson and Radke got to their feet. "We'll take off now, ma'am," the staff sergeant said. "Thank you for dinner."

"Thanks for coming along tonight," I said. "I couldn't have done it without you."

Jepson flushed. "A pleasure to help you, ma'am. Vic."

"What is this? A recruiting commercial for the Marines?" Tim punched his friend in the ribs, and added to Petra, who was trailing behind me, "We're going to Plotzky's to catch the last period of the Hawks game. Want to come along?"

My cousin smiled warmly at the two young men, glowered at me to make sure I knew I was not forgiven, and bounded out of the apartment with them. It was harder to move Mr. Contreras and the dogs, but they finally left as well.

I moved slowly through my nighttime routine. Anton didn't care about the Body Artist's website anymore, or so he said. He wanted papers he thought I had. Perhaps he'd meant Alexandra's journal. But if that was the case, it meant he'd somehow hooked up with Tintrey, because Alexandra's journal was of interest to them. Even if he was only looking for it as a potential way to blackmail Jarvis MacLean, it still meant that somehow, in the last two days, he'd learned about Tintrey's interest in the Guaman family.

September 2. Leaving Istanbul for Baghdad.

Even after I was lying exhausted in my bed, the words kept running through my head. I saw Alexandra Guaman, her dark curls damp with sweat. She'd taken the overseas job because the money would help Clara go to a good college. At least, that's what Clara believed. What else? What had happened to her? Why, with no experience as a convoy driver, had she left the safety of the Green Zone to drive a truck to the Baghdad airport?

Around one in the morning, I finally got out of bed and took the journal from between the pages of my *Don Giovanni* score. I curled up in my big armchair with it and a glass of my dwindling supply of Longrow.

September 7

Baghdad. I'm half in Iraq, half in Chicago. Everything is the same and everything is different. When I go to work in the morning, it's almost like I'm at home on a hot August day, except it's already 110. Everywhere you go there are soldiers with weapons, but inside the Tintrey building it's weirdly like being home. Same desks, same air-conditioning, same systems. People are friendly but cautious.

One of the older women in the office told us newbies never to leave the compound unless we're with soldiers or armed Tintrey personnel. No woman is safe from them, she says.

September 13

Everyone is nervous. None of us has been close to war before.

In our training before we left we were told, "We are a Team. As a Team, we will win! Stress, fatigue and terrorists cannot defeat a Team!"

When I read that to Nadia, she made a poster for me of the Tintrey Team, Mr. Scalia and Mr. MacLean behind big shields made of dollar bills. Ernest and I laughed so hard, we almost made ourselves sick. Ernest scanned it for me into the computer, but if I look at it I must be careful, everybody spies on everybody else. It's only because we're bored or lonely. Or scared. Even in the tiny apartment I share buried deep inside the compound, we hear the bombs.

At night in bed, I try not to remember my week in Michigan with Karen. Sometimes I can't help it—I go to her website, although I get no real glimpse of her, only the many masks she wears in public.

She is not worth my immortal soul—I must remember those words in times of temptation, Father Vicente said when he urged me to take this job. A chance to start over, he said, to leave your sinful tendencies in America and serve your country overseas. I thought, maybe he's right, and anyway, the money is so good! Clara is the smartest of the Guaman sisters, she deserves the chance to go to a good college. And I thought, maybe I can become a normal person if I'm far away, although, how could anyone become normal in this very un-normal place?

Everybody drinks a great deal. Even I, who used to have a glass of wine only on New Year's or my birthday, find myself drinking almost every night after work.

September 24

Mama calls twice a week. She is worried. But we are really not in danger inside our great marble compound. I didn't tell her that yesterday, I took a walk outside the compound. I went with Amani, who is one of our translators. A very serious young woman who wears the typical black covering of an Iraqi woman so you can only see part of her face. She speaks perfect English and perfect French. I trade her a few words in Spanish for a few words of Arabic.

Mama would be frightened to think of me outside the Green Zone, and why should I add to her fears? And Amani is so reliable. She made sure I was covered head to toe in one of her abayas so that we would not be targets, American and Arab side by side.

September 28

My roommates learned of my second trip into the city with

Amani and they screamed like ten-year-olds. Oh, Allie, how could you? And you put on her abaya? Weren't you afraid of germs?

Germs! I am afraid of bombs, but not of a woman's body. I thank you, Jesus, for sending me such silly girls to live with. They will not rouse any tendencies in me.

Father Vicente reminded me of the priests and nuns who wrestle with celibacy every day, sometimes every hour! Know you are not alone in your struggle. And find yourself a nice boy. You will meet plenty of young men in the middle of a war. Marry one of them, make a family. A family will cure you of your sinful desires.

I read on through the night. More trips into Baghdad with Amani. The two women went to art galleries or to outdoor markets, but never to see Amani's family—she couldn't let the neighbors know she worked for Americans or they might murder her little brothers for being related to a collaborator.

On Thanksgiving, during the boisterous celebrations inside the Green Zone, Alexandra got drunk and spent the night with someone named Jerry, one of the programmers in Tintrey's communications division.

November 26

I've been sick all day. Throwing up gin, and throwing up Jerry. I don't know which has made me sicker.

December 1

Have avoided Jerry all week. I think he told some of the other men—they look at me like a cat licking its lips over a wounded mouse. I pray I'm not pregnant.

December 9

Thanks to the Mother of God, my period arrived today. My

coworkers are all treating me as if I were a leper, I thought because of Jerry. But Mr. Mossbach, the head of my unit, took me aside today. "People are talking about you. You spend too much time with that Arab gal, and that means your teammates aren't sure they can trust you to be on Uncle Sam's side. Trust, Allie! We're a Team!"

So! Amani's neighbors may attack her family if they know she works with Americans. And my neighbors attack me because I drink coffee with Amani.

She calls me A'lia, an Arabic name. It means "exalted" or "noble." And Amani means "wishes" or "dreams," so I call her Desideria.

How can it be a sin to find more pleasure in her society than in that of silly girls or drunken boys? Of course, I have no sinful thoughts for her, only gratitude that I have found a friend in this strange country.

In January, Alexandra was transferred to another unit, to Achilles. My pulse beat faster: was this where her life intersected with Chad's? I didn't see any mention of his name. Her family, calls to her mother, e-mails to Nadia, Allie's own private wrestling over her friendship with Amani. *My desire is for my Desideria,* she wrote more than once, and then crossed out and recrossed out the sentence.

The men in Tintrey's operation outnumbered women by about ten to one, so there was constant pressure on Alexandra to date. After her Thanksgiving date with Jerry, she avoided, or tried to avoid, being alone with any of the men after work hours.

Perhaps Father Vicente is right, that all sex outside marriage is sinful and therefore without pleasure. But my roommates both have male lovers and seem to have no unhappiness. They tease me and call me the Ice Queen. As long as I do my job well and give no cause for complaint at work, surely all will be well.

February 2

Amani came to find me this afternoon. She was waiting in the shadows of the building until she found me alone in the supply room.

"A'lia, how have I offended you?" she asked, her beautiful dark eyes full of tears.

"Desideria, mi corazón, how could you ever offend me?" I said. "It is only because of my boss. He ordered me to stay away from you."

Then she asked what my words meant, not "boss," my Spanish.

"My heart," I said. "We call our sisters that. It's a pet name."

I was terrified she would think I was making an improper gesture to her.

"My heart?" She smiled and told me the words in Arabic.

And then, somehow, we were holding each other. And my own heart felt at peace.

And then began their trysts, the secret meetings in a bombed-out flat near the art-gallery district.

I took a picture through the broken window to send to Nadia. A date palm, which somehow survived bombs and lack of water. Its crown is level with the roof of the building, and in the summer, Amani tells me, boys climb to the roof and jump to the tree to harvest what fruit the tree still produces. I asked Nadia to make a painting of it, and when she did, I was able to present it to my corazón.

Allie wrote of the pleasure they had in each other's bodies, the delight in hiding from the bosses, from the soldiers, the drunkenness, the violence of the war itself. But she was always tormenting herself over her sin and wondering if she should confess it to the base priest.

*But he is such a soldier, such a military man. How could he
counsel me except with more military advice, to find a soldier
and have the children I want to share only with my heart's desire.*

And then the inevitable happened: someone started spying on them.
Allie found a crude drawing on her desk, heard snickers from her coworkers. Her roommates asked her to move out: they didn't want to
live with a traitor. Mr. Mossbach, the boss, told her no one trusted her
because she wasn't a team player.

"My work is always properly done, perfectly done. Even now when
someone on the team sabotages it, I stay late and get it all together.
How can you make this accusation?"

He laughed, suggested they have a drink after work, he'd help make
it all right for her. A drink led to attempted sex; she fought him off,
and then her life became hell indeed.

May 2

   *The weather here is as hot and difficult as my own poor life. I go,
when I can find a way to leave unwatched, to the little room Amani
found for us. But it has been many weeks now since I saw her.*

May 14

   *Today, I finally saw my Desideria. She also has had to stay
away—too many people are watching her. Someone, maybe even the
Americans, warned her cousins that she is keeping "undesirable
company." It is easy for her family to keep her almost as a prisoner
after work hours. She says she may have to quit her job, that someone
in our office has suggested to her cousins and her mother that she is
secretly seeing an American. Only the poverty of her family, their
need for the money Tintrey pays her, lets her keep the job for now.
"But my noble one, my exalted A'lia, we must be so careful. No one
must see us together in the office. Do you understand?"*

My joy with her is great. And yet my sorrow is great, too. Why is it wrong for us to meet? Because we are of different religions? Or because we are two women? Jesus, if you are the God of Love, then why is my love to be punished with so much sorrow?

That was the last entry. I flipped through the remaining pages, which were blank. And then I came upon a letter printed in black ink on a thin piece of onionskin. The ink had bled through, making it hard to read.

Dear Nadia,

I hope I may address you by your name without offense. You are the beloved sister of my beloved friend, now dead. When I heard of her death, I made my way to our room. Perhaps she told you of our room, with the date tree outside the window that told us life was still possible.

Someone had been in there. Not a drifting person, rather someone who came with the evil intent. My hands shook as I walked through the destruction of our small sanctuary. Our earthen pitcher broken, our mirror shattered, the linen cloth embroidered by my grandmother ripped in two. They had poured blood on our bed. Much destruction have I seen in this war, but this destruction was so personal, against me personally, and against your sister, that I almost fainted from the hatred that had been in a room where only love existed before.

I knew my beloved A'lia wrote in this book and kept it in a secret place we made behind the bed. Too many eyes were spying on her, in her living place and in her working place. She could not leave her writings where unfriendly eyes would see them. Thanks be to God that the evil ones did not find our hiding place.

I wish I could keep my A'lia's book, but too many eyes look upon me also: Iraqi eyes, American eyes, mullah spies. So I send this book

*of her writings to you. Keep them safe as a sacred memory of your
sister's most noble and beautiful soul. She adored you, and little
Clara, and worried constantly over your fates. But God will keep
you safe. You are in the country of safety.*

*I enclose no address, for no letter can come to me that will not be
read by many eyes before mine ever see it.*

Amani, known to your sister as Desideria

43

Othello Misfires

I'd been so absorbed in Alexandra's journal that I hadn't noticed time passing. It was almost three a.m. when I finally finished reading.

What a sorrowful document. At a time in life when Alexandra should have been glorying in the chance to explore the world and her own place in it, she'd been pursued instead by demons. The fierce teachings of her religion, the taunting by her coworkers and boss—perhaps all those things pushed her to a breaking point. Perhaps that's why she volunteered to drive a truck along the road that led to her death.

Some of the writing showed glimpses of happiness, especially the passages where she described her siblings—Nadia painting a cartoon of Tintrey for Allie, Ernest laughing with her. It was hard to think of them now, Nadia and Allie, both dead, Ernest so damaged he couldn't speak clearly about his sisters.

You live in the country of safety, Amani had written to Nadia. In the country of safety, Nadia had been murdered, Ernest severely injured.

But nothing showed a connection between Chad Vishneski and Alexandra, except for the fact that both had been in Iraq. Alexandra had worked for Tintrey's Achilles division. Chad had one of the Achilles shields in his duffel bag. Tintrey had nine thousand employees in Iraq and the U.S. had over a hundred thousand troops there. It wasn't beyond belief that Chad and Alexandra had met, but she hadn't mentioned any Chad in the journal.

If I went to Iraq and somehow found Amani, and Jerry the programmer, and Mr. Mossbach and persuaded them, by unimagined means, to tell me everything they knew about Alexandra's eight months in Iraq and her last day on earth, I still might not find out how she died. If I was going to untangle the story, I would have to do so from the evidence I could find here at home. Clara said her mother and Nadia had fought over the insurance payments the Guamans received after Alexandra's death. The parents wanted to sue Tintrey, but the lawyer, Rainier Cowles, showed up and persuaded them to accept a settlement.

There was nothing strange about that, or even unsavory, but it so angered Nadia that she walked out of her parents' home, and was still estranged from her mother when she died. And Clara believed no one was allowed to talk about Alexandra's death.

I wandered restlessly to the window, carrying my glass. The journal had absorbed me to the point where I'd forgotten to drink the whisky. I parted the blinds, half expecting to see a date tree, but of course there was nothing but snow and ice and a few late-night cars bumping through the ruts.

Rainier Cowles had come to Club Gouge with the owner of Tintrey and the head of the company's Iraq division to watch the Body Artist's homage to Nadia. The men's locker-room jokes gave lie to any notion that they were there out of respect for the dead.

Besides, when I went up to the Tintrey offices, Gilbert Scalia knew exactly who Alexandra Guaman was and how she died. Maybe Tintrey kept track of the Guamans because they feared a wrongful-death suit.

I let the curtain fall. Tomorrow—or, rather, later today—I would visit the Guamans. There had to be a way to get them to talk to me.

And then I would buy a very large crystal ball and divine where the Body Artist had gone to ground.

On that helpful thought, I stumbled into bed. This time I fell asleep. In my dreams, Alexandra and Amani were painting a picture of a date palm across my body. In the background, Karen Buckley, her transparent eyes half shut, was crying, "My sister died, too."

It was a relief when the phone pulled me out of sleep a little before eleven, even though the caller turned out to be John Vishneski.

"Warshawski, someone came after Chad, just like you thought they might. My buddy Cleon was here, and a good thing, too."

"Attacked right in the ICU? How did they get past the nurses?"

"Dressed up like a nurse. Some blond gal, looked like that actress in *Chicago*, Cleon said—all brassy hair and whatnot but in a uniform. Cleon looked through the glass and saw her holding a towel over Chad's nose, and you better believe that he busted in there fast enough to set a record, but she skittered out the other end of the ward and disappeared. What the *hell* is going on here? What did Chad get himself into?"

I didn't try to answer that. "I'll be over in half an hour," I said.

I was thoroughly awake and thoroughly scared. Why were they going after Chad now? Had they learned that I had the piece of body armor Chad had ripped open? And, if so, how?

While I made coffee, I did some stretches, gingerly, favoring my abdomen. The muscles were healing faster than I'd thought they would even though the color was still horrible. I even managed a few jumping jacks. I drank the coffee while I quickly showered, whisked on powder and blusher, put on a serviceable black pantsuit. My right hand was still tender, but I could squeeze it into a glove. I could even squeeze a trigger with it. Everything was coming up roses.

Before I left, I locked Alexandra's journal in my closet safe, behind my shoe tree. Mr. Contreras was continuing to deal with the dogs and our dog walker, which took a load off my mind. I clomped down the back stairs in my heavy boots and drove over to Beth Israel, where I made my way through the maze of corridors to the intensive care unit. The charge nurse, visibly rattled, demanded an ID from me before she'd even summon the Vishneskis.

Ex-husband, ex-wife emerged hand in hand. Whatever differences had driven them apart twenty years ago were beside the point with their son's life in danger.

"I don't understand this, Vic," John said. "Who wants my boy dead?"

"How is he?" I asked. "Has he shown any more signs of recovery?"

"He's opening his eyes more often," Mona said, "and seems alert for as much as two minutes at a time. They're saying that's a really hopeful sign. He hasn't spoken again, but Dr. Eve is pretty optimistic that he will start speaking soon. She says it's just hard to tell with brain injuries but that the scans look hopeful. Only, if he isn't going to be safe here, I don't know . . ."

She dabbed at her eyes, and John patted her hand.

"I didn't want to call the cops," John added, "because they might say he was good enough to go back to that prison hospital, and I won't let that happen. But of course the hospital filed a police report, and we've had someone here already this morning. Dr. Eve came down and told the detective Chad was still in critical condition, but—I don't know, it's all a mess."

"Yes," I said, "but I'm getting closer to some answers. I just need one or two more breaks. In the meantime, one of Chad's buddies is a Marine staff sergeant—ex-Marine, anyway. He's out of work, and I can pay him something to come up here and be Chad's bodyguard. I'll clear it with the hospital's executive director. If Sergeant Jepson takes the owl shift, maybe you can do the daytime."

The Vishneskis took me in with them to look at Chad. He'd been such a big, angry man the times I'd seen him. Lying in a hospital bed, his tattooed arms full of IV needles, he seemed to have shrunk. It was unsettling to see him like this, but I knelt next to him and clasped one of his hands.

"You don't know me, Chad, but I'm a friend," I said quietly. "I'm working with Tim Radke and Marty Jepson, and we're going to save you. You're going to be okay, so relax, and rest and get better."

I couldn't tell if he was hearing me, but I repeated the message several times. When I got back to my feet, the Vishneskis said they didn't want to leave Chad. I went down alone to executive director Max Loewenthal's office, where I spoke with his administrative assistant, Cynthia.

She knew about the attack; Max had already been briefed by his security chief.

"We're moving Chad to a private room," she said, "and we'll have someone from security there twenty-four/seven. But the cost of an intensive care patient in a private room—Chad's veterans benefits won't cover it."

"Cynthia, this is so wrecked. If someone murders Chad, his parents will sue you for negligence, and you'll end up paying buckets in damages—surely it's cheaper to suck up some of the cost of a private room—"

"Don't lecture me on costs," she broke in. "I'm on the page with you, but I don't run this circus, and neither does Max. We're doing a lot for you here, but, the last I saw, this wasn't the V. I. Warshawski Hospital for Indigent Veterans."

Beth Israel, like most other Illinois hospitals, devoted less than one percent of its patient care to the indigent. But I needed help, not combat, so I only said, "You're right, Cynthia, you're right. I'm sending a Marine up to act as bodyguard. That'll take care of some of the expense, right, if you don't have to use one of your own people?" I hesitated. "The man who stopped the intruder described her as looking like Renée Zellweger in *Chicago*. Anton Kystarnik has at least one woman on his hit team."

Cynthia had never heard of Kystarnik, but when I explained who he was she said she'd mention it to their security chief and to Max.

"If it's any comfort, this isn't going to go on much longer," I said. "I've stirred the hornets' nest, they're buzzing around like mad, stinging wherever they see exposed flesh, and that's going to lead me to the queen. Or king, probably, in this case."

"That's no comfort at all," Cynthia cried. "We can't have our hospital turned into a war zone. It's bad enough all the gangbangers coming in here who have to have their weapons pried away from them—sometimes even in the operating room! I can't worry about somebody who's supposed to be in police custody to begin with."

I couldn't think of anything to say except maybe to beseech her not to tell Lotty, and that didn't seem like the act of an optimist. Instead, I promised to wrap things up as quickly as possible.

"If there's one more incident like this, Chad will have to be moved," Cynthia warned me, "and Max will tell you the same."

With that stern valediction weighing me down, I returned to my car. I wanted to get in touch with my cousin to see if she had Marty Jepson's cell phone number, but she wasn't answering the office line or her own cell. *URGENT! CALL ASAP,* I texted her before driving to Thirty-fifth and Michigan, where I tried to see Terry Finchley.

Liz Milkova, the officer I'd spoken to the day before, came out to meet me. I went through the motions: We'd met at Club Gouge, we'd spoken yesterday, I'd worked with Terry for years.

"Several things have happened," I added, "including Chad Vishneski being attacked in the ICU. But, in addition to that, I can explain how Anton Kystarnik has been communicating with his subordinates, so any eavesdropping devices can't tag him."

"I can take a message and give it to Detective Finchley."

"I'd like to give all the details to Terry myself."

Her eyes, so dark a blue they were almost black, darkened even more.

"I may be a woman and a junior detective. But I know how to take a statement."

I felt my eyes turn hot. "I am one of the old-fashioned feminists who helped open this door for you, Officer Milkova, so don't get on your high horse with me. If you were Eliot Ness in the flesh, I still would want to talk to Terry. Unless it's *you* and not he who's in charge of the Guaman murder now."

Someone behind me started to clap, and I turned. Terry had come out into the lobby. "Warshawski, if I live to be a hundred, I'll never get more satisfaction than I've had just now, having someone hand you your own shoulder chips on a plate."

I gave a twisted smile. "I live to serve others, Finch. Did you know someone dressed up like a nurse and went into the Beth Israel ICU in the middle of the night? She tried to smother Chad Vishneski with a towel. A friend of John Vishneski's was there and chased her out."

This was news to Finchley, and he sent Milkova off to find out who in the police department had spoken to the ICU staff. He took me into a conference room, where I gave him a detailed description of the way Kystarnik and Rodney Treffer had used the Body Artist as a message board.

"That's interesting, Warshawski, but not real helpful since you say your stripper, or artist, or whatever, has vanished. And Club Gouge is closed for the time being."

"Thanks to Kystarnik!"

"You say. But the owner, that Olympia woman, says otherwise."

He held up a hand as I started to protest. "I'm not saying she's right and you're wrong. I'm just saying we don't have any basis to go collecting guys—or gals—who work for Kystarnik. And, believe me, I'd like to. These Eastern European thugs have added a whole new dimension to weapons and cruelty that our gangbangers never aspired to. As for Rodney Treffer . . . Guy took a beating the other night, and you called to report it, is that right?"

"No." I looked at him steadily. "Guy had me cuffed and was kicking me in the stomach"—I lifted my sweater to show him my color-coded abdomen—"when he slipped and hit his head on the ice. A couple of Iraqi vets came along and made sure Rodney's pals didn't finish me off."

Officer Milkova had come back into the room. She gasped at my bruises.

"You file a formal complaint?" Terry asked.

"Not yet," I said, "but I'll be happy to. The vets—a Marine sergeant and an Army systems pro—helped me persuade Treffer's subordinates to explain the code Treffer was writing on the Body Artist. It's irrelevant now, since the club's been trashed, but Kystarnik may revive his code to use elsewhere. I've written it all out for you."

When he'd read it on my computer screen, Terry nodded, and sent Milkova for a data stick so he could make a copy of it.

"You think this has something to do with the Guaman woman's murder?" he asked.

"I don't know. It's all murky right now. Everything came together through the Body Artist, but until she shows up I don't know how we'll connect those dots."

Milkova reappeared with a data stick. I copied the report, then got to my feet.

"The Vishneski kid, he's still out?" Terry asked casually.

I didn't think he needed to know that Chad had woken up long enough to ask for his "vest."

"The Vishneskis say their neurosurgeon told your officer that he's still critical. He hasn't regained consciousness as far as I know."

"As soon as he's stable, he goes back to County. The fact that Anton Kystarnik used Club Gouge as a private mailbox has nothing to do with Guaman's murder. Vishneski is still in the frame as far as we're concerned."

"Even though someone tried to smother him this morning?" I asked.

"Could be some completely different quarrel. Could be a friend of the dead woman, looking for revenge. You haven't shown me another believable perp."

"I'm working on it, Terry, and I'm pretty darned close right now." I got to my feet. "By the way, someone using Kystarnik's address plunked down twenty-three thousand in cash to cover Rodney's hospital bill. What does that tell you?"

"That Treffer has richer friends than I do."

44

A Molten House

I went with Officer Milkova to file a formal complaint against Rodney. I didn't go into every detail of the evening, especially not the part in Anton's—or Owen Widermayer's—Mercedes, but Anton was crafty enough to file a complaint against me on Rodney's behalf, so I covered as much as I could without getting Jepson in hot water on a weapons charge.

When we finished, I tried my cousin again but still could reach only her voice mail. A nagging fear that she might have been ambushed at my office made me take a detour there, but my half of the warehouse was empty and showed no signs that anyone had broken in. Before taking off again, I checked my messages. Rivka Darling had called, demanding a report on what I was doing to locate the Body Artist. My most important client, Darraugh Graham, wanted to see me at my earliest convenience. I called his assistant and said I'd be free the next afternoon.

Everything else could wait. I drove south to Pilsen to the Guaman home. Lights were on in the living room. When I rang the bell, Clara opened the door the length of the chain. When she saw me, she gasped and turned pale.

"What are you doing here?" she asked.

"I need to talk to your parents. It's time we all came out from under the cloud of secrecy we've been under the past few weeks."

She put her hand to her mouth and looked over her shoulder. I could hear the television, and Ernest laughing loudly at something he saw on it.

"Clara, I found Alexandra's journal. What other secrets are you sitting on?"

"Allie's journal? But—it was gone!"

"*¡Clara! ¿Quién está?*" her grandmother called.

"Someone for Mom," Clara said.

"So you went to Nadia's apartment after she died," I said. "When? Before or after the place was trashed?"

The grandmother appeared behind Clara. The two had a sharp exchange in Spanish, and then Clara opened the door. The grandmother looked at me puzzled, as if trying to place me.

"V. I. Warshawski," I said. "I think I saw you with your grandson at the rehab center a couple of weeks ago."

"You're with the hospital?" she asked in English.

"No. I—"

"She was a friend of Nadia's," Clara interrupted quickly. "She wants to talk to Mom about Nadia's apartment."

The grandmother's face clouded with sorrow. "Are you wanting to take over the lease for Nadia?" she asked.

I shook my head. "Perhaps you don't know this, but someone broke into the apartment. They did a lot of damage, but Nadia's artwork is still there. I'm thinking you should go soon if you want to rescue her paintings."

"Broke in? Oh, *Dios,* what next? What next?" The grandmother wrung her hands, but she tried to pull herself together, asking if I wanted tea or perhaps a Coke. "My daughter-in-law, she will be home soon. Come in, come in. It's too cold here by the door."

I followed her into the living room, where Ernest was watching the Three Stooges, clapping his hands and recapitulating the action for his sister and grandmother. Between the television and his shouts, it actually was easy to talk to Clara privately.

"Nadia told you she had the journal?" I asked.

"She showed it to me," Clara said. "A friend of Allie's sent it to Nadia, and she was so shocked, she had to talk to someone." She bit her lips. "I wish it had been someone else. I wish—I don't know—I wish I didn't know these secrets!"

"The friend—that was Amani, your sister's Iraqi friend?"

Clara hesitated, then nodded. Behind us, the grandmother had dozed off in her chair, even though Ernest was yelling, "Way to go, Curly! Way to go!"

"Nadia didn't track down the Body Artist until this past Thanksgiving," I said, "but Alexandra has been dead for nearly two years now. When did she actually get the journal?"

"It came about six months after Allie died," Clara said, "but it—at first, Nadia said she didn't want to read it. It was too hard, what with Allie dead and the fight with Mom over the insurance, so she made a little shrine for Allie instead and locked the journal in a reliquary. She made it especially so it would be the right size, out of papier-mâché, painted with roses and other symbols of Allie's beauty."

I nodded. Relatives of Holocaust victims sometimes lived for decades with precious diaries or recipe books from their dead, unable to read them. It wasn't so surprising that Nadia had waited over a year.

"So Nadia finally read Alexandra's diary," I said.

"Right before Thanksgiving, it was. It was so shocking, so hurtful, that Nadia felt she had to tell me. She couldn't bear the knowledge all by herself, that's what she said. How could Allie? How could she betray us all? And with a *Muslim?*"

I imagined Amani's sisters—*How could you—and with an American?*

And a Catholic?—but I only said, "That Muslim woman befriended your sister and kept her from feeling so lonely in a strange country."

"You don't understand!" she protested. "Allie told me she was going to Iraq to make more money so I could go to a good college. Then it turned out it was an act of penance for her—her week in Michigan with that body painter."

"Nadia was a painter," Ernest announced, catching part of our conversation, "before she went to heaven."

"Nothing is ever just one thing," I suggested. "It was penance, it was good money, she believed in you. The smartest of the Guaman sisters, she called you. She did love you, you know. She did want a bright future for you."

Clara played with the zipper on her sweater, but some of the tension in her face eased.

"And then you went to Nadia's apartment when?" I asked.

"Right after we left the cemetery. Everyone came back here for food and drinks, and I just went out through the alley and caught the Blue Line up to Nadia's place. Everything was fine—I mean, everything was awful—but you said there'd been a break-in and her apartment had been trashed. Well, that hadn't happened when I was there. Everything was just like she left it, except the little box was gone, and so was the journal."

Her amber eyes were clouded with fear.

The front doorbell rang. After a glance at her grandmother, who woke up with a start, Clara went to the door. I peered around the corner. It was Cristina Guaman, waiting for someone to undo the chain so she could get in. Mother and daughter spoke, and then Cristina came into the living room, eyes flashing, chin thrust out.

"You have no right to be here. Leave now!"

The grandmother said something in Spanish, an apology to Cristina for letting me in, but her daughter-in-law ignored her. "You take advantage of my daughter's trusting nature, but I know your kind, feasting on the bones of the dead. Leave now!"

I got to my feet and picked up my coat. "When Alexandra died," I said, "you threatened Tintrey with a wrongful-death suit, didn't you, Ms. Guaman? And then Rainier Cowles came along and offered you a settlement. Ernest needed extra care, his bills were killing you, you didn't have a choice, you took the money."

"Who's been talking to you? Clara, what have you told this . . . this parasite?"

"Please, Ms. Guaman, it's not a big secret. Why turn it into one? What kind of threat did Rainier Cowles hold over you? If it was to reveal Alexandra's private life to the world, it's not a world that cares very much about that kind of secret."

"None of this is your business. If you think you know something that we will pay you to learn, think again. We're not buying anything you might be selling."

Clara murmured a protest, but it died in the face of her mother's molten glare. Even though the accusation was unjust, it still embarrassed me, and I buttoned my coat without saying anything else.

Ernest looked from the television to me and suddenly made a connection of his own. "Puppy!" he cried. "This lady has my puppy!"

He ran from the room and came back with the picture from the pet store I'd handed him in the rehabilitation hospital. It was grimy now from much caressing.

"Allie, she's my Allie. Big Allie is a dove, she flies with Jesus. Little Allie is my puppy." He kissed the page, then suddenly turned red and shouted at me, "Where is she? You're hiding little Allie. Give me little Allie!"

He grabbed my briefcase and dumped the contents on the floor. When he didn't see a puppy, he sat on the floor and began to tear up one of my documents. Clara bent over and snatched it from him.

I gathered up my laptop, my wallet, and the rest of my possessions. Clara hunted under the couch for a lipstick that had rolled away. By the time I'd put everything away, Ernest had forgotten his outburst and was watching the Three Stooges again. I left without saying another word.

45

It's Dangerous to Know V.I.

I sat in my car for a time trying to remember why I'd thought it was a good idea to visit the Guamans or why I'd thought I had a right to intrude on the elder Ms. Guaman when she was at the hospital with Ernest, or even why I thought I should be a private eye at all instead of a street cleaner. At least at the end of a day's work, a street cleaner left things better than she found them.

I finally turned on the engine and drove up to my office, wondering what crises might await me there. Petra, for instance, had not been in touch. I owed Darraugh Graham a report. Terry Finchley still wanted to try Chad Vishneski for Nadia's murder. I didn't know where Rodney Treffer was lurking. Karen Buckley/Frannie Pindero had vanished. Plenty for the dedicated PI to do without tormenting a brain-damaged youth and his family over a nonexistent dog.

When I pulled into my parking lot, I saw Marty Jepson's beat-up truck. I hurried into my office, imagining disasters, but Petra was there with Jepson. She'd dragooned him into helping her sort the mail.

"Vic!" she said. "What a day! So much happened!"

"Too much excitement even to contact me, O Texting Queen?"

"I dropped my phone in the slush when Marty and me were roping my car up to his truck," she explained, "and that seemed to kill it, and don't worry about Marty—about paying him, I mean—because I know you didn't authorize me putting him to work. I'll split my check with him, only, I couldn't have managed the day without him!"

"Staff Sergeant," I said, "if you've spent the day with Petra, you probably deserve some kind of battle pay."

He blushed, and said, "Uh, ma'am, uh, Vic, it was a pleasure to help you out. Uh, I wonder if you can call me 'Marty.' I'm not really a Marine anymore, you know."

"People get to be called by the highest rank they ever achieve," I explained, "even if they've retired. Like, right now, Petra could be called 'pest' by anyone who'd like to know why she couldn't pick up a landline."

"Oh, Vic, don't be such a crab cake! Your phone numbers, they're in my cell-phone memory, which is as dead as my poor old car. You cannot believe how much they're going to charge, although, of course, I have insurance. At least, I'm on my mom's policy." She stopped, sticking her lower lip out as she always did when she was thinking seriously. "Maybe I shouldn't allow her to pay for it. But, gosh, with all my bills, and only this temp job for you—"

"I think your mother would be pleased to know you still rely on her," I interrupted. "But I'm the one who wrecked your car, so I'll take care of the repairs that your insurance doesn't cover."

"Vic, you're an angel. I'm sorry I called you names last night."

She launched back into a high-octane account of her day's adventures: Destroyed cell phone! Towed car! Spilled soup on new jacket! Although the stain on the cuff maybe was the pizza they'd had at Plotzky's last night—what a cool bar!

The avalanche of information was making me reel. I went to my back room, where I keep a bottle of Johnnie Walker Black for emergencies. I don't approve of drinking on the job, but responding to Petra right after my painful meeting with the Guamans felt like a medical emergency to me. I offered the bottle to Petra and Marty, but neither liked whisky.

"It's like drinking gasoline, Vic" was the fetching way my cousin put it. "Don't you have any beer?"

The whisky washed through me, and I felt warm for the first time since I'd left Mexico City at New Year's. I sat at my desk and smiled sweetly at Petra. "You'll have to buy your own beer. You towed the Pathfinder . . . Then what?"

"Oh, well," she said, "then we came here to see if you, like, needed anything done. And there was a message from Cheviot labs. Mr. Rieff, he called to say they'd found something really amazing when he ran his tests for you. Guess what they found?"

"The codes for the U.S. nuclear arsenal," I suggested.

"Oh, Vic, nothing that amazing. Just—the stuff that was supposed to be in the body armor—the, uh, ceramic or whatever it is—someone took it out and replaced it with ordinary beach sand. Can you believe that?"

I put my whisky down.

"Did he say . . . Could he prove that it was inside the shield to begin with? I mean, Chad had poked a bunch of holes in the shield. How do we know what was in it first?"

Petra hunched a shoulder. "I don't know."

"Uh, ma'am . . . Uh, Vic . . . We did get the report. Since we didn't know where you were or what you needed, we drove up to Northbrook and picked it up from Mr. Rieff."

Marty handed me a sealed envelope with the familiar crest of the Cheviot rams in the corner. I slit it open and scanned the pages, which bristled with "moieties," "van der Waals forces," "carbon 60," and other arcane phrases that I should have paid more attention to in Professor Turkevich's chemistry lectures when I was an undergraduate, but it was too late to fret about that now.

I called up Cheviot labs. Sandy Rieff was working late. That was one good thing.

"This ratio you have in the report," I asked, "seventy-five percent sand mixed with twenty-five percent fullerene, how is that different from what it should be?"

"It should be a hundred percent gallium arsenide fullerenes," said Rieff.

"And how sure are you that this diluted mix was in Chad's shield from the get-go?"

"My best materials engineer, Genny Winne, did the analysis. Winne says that she's prepared to testify on both those points. And she doesn't say that unless she thinks her results are unimpeachable."

I thought back to the *Fortune* article, to Tintrey's rush to get their Achilles body shield to market, to take advantage of all those juicy Iraqi war contracts. "So Tintrey basically put out a shield that wouldn't stop a bullet. I wonder if that was a temporary thing to grab market share or an ongoing policy. Can you order some Achilles armor from several different production runs and get your Ms. Winne to analyze the content?"

"Will do," Rieff said. "What kind of priority?"

"Priority service, but not premium."

"Have you read the whole report?" Rieff asked. "One of the oddities Winne found was scorching around the holes in the mitt. That fabric is too tough to cut without a special blade, so he must have burned it to get into it. That's the one thing a defense lawyer could jump on in claiming the contents had been tampered with."

He hung up, but I held on to the receiver, staring at the desktop. If Chad knew that his buddies had died because their armor didn't protect them, no wonder he'd freaked out when he saw Nadia paint the Achilles logo on the Body Artist. He'd accused Nadia of spying on him. He must have thought she worked for Tintrey.

I looked up to see Petra watching me anxiously.

"Vic," she said, "is there some kind of problem?"

"Not a problem," I said slowly. "Just—I think I understand what happened, but not how to prove it. Not who pulled the trigger on the gun that shot Nadia Guaman but why they did, and why they framed Chad. Marty, how much did Chad say about the body armor?"

Jepson frowned. "He never stopped talking about it, ma'am—Vic. We knew he was angry. But he was always angry about the way him and his men had been treated generally."

"But did he talk about the armor malfunctioning?"

"He said his men should be alive, that their armor didn't protect them. But, ma'am, no disrespect, you get these IEDs, and nothing can protect you."

"So he didn't say the shields were full of sand instead of the nano-particles they were supposed to contain?"

He shook his head, trying to remember. "I know he said he was going to tell the whole world how his squad got butchered, but, you know, that was just talk. It was his way of letting off steam. Least, that's how Tim and me and the other guys took it. I don't remember him ever saying he did like you did, sent the armor to a lab to get it analyzed."

"No: I think he tested it by shooting at it." That explained the burn marks around the holes in the mitt as well as the holes in Mona's bedroom wall that had bothered her so much. Chad had attached the shield to the wall and shot at it. The bullet went through the armor and destroyed the drywall behind it. That was his proof. But how had the men at Tintrey known what he was doing?

"His blog," I said. "The sections that got erased, I bet those were where he described the mitt. We need Tim. We need to see if he can resurrect Chad's blog."

I got up. "Jake's leaving for Europe this evening. I want to see him before he takes off. Can you two track down Tim and see if he'll come up to my place when he gets off work? In the meantime, make two copies of this report, will you? Send one to Murray Ryerson at the *Star*. The other goes to Freeman Carter."

I'd offered to drive Jake to O'Hare, but the packing of his basses for international travel was a painstaking, if not heart-stopping, business. With a hundred thousand dollars' worth of instruments, he bought tickets so that they could ride in the plane with him, but they required extra scrutiny and careful repacking once he'd been through security. The manager of his chamber group was bringing a roadie just to oversee the luggage.

Jake greeted me on the landing when he heard me on the stairs. "Vic, you made it. I was afraid you were shooting somebody or being shot at."

He took me in his arms and danced me into his apartment, where the living room was filled with the luggage, including his two basses—the modern one for the chamber group, the period double bass for his early-music group. In their fiberglass cases, the instruments looked like stiff elderly people at a concert. I bowed to them and sang a few bars from *"Non mi dir, bell'idol mio,"* my mother's signature aria.

Jake took me into the bedroom, where he'd touchingly set up a little table with champagne and a vase of flowers. "Three coach seats. I can't afford to take my children first-class, so we'll drink my champagne now."

He slid my heavy winter layers over my head and unhooked my bra. He winced a little when he saw the bruises on my stomach, but he didn't back away from me as I'd feared. By the time he had to get up to shower and dress for his flight, some of my earlier anguish over my visit with the Guamans had eased. I lingered in bed until the bell rang, when I pulled on my jeans and one of my sweaters while Jake went out to greet his roadie.

I stood on the landing with my champagne as the two men carted out luggage and instruments. "It will be almost April when you come home. I'll miss you. But I'll follow your concerts online when they're being broadcast."

"I hope you'll be olive-colored again by the time I'm home," he said. "This green and purple doesn't look so good on you, V.I. Try to look after yourself, okay?"

A quick kiss, and then he was gone. I lingered on the landing, but there wasn't time for me to feel sorry for myself. About half an hour after Jake left, Petra and Marty Jepson arrived with a couple of pizzas. Mr. Contreras and the dogs helped us eat while we waited for Tim Radke. When Tim showed up, around nine, he set straight to work, but even though he managed to crack Chad's log-in and password, he couldn't re-create the blog. The entries had been deleted, and that was that.

"Or he never wrote them," Tim said. "I can't tell. It's not like the Artist's website where we could see someone was issuing a command to shut down the site. Here, there's just no trace that anything was ever there."

"If we found his computer?" I asked.

He shook his head. "You'd have to hack into the blog server to see what was deleted. And even if I wanted to go to prison for Chad, which I don't, I'm not good enough to do that kind of search. The only thing we might find if we had his machine is if he sent an e-mail or wrote a letter or something about the armor."

I had to be satisfied with that, although it wasn't the news I'd hoped to receive. The young people took off to go to a club. They invited me to join them in a way that made me feel like an elderly aunt. And like an elderly aunt, I stayed home and went to bed. Oh, those days of having so much energy that I could work all day and go dancing at night . . . I wanted that time back.

It was after one when the doorbell woke me. Someone was leaning on the buzzer so hard they'd roused the dogs. I could hear the barking as I made my way to the door on sleep-thickened legs. I pulled on my coat, put my gun in the pocket, and tried to run down the stairs so I could get to the door ahead of Mr. Contreras. Petra, I was betting. Petra had locked herself out of her apartment. I rehearsed a stern speech on how she could check into a motel or sleep on the living-room floor.

The ugly words died in my throat. Clara Guaman stood outside, her right eye swollen shut, her nose bleeding. When I pulled open the door, she collapsed in my arms.

46

Our Lady, Protector of Documents

You will be well, little one. Just uncomfortable for a few days, with this packing in your nose. Now, who did this? Did Victoria involve you in some desperate scheme?"

"Lotty!" I started to protest, but the words died in my throat. If I hadn't nosed my way into the Guaman home, tonight's assault probably wouldn't have happened.

We were in Lotty's clinic on Damen Avenue, along with Mr. Contreras, who had surged out of his apartment moments after Clara's arrival.

"My God, is it Peewee?" he cried. When he saw that the face of the young woman, a stranger, was covered in blood, he'd ordered me to bring her into his place.

We laid her on his couch, and he made an ice pack for her face. "You stay with her, doll. Make her lie still. I'm getting dressed, and then we'll get her to the doc."

Clara was clutching her French textbook, and she wouldn't relinquish it. I wrapped her in a blanket and concentrated on cleaning the blood from her face. While Mr. Contreras changed out of his magenta-striped pajamas, I called Lotty from the phone in his living room to ask if she could cut through the red tape at Beth Israel's emergency room for us.

She'd been sound asleep, but years of practicing medicine made her alert at once. She told me to bring Clara to her clinic. "If nothing is broken, we'll put her together there more comfortably. And without worrying all those social workers and insurance companies about reports on injuries to a minor child."

As soon as Mr. Contreras was dressed, I ran upstairs for jeans, a sweater, and a spare coat for Clara, who'd arrived wearing nothing over her jeans and St. Teresa sweatshirt. I drove the two miles from our place to the clinic with a Lotty-like disregard for traffic laws.

Once Lotty assured herself that Clara's injuries were superficial—no broken jaw, no damaged eye sockets—she inserted codeine-laced swabs into Clara's nose and then packed it with what looked like a mile of gauze. Lotty applauded Mr. Contreras for knowing to ice the swollen eye and broken nose, then turned a stern gaze on me, wanting to know what kind of scheme I was running that endangered children.

"It wasn't Vic," Clara said. She was sitting in a big reclining chair in the examination room, knees up, head back, another ice pack pressed to her face. Her voice was a little slurred from the drugs Lotty had given her, but she seemed anxious to tell us what had happened.

"I guess they had someone watching our house, Vic," she said. "Like, you know, I told you how Prince Rainier thought we were talking to you. I guess someone told him you still were."

I felt sick to my stomach, as if Rodney were standing over me, kicking me again. Maybe I should find him and let him do it a few more times. Lotty was right—I *had* been running a scheme that endangered children. I couldn't wallow in guilt now—I needed to get Clara to tell me how bad the damage was before Lotty's drugs put her to sleep. I prodded her to continue.

"They must have waited until Papi got home from work. He was on the three-to-eleven shift today, so it was almost midnight before he got back. He was eating supper in the kitchen, and they just battered down the back door and came in. It—the noise, the shouting, these men all in black—it was so terrifying I don't even know how my *abuelita* didn't have a heart attack.

"I was doing homework, and I ran to the kitchen. Mamá and Ernie and my grandma were all asleep, but the noise woke them up. The men, they made us all come into the living room. One of them had me, he was holding me. I tried kicking him, and that's when he hit me the first time."

She was trembling at the memory, but I spoke sharply, forcing her to focus on details. How many men? Four. How were they dressed? Like Ernest used to dress when he rode his motorcycle, all black leather and studs.

"That was almost the most awful part, because Ernie started shrieking, 'We're getting our bikes out! We're going for a ride!' So these men, they yelled at him to shut up, and when he wouldn't, first one man punched him, and when he still kept yelling, this other man, he hit me. Papi and Mamá, they stood there like frozen statues."

She let out a bark of laughter that turned into a sob. Lotty wrapped her in a blanket, and forced some hot sweet tea into her. After a few moments, when she seemed calmer, I asked why she had come to me.

"Vic, she's had enough!" Lotty's voice was a whip. "She needs to sleep, and in a safe place."

"Clara's been playing with fire for too long," I said. "If she's ready to tell me what she knows, I need to hear it now, before anyone else gets hurt or killed."

"That's why I came to you, Vic," Clara said. "Because they said if we didn't give them the report, they'd burn the house down."

My stomach became a lump of ice. "What report?"

"The Army sent it to my parents after Alexandra died."

Clara's hands were shaking so badly that the tea slopped onto the blanket she was holding.

I took the cup from her and held it to her mouth. I waited while she gulped the tea down before pushing her to tell me more about the report.

"It's what started all the trouble, only I didn't know back then. I was a kid still, no one told me anything. But it's why Nadia and my mom were fighting all the time.

"My mom tonight, first she told the gangbangers she didn't know what they were talking about, only when they punched me again and my nose started to bleed, she went to get it. See, she'd hidden it inside the statue of the Virgin of Guadalupe over Allie's bed. She—I should have told her, but I thought—I don't know what I thought. I was just praying and praying that the gangbangers would leave.

"When they couldn't find it, they said we had twenty-four hours to give it to them or the house would be burned down, or blown up, I don't remember which. They left, out the front door. I just grabbed my French book and went out the back door, down the alley. I ran all the way to Ashland with Papi chasing after me, begging me to stop. But I found a cab right away and came to Vic's place."

"Your French book?" Mr. Contreras said. "Why the heck would you even be thinking about your studies at a time like that? And what about—"

"Vic gave me a twenty for an emergency."

She opened the book to the back and showed us where she'd glued a piece of notebook paper over the verb tables to make a kind of pocket.

"Yeah, but that don't explain—"

"Also, I put this inside." Clara reached into the pocket and pulled out a set of folded papers, which she handed to me.

When I opened them, I found a letter with an autopsy report

attached. I began to read—*Classic pugilistic attitude absent . . . lack of smoke stains around nostrils . . . questions about cause of death led to decision to perform autopsy . . . charring . . . made it difficult to extract femoral blood sample . . . anterior aspect of right wrist (which survived fire intact) shows a 1- × ¾-inch contusion.*

I felt my blood congeal in my arms. Dynamite. Clara had been carrying dynamite to school with her every day as if it were her lunch.

"Did you read this?" I asked.

"I tried to," Clara whispered. "I . . . They're about Allie. How she died, I mean. The report came from some doctor in Iraq who saw her body after she died. That's why Nadia and my mother fought. I think Nadia knew what was in the letter."

"But—the journal was sent to Nadia as next of kin, and the doctor wrote to your mother?" I asked.

"Can't you see the girl is worn out?" Mr. Contreras interrupted. "She don't need you bullying her."

"He's right, you know," Lotty said.

"I'm worn out, too, but we have to do this." I pushed my fingers into my cheekbones as if to push back my own overwhelming fatigue. "If Clara, if her family, are going to be safe, I need to understand this tangled mess of documents. Who hid what. Why they hid them."

"I think the Muslim lady sent the journal to Nadia because she was afraid if my mom knew about her and Allie she'd just burn everything. At least, Nadia said that was the reason." Clara was still whispering as if it could keep the reality of her family's torment at bay.

"Does your mother know you have these?" I asked.

Clara grimaced, bunching up her cheeks. "Maybe she guessed. See, Allie, Nadia, and me, we all shared a bedroom. After Allie died, Mamá, she created this whole shrine by Allie's bed. In a way, it's freaky to sleep in there, but it's also comforting. I feel like Allie is there with me, you know.

"Anyway, after Nadia got killed, I came home one night, and my mom was praying in there. She ordered me out of the room, and I thought it was, well, you know, she wanted to be private while she prayed, maybe she wanted to ask Nadia to forgive her. But later, when I went to bed, I saw the Virgin wasn't sitting flat on the base. So I went to put her back. And Mama had taken the bottom off and put these papers inside, except a bit of the paper was sticking out."

"So you put them in your French book. Why?" I asked.

She hunched a shoulder. "I don't know. It was . . . Nadia was dead, and Mamá had fought with her over Allie . . . I can't explain it . . . I thought maybe if, I don't know, if Mamá had listened to her, Nadia would still be alive. And I kept trying to decide if I should show the papers to you, if they were the reason Nadia was killed, although everyone said that crazy soldier shot her."

"Victoria, that really is enough," Lotty said. "I will call her mother, so the poor woman isn't completely ravaged by grief, and then let's get Clara someplace safe to spend what's left of the night."

"She can stay with me," I said, "but only for tonight. I'm too visible a target for the people who came after her family and her."

"Mitch could protect her," Mr. Contreras huffed. He hates not being thought strong enough to protect a girl.

Lotty gave him what Max calls her "Princess of Austria" look: *Do not argue with Royalty, back out of the room, keep subversive thoughts to yourself.* Mr. Contreras subsided into a grumble.

"It's all well and good to freeze our blood, Lotty," I said, "but it doesn't solve the problem of where she can stay."

"We're all tired now," Lotty said. "Let's get some sleep and pray that inspiration comes in our dreams. Come! My surgery schedule starts in three hours."

I started to put the documents into a large envelope but stopped and frowned over them. Kystarnik, or Rainier Cowles, or someone at Tintrey, wanted these so badly they'd gone down to the Guamans' hunting for them. I tried to imagine what I could do with them to keep them safe.

Lotty called the Guamans while I went to the clinic's business office to make copies. I could hear Lotty's voice, sharp, authoritative—*I'm the doctor, I'm doing what's best for your child*—without making out the words. I put one copy into an envelope addressed to my lawyer, which I stuck in the clinic's outbound mail basket. I mailed a second copy to myself. The others I tucked into an envelope underneath my sweater. I thought about sending a copy over to Murray at the *Herald-Star* but wasn't sure how much publicity I wanted for them right now.

"Everything settled?" I asked when I got back to Lotty's office.

Lotty nodded. "I explained we were watching Clara overnight but that you'd be down with her in the morning to talk about how to look after her. They're not happy, how could they be? But they spoke to Clara, who made it clear that she wasn't coming home tonight."

"But what are you going to do?" Clara's amber eyes were dark with drugs and fear. "They said they would blow up the house. I shouldn't have run away, I should have just given the papers to them. Oh, why was I ever born? Why wasn't I the one to get killed instead of Allie and Nadia?"

I took her in my arms. "You did the right thing, baby," I said. "If you'd given them the autopsy report . . . They knew you and your mom had read it. It's your ticket to safety, giving me the report. I'll make sure they don't know where to look for it, and I'll keep you safe. I promise."

How, I didn't know, but it was the least I could do after exposing the fragile remnants of the family to tonight's assault.

"You come on home with us," Mr. Contreras said gruffly. "Vic and me, we'll get you settled for the night. And you listen to Vic. She knows what she's talking about."

A heroic admission. I grinned at him, and he turned red, covering his discomfiture by taking Clara from me and half carrying her out the clinic door.

As Lotty locked up and we bundled into our cars, I began to worry whether the thugs who had attacked the Guamans might have tailed Clara when she ran from home. As we followed Lotty onto Irving Park Road, I tried to look for anyone who might be trailing us. I couldn't really tell in the dark which set of headlights looked familiar. Just to be on the safe side, I trailed Lotty the two miles to her high-rise on Lake Shore Drive. We bumped over the ice and potholes without incident, even when Lotty ran the red light at Ashland Avenue. Lotty is a terrible driver, the kind who insists that all her dings and near misses are due to the incompetence of every other car on the road.

Back at our own place, I circled the block, looking for anyone who might be staking out the building. All the cars on the street were quiet. Still, I sent Mr. Contreras in through the back with Clara while I parked on a side street some distance away.

Mr. Contreras and I decided to leave Mitch downstairs to sound the alarm if anyone tried breaking in. Clara and I took Peppy up to the third floor for comfort. By now, Clara was more asleep than awake, so I helped her undress, pulled a big sweatshirt over her head, and tucked her into my own bed.

Peppy jumped up and curled into a ball at her side. I remembered the grandmother saying Clara was allergic, but her fingers knotted themselves into Peppy's fur, clinging to the dog. She'd been walking on a path strewn with broken glass and boulders; a few sneezes were a small price to pay for the security of a warm puppy.

As I pulled the blanket up to her chin, Clara whispered, "I'm sorry I didn't tell you sooner. It's just until those men came tonight, I thought maybe if I didn't say anything it would all turn out okay somehow."

Her eyelids fluttered shut, and in an instant she was asleep. I double-checked the doors and windows. Everything was bolted shut. I made up the couch in the living room, put my gun on the floor by my head, and lay down with my copy of the document Clara had handed me.

47

The Captain's Conscience

Dear Mrs. Guaman

I have thought for a long time about whether to mail this letter. It may cause you great pain, and it may destroy my own career, but, after much agonizing, I have decided it would be a breach of my oath—as a doctor, as a soldier—to withhold this information from you.

It was my sad duty to examine the remains of your daughter, Alexandra, whose body was found along the verge of the Main Supply Route that connects the Green Zone to the Baghdad airport. Medics from the 4th Brigade combat team found her and brought her to our hospital inside the Green Zone, hoping to make an identification.

Forgive me for writing to you in a blunt fashion. Your daughter was found naked, with burns across her face and torso, as if she had received phosphorus burns from an IED. However, it troubled me that I did not see signs typically found in people who die as a result of burns; nor would an IED have burned off her clothes. While my staff submitted her fingerprints and DNA for identification, I began her autopsy.

The next day, her identity was determined, and we learned that she worked for the Tintrey Corporation. A representative from the company came to collect her body to prepare it for return to her family. I gave him a copy of my preliminary report. At that time, I was still waiting for results of various forensic tests, including analysis of semen found in her vagina, and for her blood work.

The following morning, I had a call from Colonel Cleburne, my own commanding officer, ordering me to destroy my autopsy report. No reason was given other than that Tintrey was a civilian operation and that the Army budget was stretched too thin to take on civilian autopsies. The Colonel informed me that he had also ordered the laboratory to end its tests on the various fluids we had sent over.

I deleted the report from my computer, as commanded, but I did not destroy my printed copies. After long and anguished deliberation, I have decided to send you my preliminary findings.

I regret being the transmitter of such difficult news, but I believe no good is ever served by burying the truth.

Sincerely,

Edwards Walker, MD, Captain, U.S. Army

Attached to the letter was a photocopy of the report. I skipped to the end, to the summary, which explained that Alexandra was a "healthy white female in her twenties, with burn marks over 30 percent of her body, whose body had been found in the midst of metal fragments that might have been the remains of a bomb blast. Medics thought at first that she had been killed by a bomb, but, upon postmortem analysis, we discovered she had been bound and strangled before death."

I flipped through the detailed medical examiner's report.

DIAGNOSES: 1. Manual strangulation. A. Petechial hemorrhages, conjunctival surfaces of eyes. B. Hyoid bone fracture.

2. Postmortem full and partial thickness burns to 30 percent of the total body surface area.

EVIDENCE OF INJURY: Distal right portion of the hyoid bone palpably & visibly fractured with prominent associated recent hemorrhage extending downward to the right thyroid cartilage.

CLINICOPATHOLOGIC CORRELATION: The lack of thermal injury to the larynx and bronchi indicates that the victim was not breathing at the time of exposure to the fire. Given the damage to the hyoid bone, and the petechiae found on the conjunctivas, the evidence is consistent with death by strangulation, with subsequent attempted disposal by burning.

On the posterior aspect of the right forearm is a linear 3- × 1-inch contusion with a 1- × ½-inch abrasion in its center. Wrists show evidence of binding ligature injuries.

The captain believed Alexandra had been sexually assaulted. He found semen in her vagina and pubic hairs of a different color than her own. However, as he had written at the end of his letter to the Guamans, the lab had been ordered to end all analyses of blood and other fluids. As a result, there was no toxicology report and no rape kit.

I lay back in the sofa bed, staring at the ceiling. There were spiderwebs in the corners and a trail of web hanging from the drapes. Cleanliness is next to impossible, one of my college friends used to say, and she was right.

I pictured Cristina Guaman and her husband reading Captain Walker's letter. Tintrey had sent Alexandra's body home to them, telling them their daughter had died of burns from an IED, burns so bad that they advised against viewing her body. With the horror of that news still fresh in their minds, they suddenly learned that Alexandra had been raped, murdered, and then set on fire and left in a public place so that everyone would assume she had been the victim of an Iraqi assault.

Who had left her there? Who had violated her, killed her, tried to cover the murder up? Her boss, Mossbach? The programmer, Jerry? Whoever it was, Tintrey knew. They had put pressure on Colonel Cleburne to end the forensic investigation and destroy the report.

When Cristina and Lazar Guaman got Captain Walker's letter, they must have tried to find out why his report was so different from what Tintrey had told them. Had they considered an exhumation so they could order their own autopsy by an impartial pathologist?

Maybe Cristina called Tintrey's office up in Deerfield. Or maybe it had been Ernest, Ernest, the good and loving brother before his injuries took his mind from him. I wondered again whether Ernest's accident had been arranged, if he'd been run down deliberately, targeted as the one person who might really push for an investigation into his sister's death. I'd never be able to prove it one way or the other, but it might be important to find out the timing of the accident—had he been injured before or after the Guamans received Walker's letter?

However it happened, as Cristina and Lazar were agonizing over how to handle the pathologist's report, Rainier Cowles suddenly arrived, waving a large check under their noses.

Take this. It will cover Ernest's medical care, with enough left over to send Clara to college as Alexandra wished. All you have to do in return is never discuss Alexandra's death with another living soul.

Nadia had been furious. Blood money, she'd called it. She and her mother fought so wildly over taking the money that Nadia felt she had to move out. Clara hadn't been privy to the details, either of Captain Walker's letter or Rainier Cowles's offer. She was told simply that she must never discuss Alexandra's death with anyone.

It had taken over a year for Nadia to feel strong enough to read Alexandra's journal. But when she did, the description of her sister's unhappiness, and Alexandra's ongoing torment over her sexuality, drove

Nadia to desperate action. She made a crucifix with a doll's head, her sister, superimposed on Christ's body.

She sought out the Body Artist, who left her feeling even more helpless. Nadia wanted someone who could talk to her about her adored sister, but the Artist was like a black hole: she drew emotions in, but reflected nothing out. Nadia's anger kept growing. She started coming to the club and painting on the Artist, painting the fire that had burned her sister, the fire that burned inside Nadia herself as rage. I could feel Nadia's helplessness and fury. I could imagine why she did what she did, but I couldn't imagine a way to prove it.

I went to my bedroom, where Clara was deeply asleep, fingers still clutching Peppy's fur. Peppy softly thumped her tail, but she seemed to realize she shouldn't leave the girl. Clara didn't stir as I tiptoed into my closet to put the autopsy report into the safe.

I went to the kitchen and surveyed the backyard, returned to the front room and looked up and down the street. No one seemed to be watching my building.

I climbed back into the sofa bed, checked that my gun was easy to reach, and switched off the lights. I was so tired that the bones in my skull felt as though they were separating, but I couldn't relax into sleep. I was trying to tie together the many threads I'd been unknotting for the last month. The threads became yarn behind my sand-filled eyelids. Olympia Koilada was scarlet, attached to the metallic pewter of Anton Kystarnik by her heavy debts so that Rodney Treffer—a nasty mustard color—had free run of the club and the Body Artist.

Everything came through the Body Artist. She was a blank canvas where people imagined whatever they wanted. Usually an erotic fantasy, but Kystarnik used her as a message board, Nadia used her to display her grief.

Chad Vishneski had gone to see the Artist for entertainment, for erotic relief from his war traumas. And then he saw the Achilles logo and thought Nadia and the Artist were taunting him. It was a typical reaction of someone in psychic distress: everything in the world around you is about you.

I sat up. Chad and Alexandra had never met. It was the luck of the draw that Chad came to Club Gouge the night Nadia began her drawings.

I imagined a scenario. When Chad was in Iraq, he had seen the Achilles logo every time he and his squad inserted the shields into their vests. Then he saw Nadia painting the same logo at Club Gouge.

He freaked out, got thrown out of the club, came home furious with the world and furious with the shield maker, and shot at the shield. He wasn't testing it, as I'd thought at first: he was taking out his rage on it. And then he saw that the bullets had gone right through the shield. And he realized his buddies had died because their protection was a sack of sand.

So he blogged about it. Someone at Tintrey, monitoring references to the company in the blogosphere, came on his postings. And then Gilbert Scalia and Jarvis MacLean actually felt afraid.

Alexandra's murder had been a minor problem. A lawsuit by the Guamans might have made for unpleasant publicity, but it wouldn't have threatened the future of the company. They'd dispatched their outside counsel, Cowles, to buy off the Guamans, and considered that problem solved. Indeed, other private contractors had been able to avoid both civil and criminal damages from claims of rape from their employees, which made Tintrey's payout to the Guamans almost an act of benevolence.

But Chad's outbursts threatened Tintrey's very future. They had grown to a multibillion-dollar empire through their Defense Department contracts. Jarvis MacLean and Gilbert Scalia could watch their stock fall through the floor if word spread that his company had sent our overstretched troops sand-filled body armor, no more protection against a sniper than a wet sock at the beach. Even if Tintrey had finally started delivering the fullerene nanoparticle-filled shields they advertised, a persnickety member of Congress might demand an inquiry, might see that they lost DOD support.

Scalia and MacLean summoned Prince Rainier to a council of war. *Chad needs to be shut up, for keeps.* No threats or blandishments, such as they offered the Guamans, would work here.

With Rainier's help, they thought it through and came up with a brilliant plan: dispose of two birds with one bullet. Shoot Nadia, frame Chad for her death, then make it look like he committed suicide by lacing his beer with roofies. Just another PTSD Iraqi vet who took the violent way out. The neighbor who thought there was too much of the MYOB said two men in overcoats came home with Chad. Scalia and MacLean? MacLean and Prince Rainier? Not Kystarnik's leather-clad thugs, at any rate.

And then they'd rummaged through his things and found the Achilles vest, which they dumped in the garbage. They just hadn't noticed the shot-up shield in the bottom of the bag. They left poor Chad full of beer and roofies, gave him six or seven hours to die, and called the cops.

Only Chad had survived. And John Vishneski had hired me.

It was seven in the morning. I could hear street noises as the neighborhood came to life. Jake would have landed in Amsterdam by now. I wished I was there, in the world of music, not here in the world of violence.

I turned off the phones and went to soak in the bath. With a hot washcloth over my eyes, I tried to imagine how I could get Rainier Cowles to tell all. Nothing came to me. I could imagine getting him to meet with me, I could imagine him ambushing and shooting me, but I couldn't think up a wedge that would induce him to talk. He was more likely to hire Rodney to kill me, Chad, and maybe even poor young Clara.

The Body Artist had her own story, her own loss, her own cons and frauds. She was the center of this particular web. Although I was pretty sure she was, well, not an innocent bystander but an unconnected by-stander, I wanted to talk to her.

As I lay in the tub, I began to try out scenarios that would flush out the Artist, get her to appear for one last melodramatic performance. As the water grew cold, one idea occurred to me. I didn't like it; it made my flesh crawl even in my tub. But it might work.

I dried off and climbed back into the sofa bed, swaddled in a soft robe that had been Jake's Christmas present to me. This time, I fell instantly down a hole of dreamless sleep.

48

Gimme Shelter

If so many lives weren't at risk, I might have slept the clock round. But as soon as I'd slept enough to take the mind-numbing edge off my fatigue, Clara's future, Chad's safety, my cousin Petra—all started tumbling through my dreams. Lives lost, lives at stake, pushed me awake. I needed to be in motion.

It was noon when I woke. I had a three-thirty meeting with Darraugh Graham. Not missable, not with my bread-and-butter client. So time to be up and doing, with a heart for any fate.

I went to check on Clara, who was still asleep, but poor Peppy was pacing around restlessly, desperate to get outside. I opened the door in my nightshirt and bare feet to let her run down the stairs.

While the dog relieved herself, I roused Clara. She woke in considerable bewilderment as well as a fair amount of pain. Lotty had left some prescription-strength ibuprofen for her, but I didn't want to give it to her until she'd eaten something.

"I hurt too much to get up," she moaned.

"Hard to believe," I said, "but moving will make you feel better. And we need to get you someplace safer than my apartment. It's going to be near the top of Rainier Cowles's list of places to look if he finds out you're missing."

"Can't Peppy look after me?"

"Peppy's a lover, not a fighter. And don't you have allergies? I thought that's why your granny said Ernest couldn't get a dog."

Clara sat up. "I'm not really allergic, at least not very—it's just that my *abuela* doesn't want a dog. She thinks she'll be stuck looking after it."

Clara's skin was puffy, and the broken nose was radiating bruises out under her eyes. Just as well Lotty had taken care of her at the clinic. Clara would have been whisked off by Child Protective Services faster than the speed of light if a hospital social worker had seen that face.

I dug out some clean jeans and a sweater that I thought would fit her. "You need to get dressed, and get some food. Then we'll talk to your mom and your school and figure out how to navigate the next week or so until we get this nightmare all sorted out."

"I can't go home! Mom is so furious with me. And those people, they'll be watching for me."

"That's why you need to move. Because as soon as I have you squared away, I'm going to call Prince Rainier to tell him I have the documents. That will bring him hotfoot to my side. Where you *definitely* don't need to be."

"But where can I go?"

"I have an idea on that, but I need to see your mom first. Meanwhile, time's a-wasting. We have three hours to accomplish our whole agenda. You get dressed while I organize some food. Come on, up and at 'em. It's not the size of the dog in the fight but the size of the fight in the dog, and all that good stuff."

Between a laugh and a snarl, Clara finally hoisted herself out of bed and shuffled off to the bathroom. I phoned down to Mr. Contreras, who was vociferous in relief at hearing from me—*Didn't want to call up in case you was sleeping in, but I been worrying about the kid. She okay?*

As I'd shamelessly assumed, he was glad to provide breakfast—French toast, his specialty—and the kid wasn't one of those teens who starved herself, was she, whatever for, healthy girls thinking they had to act like they lived in Darfur?

"Give us half an hour."

Clara was spending a teenage eternity in the bathroom. I put on coffee and got dressed for my meeting with Darraugh. The current pride of my wardrobe was a burgundy Carolina Herrera pantsuit that I'd found in Mexico City at Christmas, cut on the bias so that the wool jacket fell in a flattering line from the high-standing collar to the hips. My gun made an unsightly bulge at the waist, so I dug an ankle holster out of my closet.

I rapped on the bathroom door.

"Come on, Clara. I need to get in there to put on makeup."

"I can't come out, I look like I've been attacked by gangbangers. What will the kids say when they see me?"

"I already know what you look like, so your face isn't going to shock me. We'll figure out the rest after breakfast."

There was silence for a few more seconds on the other side of the door, and then Clara switched on my hair dryer. I packed a suitcase with enough clothes for a few days away from home. A box of shells and a spare clip for the Smith & Wesson. My laptop and my backup drive. By the time I'd done all that, turned down the heat, and parked my mother's Venetian glasses and my personal financial documents in Jake's front room, Clara finally emerged.

She'd used my foundation with a lavish hand, covering the spidery network of broken blood vessels so thoroughly that her face looked startling, like a Kabuki mask.

"Well done," I said briskly, collecting what was left of my makeup and sticking it in my bag. I'd finish my own face later.

Before she could come up with any more delaying tactics, I picked up her French book and ushered her down the stairs toward Mr.

Contreras. My neighbor had breakfast laid out on his kitchen table. It wasn't until we were facing each other across his wife's old checked red tablecloth that I remembered her name had also been Clara. This would add to his already strong interest in the youngest Guaman sister's welfare, and it would make it harder for him to let her go back into the world.

"We are going to have a long day," I told him. "We're going to Clara's school to explain why she's tardy and see if it's a secure enough campus. Then we're going to see her mother and find a safe place for them to sleep."

Mr. Contreras said there wasn't any place safer than his apartment, and I had to go through a longer version of the litany I'd just covered with Clara, including the fact that I was going to announce myself as the tethered goat.

He didn't like any of it, sending Clara away, letting her go to school, or even me using myself as bait, although that was at the bottom of his list of objections. I finally suggested he accompany us to her school.

"I'll go get the car and meet you in the alley in twenty minutes. Clara can finish her breakfast and say good-bye to Peppy."

I went out the back way and down the alley to the side street, where I'd parked early this morning. The car didn't blow up when I unlocked it or even when I turned over the engine. Good signs. And, even better, Mr. Contreras and Clara arrived within a minute of my pulling up behind our building.

We had a quick run down Ashland to St. Teresa of Avila. It was after one-thirty now, and I was starting to worry about the clock. Clara's principal, Dr. Hausman, turned out to be a sharp, intelligent woman who quickly took in the details of what had happened. Hausman was cautious at first about talking to me, which made Mr. Contreras bristle. As soon as I put her in touch with Lotty, though, the principal became briskly professional.

"We did call your mother when you didn't appear this morning,"

Hausman said to Clara, "and she was quite upset but didn't give me any details. I can see why now. We'll give you a pass for today, but I'm going to send you off to your counselor to work out how to make up your missing assignments for today. Ms. Warshawski and I will figure out the best way to keep you in school and keep you safe."

Dr. Hausman had the happy notion of sending Mr. Contreras with Clara. As soon as they had gone down the hall to the counselor's office, she said, "I've been here long enough that I knew both Alexandra and Nadia. Their deaths have been a heavy burden on Clara, and she's taken refuge in sarcasm and hostility, but, mercifully, she's also taken refuge in her studies. I don't want her class attendance to suffer, yet I also don't want her in the kind of danger that cost her sisters their lives."

"I'm going to try to persuade her mother to go to Arcadia House," I said. "It's a shelter for domestic-violence victims, and I'm on the board. If I can line up someone to act as a bodyguard to and from the shelter to the school, will Clara be safe here during the day or should I try to have someone sit with her?"

The principal thought it over. "How secure did you think we were when you got in just now?"

"It wasn't bad, as far as it went—we came in through the main door, and we had to show some ID. I don't know what the rest of your campus is like, how many open doors there are, and I don't have time to look around this afternoon."

Hausman nodded. "I'll talk to my security staff and arrange for someone to be outside any classroom where Clara is for the next week. If it goes on longer than that, then you'll have to hire guards. It's not fair to the school as a whole to divert resources to one student. We had an Israeli diplomat's child here for a semester, and he'd brought in his own guards. The kids took it in stride, once the initial excitement died down, so I don't think they'll overreact to anyone you bring in for Clara."

She walked with me down to the counselor's office, where we

collected Clara and Mr. Contreras. As we walked through the high limestone gates separating the school from the street, I put my gun into my coat pocket and kept my hand on it, but the only people on the street were waiting at the bus stop at the corner, and none of them paid us any attention.

If our meeting at the school went more easily than I'd feared, our conversation with Clara's mother was more difficult. When we got to Twenty-first Place, it was clear that someone was watching the house and not making any secret of it. A late-model black Lexus was parked in front, engine running, with either Konstantin or Ludwig at the wheel.

I didn't slow, just went straight on to Ashland, where I parked near a busy coffee shop.

"That car in front of the house," Clara said, "that was one of the men who hit me last night." Her eyes were big in her Kabuki face.

"Yes," I said, "I know who he is. I need you to call your mother, see if she's home or at work, and get her to meet us here." I put the battery in my cell phone and handed it to Clara.

After a moment's hesitation, looking from me to Mr. Contreras, she typed in the number. "Ma, it's me . . . I'm fine, just sore. Dr. Herschel, she did a great job fixing my nose. She says I shouldn't even need surgery . . . No, I can't come home! . . . No, he's in front of the house, waiting for me . . . No, Ma, if I come home, he'll kill me. You want all your children gone? . . . I'm sorry, I'm sorry . . . Please, Ma, come to me. I'm at Julia's Café con Leche on Ashland . . . No, now. Please, Mamá!"

The incipient hysteria in her voice was genuine and apparently got through to her mother. Clara handed me back the phone, saying Cristina was coming. I removed the battery again and hustled our little group into Julia's to buy coffee and sandwiches. I insisted that we eat in the car. I didn't want a row of sitting ducklings inside the coffee shop if someone trailed Clara's mother here.

We had an agonizing half hour before Cristina appeared. As soon as

Clara saw her mother, she jumped out of the car and ran to embrace her. I hurried after, anxious to get the Guamans off the streets.

Cristina Guaman's face was as gray and puffy as her daughter's. "Why are you torturing my family?"

I surveyed the street behind her. "Were you followed here?"

"I don't know. I hope not. I went out the back door and crossed the neighbor's yard to come out on Twenty-second Street. Why are you putting Clara in harm's way? Why did you get my Nadia killed?"

Mr. Contreras said, "She ain't the person killing your children. If you'd been a better ma to your girls, not blaming them for the lives they were leading, your oldest kid wouldn't never have gone off to Iraq in the first place."

"How dare you!" Cristina said to him. She turned to me, "Is this your husband?"

The question embarrassed me almost as much as it did the old man, but I didn't bother to answer. We were starting to draw an audience, people wanting to know who was attacking who here—and it *was* hard to tell, from the way we were standing, who was the assailant, who the victim. Since I was a well-dressed gringa in a poor area, I didn't want to push my luck.

"We need to get you and Clara and the rest of your family to a safe house," I said. "I want to take you to Arcadia House. It's a women's shelter, and they are expert at keeping their residents free from harm, as long as we can think of a place for your husband to stay."

"Papi could sleep with his cousin Rafi," Clara offered. "He does, sometimes, if the weather is too bad for him to make it home. Rafi lives in Bensenville, up by the airport."

"We can look after Clara," Cristina Guaman said fiercely. "I will not have her stay with strangers, especially strangers who will judge us. I know the kind of shelter you mean, where they look down their noses at us for being Latinas."

"I don't think the staff at Arcadia House behaves that way," I said, "but, even if they do, better to be in such an environment for a week than face those thugs in your house again tonight."

Cristina Guaman looked at the group on the sidewalk, who continued to interject their own comments and queries—some of them knew her from the hardware store—and told them in Spanish that she was all right, just distracted with worry over Ernest's health and Nadia's death.

That marked the turning point in our confrontation, although it took another minute of cajoling before she and Clara got into the backseat of the Mustang. I drove to the house behind the Guamans', to the neighbor whose yard Cristina had used when she left her own house. She crossed their yard to her boarded-over back door and returned in fairly short order with Ernest, her mother-in-law, and a couple of suitcases.

I drove a circuitous route to Arcadia House's shelter, an anonymous building that lay just beyond the big medical complexes on the near West Side. It took some time to explain the Guamans' situation to the staff. Arcadia House was bursting at the seams, and they weren't happy about offering an adult male shelter, but after a prolonged conversation with him, and among themselves, they finally agreed to let the four Guamans stay for a few nights.

"If it's any longer than that, Vic," the executive director said, "you're going to have to make other arrangements. In this economy, more and more families are breaking down into violence, and we're overcrowded as it is."

"If I can't fix this situation within a week," I said, "I'll probably be dead, anyway. I'll be in touch later today to tell you who will show up in the morning to escort Clara to school."

49

Darraugh Gets Things Done

I was running out of time to make my meeting with Darraugh. I told Mr. Contreras I'd get out at Darraugh's building on Wacker Drive.

"Can you take the car home?" I asked. "I'll be checking into a hotel tonight, but I'll get you word somehow about where I am and where to meet me. There's a lot of work to do and not much time to do it in. Will you call Petra, too, and tell her to lie low for now? I don't want her running around town, exposing herself to danger."

Mr. Contreras was delighted to be part of the team. When we reached the building on Wacker where Darraugh had his headquarters, my neighbor gave me a rough hug and told me not to worry about Petra, he'd take good care of her.

I jogged inside, trying to comb my hair while I waited for the elevator. As I got off on the seventy-third floor, I thought it was a pity Arcadia House couldn't lease Darraugh's lobby. It seemed to be bigger than the entire shelter on Taylor Street.

Darraugh's assistant ushered me into the conference room and sent a message to his office to let him know we were ready when he was. Darraugh ran through the meeting with his usual briskness. I managed to be focused enough to cover my part of the agenda, which seemed like a major achievement, given my ragged condition. While Darraugh's vice president for overseas operations wrapped up—at such length that Darraugh cut him short with a pithy remark—I thought again about the building's beautiful, well-guarded space.

Everyone got up to leave. The chief of operations started a private conversation with Darraugh, but I interrupted, asking if I could have five minutes alone.

Darraugh's brows went up, but he took me into his own office and shut the door. "Well?"

"I'm working on a case that is really scaring me, and I have an extraordinary favor to ask."

I gave him a fast précis of how Chad Vishneski and Nadia Guaman had met, and why—at least in my opinion—she'd been murdered and he'd been framed.

"Tintrey has access to America's most sophisticated tracking systems, and I need a secure place where I can meet with my team. I'm hoping— begging you, really—that we could use one of your conference rooms . . ." My voice petered out under his cold blue stare.

He didn't speak right away, looking me up and down as if assessing my competence.

"You know why I work with you when I have companies like Tintrey on retainer as well?" He finally said. "Their size—I mean, their global scope. I don't do business with Tintrey. Don't like Jarvis MacLean. We're on civic committees together. He always manages to duck his pledges."

"I assumed it's because when you work with me, the right hand knows what the right fingers are doing." I said stiffly. I knew I couldn't compete with the global monsters, and that without Darraugh, I wouldn't be able to pay my bills very easily.

He produced his wintry smile. "Right fingers, right hand—yes, I suppose that's part of it. When I was a boy, I found a stray dog on our land. Someone had dumped him there with a broken leg, and I brought him inside. Mother's chauffeur showed me how to set the leg. I've never known why Mother and my grandmother let me keep him. My grandmother despised sentimentality, hated the whole idea of pets. Unsanitary, she said, but the truth was, she hated the idea that any creature under her roof might show my mother or me affection.

"Some adult intervened," he continued. "Don't know who to this day. I called the dog Sergeant Rock, a comic-book hero when I was seven. Rock was small, some kind of terrier mix, but he took on anyone or any animal he thought was a threat to me. Growled whenever my grandmother came near me. Saved me once when I got cornered in the woods by some passing tramp who kicked me hard enough to break a rib. Died when I was fifteen. Broke my heart.

"You remind me of Rock. Scrappy. Sink your teeth into anyone's calf if you see them kicking a kid."

I felt myself flush but didn't say anything.

"When do you want your team here?" he asked.

"Tomorrow. Maybe around noon."

He nodded. "I'll tell Caroline to let you have a room. She'll clear it with security. She can get your people up here without leaving a trail. Just give her a list of names, phone numbers."

I started to thank him, to offer him a month of free detecting, but he shook his head and took me over to his assistant.

"Vic's going to give you a list of names and phone numbers. People we're hosting tomorrow at noon. A number of competitors are interested in the attendance list and the agenda, so do your usual security magic for us, right?"

Caroline Griswold had been with Darraugh for nearly a decade. She spoke fluent French and serviceable Chinese, and often entertained Darraugh's overseas clients or competitors. Two secretaries worked for her, but when Darraugh needed to be confident that security arrangements had been properly made, she handled all the clerical details of the assignment on her own.

While Darraugh went into his boardroom for a video conference, Caroline took me into his inner office and shut the door. I gave her a quick summary of the problems I was working on, then turned on my cell phone long enough to look up the names and phone numbers of everyone I hoped to see tomorrow: Petra, Murray Ryerson, Rivka and Vesta, the Vishneskis. Mr. Contreras, of course. Tim Radke and Marty Jepson. Even Sanford Rieff up at Cheviot labs. I put Sal Barthele on the list, but said I would speak to her privately ahead of the meeting.

Finally, I thought about the ultimatum the thugs had given the Guamans: Produce the autopsy report by tonight or watch your house go up in smoke.

"Do you have a way to make a call to a lawyer here in the Loop so that it's impossible to tell what city it came from?" I asked.

Caroline's usual face is the smooth mask of the high-stakes corporate poker player, but after a moment she smiled mischievously. "Tell me what you want to say, and I'll send an e-mail to our agent in Beirut. He'll be happy to place a call from his cell phone. He's used to dodging bullets, so he knows how to talk from an untraceable line."

"That will be especially fitting. This whole situation has its roots in our war in the Middle East. The lawyer is Rainier Cowles, a partner at Palmer and Statten. I want him to know that the Guamans *do not* have the material his clients are looking for. V. I. Warshawski has taken the papers with her to a remote location, and no one knows where that is. Any communication with Ms. Warshawski should go through her own attorney, Freeman Carter."

Caroline wrote it up in an e-mail to their Beirut agent and had me read it before she sent it.

Since I was already begging so many favors, I asked to use her phone so I could try to organize the bodyguards I wanted for Clara. I started with the Streeter brothers, who I know are both skilled and reliable. Only Tom was available, and only afternoons, but I turned down his offer to find someone else for backup. I needed to know the guards I used.

I scowled in thought, then remembered the Body Artist's friend Vesta; she was a third-degree black belt. I reached her at a law firm where she was temping.

"Have you found Karen?" she asked.

"Not yet. But I have the youngest Guaman daughter, and I'm wondering if you'd have the time or the inclination to do a little babysitting." Before she could protest, I explained what had happened at the Guaman house the previous night and how I wanted Clara to be able to go to school while I tried to resolve the crisis in her family's life.

"I have someone who can see her home from school," I said, "but if you could get her there in the morning it would be a huge help. I pay twenty-five an hour, going rate for experienced guarding."

"How much risk is there?" she asked. "Really. Not glossing over it to get me to do what you want."

"I don't know. The people trying to get at Clara work for the same outfit as Rodney Treffer. He's the man who was always putting those crude numbers on Karen. If you are skillful at choosing your route, you should be safe. If they get a whiff of where she's staying, it could be awful."

"I don't owe the Guamans, or even Karen Buckley, anything."

"I know that."

"And I know how to spar, how to conduct myself, under attack, but I'm not trained as a bodyguard."

"I understand."

"But I also know what it's like to be powerless when someone's beating on you. No girl should have to walk the streets in fear. Let me know where to pick her up, and I'll do my best."

I found I'd been holding my breath and let out an audible sigh. Before we hung up, I told her about the meeting I wanted to hold in

Darraugh's office the following afternoon, and she promised to arrange her lunch break so she could attend.

I got up and thanked Caroline for her help. "Although 'thanks' is a pretty feeble word, for all you've done."

She smiled, her brisk, corporate smile. "All in a day's work, Vic. But if we need to reach you, where will you be?"

I shook my head. "I don't know yet. I'll try to get a room at the Trefoil Hotel, using my mother's birth name, Gabriella Sestieri, but I can't afford more than a couple of nights there."

Caroline thought for a moment. "I'll check with Darraugh, but we keep an efficiency apartment in the Hancock building for overseas staff who have to spend more than a few nights in Chicago. It's free now. I can book you in as Ms. Sestieri."

I felt my eyes grow wide. "It's extremely generous. But, Caroline, it's not just beyond the call, it could expose you to danger, too."

She shook her head. "My sister's only son was killed in Iraq, blown up in Fallujah. He was a reservist, and he had a new baby he never even saw. I can't stand the thought that companies like Tintrey have been making money on his body."

She looked at the console on Darraugh's desk, saw that he'd finished his video conference, and took me into the boardroom so she could explain what she proposed. Darraugh grunted an agreement, and Caroline told me to stop back by in the morning to pick up a key and a photo ID for Gabriella Sestieri.

Darraugh escorted me to the elevator; he believes in old-fashioned etiquette and decorum. As I was getting into the car, he let out an unexpected bark of laughter and brushed a finger across my cheek.

"You are Rock to the life. I don't know why I never thought of that before."

50

Phew! Around the Sal Corner

I didn't feel very Rock-like crossing the Loop. Rainier Cowles and Kystarnik had me so spooked that I stopped in my bank to cash a large check; I didn't want to take the chance that they might be able to track my credit card or ATM transactions. That's the trouble with the Age of Paranoia—you know people can trace you, given the resources, but you don't know if they are actually doing so, not unless you're a whiz like NCIS's Abby Sciuto, who can back-trace anyone who's looking at her records.

When I finally reached the Glow, it was half an hour after the closing bell, and the traders were packed three-deep around Sal's famous mahogany bar. Sal saw me, nodding as she directed traffic. Within two minutes, a minion appeared with a glass of Johnnie Walker Black. I left the drink on the bar, not wanting alcohol to take the edge off my awareness. I also resisted the temptation to pull out my cell phone and reconnect to the world. I was anxious about Chad Vishneski's safety as well as the Guaman family's, but I couldn't take any chances right now.

When the traders, exhausted by a day from hell in the markets, had finally drunk themselves into enough oblivion to manage a commute home, Sal came over to my perch at the end of the bar.

"I hear Olympia's had to close the Gouge," she said. "Bad fire in there."

I shrugged. "Not that bad. She needs to redo her stage and her electrics, but the structure's okay. Question is, where she'll find the money, since she's already in way over her botoxed forehead to Anton Kystarnik."

Sal's lips rounded in a soundless whistle. "So the rumors were right this time. I couldn't believe anyone would be such a complete idiot. Still, as my mother says, a fool and her wits are soon parted."

She paused, measuring me. "You'd probably better know there's another story running around the club scene. Some people say you started Olympia's fire."

"People will say anything, won't they? Especially Olympia Koilada. I did threaten her with legal action if she kept slandering me, but she probably knows I don't have the time or patience for a civil suit."

"So how did the fire start?"

"Actually, I sort of *did* start it."

Sal threw up her hands. "Oh, Vic, why? I'm sure it wasn't the kind of pedestrian reason most of us would have: she dissed your cousin, she kicked your dog, or, in my case, the last time I had a fire here some idiot had left her curling iron on a stack of towels in the women's toilet."

"I didn't do it on purpose. It was sort of collateral damage."

I described the night at the Club Gouge, with Kystarnik's thugs beating up the Body Artist and Olympia because they couldn't run their message board on the Artist's body.

"So where is Buckley doing her show now?" Sal asked.

I shook my head. "She hightailed it. No one knows where to find her, but she's a woman with more than one identity. I know two of them, and wouldn't be surprised if she had a third to use as a bolt-hole in a situation like this."

Sal's shaved and painted brows lifted so high they looked like cathedral arches. "You looking for her? What's Kystarnik going to do if you find her?"

"That, my dear friend, is the question of the hour. They have history, Anton and the Artist. The Artist and Zina, Anton's only kid, were so close, they OD'd together. Zina Kystarnik died, but the Artist pulled through and then disappeared. Where she spent the next thirteen years is a total mystery, at least to me, but Kystarnik apparently knew. At least, he knew she was doing her act at Olympia's. He's been using her, I just learned, but does he hate her or love her? Will he kill her or protect her? I'm betting the first, but he's a psychopath and they are like tornadoes, you don't know where they'll go."

"Kind of like you, Warshawski," Sal said. "Is anyone paying you to look for the chick?"

"Not exactly. Someone is paying me to show that Chad Vishneski didn't kill Nadia Guaman. Kystarnik and the Body Artist don't connect the dots, but they sure have enough dots on them to look like a measles epidemic. Kystarnik wouldn't have wanted a spotlight on Club Gouge and the Artist, so I don't think he was behind Nadia's murder. I'm convinced the killer was hired by Tintrey. Or maybe even Rainier Cowles himself."

I stopped to count on my fingers. "So many parties to this horror show. Besides Cowles and his pals at Tintrey, there are four others: Nadia, Chad, the Body Artist, and Kystarnik. When a fifth party blocked embodiedart.com, Kystarnik was beside himself. He roughed up the Artist and slapped Olympia around. He wanted that communications network up and running."

I brooded over my drink. "I'm sure it was Tintrey that blocked the site. Only now they seem to be happily doing business with Kystarnik. It was Anton's thugs who were parked outside the Guaman house this afternoon, but a week ago they didn't know each other's names. I don't know how it happened, although I'm wondering if Olympia brokered that marriage. And how it happened isn't important—it's what they'll do next that scares me."

"You may make sense to yourself, but it's gibberish to me."

Sal went over to talk to a couple of new arrivals whom she knew. Erica, Sal's bartender, came around with the Black Label bottle.

"You okay, Vic? You haven't touched your drink."

"One of those days, Erica. Just not in the mood." I'd never be able to prove I was right, not unless I found a way to make Prince Rainier speak. I laughed to myself, thinking of Darraugh calling me after his mongrel terrier. *Speak, Prince Rainier! Or I will sink my teeth into your calf.*

However it had come about, Kystarnik and Tintrey had joined forces. Rainier Cowles didn't want to beat up the Guamans in person, so he hired Kystarnik's muscle to force the family to turn over their copy of Captain Walker's autopsy report. Cowles, or the Tintrey executives, thought this would end their problems. Apparently it never occurred to them that the Guamans might have made other copies. Or maybe they thought beating up Clara would persuade the bereft parents to keep Tintrey's dirty secrets to themselves. Or maybe they planned to kill all the Guamans once they had the report.

When Sal finally returned to my end of the bar, I spoke without preamble. "Have I ever put your life or your bar at risk?"

"Nope. And you're not about to start now, Warshawski."

I looked around the Glow, at the Tiffany lamps on the tables and the racks of glassware hanging over the horseshoe bar. Erica was polishing the glasses methodically before putting them up in the manner of bartenders all over the world when business is slow. Each glass wiped obsessively until it reflects the light in the room.

"You'd want to put the lamps somewhere safe," I said, "and maybe move those racks of glassware out of fighting range. You could rearrange the tables, create an open space for a performance. And if you let me cover the windows with sheets, they'd do nicely as projection screens."

"V. I. Warshawski, I don't care if you are on a Carry Nation mission to torch the nightspots of Chicago as long as you leave the Glow off your list."

I tilted my glass, watching the surface of the whisky retain its flat surface while changing shape. Gravity was amazing.

"For one night, Sal, one night only, I need to resurrect the Body Artist."

"Rent the Art Institute. They have better insurance than I do. And a real stage."

"What's your deadest night of the week? Sunday? If I publicize this right, with a cover charge of twenty bucks, or even thirty, you could make your week's profit in two hours."

"Are you listening?" Sal said. "The answer is no. Any profit would vanish in two minutes if Kystarnik came in here in an ugly mood. Which, what I know of the boy, is the only mood he's got, the question being is it mean ugly tonight or plain vanilla."

"Sal, let me tell you the story of three sisters. Call them Alexandra, Nadia, and Clara."

I told her the story, as much as I knew, starting with Alexandra's journal, her journey to Iraq, the Guamans, Chad, the Body Artist's disappearance, ending with my own flight.

"Clara's sixteen. She got her nose broken last night, and that was after burying her two sisters and watching her brother live in the nightmare of a badly damaged brain. I'm not asking you to do this for me, you know."

"Oh, I know, Warshawski. All I want is to run my bar in peace and maybe die in my bed, not from a stray bullet. But you always have some cause that's bigger than the rest of us."

My face turned hot, but I tried to keep my temper under control. "That comes mighty strangely from you, my sister, being as you're the one who dragged me onto the Arcadia House board."

Sal chairs the board. It was because I'm on the board and known to be Sal's friend that Arcadia squeezed in Ernest Guaman along with his sister, his mother, and his grandmother.

"Yeah, I chair the Arcadia board, and I give money to causes I care about. But with you, it's always different, it's always some damned crusade or other. It's like you want the rest of us to think that, next to you, we're a bunch of worthless slackers."

"Most of my work is for corporate clients who pay me with money they get from grinding the faces of the poor in the dirt. Does that make me acceptable as a human being, that I'm just as much a part of the system as everyone else who comes into your bar?"

Sal drummed her long fingers on the bar, still watching the room under her curling lashes. Something was in the balance here, I wasn't sure what—my sense of myself as a person, my friendship with Sal maybe. If I survived Kystarnik and Rainier Cowles, maybe I'd find a place in the country where Mr. Contreras and the dogs and I could live a simple life, growing our own vegetables and offering shelter to runaway farm animals. No more spikes in the hand or boots in the belly.

Sal twisted on her stool to look at the fake Gothic windows that fronted Van Buren Street. Snow was starting to fall again, creating a furry glow that almost blotted out the blackened fronts of the old buildings across the street.

"It's not such a great view, is it?" she said. "The L tracks, that OTB shop over there, and all the paper and chicken dinners and whatnot. I guess I'm so used to it, I never notice how tawdry it is. Maybe if I close the shutters for an evening, it'll cheer the place up. Better tell me what you're up to, and why."

I felt sweat drip between my shoulder blades. Whatever dire outcome I'd been fearing, it wasn't going to happen tonight.

Even though Sal raised a dozen objections, about everything from not having a dressing room to where to set up the Body Artist's webcams, she was on board. When I held my strategy meeting at Darraugh's the next day, Sal helped me push the project forward.

51

Mad Preparations—
Then What?

Looking back, that meeting with Sal in her bar seemed to be the only time I sat still for a week. Organizing the performance, keeping Clara and her family safe, watching my own back, trying to stay in touch with my regular clients while doing business on the fly at Internet cafés, I felt like a hamster on a jet-propelled treadmill.

For our initial meeting, Darraugh's assistant, Caroline, supplied us with food and drink and sat in for several long stretches to help move us along when we got bogged down. Darraugh himself wisely steered clear. He was going out on a very long limb letting us use his corporate headquarters. If his directors learned about it, they might have a few words with him.

Petra thought it was all a great game. Staying at Tim Radke's place made her feel safe and therefore cocky.

"Don't worry, Vic," she assured me. "Me and Tim, we'll take care of publicity. We'll Tweet and network and get this all over town. I still have some media contacts left over from when I worked on the campaign last summer."

"Let's take this a step at a time," I said. "We need to figure out who we want to reach out to. We aren't selling Wheaties here, hoping everyone in the world gets our message."

"The Glow holds a hundred thirty-seven, tops," Sal added. "And I need serious crowd-management help if it gets up to that many."

Tim Radke assured me that his and Marty's friends would turn up in good numbers to make sure no one got too violent.

"We don't want a free-for-all," I said, "with arrests and broken heads. The whole purpose of getting the Body Artist back onstage is to stop the torment of the Guaman and Vishneski families."

"How can you be sure she'll come?" Rivka said. "You haven't been able to find her. I don't think you've even been looking."

"I've been searching like mad," I assured Rivka. "I even found her apartment."

Rivka's face lit up. "What did she say?"

"She'd fled before I got there, but she'll show up Sunday night. No artist wants to be plagiarized or have her work attributed to someone else."

I spoke with a confidence that I was far from feeling, but the whole scheme wouldn't work without someone like Rivka, who was both talented enough and experienced enough to re-create the Artist's images.

Most anxious was John Vishneski, who felt I was giving his son short shrift. "I'm the client here, the one paying your bills. And it's my boy who's still on the critical list at the hospital—my boy, who someone tried to kill two days ago. But this seems to be all about that gal who died in Iraq."

I nodded sympathetically. "There are two halves to the story, your son and Nadia Guaman. I need the real killer to make a move in public, and focusing on the Guamans seems to me the best way to force the murderer out into the open. But if you have a better plan, please, let's hear it now. No Monday-morning quarterbacking. Too much is at stake."

Mona patted her ex-husband's arm. "John, you know you don't mean to be selfish. That poor family, losing two daughters. And who knows what will happen to the third girl!"

The Guamans' situation had me badly worried. The day of our first meeting in Darraugh's offices, Tom Streeter had called to say that Lazar Guaman had come to St. Teresa's and insisted that his daughter and wife return home.

I took a cab to the school and found Lazar in the principal's office with Clara. Dr. Hausman seemed worried, even frightened, when she introduced us.

"Perhaps you mean well, Ms. Detective—I can't say," Lazar Guaman said. "Clara seems to think that you do. We won't try to stop you. But we do belong under our own roof."

"Why not let her be safe with your wife and mother?" I suggested. "For just a few days. All this should end on Sunday."

"We are a broken family," he said, "I know that. My girls have been killed, I could not protect Clara when those men beat her up. But I won't cower in my cousin's home while she's in danger here in the city."

I tried to argue with him, but his mind was made up. He insisted that Clara call the unlisted number at Arcadia House so he could speak with his wife, and the family returned home. My one hope was that Rainier Cowles would leave the family alone now that he knew they didn't have Alexandra's autopsy report. Caroline told me at the meeting that Darraugh's agent in Beirut had duly delivered the message. Still, I had to take Vesta off bodyguard duty. It was just too much to ask of an amateur in case Cowles—or, even worse, Kystarnik—wanted to attack the family.

I bought several disposable phones for my outgoing calls while my answering service was fielding all incoming ones. As long as no one could find me, they couldn't deliver threats. *Turn over the report or we will hurt Petra*—or *Clara*—or *Lotty*—or *Mr. Contreras*—or *the dogs*. I was a Swiss cheese of vulnerability, thankful that Jake was on the other side of the world.

Although I didn't hear from the Body Artist, I knew word about the performance was getting out around town. For one thing, we had a lot of hits on our website. For another, I got a call from Olympia. Actually, I got many calls from her. After her third, and most emphatic, message, I called her back, sitting in a window seat in Darraugh's Hancock Center apartment.

"What are you doing?" she said. "Advertising the Body Artist's final Chicago appearance?"

"Olympia! How are you? How are repairs to Club Gouge coming along?"

"Never mind the club. What the hell is the meaning of this announcement I saw?"

"I don't know what you see or where you look," I said, "so you'd better give me a hint."

I thought I could hear her teeth grinding on the other side of the ether.

"I've seen the advertisements that the Body Artist is going to be at Sal Barthele's joint on Sunday. What is the meaning of this?"

"Gosh, let me look at some tea leaves. Yep, here it is. It means that the Body Artist is going to be at the Golden Glow on Sunday."

"Buckley is under contract with me," she said, "and any bookings she makes—"

"Talk to the Artist or her agent. Don't talk to me. If she has to wait for you to fix up Club Gouge before she can perform in public again, it seems like a mighty poor contract, but, not my business."

"It's your business if you put Sal Barthele up to it. I've been asking around, and everybody who knows Sal says you two are really tight."

"Still doesn't explain why you and I need to talk about it," I said.

Olympia was silent. A field of gray-white clouds floated around Darraugh's sixty-seventh-story apartment so that the city, with all its art and music and corruption and gang wars, seemed as silent and distant as if it existed only in a child's pop-up book. Open the cover, and the characters and their world spring to life. Shut it, and you float off into your own private space.

When Olympia still didn't say anything, I added, "By the way, I drove by the club last night, and it didn't look to me as though anyone was doing any work. Did you know that? Or has Kystarnik cut off all your cash until you jump through some big hoops for him?"

"Where is Karen Buckley hiding, Vic?"

"Don't you think she'd be in touch if she wanted you to know, Olympia?"

Some swallows had ventured up as high as our windows, looking for the insects sucked toward the building by the wind currents. Funny how much of nature there is to see, even from a skyscraper.

I said, "What did Anton offer you in exchange for getting her location from me? To cancel all your debts? To repair the club?"

She hung up with a bang. I laughed to myself, but not for long. I had too much work to do.

I had called Trish Walsh, the Raving Renaissance Raven, to see if she would play music as a warm-up for the show. It was her performance back in November that had brought me to Club Gouge the first time, and it seemed fitting, somehow, for her to open for the Body Artist on Sunday. I knew Trish was flying over to London to join Jake's early-music group, but she wasn't leaving for almost a week.

Trish readily agreed, but I had to warn her that I didn't know what to expect—there might be a hundred people or five, the crowd could turn violent, but I hoped not.

"Vic! You're making this sound like a *Buffy* melodrama. I'll play for this event—I can't wait to tell the rest of the group that I've been close to bloodshed—but you'll have to write in a guarantee for my instruments."

Her lute and hurdy-gurdy were valued at twenty thousand, for insurance purposes. I gulped, but told her to add the guarantee to the contract.

Tim Radke and Sanford Rieff from Cheviot labs were creating high-quality images for the slide show that the Body Artist had always run on big screens during her performances. Tim called in sick to his day job to help us out, and he wasn't letting me pay him for his time. He insisted he was doing it for Chad, that I shouldn't worry. Still, I felt a bit guilty.

Rivka was creating stencils for use in the show, although it took Vesta's and my combined efforts to keep her working on something the Artist had never authorized. "She won't be happy when she sees these," Rivka grumbled every time I asked her to prepare a new figure.

She was working in the basement of the Golden Glow, where Sal stored her overstock. Marty Jepson and Mr. Contreras had moved all the cases around to create room for Rivka to spread out her materials. They'd installed floodlights and a mirror, so that the space could be used as a dressing room.

Even with Darraugh's help providing me a place to stay, the expenses were staggering, and I knew I could pass very few of them on to the Vishneskis. They were uneasy enough with what I was doing without my suggesting they pay for messenger service between the Gold Coast and the northern suburbs, rental of the Glow, insurance on the Raving Raven's hurdy-gurdy. I entered the figures by hand on a spreadsheet, and the totals made me feel faint.

Every morning that I woke up without anyone on my team having been shot or stabbed, I was relieved. And every night when we'd made it through yet another day intact, I had a moment to relax, however short, before the next day's maniacal routine began again.

Chad Vishneski's welfare was a big worry, too. John and Mona Vishneski decided to take him to John's apartment for the weekend. Chad was definitely on the mend. He was alert for as long as fifteen minutes at a stretch now. But he had no recollection of the night of the murder, and there were big gaps in the rest of his memory, too.

John and Mona wanted to see the show, and two of John's construction buddies agreed to stay with Chad, but it made me nervous to move a vulnerable man away from a doctor and closer to killers. Lotty wasn't happy, either: although she didn't want the burden of his protection falling on Beth Israel, she also didn't want him far from medical help at such a fragile stage in his recovery.

When Sunday afternoon finally arrived, when the webcams and the security cameras were in place, the microphones set up, the screens for projecting the images hung over the shuttered windows, I couldn't sit still.

Rivka didn't help: she kept saying, "I told you she wouldn't come. I don't know why I believed you and did all this work when it was all just a big con job."

By eight-thirty, when the doors opened, I felt as though every nerve in my body had pierced its sheath and was dancing naked on the surface of my skin.

TONIGHT *and* TONIGHT ONLY

At the

GOLDEN GLOW

...

The Body Artist

...

in her FINAL CHICAGO APPEARANCE

THE RAVING RENAISSANCE RAVEN at 9

THE BODY ARTIST at 10!

Doors open at 8:30 P.M.

$20 COVER

52

The Naked and the Dead

Under the bright spotlights, the thick foundation stripped the Artist's face of expression. The cream paint covered her completely, obliterating her race, her age. Her hair was pulled back from her face, lacquered heavily so that it stood straight up like a small shrub. Peering out from the middle of its leaves were a couple of Barbie dolls. Their plastic high heels bit into the Artist's scalp.

The crowd on the other side of the lights whistled and catcalled. The Artist turned slowly. She felt exposed, powerless, and it took all her concentration to hold herself upright, to pretend that if she noticed the audience at all, she disdained it.

Behind her, two giant television screens kept changing slides. One zoomed in on a pink-and-gray fleur-de-lis on her left breast, another showed her shoulder with Alexandra Guaman's face, surrounded in flames, as Nadia had painted it.

Off to one side, the Raving Renaissance Raven played her amplified hurdy-gurdy. The words were so out of harmony with the Purcell-inspired melody that it took some time for the audience to realize what they were hearing:

Little girl, little girl
What's your sister?
A toy
Played with by big boys
Until she's broken
Little boy, little boy
Where's your brother?
Dead
Blown up by big boys
Into small pieces

As the Raven sang, the images on the screen began to change from the pictures painted on the Artist's body to shots of soldiers' bodies, maimed and charred, in a desert; a woman clutching a torn dress around her bleeding body; a group of men, roaring with laughter, toasting one another at a black-tie dinner.

Text replaced the images.

Will a Change of Owner Change Achilles' Fortunes?

Someone in the audience yelled, "Get to the show, get to the show," but at a table near the stage three men stopped drinking and began looking around the room, as if checking for anyone who recognized them.

The Artist—a giant doll, really, not a woman at all—perched on a high stool in the middle of the jerry-rigged stage and sucked in a breath. The Raven wound her hurdy-gurdy more slowly, and after another few seconds fell silent. The Body Artist's program began.

It's story hour, boys and girls, girls and boys. And everyone's stories come together through the Body Artist. She is the blank canvas where your dreams come to life. Your dreams may be nightmares, but you'll realize them all in the Artist's body.

The screens began flashing images from embodiedart.com, first the Body Artist's original *Pieces of Flesh*, the field of lilies growing from her vagina, the tiger mask, the winking eye. They switched to the more disturbing images of the woman-faced deer being savaged by dogs, the crucified woman with a spike through her vulva. A horrified murmur ran through part of the crowd, but others began yelling explicit sexual commands. At me. At my body.

"For the Body Artist's final Chicago appearance, I'm going to treat you to a fairy tale. It begins, as all good stories do:"

Once upon a time, there was a Chicago boy who loved to play football, loved to fool around with his buddies, loved beer. But, above all, he loved his country. So when his country invaded Iraq, he dropped football and a college scholarship and went off to war.

The screens showed pictures of Chad as a small boy splashing in a wading pool, then in his Lane Tech football uniform, finally as a soldier heading for Iraq.

He served cheerfully through his first two deployments, but the third time he was sent, his squad came under fire, and every one of them died except for him. They'd all worn body armor, but the armor had failed them.

Losing all his buddies at once, that was hard. Our hero served yet a fourth deployment before he was finally released, but he was never the same happy-go-lucky guy he'd been before. He was angry. Odd things set him off.

One of the odd things that set him off was seeing someone paint the logo of the body armor that he and his squad had worn across the Body Artist's back.

I got up and began slowly revolving as Sanford Rieff followed with a spotlight. Rivka had covered my body with the logo for Tintrey's

Achilles shield, using a paint that showed up under an infrared light. There was a ripple of amazement at the display, while someone who had been to the shows where Nadia did her paintings cried in surprise, "That's what that dead woman was painting over at the other club, remember?"

My soldier was so angry that he took out his old body armor and shot it. And that was when he saw his armor could no more stop a bullet than—my bare hand. This so enraged him that he wrote about it in his blog.

Man, there's something I gotta get off my chest. There's something I gotta get off your chests. All you out there, look at your armor. If it's got that funny logo that looks like an ear of corn sprouting, get yourself new armor ASAP. My whole squad was killed on the road to Kufah because our armor wasn't worth shit, and we all wore those corn shields. They're made by Achilles. So go get yourself Ajax or any other brand and GET RID OF THE SPROUTING CORN!

The blog posting had taken a lot of work. I'd written out what I wanted it to say, and then John Vishneski and Marty Jepson kept rewriting it until they thought it sounded the way Chad would have written it.

I paused, hoping for an outcry from Rainier Cowles or Jarvis Mac-Lean, but they were holding themselves still. Squinting through the spotlight, I saw Gilbert Scalia half start to his feet, but Cowles pulled him back down.

I took a deep breath to steady myself. Off to one side, I saw my cousin's unmistakable spiked hair. She was helping wait tables.

Well, boys and girls, you can imagine how happy—or not—the sprouting-corn company was to see this story going round the blogosphere. The company was making out like bandits, selling the Army sand-filled armor instead of the real deal. They began having corporate meetings, the kind where they muttered, "Can no one rid us of this meddlesome vet?" They didn't know what to do. Then Fate intervened and played a rotten trick on the soldier.

You see, once upon the same time that our soldier was serving his country, there were three sisters who all shared a bedroom in a bungalow on Chicago's South Side. Unlike Cinderella, or other fairy tales about sisters, these girls loved each another. Sure, they argued, as sisters do, but each was more beautiful than the other, and each worked hard to help the other two. They had one brother who laughed with them and kidded them and made them feel special the way a good brother can. The oldest sister was called Alexandra, the middle sister was named Nadia, and the baby, we'll call her Clara, the bright one.

The Guaman sisters' faces were flashing on the giant TV screens.

The eldest sister led the way for the younger two, going to a good prep school and off to college. She took a job at the same company that made the Achilles shield.

The world should have been golden to Alexandra, but she had a secret that weighed heavily on her, and that was the secret of her sexuality. Her priest told her to go to Iraq because her company had high-paying jobs in the war zone. She could start a new life there, a life untroubled by what her priest told her were her sinful desires.

Alexandra obeyed him, but, for better or worse, she made friends with an Iraqi woman, who found a small room, with a date tree outside the window, where they could leave the atmosphere of war and occupation behind and sometimes just rest and pretend they lived in peace.

But Alexandra's coworkers harassed her over her friendship with a local woman. And her boss, who tried to assault her, was furious that she turned him down.

The day came when men in her office took Alexandra away and

raped her. Perhaps their assault got out of control, or perhaps they thought they needed to silence her. Whatever the reason, they strangled her. They then set her on fire so they could pretend to her bereaved parents that she had been killed by an Iraqi bomb.

The company sent her home and told her parents she was so badly damaged by fire that they should not look at their dead daughter's body. But a military pathologist had seen Alexandra after her death, and he could read the story of her murder by the marks on her body. His conscience gave him no rest until he wrote her parents. You can imagine their shock. You can imagine the phone calls they made to the people for whom their daughter had worked. And these people told the parents that they would pay them a lot of money if they never mentioned Alexandra's name again in public.

The screens were showing battle scenes and then a drawing Rivka had made of Alexandra and Amani, sitting under a date tree. On the left screen, Captain Walker's autopsy report was displayed, slowly, paragraph by paragraph.

"No!" Lazar Guaman was on his feet. "You cannot speak like this about Allie. She was not that kind of girl. She was a saint on this earth!"

Tim Radke was at his side, arguing with him, but Lazar was frantic.

"They murdered her—yes, it's true, the Tintrey people murdered her—but this woman, this whore, standing in front of you, she is telling you lies—all lies—about our blessed one."

A hubbub broke out in the audience. People began repeating Lazar's words, began realizing they were hearing a true story. Beth Blacksin from Global Entertainment tried to get a mike in front of Lazar's face. Murray Ryerson had spotted Rainier Cowles with the Tintrey execs. He leaned over them with his cell phone.

"But what happened?" a woman cried from one of the side tables. "What happened to the soldier?"

In the shadows, the Raving Raven began playing "He Had It Comin',"

Sara Paretsky

from *Chicago*. She sang at full volume until the uproar subsided to a buzz. When I began speaking again, she lowered her sound so that it became part of the background.

My naked body under a spotlight, a perfect target, nothing between my heart and a bullet but a layer of paint. My palms turned wet, and sweat began to seep down my neck from my lacquered scalp.

Nadia, the second sister, and the angry soldier ended up at the same nightclub, the nightclub where the Body Artist was performing. Poor things: each thought the other was spying. The sister thought the soldier was a spy from the company, checking to see if she'd violated their order not to talk about Alexandra in public. The soldier thought the sister was a spy for the armor maker, checking to see what he was saying about their body armor.

Ever since our soldier wrote in his blog about the defective body armor his outfit had been given, the manufacturer had kept track of him. Because they had the highest level of clearance, they had access to the Defense Department's most advanced technology. It was a piece of cake for them to go into people's computers and erase their websites or their blogs. That's what they did to our soldier: erased his blog.

The company heard how enraged our soldier became every time Nadia painted their logo on the Body Artist. So they worked out a sweet plan: Kill the sister, frame the angry soldier, give him roofies, and make it look like he committed suicide out of remorse.

And where do you get roofies when you need them? You go to your local drug dealer, to the Body Artist. The Artist was working for a notorious mobster, letting him use her body to send messages to his team of thugs. She'd made a name for herself years ago on the North Shore as drug dealer to the rich and famous, the rich and notorious. When someone came to her asking for Rohypnol, the date rape drug, she knew just where to send them.

"No, you ignorant bitch!" The shout came from the back of the room. "I never gave anyone drugs. You know nothing about me. If they wanted drugs, they wouldn't come to me, they'd go to the source. They'd go to Anton. Ask him! Ask him how he treated his own daughter!"

The room was briefly silent, and Rivka's voice rose from somewhere near the bar, "Karen! Karen! It's me, Rivka. Where are you, oh, don't go away!"

The audience erupted into noise. I shielded my eyes from the spotlight, but could make out only shadows of people rising from their seats, necks craning. I saw Murray's unmistakable bulk trying to carve a path through the crowd toward where Karen had been standing. I hoped one of the Streeter brothers would make sure she stayed in the bar until I could talk to her.

Above the roar, I heard a louder roar, the unmistakable sound of a gun, and glass shattering. A second shot, and then screams. In the small space the sounds echoed and bounced from the glassware hanging over the bar; I couldn't tell where the shots had been fired, but the screams had come from the back of the room, where I'd heard Karen's voice. Rodney or Anton, they must have tried to kill her. I forgot I was naked. I ran into the crowd, tried to muscle my way toward where Karen/Frannie had been standing, but my painted body was slippery, and I couldn't make any headway.

Another shot sounded, so close to me I knew at once it had come from my left. I whipped around and saw a cloud of smoke rising near where the group from Tintrey had been sitting. I managed to push through to their table.

Rainier Cowles was slumped in his chair, blood pouring down his back. His tablemates sat frozen, their eyes on Lazar Guaman, who was pointing a gun at Jarvis MacLean.

"Enough!" I shouted. "Enough bloodshed. Put your gun down, Lazar."

"They killed my girl," Lazar said to me, his voice calm, just explaining the situation. "They killed my princess."

I stepped behind him and chopped my hand down on his arm, hitting the nerve hard enough that he dropped the gun.

"One of you, call 911!" I cried. "Don't sit there like stuffed frogs!"

I shoved the gun out of reach with my bare foot. "You're such war heroes when kids are dying far away, do something now! Fold a napkin into a pad for the wound. Call an ambulance."

Neither of the men seemed able to move. They stared at me glassy-eyed. I put a finger to Cowles's neck. He still had a faint pulse. The bullet had gone through the side of his head and come out through his jaw. I grabbed a couple of napkins from the table, made pads, and started pushing them against the two wounds. It was a nightmare, a repeat of the scene in the alley when Nadia died. I kept screaming for someone to call 911.

Behind me, I heard John Vishneski come up to Lazar. "Man, it isn't worth it," Vishneski said, "spending your life in prison for these scum. You go back to your wife. She's been through enough, okay?"

Out of the corner of my eye, I watched him ease Lazar away from the table.

Marty Jepson materialized next to me. "Vic, what do you need?"

"Call 911. Get a medical team here. Page Dr. Herschel over the loudspeaker. Get me more linen."

Jepson took out his cell phone. He started to explain our emergency to a 911 dispatcher, then I heard the phone drop.

"That man," Jepson said. "He was outside Plotzky's that night. Chad left early, and I saw that man come over and start talking to him."

I looked up. "Which one?" I demanded.

Jepson pointed at Scalia. "And what the fuck are you doing with an Iraq service medal?"

Vishneski stared from Jepson to Scalia. It took him a moment to realize what Jepson meant, but he suddenly roared with anger and flung himself across the table. Glassware crashed, and bourbon spilled across my bare thighs.

"Was that you?" Vishneski grabbed Scalia's neck. "Was that you who killed that gal and tried to kill my boy? You chicken shit, you fucking coward, you send my boy and his friends to war without protection so you can make a few extra bucks and then you flaunt a medal?"

I was struggling to my feet when a welcome voice bellowed through the room.

"This is the police. We have closed the doors. Return to your seats. And one of you people behind the bar, turn up the lights."

It was Terry Finchley, standing under the spotlight on the stage with a bullhorn. Officer Milkova was behind Vishneski, pulling his hands from Scalia's throat. Terry tossed the horn to the floor and came to our table.

"An ambulance is on its way, Warshawski. Go put on some clothes. And then you'd better be prepared to tell me all about it."

53

After the Brawl

As the night wore on, events began to blur. Ambulance crews came for Cowles and for a woman who'd been shot when one of Anton's thugs tried to kill the Body Artist. Someone—it might have been the Renaissance Raven—wrapped me in a big furry coat. I never did learn who it belonged to.

Terry Finchley had set up operations at the end of the bar. He demanded I give him the names of any key players, besides the group at Tintrey's table, but I had told him only about the Body Artist and Anton's creeps. I was pretty sure I'd seen Rodney in the crowd, but he'd managed to slide out ahead of the cops along with Anton. They'd left Konstantin and Ludwig to take any heat coming Anton's way.

Jarvis MacLean demanded that Finchley arrest Lazar Guaman for shooting Cowles. When MacLean turned to me, insisting that I confirm that Guaman had shot Cowles, I shook my head.

"Can't help you there, Mr. MacLean," I said. "I had my back to your table when the gun went off. I didn't see it."

"Damn it," MacLean said, "he was holding the gun. You made him drop it."

"Still can't help you," I said. "Gilbert Scalia might have shot Cowles, the way he shot Nadia Guaman. He framed Chad Vishneski for Nadia's death, and now he could be trying to frame Nadia's father for shooting Rainier Cowles."

That got Terry's attention in a hurry. He had been prepared to let MacLean and Scalia rush off to their waiting limo, but he ordered me to repeat the accusation.

"What are you basing that on, Vic?" Terry asked. "Your woman's intuition or actual evidence?"

I gave a tight smile. "Marty Jepson ID'd Scalia as a man who accosted Chad outside Plotzky's bar the night Nadia Guaman was shot. And one of Mona Vishneski's neighbors saw him and a second man escorting Chad home about half an hour later. The neighbor recognized Scalia's Iraq service medal. Maybe he can pick Scalia out of a lineup."

"I have major responsibilities in a war that the U.S. is waging against our most ferocious enemies," Scalia said. "I can't be bothered with this kind of crap."

Terry's eyes narrowed. "Murder is a kind of crap, Mr. Scalia, the worst kind. If you've shot someone in my city, then you'll have to take time away from your heavy duties to answer my questions."

Terry told Milkova to see that Scalia and MacLean were driven to his office at Thirty-fifth and Michigan. "Let Captain Mallory know what we're doing. And, of course, let them call their lawyers. I gather their chief counsel is over at Northwestern getting his head sewn back together, but they must have other lawyers at their disposal."

Finchley told me I could sit down until he was ready for me, and I retreated to the stool the Renaissance Raven had used. After that, I remembered things only episodically. Jepson and Radke smuggling the Raven out of the bar through the basement service door. Perhaps she was afraid a police inquiry might keep her from her European tour.

Petra shrieked at the blood from my left foot pooling on the floor. I hadn't noticed it until then. "Vic! You've been shot!"

I pulled my foot up and looked at it under the spotlight. A piece of glass was embedded in the ball. I hadn't even felt it when I walked away from Rainier Cowles.

"Don't worry about that now. What I need is for you to make sure the Body Artist hasn't left."

Petra gulped. "Vic, you can't just sit there with glass in your foot."

"Then pull it out and go find the Body Artist."

Petra disappeared into the crowd, which was sounding like the herd in one of those old John Wayne movies: low mooing, restless movement, prelude to a stampede. Now that I knew about the glass in my foot, I couldn't bring myself to get up to look for the Artist. I tried to scan the crowd to see if I could spot her, but it was impossible with so many bodies crammed together.

I must have dropped off to sleep, because the next thing I remember was Lotty holding my foot while Vesta pointed a flashlight at it. "Yes, it is just glass, not a bullet. And Sal has a good first-aid kit. This will hurt: I don't have any topicals with me—I don't go to nightclubs expecting to need them. Vesta, a little lower and to the right."

The pain as she pulled the glass out shot through me like an electric current. Lotty's expert fingers probed the area, didn't find any more fragments. She swabbed the wound with antiseptic, which jolted me again, and pieced the gaping pieces of flesh together with tape before wrapping the foot up.

"Thank you, Lotty," I said weakly. "Sorry the evening's entertainment took such a shocking turn."

"Why would I expect otherwise when you're in charge? God forbid that the Chicago Symphony ever hires you to run a program for them."

The words were harsh, but her tone was affectionate. She squeezed my shoulder and ordered Petra, who'd hovered, white-faced, behind her, to bring me a hot, sweet drink. No alcohol! Lotty waited until Petra returned with some hot cider and stood over me while I drank it.

"You have to stay?" Lotty asked when I'd finished the cider. "I'm getting Max to take me home. You know, men in uniform. I think I've seen enough of them for the evening. You have someone to see you home when they let you go?"

"Plenty." I got up to kiss her good night and ask her to take Mr. Contreras with her. He had been buzzing around the perimeter while I talked to Terry and while Lotty worked on me. It wasn't just that I didn't have the energy to talk to him right now, but I wanted to stay until I could see the Body Artist alone. I didn't know if I could even keep her in the bar when the cops finished with her.

"Petra needs to go home," I said to my neighbor when he started to reject Lotty's offer of a ride. "She's seen way too much violence tonight."

That suggestion brightened his face: looking after Petra was a pleasure as well as a duty. As soon as he left with Lotty and Petra, I turned to Vesta. "If Karen is still in the bar, if the cops don't send her down to Thirty-fifth and Michigan, will you hold on to her for me? I want to talk to her alone and may never find her again if she gets away tonight."

Vesta's mouth twisted into a wry smile. "You're half dead where you're sitting, you know. But if it'll cheer you up to talk to Buckley, or whatever her name is, I'll sit on her chest until you're done here."

When Terry finally finished with me—"I saved the worst till last, Warshawski"—and the last of the cops disappeared, Vesta stepped out of the shadows inside the mahogany horseshoe and brought the Body Artist over to me. Marty Jepson and Tim Radke followed. I wondered where Rivka was, but Vesta told me she'd made Rivka leave an hour or so earlier while the cops were interviewing the Artist.

"We'll go down to the basement and talk while I clean up and change," I said to the Artist. "Vesta, can you escort her down? And Tim, Marty, why don't you hang around up here? If she decides to run up the stairs, I've got this gimpy foot—I can't stop her."

"I have nothing to say to you," the Body Artist said, "so you might as well let me go now." Her chin was high, defiant, Joan of Arc confronting her Burgundian jailers.

"Then you can sit in lofty silence, while I clean up and dress. And I'll talk to you."

54

The Body Artist's Tale

The concrete floor and walls were just about at the freezing mark. I turned on a space heater full blast, but I was still shivering. I began rubbing cold cream on my legs. Vesta retreated into the back, sitting on a crate of beer bottles. She stayed so quiet during our conversation that, after a few minutes, both the Artist and I forgot she was there.

"Let's see," I started, "you were born Francine Pindero, you and Zina Kystarnik sold drugs to the rich kids on the North Shore until you and she overdosed. She died but you survived. I guess that proves how ignorant I am because I always thought dealers were too smart to use their own dope."

"How did you know my name?" she demanded.

"I'm a detective. I detect things."

"Then how did you detect I'd given roofies to your tame soldier?"

"That was a guess."

I ran a facecloth under the tap in a sink that stood in one corner of the basement and soaped my breasts. It felt wonderful, like being newborn, to see my own skin again.

"You guessed wrong. Like you guessed wrong about Anton and me."

Her arms were folded across her chest, her mouth a thin uncompromising line.

I dried off and pulled on a T-shirt and a sweater. My hair, stiff with the hair spray Rivka had used to hold the Barbie dolls in place, felt heavy and filthy, but I'd wash it at home.

"You let Rodney Treffer use your ass as a billboard for Anton Kystarnik."

"Wrong," she said.

"Okay, what's the right version?"

"Why should I tell you one damned thing?"

"No reason," I said. "My version is the one that will go out in the *Herald-Star,* and then it will be all over the blogosphere. But if you're cool with that—"

"You can't be putting out lies about me," she interrupted. "I'll sue you."

"And then you'll have to tell the truth in court, and everyone will know your real name. So why not do it here and now?"

She looked around the cold basement as if hunting for an escape route. The service door to the stairs leading up to the street was behind me. The stairs going up to the bar were behind her, but she knew Marty Jepson and Tim Radke were waiting there.

"Let me tell you a version," I suggested, "and you tell me where I'm wrong. You recovered from your overdose all those years ago and knew Anton was out for your blood because his kid had died, so you took refuge in a second identity. Leaving your dad with a basement full of drugs."

"Wrong, wrong, wrong, wrong!" The last "wrong" came out as a scream, and her transparent eyes flooded with color as violent emotion swept through her. "My dad—I would never have done that to him. It was Anton. Where do you think Zina and I got the drugs? Anton thought it would be good fun for us to sell them to our friends, and their parents. Why do you think we got away with it for two years? Because he was covering for us!"

She began to pace the small basement, frenzied, a panther in a cage. "I got out of the hospital, and cops were waiting to talk to me, and Dad, he was shaking, he looked like an old man. I see him in my nightmares to this day—not just how afraid he was for me, whether I'd ever recover, but because he hadn't known what Zina and I were doing. He was so disappointed in me. He had big hopes for me, I was going to go to college, I was going to be a painter—I was going to be his special success in the world! And then the cops got a tip, probably from Anton, and suddenly this whole pharmacy appeared in our basement."

She gulped back hysterical laughter. "And then Anton showed up. He waited till Dad had left for work, then he beat me up and said I was lucky he didn't kill me. He said it should've been me who died, not Zina, and if I told anyone where we got the drugs, he'd see that my dad was arrested, not him.

"I didn't know what to do. But—my mom was dead. Her name— before she married, she was Karen Buckley, and my dad still had her old high school yearbook and her old high school ID. I took them and ran away, and called myself Karen Buckley."

She'd spent so many years with her story locked inside her that once she started talking, she couldn't stop. I sat quietly on the stool in front of the space heater.

"I couldn't even tell my dad what I'd done because I was afraid he'd try to go after Anton, and Anton would have killed him, like swatting a fly. So I disappeared. I bummed around the country just living on what I could live on. I cleaned houses, I did some carpentry—I learned how, working with my dad in the summers—but I couldn't get a regular job, I couldn't do anything where they needed a Social Security number because then Anton would know where to find me, and I didn't want to ever see him or hear from him again. I took some painting classes at local community colleges and worked on my art, but nothing was right in my life.

"Then I came back to Chicago and started this body art gig. I thought, I can be anonymous here behind all this paint, so I started doing it in public."

"How did Anton find you?" I asked when she paused.

"Because my life is crap and nothing turns out right! It was that idiot bitch, Olympia. If I'd known she'd borrowed money from him, I never would have set foot in her goddamned bar! But she always did these kind of edgy acts, music and performance both, and when I pitched my body-painting idea she thought it would work because it was novel. That's what you need in the club business, something new all the time. And it was starting to work, except Rodney came around. By now, he was Anton's enforcer, but he'd been strictly junior grade when I was in high school. He recognized me from the sex parties."

"Sex parties?"

"Oh, you know, Anton liked Zina and me to help entertain his friends. His wife was usually pretty stoned by the time night rolled around, and we thought at first it was fun. We made so much money, you can't imagine—for a teenager to have a thousand dollars in cash—but sex with those guys—it's why Zina and me, why we started using. Had to be high to get through the night. Anton, he had pictures, that's why I couldn't move without being afraid of him and blackmail." She began chipping at her fingernails, tearing off little pieces and throwing them to the floor.

"So it must have been horrible when you saw Rodney at Club Gouge," I said.

She looked up. "I'll tell you what was really horrible. He knew me before I knew him on account of he'd put on about a hundred pounds. Anton had been sending him to Club Gouge just to keep the heat on Olympia about the money she owed. But when he recognized me, it all started again. Anton had this idea, he thought it was so damned funny—"

"Yes, to use you as his message center. I got that much. And that's why you were so angry the night they came in and started beating on you."

"I wanted to kill you," she said. "If Anton thought I'd ratted him out to a cop, even a private one, my life was worth less than the paint covering me. So I ran home and grabbed my stuff and hid out. But then I saw your ads on the Net and I couldn't stay away—I needed to see what you were doing in my name. I guess you were counting on that, weren't you?"

She looked at me in surprise, as if startled to think I could be that clever.

"Hoping for it," I said, "not counting on it. I didn't know what would happen tonight. I wanted the cops to see an alternate version of the story of Nadia's murder. I thought if you were here, you could fill in some critical blanks."

The Artist began fiddling with the paintbrushes I'd left out on the counter.

"Yes, poor Nadia. I thought she was full of drama—self-drama—over her sister. Poor Allie, too. Is that really what happened to her? Raped and murdered in Iraq?"

"It's what really happened to her. The wrong guy got shot tonight. Just my opinion, but the corporate guys, MacLean and Scalia—nothing will happen to them. Once the Guamans threatened legal action over Alexandra's death, they must have talked to her boss in Iraq, that guy Mossbach. Scalia and MacLean are the ones who got Cowles to pay off the family. In my book, that makes them accessories to Alexandra's rape and murder. Well, maybe Finchley will get enough evidence to arrest Scalia for Nadia's death, but I don't see a murder charge sticking. Meanwhile, Scalia and MacLean are responsible for hundreds of American dead because they substituted sand for gallium in their body armor."

The Artist had limited interest in any life other than her own, certainly not in Tintrey, or unknown soldiers overseas. She flung the brushes down and walked over to the stairs leading up to the club.

"Not quite yet, Ms. Pindero. I need to know how Tintrey and Anton came together. Tintrey was blocking your website, I'm pretty sure of that, and Anton didn't know it the night he came to Club Gouge to try to force you to bring the site back online. Yet two days later, Anton was providing MacLean backup at the Guaman house."

"Anton will kill anyone for no reason," she said. "Or break their necks just for fun, if he's in the mood." Her voice had gone flat again, and all expression had left her face.

"Yes," I said, "that's pretty much how I have him pegged, too. That's why I figured you needed an insurance policy after you ran away. You were scared, that was obvious from the way you'd recklessly jumped through the back window of your apartment—"

"You found my home?" She came back into the main part of the room, her face white. "How?"

"I'm ignorant about a lot of stuff, Ms. Pindero," I said, "but I've been tracking missing people for a long time. When I saw the frenzied way you'd come and gone, I thought you might call Anton, keep him happy by telling him that it was Tintrey blocking the site."

She stood perfectly still, not even seeming to breathe. There was a piece I was missing, a piece she didn't want me to figure out. I tried to relax, to let go of my anxious thinking, to recall what had happened the different times I'd seen her perform in the club. The night of the memorial for Nadia Guaman, I'd seen Vesta and Rivka. And the boys from Tintrey had been there.

"Rainier Cowles was in the club when you did your memorial," I said slowly. "You denied knowing him."

"I'd never seen or heard of him." Her eyes were wary.

"No. But Vesta looked at him through the curtains, and you asked her to point him out to you. A day or two later, you went to his office.

You didn't know if he could be useful to you or not, but he was an important lawyer. And he had a connection to the Guaman sisters."

She sucked in a breath, and I knew I'd made a lucky guess. "So what if I did?" she said. "Is that a crime?"

"I don't know anymore what's a crime, what's stupid, or what's just plain wrong," I said. "Lazar Guaman—was he stupid to say yes to Tintrey's money? He had a brain-damaged kid to support and no power to go up against them to fight over Alexandra's death. Was it criminal to shoot Rainier Cowles? A jury may say so if the police make an arrest, but I'm not so sure. Was it just plain wrong of you to go to Rainier Cowles? I don't know. You tell me."

The Artist kneaded her fingers together. "It was wrong and stupid and criminal to sell drugs with Zina, I know that. And I didn't go to prison, but I might as well have, the life I've been living the last thirteen years."

"Maybe you've been a prisoner of your fears, but it still beats an orange jumpsuit and sexual assault by guards when they're in the mood. What did you tell Cowles?"

"I said I'd call Anton for him if he needed any extra muscle for anything. Okay? Are you happy now?"

"I'm ecstatic. Is there anything else I've been too ignorant to know before you take off?"

She paused, one foot on the stairs. "Alexandra Guaman was incredibly beautiful and very sweet. Even I—fell for her the one week of her life that I spent with her. She made me so angry, not wanting to meet me in Chicago. I wanted to out her to her family! But she didn't return my calls. And then she disappeared."

"She didn't disappear, not the way you do."

"How was I to know that? It wasn't until Nadia showed up that I learned what happened to Alexandra. When Nadia introduced herself to me as Allie's sister, I hoped—I thought, maybe—she would be the same. They looked alike, and Nadia even seemed to want to go to bed with me. Then it turned out she was using me! She didn't care about me at all. She was using me just to get answers about her sister." Her colorless eyes turned dark again.

I smiled sourly: only Buckley, or Pindero—or whatever her name was—got to use people. Nadia had broken the rules. A modest revenge for a modest girl. I didn't say any of this—I wouldn't get anything more out of the Artist if she felt I was judging her.

"So she made you really angry. Did you finger her? For Anton?"

"Don't you understand anything? Anton is poison. I try to stay out of his way. Just—when I saw those two guys hanging around the alley after my show the night Nadia was killed, I thought, Oh, let them jump her. I didn't know they were going to kill her. But once she was dead, what was I supposed to do? I couldn't go to the cops. Not with my past, not with Anton and the drugs and everything. No one would come forward for me, none of those North Shore snots who used to come to Anton's pill parties. They'd be glad to see me go to prison."

She had come back into the room, her pale face flushed, animated in a way I'd never seen before. Nothing like the need for self-exculpation to get your blood pressure up.

"So those were Anton's men who killed Nadia?" I couldn't believe it. I couldn't believe I'd been so wrong about Rainier Cowles and Scalia and the rest of the Tintrey gang.

"I don't know who they were," she said. "I just could tell they were bad news, the way they were lurking in the alley, ski masks over their faces, leaning against this old Jaguar, like they thought they were in a movie or something. At first, I thought they were after me. I was really panicking, but then I saw they'd spotted me. They looked me over, the way guys do, and shook their heads. That made me see they were after someone else, so I went onto Lake Street and got in a cab for home."

I wanted to shake her or smack her, something that would force some kind of empathy into her. Didn't she care that five seconds could've saved Nadia's life? All she needed to do was ask the valets to call the cops—she didn't even need to put herself on a 911 tape.

I swallowed my bitter words. Nothing I said in this cold basement tonight would change Karen Buckley, but an angry tirade would drive her away. She'd said something else that was more to the point.

The men were leaning against an old Jaguar. I'd seen an old Jaguar, a beautiful one; I'd been coveting it. Where? I squeezed my eyes shut, trying to think back over the past month. There had been one outside the Tintrey offices. The day I went up there and Scalia threw me out, I'd seen it in the executive parking area.

"So you let Chad Vishneski take the fall," I said. "It looks like, after tonight's charade, the police may pressure the state's attorney to drop charges against Chad. But if they don't, I'm making sure that you, my sister, are in the hot seat as a witness."

"Not if you can't find me." The Artist smiled naughtily like a toddler in a game of "I dare you."

"I'll find you," I said drily. "I've done it once; the second time won't be nearly as hard. That car in the alley, the Jaguar. Do you know enough about cars to know the make? Could you see the color?"

"It was in an alley, it was night. I couldn't tell the color, just in the street light I could see it said Jaguar on the trunk and then a letter, E, and I thought, oh, gross, another code. Just like what Rodney was always painting on me. And what does that have to do with anything, anyway? . . . I'm leaving now. So tell your goons not to try to stop me."

An E-Type Jaguar. The car of my dreams. The car I'd seen at Tintrey. "Do you enjoy living on the run?" I asked. "Wouldn't you like to get Anton off your back, take your art to a bigger stage?"

"If you think you're stronger than Anton, you're even dumber than I thought you were."

I laughed. "Not possible. But the feds are hot on his trail. He's not long for this world. If you know anything, the least thing that could tip off the FBI to—oh, I don't know—how he killed his wife or some other murder we've never heard of, you wouldn't have to come forward, you wouldn't have to talk about your dad and the drugs and all that ancient history. Just a tip that would send an investigator in the right direction. Once Anton's out of the picture, the rest of his goons will melt like this snow is going to one of these days. And I'd run interference. I'd leak the tip and wouldn't reveal you as a source."

"How do I know I can trust you?" she asked.

"You don't. You can only go with your gut. And what you've seen of me. That I took a beating from Rodney and didn't stop my investigation. That I did the best I could for Clara Guaman and Chad Vishneski."

"You took a beating from Rodney?" She was suspicious.

Once again, I showed off my discolored abdomen, although, ten days out, the bruises had faded to a dull yellow.

"Didn't you wonder tonight how I knew about the messages they were sending through your body? After Rodney jumped me and tried to kick me into submission, I managed to leave him unconscious on the street. And then I persuaded two of his team to talk to me."

It sounded more impressive that way, leaving out Tim Radke's and Marty Jepson's help, and my pure dumb luck when Rodney slipped on my vomit.

"If you rat me out and Anton gets wind of it, I'll send him after you," she warned me.

"I'm not afraid of the big bad wolf," I lied. "Any thoughts on how he might have offed his wife?"

She held her breath, shut her eyes, ready to jump off the high dive. "Acid. It's how he made a helicopter go down when I was in high school. He put acid on wires running from the master switch to the solenoid, and it ate through the insulation about twenty minutes after the chopper took off. Anton was laughing about it on the phone one night during one of his horrid parties. Zina and I were hiding behind the couch, where his pals couldn't see us. As soon as he left the room, we ran like hell. Even Zina didn't want Anton to know she'd heard something like that."

"Acid on the wire from the master switch to the solenoid? How'd you know what that was?"

She shook her head. "I didn't. I asked my dad. I didn't tell him why I wanted to know—I let him think it was for a physics project at school. Even so, he might have guessed. He was a smart guy, my dad, but he died thinking I was selling drugs."

"He loved you," I ventured. "He certainly would have forgiven you."

"I was so stupid," she whispered. "So greedy. I wanted the stuff that all those rich brats had—their horses, their clothes, and when I started hanging around with Zina, Anton, he saw my greed. I made it so easy for him. So goddamned fucking easy. 'Is not taking candy from baby,' he said. 'Is giving baby candy and giving you power.' I loved it. I've always loved power. It was only later, when I was in too deep, that I saw he had all the power."

The story was almost more than I could bear. Anton's vileness, using his own daughter and her friend as a private brothel—Scalia and Mac-Lean, casually murdering Nadia Guaman to keep her sister's destruction a secret—I didn't think I could continue living in a world with people like this in it.

And Karen, her adolescence shaped by Anton. No wonder she kept people at a distance.

My feelings must have shown in my face because she said, "Don't go feeling sorry for me. I hate that worse than anything. Tell your cop friend about the solenoid. If Anton really goes to prison, then, yes, I'd like to come home, be Francine Pindero again. If you want to send me any news about it, e-mail steveskid80@yahoo.com."

Vesta emerged from her crate at the back of the cellar, surprising both of us—we'd been so intent on our talk that we'd forgotten her. She put her arm around the Body Artist.

"Come on, Buckley," she said. "Or Frannie. Maybe I'm a fool, but I'm taking you home with me."

I turned off the space heater and followed the two of them up the stairs. When I got to the top, Tim and Marty were holding the Artist. I told them we were done—she could vanish into whatever shadows she chose.

55

There Is Some Justice in This World, Just Not Enough

Marty Jepson and Tim Radke were heading to Plotzky's to join their other friends for a drink or six and wanted me to join them.

"Chad's off the hook," Tim Radke said. "You were awesome, Vic. Wish you'd been with our squad in Iraq."

I told them that they were pretty awesome themselves, but that I'd take a rain check for now. "Drink one for me. We'll catch up soon."

Marty stayed a moment to apologize for losing his cool. "Man, I watched Chad disintegrate into that kind of rage a hundred times and never thought it could happen to me. But when I saw that guy—and wearing the Iraq medal—if Chad's dad hadn't beat me to it, it would've been me with my hands around his throat."

"You saw someone getting away with framing one of your buddies for murder. Most people would have had a brainstorm under those circumstances. I wouldn't worry that it'll keep happening to you."

"I—" His voice cracked, and then he surprised us both by pulling me close and giving me a full-treatment kiss. "You take care, Vic. And if you ever need help—any help with anything—well, you know how to send for the Marines, right?"

He turned and ran across the room after Tim Radke.

Sal was waiting to close. She and Erica had swept up the debris, but a decontamination team would have to come in before she could re-open the Glow.

I took a stool next to her at the end of the bar. "You were right, Sal: I should have rented a theater. I somehow wasn't imagining that there would be people stupid enough to fire guns in a crowded room."

Sal poured me a slug of one of those liquid-gold single malts that I can't afford to get used to. "The damage wasn't as bad as it might have been. A table, some glassware, and that light fixture near the exit. Which, thank the goddess, wasn't an original. I guess that was when that guy was trying to shoot the Body Artist. As long as Rainier Cowles and the woman who got shot instead of the Artist don't sue, we should be okay."

"If your insurance doesn't cover the decon team, I'll take care of it. And the chandelier and table." I couldn't bear to think about my ex-penses on this venture.

"I'll make that my donation to truth, justice, and the Warshawski way," she said drily. "You pulled it off, girl. When you came out under the spotlights, I was completely convinced. You were the Body Artist."

"Yeah. We're just a bunch of interchangeable parts, aren't we, under our clothes."

"Don't go down that road, at least not tonight. Go back to your own crib, get your life back in order. Get on a plane and surprise Jake over there in Amsterdam, or wherever he is right now. Do something good for yourself, you hear?"

My smile felt lopsided, but I squeezed her hand, drank up, went back to my own place for the first night in a week. My neighbor had stayed up until he was sure I was home safely. I hugged him but went on up the stairs to shampoo the heavy lacquer out of my hair. When I got out of the shower, Mr. Contreras was in my dining room with the dogs and a plate of scrambled eggs. Mitch and Peppy were ecstatic to see me again, which brought as much comfort as the late-night supper and Mr. Contreras's affection.

I knelt to fondle Peppy's ears. "If you'd been in the Golden Glow tonight, you'd have known right away it was me. Not a body, but me, V. I. Warshawski."

Mr. Contreras had a thing or two to say about me being naked on the stage. "I told you two months ago, women who sit around naked onstage get what's coming to them."

"And how reassuring it is to hear that again. Although Terry Finchley seems to think that not knowing who was naked under all that paint is what unnerved Anton. Anton thought I was the Body Artist. And then when Karen, or Frannie—or whatever we're going to call her—had her outburst at the back of the room, Anton was so surprised he lost his cool and sent Rodney after her."

"So I guess your stunt worked. Guess you're happy as all get out. Just do me a favor, keep your clothes on in public in the future."

"Yes, sir," I said meekly.

"Oh, you don't fool me none with that butter-wouldn't-melt attitude. I know you. I know you do what you damned well please no matter what I say."

He spoke roughly. My well-being mattered greatly to him, and he hated knowing he wasn't fit enough or fast enough anymore to keep up with me, let alone look after me.

"I listen to you." I put my arms around him. "My mother would be glad to know I have you to counsel me."

He brightened, thinking that I loved him well enough to compare him to my beloved mother. He bustled about cleaning up the table. *It was two-thirty, time we was all in bed, anyway, doll. So what's the point of fighting when it's all water over the dam, anyway.*

Mr. Contreras was right. The stunt had worked. At least, up to a point. The results, however, didn't leave me happy as all get out, except for how they affected Chad Vishneski. Two days after my show at the

Golden Glow, John Vishneski came into my office, Mona at his side: the state's attorney had decided to drop charges against Chad.

"We can get him into a proper rehab hospital," Mona said. "You worked a miracle for us, Ms. Warshawski. I didn't know what to think when we got to that bar on Sunday, but you knew what you were doing."

Vishneski grinned. "You ever want to take up that line of work more seriously, let me know. I can play the clarinet for you instead of that gal on those old-time instruments . . . You let me know what all your time and work came to. We'll settle up."

I was working on the bill between my endless interviews with local, state, and federal cops. Grateful clients pay up, but the longer you wait between results and invoice, the more their gratitude fades. The trouble with the Vishneski bill was I had to sort out what belonged to the Guaman inquiry—which no one was paying me for—and also subtract items the Vishneskis really couldn't be expected to cover, like the extra security I'd brought into the Golden Glow Sunday night, or insurance for the Raving Raven's instruments.

I called Terry Finchley to thank him for getting the state's attorney to drop charges against Chad. "Does this mean they're going to charge Scalia, and maybe Rainier Cowles, for killing Nadia Guaman?"

"The state's attorney is an elected office," Finchley said at his most wooden. "The incumbent has received great support from the Tintrey Corporation, as Scalia's mouthpiece reminds me every hour on the half hour. The evidence isn't great."

"Marty Jepson can ID him talking to Chad the night of the murder, and maybe one of the tenants in Mona Vishneski's building can recognize him, too. The Body Artist saw an E-Type Jag in the alley the night Nadia was killed. Oddly enough, Gilbert Scalia owns the same make and model."

"Marty Jepson is a stressed-out vet who saw someone through a bar window," Finchley said. "He's like a lot of our deserving vets pummeled by their time in the desert and prone to confusing reality and imagination. And before you jump down my throat, Warshawski, I'm just quoting the lawyer. As for the Jag—who's the state's attorney going to listen to, a stripper who used to work for Kystarnik or the senior veep at a billion-dollar company?"

"So it's going to be left an open investigation." I couldn't keep the bitterness out of my voice.

"You came away better than you thought you would when you started out," he said. "Not such a bad deal, even if it does grind my bones to see the Tintrey boys skate. But speaking of open investigations, I need more from you about Lazar Guaman and the attack on Rainier Cowles."

"You know as well as I do how a good defense attorney would shred me on the stand, Terry. I heard a shot, but I didn't see anyone fire it. If Lazar Guaman was standing at Cowles's table, so were a lot of other people. I am not going to get up on the stand to perjure myself or to be made a fool of—either way, it's bad for business."

Rainier Cowles wasn't going to die. The bullet—whoever had fired it—had shattered his jaw, and he would need extensive reconstructive surgery. Who knew, though—maybe it would make him a more fluent litigator. Perhaps even an empathic one. Maybe the Cubs would win the World Series in my lifetime.

The gun used to shoot Cowles had been one of the millions floating around the country without proper registration, so it was impossible to trace it to Lazar Guaman. But Jarvis MacLean had identified Lazar as the shooter. Other people identified me, and still others had chosen a twenty-something guy who'd sat at the next table with a group of buddies, so it was hard for the cops to make a cast-iron case.

It made me wild to think that the Tintrey crew would get a free ride. Terry's implication that there was a quid pro quo between the open investigation into Nadia's death, and the investigation into the shooting of Cowles, carried no weight with me at all. Guaman acted out of the personal pain of his daughters' deaths. Scalia and MacLean were trying to protect the value of their stock options.

Not to say that Tintrey's CEO didn't have a few troubles. Murray Ryerson and Beth Blacksin made sure that the story of sand in the Achilles shields got wide circulation. Illinois's congressional delegation began making noises about hearings that would look into Tintrey's billions of dollars' worth of contracts with the Defense Department. The stock price was already dropping.

There were some other bright spots. Of course there were. Chief among these was Chad Vishneski's vindication. I also managed to get the Body Artist's tip about acid in the solenoid wires up the chain. I suggested it to Murray—"Wasn't there some story about Anton and a chopper ten or fifteen years ago? He brought it down by painting acid on the wires, which ate through the insulation when the chopper was in the air?"—and he was on that tidbit like a flea on Mitch. I had the satisfaction of reading that the FAA and TSA were taking another look at Anton's wife's airplane.

A smaller spot, but one that warmed me personally, came from Darraugh. He hadn't been at the Golden Glow Sunday night, but Caroline Griswold, his personal assistant, had been there. I hadn't noticed her in the densely packed room, but after Lazar shot Cowles, she had slipped out a side door before the cops shut off the exits. Caroline apparently had given Darraugh a comprehensive report because on Wednesday I got a giant basket of flowers with the note "Good Girl, Rock."

In between talks with cops, sending Darraugh a handwritten note, and cleaning up my apartment, I answered e-mails and tried to pull together the threads of some of my other investigations. Clients were getting huffy. They thought I was being a media hound and not tending to their needs.

Olympia came to see me one day, hoping I would "let bygones be bygones." The federal prosecutor for Northern Illinois was nosing around in her books, and she was getting scared. I told her I couldn't possibly help her, but I didn't preach at her—she'd dug herself into such a deep hole, she was lucky to be alive.

"I hear you let Buckley walk away into the night," she said. "Why won't you help me?"

"One of those things, Olympia."

I didn't say it was because Francine Pindero had taken refuge in her dead mother's name. If I'd lost my mother at eight, the age when Frannie lost hers, my dad, working long hours, couldn't have kept me out of trouble in the neighborhood I lived in. We needed our mothers, Frannie and I. I'd been the lucky one, getting to live under Gabriella's fierce protective wing until I was old enough to fly on my own.

56

A Song Across the Ocean

I drove down to Pilsen the day after my show at the Golden Glow. Cristina, in her own way, had been tough and cold. Or at least bitter and hostile. She didn't want to thank me for clearing up the search for Nadia's killer or even for focusing a public spotlight on Tintrey for their treatment of Alexandra.

Instead, Cristina blamed me for her husband's behavior—the police were circling around Lazar Guaman as a "person of interest" in Rainier Cowles's shooting. I suggested to her that the Guamans hire a criminal defense lawyer, to be on the safe side, and she threw up her hands. "Why not say he is guilty and run an ad in the paper? Having a lawyer makes him look like he has something to hide."

"Having a lawyer means he won't get tricked into saying something that can be used against him in a trial. I know a first-class criminal defense lawyer. She just joined my own lawyer's practice, and I'll be glad—"

"No more favors, *por favor*! Haven't you done enough harm to us already? Did you think we were a house full of puppets, that you could just pull our strings and make us dance? My two daughters lie dead.

And now what will become of us without the money we were getting from Alexandra's company?"

"Ma!" Clara was red with embarrassment. "How can you say that? Prince Rainier killed Nadia! His bosses murdered Allie! We were like—like slaves, bowing down to them. We're better off without their money. Nadia was right—it was blood money!"

"Of course you'd take this detective's side over your own mother's," Cristina said. "You ran off to her. You left your own family to run off to this woman. And now your papi could be in jail for murder. What good have you done, the two of you?"

The world was a weight on her head—I could understand that, with the wrecked remains of her family around her. "But Clara deserves all our best efforts to have the bright future Alexandra wanted for her," I said. "And it will be easier for her to go to school now that this heavy load of secrets has been taken from her shoulders."

"She's right, Ma, and when I finish college, I'll get a good job and look after you and Ernie, and even Papi, if they don't send him to prison. And maybe they won't. By the time everyone hears what Prince Rainier and his pals did to Allie and Nadia, they'll give Papi a medal, you'll see. Stop trying to make Vic and me feel guilty for stepping forward."

I grinned at Clara and hugged her, but her mother's words haunted me as I tried to clean up the residue of the case. I hung out some with Sal, and the two vets came around to check on me once or twice.

The three of us went to visit Chad in the rehab hospital where he'd been transferred. It was a relief when he instantly recognized his friends: I'd been afraid that he'd be like Ernie, with lasting brain damage. The three men greeted each other awkwardly. It's so much easier for women to hug and show emotion.

"I hear you guys saved my ass," Chad said.

"This lady here is the one you need to thank," Marty said.

After a few more awkward exchanges, I left them to catch up and took a cab home. I felt like an invalid myself these days, like someone who needed a lot of tender care, so I was treating myself to things like cab rides. I cut back on my hours and lounged around with the dogs. I missed Jake and his music more than I had expected. The dogs were physically taxing but emotionally rewarding, what I needed these days.

I was a bit gimpy on my cut foot, but as the days grew longer and the temperatures rose to the freezing level for the first time in five weeks, my solace was in the parks along the lakefront. The dogs and I went south to the wilderness preserve near the University of Chicago, where Mitch chased a coyote for half a mile. Peppy followed as fast as she could, while I limped along in her wake.

Petra helped me get my correspondence back in order. At the end of the week, though, she came to me, very solemn, and announced her resignation.

"I don't want to leave you in the lurch or anything, but, Vic, I don't think I'm cut out for detective work. People getting shot or cut to bits, I hate it. I was so scared last Sunday. And then I saw how tough and cool you were, and, don't take this the wrong way, I don't want to be like you when I'm your age. Like, living alone, and being so hard that violence doesn't seem to bother you."

"How could I possibly take that the wrong way?" I said in my hard fashion. "You going back to Kansas City?"

"No. The company where Tim works, they're looking for a publicity person, and it seems like a good job for me. And, well, Tim and me, we really hit it off. So that'll be fun."

I wrote out a check for the hours she'd worked. "Just don't blow hot and cold on me, Petra. You came to me for help, and I helped you. Now you're leaving me high and dry. Maybe you don't want to become tougher. But you do need to become more thoughtful, more responsible."

She nodded solemnly but didn't even bother to answer me. I went home that night close to tears. Not because Petra was quitting—she was too impulsive to be an asset to my business—but I couldn't help feeling demoralized by her take on my personality.

When I reached my building, I thought I really might break down. Clara Guaman was sitting on the single front step with her brother Ernie. On this cold February night, after hearing my cousin's take on my character, I didn't think I could cope with any more Guaman crises, but I held the lobby door open for Clara and Ernie and forced myself to smile.

"How are things?" My voice must have been harsher than I'd intended because Clara cast me a nervous glance.

"This isn't a good time, is it?" she said.

"No, no, it's fine. I'm just tired . . . Your dad okay? Have they arrested him?"

"He's a wreck, he wants to confess. Ma wants him to run away—to Cuba, even. And everybody's fighting—it's like it was when Nadia and Ma were fighting all the time. I thought it would all be better now, but it's not. And tonight, Papi said if he had to hear Ernie's laugh one more time he wouldn't be responsible for what he did next. I didn't know what else to do. I couldn't take Ernie to any of my girlfriends, so I brought him here."

The dogs heard us and began barking and whining. Mr. Contreras opened his door, and Mitch and Peppy bounced into the hallway.

"Peppy!" Clara's face lit up. "I hoped she'd be here."

"Well, Clara, look at you. That black eye all gone, you're pretty as a picture. Ain't she?" Mr. Contreras beamed at her, and she blushed.

I worried what would happen when Ernie encountered the dogs—if he tried to hug or squeeze Mitch, it could end in disaster. However, the animals seemed to understand his disability. While Clara knelt and crooned over Peppy, Mitch jumped, paws on Ernie's shoulders, and licked his face.

"She likes me, she likes me! Did you see, Clara? She kissed me. The Allie dog kissed me."

Ernie's shrieks of delight echoed up and down the stairwell. I didn't try to tell him that Mitch was a male.

I took all five of them, young people, old man, dogs, upstairs with me while I changed from corporate to exercise clothes. I showed Ernie how to hold Mitch's leash when we went back outside for a run. He needed reminding at each intersection that we stopped at, the dogs sat down, and they waited for the command to heel before moving again. But, in the park, I let Ernie tear up and down the lake path until he and Mitch were both exhausted. Clara played more quietly with Peppy. Both Guamans came back to the house happier than when we'd left.

I had bought a salmon fillet to share with Mr. Contreras for dinner. We stretched it into a meal for four by adding pasta and a head of broccoli, but Ernie was too excited to eat much.

"My Allie dog, my Allie dog," he kept crying, jumping out of his chair to hug Mitch.

"Ernie should get a dog," Clara said. "He hasn't been this together since before his motorcycle wreck."

I nodded. "I know someone who trains dogs for hospital visits. We'll go see her on Monday and get her help in finding the right dog and the right training for Ernie. I'm also going to give you Deb Steppe's contact information. She's a crackerjack defense lawyer. We'll call her, you and I; I think if you can bring your father in to see her, he'll feel better, and then things will calm down at home."

Clara played with the feathers in Peppy's tail. "Did my dad—did he really shoot Prince Rainier?"

"Sweetie, I can't answer that. I didn't see him fire the gun, and if I say more than that, you may be forced to repeat it under oath."

"But—half of me wishes he did, to avenge Allie and Nadia. Half of me wishes he didn't, because it's terrifying to think my own father could shoot someone."

I took her hand. "What you and your family endured for the last three years, no one should have to live through. There are so many casualties of war, and many are far from the battlefield. If your father did shoot Rainier Cowles, you should think of it as post-traumatic stress, the same way poor Chad Vishneski suffered from it. I don't think your dad will go around attacking other people. Once he talks to the lawyer, things will settle in his mind about what the right course of action is for him and for what remains of his family."

We called Deb Steppe. She listened to me and then spoke privately with Clara. The conversation seemed to help Clara feel ready to go home again, although she and Ernie stayed until after eleven. It was hard to dislodge Ernie from Mitch—without Mr. Contreras's help, I'm not sure we could have—but the promise of more time with Mitch and the promise of finding him his own true Allie dog very soon, finally got through to him, and I was able to drive the two Guamans home.

When I got back to my own place, my melancholy mood settled on me again, and I found myself writing a long e-mail to Jake. He had finished his tour with the contemporary group, playing Berio's *Sequenze* in Berlin, and was heading to London with his early-music group, High Plainsong. The Raving Raven had flown over on Wednesday to join them with her historically correct, unamplified period instruments.

I'd written Jake once, briefly, to tell him the highlights of Sunday's show, trying to make it humorous. Tonight I wrote more honestly. Or maybe with more self-pity. Hard to tell, sometimes.

> The fact that the Guaman kids turned to me in a time of trouble should make me feel better, but the truth is, I don't know if I do more harm than good. Cristina Guaman said I treated her family like a stage full of puppets, and maybe I've done that again, finding a lawyer for them, promising to get Ernie his own dog.
>
> Sometimes I think the fact that I'm so willing to act is a danger to the world around me. Like Sal's criticism a few weeks ago that I seem to put myself on a plane above everyone else. It's not that. I don't. I think I'm driven more by despair, even, than confidence, especially the despair

of seeing so much misery around me. And then I leap into action and make it worse. But at least Ernie will get his dog. Surely that will be better, but the law of unintended consequences, that's what seems to bite me time and again.

I wish you were here or I was there. I wish that my life had followed a calmer path.

I hoped to hear back from Jake the next day, although between the time difference and his work schedule I knew he might not even be looking at his mail. I went to the gym and took part in a pickup basketball game. I went to my office but decided I was sick of work. I went to a spa in my neighborhood, got a massage, lounged in the pool.

When I got home, I found a message on my machine from Lotty.

"Max and I are coming over for breakfast tomorrow. Be up by a quarter of seven."

When I called her back, she only laughed and told me to be up and have my computer turned on. Before I could beg or wheedle any other information out of her, she hung up.

Sunday morning, I was so curious I got up early enough to run the dogs. When we returned, Max was just pulling up across the street from my building. He and Lotty followed me up the stairs, exchanging reminiscences about wartime concerts in London, a night at Wigmore Hall when they'd held candles for their performing friends because the power had gone out.

While I made coffee, Lotty unpacked a hamper with fruit and rolls, and Max fiddled with the Internet on my laptop. A jangling Prokofiev concerto was coming to an end, and then an announcer stated the time, just after one o'clock, and the station, BBC Radio 3. He read the news, and then said he was turning us over to the *Early Music Show.*

The presenter's rich contralto filled the kitchen. "Today we're delighted to have the American group, High Plainsong, in the studio with us."

I felt myself grinning in surprise. "You knew! How did you know?"

"Jake called Max when he knew they were going to do it and asked us to surprise you." Lotty smiled at me.

The presenter introduced the members of the group. They discussed their instruments—Jake played a bass viol for High Plainsong—and the special repertoire they'd prepared for the trip. Trish Walsh, the Renaissance Raven, sang and played an ancient lute, one that didn't have a power cord stuck into it. It was odd to hear her speaking in her "high-culture" voice after listening to her heavy metal performance at the Golden Glow on Sunday.

"We're going to start with works by some of the *trobairitz,* the women troubadours of the twelfth and thirteenth centuries," Trish said. "There were several dozen of them, but very little of their work survives, and out of that whole group we have music for only one poem. However, we've taken some of the surviving poems and set them to the music of the period."

"I chose the first song Trish is going to sing," Jake said. "The words are by Maria de Ventadorn. I've always loved the poem itself—a dialogue Maria wrote with a poet named Guy d'Ussel. She tells him that a lover should respond to a lady 'as toward a friend' and 'she should honor him the way she would a friend, but never as a lord.'

"I put together the music as a salute to a lady of my acquaintance. Like the *trobairitz,* she's a woman of high courage. She just saved a girl and rescued a soldier, and did so with all her usual spirit and guile. V. I. Warshawski, I hope you're listening."